# SIXPENNY GIRL

Saran Chandler sees her mother and baby sister sold by her evil stepfather, Enoch Jacobs, and only escapes the same fate when Enoch drowns in the canal. Determined to reunite her family, she teams up with Luke Hipton and eventually they start their own business. Then she meets local businessman Zadok Minch, whose god-fearing exterior conceals a cruel and depraved man, and realizes he is the man who bought her family. His insatiable lust and greed lead to his castration and death – too late for Saran to save her mother. Can she find her sister – and true love?

Please note: *This book contains material which may not be suitable to all our readers.*

# SIXPENNY GIRL

# SIXPENNY GIRL

*by*

Meg Hutchinson

**Magna Large Print Books**
Long Preston, North Yorkshire,
BD23 4ND, England.

British Library Cataloguing in Publication Data.

---

Hutchinson, Meg
Sixpenny girl.

A catalogue record of this book is
available from the British Library

ISBN 0-7505-2110-4

First published in Great Britain 2003 by Hodder & Stoughton
A division of Hodder Headline



Published in Large Print 2003 by arrangement with
Hodder & Stoughton Ltd.



Magna Large Print is an imprint of Library Magna Books Ltd.

Printed and bound in Great Britain by
T.J. (International) Ltd., Cornwall, PL28 8RW

'Nail making is one of the worst trades in the kingdom. There are scores of men in this parish who are not earning nine shillings a week for seventy, eighty, or ninety hours work and out of these earnings are made to pay from one shilling to eighteen pence a week for firing, and about sixpence a week for keeping their tools in order.'

Robert Sherard, 1896

To the memory of those men, and so many like them, who worked their lives away in coal mines and iron foundries, I dedicate this book.

Meg Hutchinson

With thanks to the Walsall Local History Centre
whose help and research supported an 'old tale'
often told by my grandmother.

In November 1837, the *Wolverhampton Chronicle* reported what is thought to be the last documented case of wife-selling in England. A man travelling from Burntwood led his wife, a halter tied about her waist, into the market place at Walsall. There she was sold to a man, also of Burntwood, for the sum of half a crown.

Walsall Local History Centre

# 1

'Shut yer mouth, you mewlin' bitch!'

Enoch Jacobs snatched the broad leather belt from around his waist, cracking it several times and savouring the sound.

'You don't ask no question o' Enoch Jacobs.' The belt whistled on the air before slicing across the shoulders of the slight figure crouched on the ground. 'You don't ask no question...' the belt rose and fell, 'no question ... no...'

Breathless with the effort, Enoch Jacobs's heavy-set figure slumped back against a tree, sliding downward as his legs folded.

Curling her body tightly against the savage fury of the man, her arms thrown protectively about her head, Saran Chandler waited for the next slash of the belt, the next of the stinging blows that followed through her every day.

Where had the money come from? How had he paid for the ale that had him roaring drunk? She had not dared ask those questions ... not this time!

Folded in on herself she held back the tears, her teeth clenched against the smarting pain burning across her back and shoulders, breath held against the next onslaught. But the whine of leather slicing the air had stopped ... the next blow had not come. As the realisation seeped into her brain she waited a moment then slowly raised her head. Sagged against the tree, his heavy-jowled face flushed, the belt fallen from thick fingers, Enoch Jacobs snored loudly.

If only she could run away now, leave and never have to look upon his face again; but while Enoch Jacobs took care always to find a tavern to satisfy his thirst, he was just as careful to make sure that what he saw as his property remained that way.

Easing her cramped legs, Saran felt the rope bite against her neck. Yoked like an animal, the slightest movement had the knot slip a little tighter against her throat.

Where had the money come from? Leaning her head against the trunk of the tree Saran thought of that day a week ago when she had dared ask that question. He had been an hour in the alehouse, an hour drinking away the last farthing they had, a farthing that could have paid for a loaf of week-old bread, bread that would have fed her mother and her sister. Then he had come outside. The ale already telling on him he had hit against the doorpost before staggering across to where he had tethered them like beasts, his heavy face flushed, his eyes bloodshot.

She had thrown an arm about her mother and sister, holding them as close as the rope about their necks would allow, her own body tense as it waited for the blows that followed them through the days like a constant companion. A beating was what they had come to expect almost from the day her mother had remarried. *'Let me take care of you all,'* Enoch Jacobs had said, smiling, the day of his marriage; but the only care he had taken was of himself, selling every stick and stone, every item they possessed to satisfy his own needs, quieting any objection with blows. That had become the pattern of their lives. When sober, Enoch Jacobs delivered those blows with an air of regret, as if the pain of driving evil from them was a more bitter pain for himself, but she had known the true force behind them was self-gratification, every punch, every slash of his belt an outlet for a wickedness that consumed him; and when drunk that gratification glowed with an intense pleasure.

*'On yer feet you mewlin' bitch!'*

Her stomach churning at the remembered words Saran stared at a sky strewn with a million stars. Such a beautiful world, yet so full of misery ... knuckles pressed against her lips she tried to stem the pictures in her mind but, relentless, they flooded on.

He had cut away the length of rope holding her mother and sister, kicking away the hands that tried to hold on to them, then yanked the thin figures to their feet dragging them behind him into the beerhouse. He had ignored the sound of her mother's choking – the cord digging so savagely into raw flesh she could not breathe – and the cries of an eight-year-old.

It seemed a lifetime later her mother and sister had emerged, their yoke held by another hand, a hand that tugged hard on the rope as her mother had turned to look at her. She had tried to call ... to speak ... but only her eyes had said the words.

Pressing her fingers so hard against her lips her teeth cut into them, Saran could not stop the sobs trembling in her chest.

The afternoon sun had sparkled on the tears filling those gentle eyes, eyes that had said good-bye. That same day she had asked the questions, where is my mother and my sister ... what have you done with them.

He had been even heavier in drink, his words mumbling from a saliva-drooling mouth, his small eyes bleary as he had looked at her. Then had come the blows. Like savage rain they had fallen on her head and body as Enoch Jacobs had sought to relieve his own guilt by beating her senseless.

It had been during that same night she had learned the truth. Closing her eyes against the agony of it, Saran remembered the drunken mumblings.

*''Alf a crown...'* Enoch Jacobs had twitched and moaned as he lay sprawled on the ground, *''alf a crown for the woman ... bloody daylight robbery, should 'ave bin twice that, got years of work in 'er...'*

With every bone screaming its own pain she had scrambled as close as her tethering rope allowed, straining to catch each muttered word.

'*...but it weren't work 'e 'ad in mind fer the little 'un, 'e wanted 'er for 'is own pleasures; I seen that when I set 'er on the table... Zadok Minch's eyes glowed when they lit on 'er, likes 'em young, do Zadok Minch...*'

He wanted her for his own pleasures? Her blood had run cold as she had listened. What had this brute of a man done with her family?

'*...come close to that table, then, 'e did...*' the mutterings had gone on, '*...couldn't resist runnin'* *'is 'ands over that body, feelin' the buds just beginnin' to pop, strokin' up them legs to the very top, knowin' by the way the kid squirmed and cried out that he was first man to play his fingers in that tight little 'ole...'*

She had wanted to kill him then, wanted with every fibre of her being to grab a stone and dash it hard against that heavy-jowled face, to keep on smashing it down until no trace of life was left in the man she hated; but the rope had held her too tightly and all she could do was listen.

'*...'elp in the 'ouse was what 'e were buyin' 'em for...*' Enoch Jacobs's laugh had snuffled in his throat, '*...that might 'ave fooled the others who were bidding for the goods on offer but it d'ain't fool me, I knowed what the wench were wanted for an' I med Zadok Minch pay; I let 'im feel 'er all over, then when 'is mouth were waterin' I med 'im pay ... 'alf a sovereign was what I asked, 'alf a sovereign for a babby to play with in 'is bed...*'

As if guessing that she already knew what had transpired the afternoon before, Enoch Jacobs had smirked when dragging her to her feet next morning, had taken a cold sadistic pleasure in retailing the account in full. He had led her mother and sister into the beerhouse, shoving first her mother on to a table shouting loudly she was for sale to any with money to buy. They had bid in pennies and halfpennies, gloating as her skirts were lifted to show her legs were capable of 'carrying a load during the day an' spreadin' wide enough at night to take the load of any man 'ere'.

He had enjoyed seeing the blush of colour that had brought to her cheeks, but Saran had known his real enjoyment had lain in seeing the pain she could not keep from showing on her face.

*'Then come the wench's turn...'* The words sounded again in her ears as though they were still being spoken. *'Lifted 'er on to the table, I did, pulled 'er frock up to 'er face ... let the fox see the rabbit. Them little tits just startin' to sprout set the bids comin' thick an' fast but Zadok Minch were the only man could spend 'alf a sovereign. That be what I done wi' yer mother an' sister, I sold 'em, sold 'em as any husband and father 'as the right to do.'*

*Sold them!* Hard as stone the words settled on her heart, stilling the sobs in her chest, banning the tears from her eyes. Only hate remained, cold impervious hate coupled with a burning desire for vengeance.

The thick cord biting into the soft flesh of her neck, Saran stumbled as it jerked almost pulling her off her feet. Enoch Jacobs had slept fitfully, crying out at intervals as some unseen dread plagued him, a dread the constant spending from the money got from the sale of her family did nothing to abate.

'Pick yer bloody feet up, you clumsy bitch!'

Jacobs snatched again on the rope he never removed from her throat, mumbling to himself as he walked. He had not been properly sober from the day he had sold her mother and sister, auctioning them like cattle to the highest bidder; nor, since that day, had he once settled to sleep until he had tied her hands together then secured her to a tree. And she knew the reason for this; the reason, despite the ale he consumed, was fear, fear of her. Enoch Jacobs had seen what gleamed every day in her eyes, heard what laced each word that left her mouth, knew what rested in her heart, the prayer that rose nightly from her soul, the yearning to see him dead!

Six steps in front of her, he paused. Saran turned her head away as, making no attempt at privacy, he relieved himself. The man was an animal! Keeping her eyes tight shut she swallowed hard. What lies had he told her mother when persuading her to wed him?

'I needs a bite o' summat to eat.'

The rope jerked again and Saran caught the sneering look as she opened her eyes, the look that said she belonged to Enoch Jacobs to do with as he pleased; and what did he intend to do with her? Trailing her around the country would bring him neither peace nor profit so what was to be her fate ... auctioned off in some beerhouse as her loved ones had been?

'There be a tavern up ahead, I'll get meself a meal and a bit o' decent company, an' a bit o' decent company will mek a fine change from looking at your surly face the day long. I'll find somebody as knows 'ow to smile at a man.'

How could he call himself a man! Three people tethered like beasts for market, two of them sold into God only knew what sort of existence, herself dragged from tavern to tavern then staked to the ground or tied to a tree while he drank himself into a stupor. But at least the hours spent waiting were hours when she did not have to look up on that hated face, when her ears were free of a voice that scarred her soul.

'Sit you 'ere.'

Tugging viciously on the rope, Enoch Jacobs hauled her to where a group of tall bushes stood a little way off from a low-slung building, small-paned windows glinting in the late spring sunshine. Checking her hands and assuring himself they were still firmly tied he smirked.

'Mebbe I'll bring you a bite o' summat out ... mebbe!'

Laughing loudly he swaggered away, the first of his remaining coins already in his hand. Watching him bend to enter the low doorway Saran felt her stomach rumble. He had not brought her more than a crust in days and there was little doubt but he would not bring her anything today, his own needs were all that occupied the mind of her stepfather. But hunger she could cope with and she thanked heaven for these precious moments when she was alone.

Drawing up her knees she rested her forehead on her tied hands. What had happened to her life? One minute they had all been so safe and secure, so happy in their small house in Willenhall, her father's locksmith workshop attached to its rear. Then had come that accident. Her father had gone to the steelworks as usual to order a fresh supply of metal for his business, and it was whilst he stood talking to the overseer in the yard that a loaded cart overbalanced, tipping its load of metal bars. There had been no warning, her mother had been told by men carrying her father's broken body home on a door used for a stretcher, no time for her father to escape the rush of heavy steel, he had been killed almost instantly. Two weeks on from the burying of the father she loved, Enoch

Jacobs had come upon the scene. What money they had could not last many weeks ... eyes tight shut, Saran remembered her mother's words.

*'Mr Jacobs is a locksmith, he has served his years of apprenticeship and he will work for us.'*

But Enoch Jacobs had worked for himself, duped her mother with his quiet concern for the welfare of her family and the business that supported them, inveigled himself so deeply in her trust that she turned more and more to him, asking his advice, following it to the letter even though in her heart she must have known it was not always sound. But her mother had in turn been taught by her mother always to believe that a man was superior to a woman, in mind as well as in body, so she had refused to listen when Saran had tried to point out that Enoch Jacobs was not conducting the business as her father had done, nor would he any longer have herself keep the account books; in fact, he had gradually drawn more and more into his own hands until finally, with marriage to her mother, he had it all.

Life for her family had gone downhill from that point. Less and less of the money from the business had been given to the housekeeping and more and more to the tavern-keepers and brothels, with any complaint bringing a blow to the mouth.

It had been one such blow had brought on her mother's miscarriage. Now clenching her fingers tightly where they rested on her knees, Saran tried unsuccessfully to wipe the pictures from her mind. There had been no fire in the grate the night Enoch Jacobs had staggered home from the tavern, the small house was cold with the frosts of January. He had ranted and raved, demanding a fire be lit and a hot supper produced. Her mother, seven months gone with his child had trembled as she answered that there was neither food nor coal in the house. He had stopped shouting then. Beer-dulled eyes had rested on her mother then he had swung a doubled-up fist, hitting her full in the face and sending her crashing backward into the fireplace. Minutes later her mother was gasping with the pain of childbirth.

She had not known what to do. Saran flinched, seeming to feel again her mother's hands clawing at her arm as she writhed. Jacobs had left the house as her mother had fallen; only Miriam was there. But Miriam was no more than eight years old. Her mental vision switching, Saran saw a small white-faced girl, her dark eyes wide with terror as they looked at the woman groaning with pain.

*'Fanny Simkin...'* her mother had gasped between spasms that left her breathless, *'send for Fanny Simkin!'*

Should she go? Leave her mother like this with only a terrified child to care for her? What could Miriam do should anything happen? Saran remembered the thoughts that had been a whirlpool swivelling her brain... That was when she had made her decision. Miriam must go fetch the woman who acted as midwife for half of the town. Tying her own shawl over her sister's head she had told her to run, to find Fanny Simkin and bring her to the house. She had looked at the prettily enamelled clock stood on the mantelpiece as the child had fled from the house. It had showed a little after ten. Somehow she had got her mother to bed; holding the worn figure, taking the weight against her own, they had paused on almost every step for waves of pain to subside. And the time had rolled slowly by, each minute seeing her mother's agony grow. But Fanny Simkin did not come.

*'Help me, Saran ... help me, child!'*

Tears hot against her closed lids, Saran heard the cry again in her head. She had never seen a child birthed, how could she help? But without assistance her mother might die. That one thought had quieted the doubts, stilled the chaos in her brain. She had run to the room she shared with her sister and snatched a clean cotton nightgown from a drawer of the dresser, laying it across the foot of her mother's bed; then she fetched the threadbare sheet they had washed and set aside for the purpose, and spread it beneath the panting figure. If only her mother had explained the process of childbirth as she had spoken of the need for the sheet ... but she had not. Saran remembered the desperation that had swamped her. But somehow she had kept it a controlled desperation. Outwardly calm she had talked quietly to the heaving figure, soothing ... quiet ... holding an air of reassurance she herself had been far from feeling. Praying for guidance, asking heaven for the help she needed, she had placed her mother's legs so the knees pointed to the ceiling, then, speaking with a new-found authority, had told her to breathe long and slowly, doing it with her while the pain-filled eyes had clung to her face. Then the child had come. Exhausted, her mother had sunk into the pillows and she, Saran, had washed the tiny dead body of her half-brother.

It had been all over when, at one o'clock in the morning, Miriam and the midwife had returned, the older woman saying she had been at a birth on the far side of Shepwell Green.

*'There were naught you could 'ave done that you didn't do.'*

Fanny Simkin had looked at the marble-cold body of the newborn baby.

*'At seven months they don't stand a lot o' chance o' bein' born alive. You need set no blame agen yourself for 'twas a deal o' sense you showed and 'tis like enough you 'ave your mother's life to show for it.'*

She had looked once more at the poor little body, marking the sign of the cross on forehead and chest before wrapping it again in the cotton nightdress.

*'Where be Enoch Jacobs?'*

Stunned as she had been by all that had happened, Saran had not failed to notice the woman did not afford him the usual courtesy of calling him 'the man of the house'. Hearing he had not returned as yet she had simply looked at the tired figure in the bed then back to Saran.

*'When you hears the whistle along of Priestfield pit calling the miners to their shift you get yourself to Lizzie Beckett's grocer shop along of Froysell Street; tell 'er Fanny Simkin sent you, 'er'll gie you a soapbox to lay the child in, and for sixpence Joby Grump will see it laid in 'oly ground.'*

She had thanked the woman, moving with her to the bedroom door. There Fanny Simkin had paused, her voice lowering as she glanced back over her shoulder at the bed. '*Your mother be worn out ... 'er don't be well enough for the kind o' attention Enoch Jacobs be interested in, you understands me, wench? Your mother be too weak to carry more babbies, the next one be like to see the end of 'er.*'

The woman's words had been more than kindly advice, they had been a warning, one Saran had done her utmost to heed. Beginning that same morning she had begun to sell everything which belonged to her personally; the locket her father had given her to mark her thirteenth birthday, saying proudly his little wench were now a young lady, the ivory bracelet that had been a gift on her Confirmation. One by one they had gone and after them had gone Miriam's little treasures, the doll she cherished going last of all.

Lifting her head Saran gazed at the sky, the last of the sun's scarlet setting spilling like blood on the horizon.

Selling the doll had been the hardest task of all. Miriam had tried not to cry but tears had trembled in her soft eyes. It had all but broken her own heart and their mother had pleaded with her to give the toy back, yet Fanny Simkin's warning had been stronger. While there was one item in the house, one thing that would bring money to pay for Enoch Jacobs's beer and women, then it must be sold; only that way could she keep him from taking his pleasure from her mother, only that way could she keep her safe.

# 2

Shivering with cold, Saran jerked awake. Overhead the blackness of the sky was pierced with pale lemon silver ribbons of moonlight rippled on the dark waters of the canal. Enoch Jacobs had kept close to the waterway, shunning the villages, avoiding being seen with a girl he kept yoked and bound.

He had first fastened them together after he had caught them running away. There had been nothing else to sell and, desperate for her mother and sister, she had talked them into leaving. But Enoch Jacobs had found them soon enough and roped them together, not even freeing them to make their toilet. It had been her fault; the indignity her mother had suffered had been her fault!

A sob catching in her throat, she pulled at the rope holding her to a tall bush but all it did was bite into her flesh. If only she could sever that cord, get away from Jacobs, she could find her family.

'I tells yer, if you wants it then yer must bid forrit along o' the rest.'

Hearing the raucous voice grating the quietness of the night, Saran glanced to where the canalside alehouse gleamed in the darkness.

'My offer be a good 'un.' A second voice, equally rough, answered the first.

‘I ain’t sayin’ it don’t be, what I do be sayin’ be this, mebbe somebody else’s offer’ll be better.’

‘Oh ar! An’ mebbe’s nobody else’ll bid at all!’

The strident laugh Saran recognised as her stepfather’s echoed in the shadows.

‘Could be as yoh’ll be proved right, an’ then agen it could be as yoh won’t; we’ll ’ave to wait an’ see.’

They had reached the bush he had left her tethered to, his hand releasing the rope and jerking her to her feet as he laughed again. Outlined against the moonlight, their faces hidden from its glow, two men of roughly the same stature stood over her but Saran had no need of light to know the face of one, heavy-jowled and by this time red and suffused with drink; but the other ... why had he come?

‘I puts another shillin’ on my offer ... that meks it five, ye’ll get no more from the men as teks their ale in the Navigation.’

The words had come after a lull during which Saran felt herself scrutinised.

‘Five shillin’!’ Enoch Jacobs turned to the man stood beside him. ‘That be yer bid ... but ye’ll mek it in that tavern where others ’ave the same chance.’

His bid! Snatched along, Saran prised her fingers beneath the rope which was choking off her breath. Bids ... auction! The awful truth hit like a sledgehammer. He had sold her mother and sister ... auctioned them as you would an animal ... and now it was her turn!

Inside the low-ceilinged tap room, smoke from clay tobacco pipes curled thick on air warmed by the large open fire. Pulled to a table placed in the centre of the sawdust-covered floor, Saran was shoved on to it while Enoch Jacobs called to the tavern's occupants to draw closer.

Blinking against moisture the bank of smoke brought to her eyes, she kicked at a hand touching her ankle.

'Yer don't want to go biddin' for that, Zeke. One night ridin' a filly wi' such blood'll 'ave yer on yer back fer weeks!'

The laughter following the taunt rang against blackened roof timbers but the calls came louder still.

'It don't be yer back yer should worry over, Zeke, it be yer front pervides the pleasure, an' I reckons that wench'd wear yer'n out wi' in a couple o' nights.'

'That be just like yoh, Jake Pedley, yer gives advice cos yer be past settin' Zeke an example.'

'Oh ar, if yoh knows so much about advice then act on it 'stead o' talkin' on it!'

Cheers ringing around the room had Enoch Jacobs shouting for order. Stood on the table, Saran looked at the faces of a dozen or so men all staring at her, men whose eyes stroked her body. A shudder racing through her, she felt panic clog her throat. This was no play on Jacobs's part, he would sell her as he had the others.

'A man don't buy goods 'e ain't examined.' Grey-whiskered, a muffler tied about his neck, a squat-looking man pushed closer to the table. 'It be one thing lookin' at a frock but what lies beneath ... yer wants our money then I says yer shows what it is we be buyin'.'

'Perkins be right.' A voice rose at once to champion the grey-whiskered man. 'No man buys a pig in a poke.'

'Well, one thing be certin...' Zeke grinned, showing black-rimed teeth, 'yoh can't lose wot ain't in yer pocket, Jake Pedley, yer don't 'ave tuppence to bless yerself wi' let alone money enough to buy yerself that little bed warmer.'

'An' I supposes it be a full pocket meks yoh talk so cocksure!'

'Be it an auction yer wants or a slangin' match!' Enoch's closed fist came down hard on the table. 'If it be the last then I'll be tekin' my sale further along the cut for–'

'Five shillin'!'

Eyes closed against the shame of standing on a table being ogled by those men, Saran recognised the voice she had heard outside.

'Five shillin' ... that be my offer, tek it or not as yer pleases.'

Several moments of silence passed, marked only by the puff of tobacco pipes and the occasional sizzle of saliva spat into the fire.

'Five measly bloody shillin'!' Jacobs found his tongue. 'This 'ere don't be no bawdy 'ouse wench...'

'Nor do five shillin' be the price yer would pay for one of 'em!'

Cries of assent issuing from the gathered men told the offer was not likely to be bettered, not here in the Navigation. But like the half a crown got for her mother, the money would not last long and then how would his comfort be bought? Unless... Enoch Jacobs smiled to himself as the solution crept into his brain ... unless instead of disposing of his asset in one final sale he sold it a little at a time ... or rather he didn't sell the wench at all but hired her out at every hostelry he cared to call at... Many a man would pay for a tumble and a few shillin' a night would amount to a satisfactory living for Enoch Jacobs.

'I pleases not to tek yer offer...'

A wave of relief sweeping over her, Saran released the breath she had not realised was imprisoned in her chest. He was not going to submit her to such barbaric treatment!

'...but to mek another one altogether.' Enoch Jacobs's voice was suddenly the only one in that murky, smoke-filled room. 'I wishes to give every man 'ere a chance o' a little pleasure. For a shillin' yer gets to lie wi' the wench ... gets to strip off all 'er be wearin'... do what yer've often dreamed, an' all it'll cost be one shillin'...'

'A shillin'! I can get an hour fer a tanner along o' Willenhall town ... there be many a floozie there be only too glad to tek it.'

The smile breaking on to his mouth, Enoch looked in the direction of the shout. 'Yer would be wastin' yer money; judgin' by what I sees o' you I reckons what you got atwixt your legs would be spent an' empty afore the woman 'ad 'er drawers off!'

'I'll pay yer a shillin'.'

Tears of fright blinding her vision, Saran could only listen, her heart pounding with every word. Was this what had happened with her mother and sister, had they been stood on a table, had they been pawed and humiliated while men bid against each other, as she was? But Jacobs said he had sold them outright, she had seen another man lead them away, seen her mother's tears, tears of sorrow at parting from a daughter... But was that all that lay behind her sobs? Every sense, every nerve in Saran's body jarred as the next thought entered her mind: could her mother's tears have been more for her younger daughter, for an eight-year-old girl bought for the purpose of prostitution? Not that! Her tears spilling, Saran lifted her shackled hands to her face. Dear God in Heaven, not that!

'A shillin' be the payment for entry *after* the amusement 'as bin opened.' Jacobs grinned at the listening group. 'But for the privilege of bein' the first to go in, the one who opens it as yer might say, then the price be 'igher, an' afore yer goes complainin', let me remind yer it ain't no carpet bag yer be layin' yer money out for, it can't go bein' closed after tekin' what yer wants, yer can only pick a flower from its stalk once an' this 'ere wench be a bloom as ain't never bin picked afore.'

'I still says that when a man offers goods fer sale 'e should let the buyer see what 'e be offerin' for.' Jake Pedley sidled to stand beside the grey-whiskered man. 'I says we should see fer us selves if what yoh 'ave on that there table be worth our money.'

There were two ways to go. Jacobs's brain struggled with his body's clamour for drink. He could walk out of the door taking the girl with him. But that way he must wait for the sweet ambrosia, the ale that brought him so much pleasure, for he had not a penny remaining of that money and this landlord allowed no tankard to be filled until payment was in his pocket; that left only the selling of the wench and that was like to take some time, seeing the tight-fisted attitude of the men collected around her ... unless he whetted their appetites!

'Never say Enoch Jacobs was one to pull the wool over anybody's eyes–'

'Never mind the wool,' a voice from the rear of the room cut through the smoke haze, 'just lift that frock over *'er* eyes.'

Laughter ringing in her ears Saran dropped her hands, holding her skirts against her knees, but as a sharp blow from Jacobs sent her almost toppling from the table, she had to lift them to steady herself, and in that moment her skirts were thrown high.

'A man buys 'isself a mare to ride only after he feels the flesh be sound.'

As he spoke the grey-whiskered man ran a hand up along Saran's leg, shoving it beneath her bloomers rubbing his fingers over the soft mound that topped her legs.

'And the tits,' Jake Pedley's lips slavered, 'gie we a peek at the tits!'

What were these men doing to her ... had they done the same things with her sister, a child who knew nothing of their sordid purpose? For a moment she saw the small face, fear robbing it of colour, confusion widening gentle blue eyes, and in that moment her own fears disappeared, leaving in their wake a raw, biting fury, an ice-cold repugnance, an abhorrence of the man who had plundered her life, robbed her of everything she loved in the world and now was robbing her of common decency. Loathing rising like an iceberg in her heart, she snatched her skirts from Jacob's grasp, at the same time lashing a booted foot towards that grey-whiskered face.

It had been bedlam, the smoke-filled room had erupted as her foot had sent that man falling backwards, fists flying as those at the edge of the crowd had surged forward to obtain a better view while others bayed for blood. And it was her blood they had called for: how dare a woman strike a man! How dare a woman do anything? Saran touched a cheek still swollen from Enoch Jacobs's beating. It was 1837 and England was a civilised country, yet still a woman could not count her life her own.

Enoch Jacobs had grasped the rope that held her, hauling her from the table as those cries had broken out, dragging her behind him out into the night; but not before he had snatched a pot that held the stake from a card table. The money had kept him in ale that following night and her with a slice of bread and cheese; Jacobs realised he must at least feed her his leavings if he was to reap the harvest he had set himself.

He had not attempted that again as yet, but he would. Saran knew it was only a matter of time; once his stolen funds were exhausted it would begin all over, the taunts, the pawing, the humiliation!

She prayed with every nightfall that he would fasten her hands and neck less securely, that just one time the ale he consumed in the daytime would have his brain so fuddled he would forget to tether her at all; but he never did. Always he checked her bonds before leaving her to enter some tavern, to ensure they were firm, just as he had checked them tonight.

*'Always say your prayers, trust the Lord and He will take care of you.'*

How many times had her mother murmured those words when saying goodnight to Miriam and herself? Saran tasted the bitterness in her throat. Was this the care He gave, was allowing women and children to be sold like animals the care He gave! Were they lies they had been told during those long Sunday sermons in St John's church, lies like those told by Enoch Jacobs when courting her mother? 'Come to me and I will take care of you'. Was there no difference between God and man, were they both liars?

Huddled into herself for warmth Saran tried to sleep, but the coolness of the night breeze coupled with her misery defied the effort. If only she were given the shelter of a doorway but, from the first day of leaving Clemson Street, Jacobs had avoided villages keeping strictly to the canal towpath, always forcing her to sit on the ground, ensuring her clothing covered the bonds set about her hands and throat, hiding them from view when any narrow boat passed.

The sound of voices calling goodnight had her raise her head. Drunk as she knew he would be, Enoch Jacobs stumbled across the empty ground waving a bottle as he came towards her.

'Shgone ... sh'all gone.' He sagged to the ground,

swigging from the bottle. ‘Money’s all gone but Enoch Jacobs’ll get sh’more. He be sh’mart, do old Enoch, knows ’ow to get money ’e do.’

The face was lost in shadow but Saran knew it would be heavy with drink, the eyes bleary and half closed, the words coming from wet lips slurred in their boasting.

‘’E’ll find ’ishelf another Zadok Minch.’

The bottle lifted, wavering with every rise and fall as Jacobs tipped more and more of the contents into his mouth. What did he mean when he had said he would find another Zadok Minch? Had someone else been robbed of their money? Had he stolen another stake from a card table? But there had been no sounds of rumpus from the tavern, no angry shouts or crash of falling men and furniture; so what had he meant? Alert now, Saran listened closely but the mumbling ceased, drunken snores taking their place. Grateful for the few hours of peace his stupor would give she rested her head on her drawn-up knees. Perhaps tomorrow would see a change ... perhaps tomorrow she would be given a chance to escape.

‘’S beautiful!’

Saran woke to the sound, not sure she had not dreamed it.

‘Sho beautiful!’

It was no dream. She lifted her head warily. Had someone come across them on the canalside?

‘It’sh lovely, they be danshing.’

It was no stranger had wakened her. Saran watched the figure of Enoch Jacobs swaying unsteadily on his feet. He did not usually wake halfway through the night nor had she known him to sleepwalk, no matter how drunk.

But he was sleepwalking now, acting out the dreams flitting through his brain. Should she call to him? Or had her mother not told her once that sleepwalkers should not be roused but led gently back to their bed? Fastened as she was to a clump of gorse that would be impossible.

'Enoch wantsh to dansh...'

Caught between wanting to call out, yet afraid of the harm a sudden waking might cause, Saran stared at the figure silhouetted against the night.

'...Enoch wantsh to dansh...'

Repeating the slurred words he lifted his hands, holding them half raised to the shoulder as he cavorted. Saran clenched her teeth on the disgust the scene aroused in her. He looked like a devil; black against the glittering moonlight he looked what he was, a devil from hell.

As suddenly as he had begun to shamble about, Enoch Jacobs was still, his hands lowering to his sides. Saran felt a swift surge of relief. He would return to his spot now, lie down and sleep to near midday. That was many blessed hours from now. She glanced to where the moon, full and golden, gleamed serenely from a blue-black sky, and drank in its beauty, feeling her heart respond to its lustrous radiance. It had aroused such feelings in her for as long as she could remember; in childhood she had pretended it was a land of fairies, a wonderful magic world where dreams came true. The fancies had gone, passed with childhood, but the admiration of the luminous orb, of its incandescent perfection had never left her. Gazing at it now as it spilled sparkling streams of brilliant gold that reached to the water and reflected off its dark surface, glittering like jewels on the stillness, she hoped she would never lose her appreciation of such beauty.

Across the sky a small cloud moved floating into the gilded nimbus, touching the great lambent circle teasing the light with its own diaphanous grey veil until the beams shimmered on the water, twisting, reaching downward and then twirling upward twining sinuously with and around each other like some beautiful gold-clad dancers.

'You be sho lovely...'

Lost in the vision of loveliness Saran had not seen Enoch Jacobs move. Glancing at him now she saw him standing on the very edge of that dark glassy ribbon, his arms reaching out over it.

'...Enoch wantsh to dansh.'

Her breath caught in her throat as she tried to shout, to call out a warning, wake him from the dream that had him in such danger, but the words were no more than a whisper.

'Enoch wantsh to dansh wi' you, he–'

But the remainder was lost in the splash as he stepped into the water.

# 3

He had walked into the water, arms stretched out before him as though reaching for something. Enoch Jacobs had stepped straight into the canal! Saran stared into the paling dawn. She had tried calling to him but after so many hours without a drink her throat had been hoarse and dry, so her call sounded little more than a croak; but had it been the roar of a bull it was doubtful it would have turned him from his purpose for Enoch Jacobs had seemed like a man deep in a trance, mesmerised by something only he heard and saw.

She had wanted to help, despite his cruelty she had wanted to save him pulling against the rope yoking her to the bushes until it had rubbed her flesh raw, but it had been hopeless, he had knotted the rope too well. She had heard the thresh of the water. Closing her eyes Saran tried to free her mind of the picture that had played there over and over through the remaining night hours and now was repeating again, but it was no use, the horror just went on and she saw again the stocky figure etched black in the moonlight, arms straight out in front of him ... and the voice ... she had not realised last night but, though the slur of a drunken man, it had held a note almost of ecstasy, as if he were watching something beautiful; then, drawn by a desire that echoed in his last call, he had deliberately stepped from the towpath!

'Cripes, missis, yer frightened the life outta me!'

Her eyes springing open, her heart drumming like the hoofbeats of a galloping horse, Saran instinctively drew back against the bush.

'I d'ain't see you sittin' there ... Lord, you give me a fair shock.'

'I ... I'm sorry.' She swallowed hard, trying to still the shaking of her voice as she looked at the boy who had spoken to her.

'T'ain't your fault.' He grinned, showing strong teeth. 'It was just I weren't prepared, like... I'd expected to see yer gone.'

Gone? Saran was confused. The lad spoke as if he knew her but they had never met before this moment.

'How come your old man d'ain't tek you as bargained? Or mebbe 'e did then come back to this place for a second sale. I 'ave to say there was more than one with 'is coppers in 'is 'and. Where is the old bas– your father? Can't say I be in a monkey's wrostle to meet 'im.'

She had been in no hurry to meet with Enoch Jacobs either. Saran got to her feet as the lad turned to go.

'Wait ... please ... what did you mean when you said you did not expect to see me here?'

Glancing both ways along the towpath the boy hesitated. It was obvious he was nervous, that he wanted to be off, but when Saran repeated her question he moved a step closer into the shelter of the clump of bushes that hid them from view of the tavern.

'I 'eard 'em talkin'.' Hands shoved deep into

the pockets of his jacket he squatted beside her. 'I'd done a job for the landlord and in return 'e let me sleep the night in a cubby 'ole next to the chimney. It was from there I 'eard 'em, two men talkin' of a sale of some sort ... one were sayin' that six shillin' were too much even for one which hadn't bin tried. I wondered what it were they were on about so I listened some more. "Never had a man astride 'er," so the first voice said but the second were quick wi' an' answer: "If that be the case," 'e said, "how do I know her will come up to scratch?"' I took a peek then, seen the red-faced 'un laughing. He took a swig from his tankard then said her'd go the same way as her mother and sister; if the wench d'ain't prove as he'd promised then he'd sell 'er for half a crown. That were when it were agreed; for five shillin' the second one had 'imself a vir–' The boy paused, his sharp-boned face blushing deep pink. 'Had a wench he could keep forra whole night.'

It was her! The boy was talking about her! Saran felt the blood slow in her veins. Enoch Jacobs had intended to trade her for a few shillings. But he had come from that tavern alone ... why had the other man not come with him?

Unaware she had whispered the words aloud she only half heard the quickly spoken reply.

'That was what I thought meself when they went on drinkin', he's paid his five bob so why not collect the goods, so to speak. But they both went on swillin' ale like there'd never be another drop; the red-faced 'un spendin' the five bob quick as he'd come by it, payin' one round after the t'other wi'out a thought to keepin' a penny of it for the next day.'

Why would he? Saran sank to the ground, staring again at that spot on the water. Why would Enoch Jacobs have had a thought for money when he could make more by using his stepdaughter as a prostitute?

'I reckon them goods bein' hired out were you.' Beside her the boy talked on. 'That 'eavy-jowled one, the one free an' easy in his spendin' said 'e had the wench fastened up good and tight close by and that rope around your neck and 'ands tells me I ain't no mile off the mark.'

He was bang on the mark. Hot tears scalding behind her lids Saran stared helplessly at the bonds that had bitten deeply into her wrists as she had struggled to reach the figure on the towpath. She had been hired out...

'Look,' the lad twisted to look at her, 't'ain't none o' my business, that I knows, but it don't seem right for a wench to be trussed like a sow for market... I could 'ave that rope off and chucked in the cut afore old beer guts gets back from wherever it be he's gone to.'

'He ... he won't be back,' Saran murmured, 'he won't ever be back.'

'Left you, 'as 'e?' Nimble fingers busy with the cord that held her wrists, the boy talked hurriedly as though every second he stayed with her placed him in danger. 'No loss to my way of reckonin' but the other one still be in that tavern; he passed out dead drunk an' the landlord said to put 'im to bed and set the cost to his bill, but 'e won't sleep the 'ole day so unless you feels like honourin' a bargain you d'ain't 'ave the mekin' of

I suggest you hop it sharpish.'

Removing the cord as he finished speaking the lad coiled it, then, tucking one end between the loops so it would not undo, he hurled it into the centre of the canal glittering now as the newly risen sun dappled its surface.

'I have nowhere to go.' Watching the rippling circles spread and disappear, leaving the ribbon of water smooth and calm as before, Saran felt the strike of true emptiness. She had hated Enoch Jacobs and, yes, she had wanted him dead, but his presence had been a strange comfort, it had meant she was not entirely alone. But now that reassurance was gone and life was showing her a new fear.

The lad was on his feet, his glance travelling the towpath. 'Ain't you got no relations ... somebody who would tek you in?'

'I ... I have a mother and a sister...'

'Well, theer you am then ... all you need do is–'

'I don't know where they are.' Saran went on like someone caught in a horrible dream, a nightmare that shut out reality. 'Enoch, my stepfather ... he ... he...'

Watching the tears break free coursing down Saran's cheeks the lad seemed suddenly a man. 'You don't 'ave to tell me,' he said quietly. 'The old swine has them hired out as he intended doin' with you.'

If only that were true it would be better than it was now, for at least she would see them, know if they were well! With sobs thickening her throat, Saran shook her head. 'He did not hire them out.' She stared again at the glistening water, and when she spoke it was a trembling whisper. 'Enoch Jacobs sold my family.'

Following the narrow strip of ground worn bare of grass by the tramp of men leading barge horses, Saran glanced at the lad trudging beside her. Taller than Miriam and possibly a year or two older, he had taken command of the situation. Catching her by the hand he had pulled her to her feet, running with her until that tavern was not even a speck on the horizon. But she ought not to have left that place, she should have gone to the nearest town and explained to the constable there what had happened.

'I reckons we should leave the cut.' The lad glanced behind, clearly ill at ease. 'We sticks out like a sore thumb walking this towpath, best mek for a town; we'll be less likely to be taken note of among a crowd.'

His eyes were blue as Miriam's! Saran caught his quick glance then shook her head. 'I have to go back,' she said quietly, 'my stepfather...'

Quiet and assertive as he had been when pulling her to her feet outside of that tavern, the boy's youth fell away from him once more. 'Your stepfather be dead and there be nuthin' you can do to alter that. You 'ave a life to lead and a family to search for; go back to that beerhouse, send for the constable and by the time you've told him what was done to you and your'n you'll find yourself up afore the bench accused of murder.'

'Murder!' Saran gasped. 'That's ridiculous, I couldn't... I wouldn't...'

Coming to a standstill the lad half laughed.

'P'raps not but who do you think will believe that? And while we be on the subject, tek this into consideration: there were nobody to see what truly 'appened, nobody to swear on the book they seen your stepfather *fall* into the cut. The coppers and magistrate will want somebody to answer for a dead body found floatin' and you'll do very nicely. I say forget him!'

Would it happen as he had said, would she be suspected of murder? Saran's feet moved slowly behind the lad now moving on. An enquiry could take weeks, possibly months ... she might be kept locked away in prison and in that time her family could be taken anywhere!

'Luke!' Calling the name the lad had told her was his, she caught up when he turned to wait. 'Luke, I–'

Luke Hipton pushed a welter of brown hair back from a broad forehead with a movement of exasperation. 'Look,' he said flatly, 'I've told what it be I thinks you should do, whether you does it or not that be up to yourself; as for me I'm goin' to ask at yonder cottage for a drink of water then I be mekin' for a town, like I said.'

Following the line of his finger, Saran saw the tiny house that, but for his sharp eye, would have gone unnoticed, set as it was in the curve of a low hill. Smoke curled thinly from its chimney and was immediately lost in cloud lowering in the sky. A drink of water would be welcome.

There was no fence about the low-roofed cottage, no gate or path leading to its door, while an overgrown patch of wild flowers claiming to be a garden nestled beneath the minute window.

Waiting some way off, Saran watched the lad knock at the door, then moments later turn and shrug his shoulders with a gesture that implied there was no one at home.

'Come on,' he called, smiling, 'they won't mind we tekin' a drink from their well.'

Luke should not be going to the rear of the house ... they should not be here at all ... taking that which was not offered was like stealing...

'He be right, Harriet Dowen refuses no traveller a drink.'

Startled by the quiet voice Saran swung round, catching her breath at the sight of a face of which half was blemished with the deep red stain of a birthmark. 'I ... I ask your pardon,' she stammered. 'Luke ... we ... we meant no harm.'

'That I knows,' the woman answered. 'Yourself would have passed on by but the lad...'

'Luke would not steal anything, he ... he only wanted a drink of water.'

Sharp eyes glittering beneath her cotton bonnet the woman nodded. 'That also I knows and you both be welcome to it but there be a kettle boiling atop the fire and a slice of bread and a bite o' roast fowl in the larder if you have a mind for it and I reckons it wouldn't go amiss for there be a look of weariness about you.'

'There be only a bucket so if you wants a drink you'll 'ave to come round...' Luke's words died on his lips as he rounded the corner of the cottage.

'I think the wench would manage better if'n her drinks from a cup, and if you would prefer tea then we could find one for you an' all.'

If only he would look at her ... if she could

catch his eye, tell him with a look she would rather not stay, that she felt uncomfortable imposing on a woman she had never met before and would rather he took his drink of water and they could move on. But he had already decided otherwise; grabbing her wrist as he followed the dark-skirted figure, he drew her after him.

Inside, the room was dim after the stronger light of day but the fire burning in the grate flickered over pretty chintz and cupboards gleaming from daily rubbing away of dust. Laying her basket on a table covered with a spotless cloth the woman removed her shawl, hanging it on a peg beside the door.

'Sit you down at the fireside,' she said, reaching for a teapot covered with brightly painted flowers.

Twisting her fingers awkwardly with her skirt, Saran asked, 'May I help ... please, I'd rather.'

'I understands.' The blemished mouth gave the shadow of a smile. 'Busy fingers helps lift a load from the mind. See you then to the mekin' of a pot of tea, you'll find all you needs in that cupboard and I'll bring milk from the scullery.'

Taking up her basket the woman drew aside a heavy chenille curtain draping a tiny square passage, which no doubt gave on to a scullery. Watching her go, Saran reached cups from the dresser, setting them on the table before reaching for a pottery jar painted with the same array of brilliant flowers as the teapot. Finding her guess correct that this served as a tea caddy, she spooned some of the dark leaves into the pot then scalded it with water from the kettle. Brewing tea would keep her fingers busy, she thought, putting the teapot on the hob to infuse, but nothing would lift the burden from her mind. Enoch Jacobs was dead, drowned, and evil as he had been to her and her family, she should have seen to the recovery of his body, seen to his burying, but instead she had run away. Guilt at the wrongness of her action making her hands shake, she took the jug with its beaded cover, avoiding the eyes of the woman handing it to her.

If her trembling hands had been noticed they brought no comment. Placing the food on the table the woman waved Luke to a chair beside it then bowed her head, offering a prayer for the bounty of heaven and the grace of the Lord.

'Amen.' Saran added her own whisper to Luke's enthusiastic reply.

'The meal be sparse but the welcome be plentiful.' The woman placed thick slices of meat on blue-rimmed plates, passing one to each of them.

After the long days of hunger the meal was a banquet, but the kindness with which it was given filled her throat and Saran could not eat. Knowing it must appear gross ingratitude she tried to apologise, but the older woman dismissed it with a quick wave of the hand.

'That there chicken don't be going to get up and run from your plate, wench, so you tek the time you needs. There be no hurry.' Turning her attention to Luke she placed another slice of meat on his plate, meeting his approving grin with a nod.

Beyond the window the sky darkened suddenly and a distant roar of thunder rolled from the distance.

‘Seems there be the mekin’s of a storm.’ The woman glanced at the ceiling then back to Saran. ‘If it be you have no liking for being soaked through then you be welcome to bide ’til it be passed and should it be it carries ’til the morning, well I ’ave no bed to offer but the fire will burn all night and there be a blanket apiece.’

A few hours beneath a roof, sheltered from the chill of night, a fireside in place of a hedge! It all seemed too good to be true, but the delighted look on Luke’s face said the offer was genuine and he, if not herself, would accept it. Perhaps she could stay for just a little while, a few hours’ rest, then she would go back the way she had come, go to a magistrate and tell what had happened, and somehow she would see Enoch Jacobs’s body buried in church grounds.

She had slept. Warm in the sweet-smelling blanket, Saran listened to the drum of rain against the tiny window. The storm the woman had foretold had broken but its sounds had not disturbed her. Nor had it wakened Luke. Sitting upright she glanced at the figure curled in a corner of the room. She would have liked to stay with this cheerful lad, been glad of his company for a few days more, but he would go on to a town while she must return to Willenhall. There was no need to rouse him, no need to explain her leaving: he would know the reason. Rising quietly, she folded the blanket then paused, holding it draped over one arm. What was said of Luke could not be said of Harriet Dowen. Luke would place no concern on being given no word of goodbye but that woman's kindness did not deserve to be repaid in such a way; if nothing else, she deserved an explanation.

A movement of the curtain closing off the scullery had Saran turn quickly. The woman's bright eyes were watching her.

'I ... I want to thank you, Mrs Dowen...'

Moving to the fire the woman poked the embers, freeing them of grey ash before feeding it fresh coals. 'It don't be Mrs.' She straightened, holding the empty coal bucket in one hand. 'I were never wed and never expected to be, for what man would tek a wench with a mark such as I carries? There was none in the hamlet of Bentley nor in the towns that stand beyond. Seems no man were willing to take on a woman scarred as I be.'

'Then there was no man with sense!' Saran answered quickly.

The smile touching the blemished mouth hinted at long-passed sadness. 'Maybe ... maybe.' Gentle as the smile, the words came softly. 'Whichever the reason, I were never offered for ... but I be happy enough with life, I have my herbs which people often come here for, and helping them gives me content; it might be you could find a bit of the same before you returns the way you came. Oh there be no need of telling me your intent! It be obvious in your face. You carries a guilt, could be Harriet Dowen could ease it a little.'

How could this woman help her? Saran laid the blanket aside. Could she tell her where money enough could be earned to pay for Enoch Jacobs's funeral ... or where she might find her mother and sister?

'You have your doubts as to what I says ... that be your privilege.' The woman turned towards the scullery. 'Harriet Dowen don't give where her don't be asked.'

She had hurt the woman's feelings. Harriet Dowen had read the guilt she carried and had offered help but she had also seen the refusal Saran knew showed in her eyes.

'Mrs– Harriet,' she said as the figure returned from setting the empty bucket in the scullery, 'I didn't mean...'

'I know, wench, I know.' Her smile emerging once more, Harriet Dowen nodded. 'You've given no offence but I'd tek it kindly if you'd share a pot of tea with me afore you goes on your way for it's been a day or two since I had the pleasure of company.'

She could not refuse. Murmuring her thanks Saran set the cups while the older woman lifted the kettle from the bracket swung over the fire.

Minutes later, handing a cup to the seated woman, Saran felt their fingers brush and Harriet Dowen gasped as she drew her hand back.

'Harriet!' Saran swung the cup back on the table, ignoring the stain as it spilled tea on the white cloth. 'Harriet, what's wrong ... are you ill?'

Harriet Dowen's face had become chalk white, its red birthmark glowing a deeper crimson while her eyes seemed to stare into a space beyond her own room.

'Oh, sweet Mother of Jesus!' she gasped. 'Oh, dear Lord, have mercy!'

# 4

'Saran, Saran, what be wrong ... be you all right?'

Awake in an instant, Luke was on his feet and across the room.

Still staring at Harriet, Saran did not see the lad's face, anxious as her own, as he looked keenly at her.

'It isn't me,' she answered, 'it's Harriet, she ... she's taken some sort of turn.'

A little colour returning to the white side of her face, Harriet Dowen pulled herself together, but she could not still the trembling of her hands as she asked for her cup. 'No need for worrying,' she said shakily, 'and I be sorry to have wakened you, lad.'

'But what happened ... will I go for a doctor?'

'No, lad, 'tis kind of you to offer but there be no doctor can cure Harriet Dowen of the mark her carries on the outside nor that which be inside.'

Was the woman who had been so generous to a couple of strangers ill ... could it be she suffered from that same falling sickness a girl in the street next to theirs had suffered from, often taking a fit that left her trembling and drained of colour? Saran bent forward.

'Can I get you anything ... perhaps some potion?' Concern uppermost in her mind she laid a hand on the woman's arm, withdrawing it at the sharp gasp. 'I'm sorry...' Perplexed, she took a step backward her hazel eyes troubled. 'I should not have touched you.'

'Saran child, sit down.' Harriet laid her cup aside. 'There be something I would have you know ... no need for you to go out of the room, lad...' She glanced at Luke who had started towards the door. 'I wants you to hear what it is I have to say for I feel it circles yourself.' Returning her bright look to Saran, she went on. 'What you just seen, the shock that took me when your fingers touched against mine, be a thing which has happened to me since I was naught but a little wench stood at my mother's knee. Sometimes when people touched me I would see things in my head, things that had to do with them, oft time it were their past that were shown me and other times it would be what was yet to come. That is how it be with you. Your fingers brushed mine and it was there, pictures vivid and clear, pictures of a woman lying atop two wenches, one no more'n seven or eight years; her were trying to protect 'em from the lash of a belt ... a belt wielded by a thickset man, heavy-jowled, hair flaming like dull fire.'

Enoch Jacobs! Saran felt her insides tumble. The woman was describing Enoch Jacobs!

'The man be known to you...' Harriet was still speaking though the trembling of her hands was gone, 'but he be no more, he was called – called to join the moon dancers.'

'Who be the moon dancers? I ain't never seen 'em. Be they an act at the Palace of Varieties?'

'They be no act on no stage, lad, you'll not see them in any music hall.'

'But you said the man you seen in your 'ead had bin called to join the moon dancers!' Luke was clearly dissatisfied with the answer he had received.

Harriet nodded but her eyes did not leave Saran's face. This wench knew well the man spoken of, her body bore the marks of his brutality and her soul the scars of his malevolence. 'What I said were what I saw.' She spoke slowly, the words directed at the girl. 'The man I speak of were called by the moon dancers; you think to return to the place where he stepped into the water, to find his body and see it set in holy ground, but them as frolics wi' the moon dancers be many days in the finding, sometimes it be far from the spot they was called, sometimes they don't be found at all.'

'Be these moon dancers real?'

'Real enough to the poor unfortunates as sees them at their revels.' Harriet reached for the teapot. 'Now, lad, you fetch a bucket of coal from the backyard and I'll see about mekin' you both a bite of breakfast, the day be sharp as yet and an empty stomach will have it feeling no kinder.'

Her mind in a turmoil, Saran followed the woman's instructions, setting a pan of water to boil, adding oatmeal and salt, then stirring the mixture with a wooden spoon.

*'many days in the finding.'*

The words turned in her mind.

*'sometimes they don't be found at all.'*

Was Harriet Dowen telling her that Enoch Jacobs would not be found ... to search for the body would be fruitless? But that could mean he had not drowned, for if he had then his body would float. It would rise to the surface ... be seen by the first person to pass on the towpath. With a breath suddenly held in her throat, fingers gripping the long-handled spoon, she stood motionless, one thought dominating every other. Maybe she was wrong in assuming Enoch Jacobs had drowned, perhaps he had managed to crawl out of the water, drag himself on to the opposite bank! The moon had been brilliant but its light had seemed to play only over one patch of the canal, centred in one small area, leaving the towpath and surrounding land in thick dark shadow. He could have hauled himself out, she would not have seen him in the blackness; and if he had woken some time later and stumbled away that would explain why neither she nor Luke had seen him that morning. He was alive! Enoch Jacobs was alive and she must find him, for only he could tell her who it was had purchased her mother and sister, only he could tell where they would be found.

Turning quickly, the hand that held the spoon caught against that of the woman setting bowls on the table. Catching her breath Harriet pulled back, her face paling as she clutched the angry red mark already visible on her skin.

It had been no scald had that mark appear on the back of Harriet Dowen's hand. The porridge bowls washed and returned to their place on the dresser, Saran turned her attention to the table. Gathering the cloth she took it outside, shaking its white folds free of crumbs. The woman had been more than kind to them. Standing a moment,

Saran stared over the barren stretch of ground empty of any other dwelling. She had come here to live, to escape the cruel jibes of children, so Harriet had told her as they had talked the night before. But had that truly been the reason she chose to live in isolation with only the brief visit of women wanting potions, or was it the heartache of having no man ask her to be his wife? It was a cruel trick of fate that had half of her face covered with a terrible birthmark.

'Darlaston, you say that be the nearest town?'

Luke's voice floated out followed by the quieter tone of Harriet.

'One way be Darlaston, the other leads to Wednesbury. You'll come to the spot where the track divides – it be marked with a signpost – but it's nothing either promises 'cept toil and sweat. Life be hard for the folk there and 'tis not much they have to feed their own and less to give to strangers ... so you tek the bread and cheese I've wrapped in that cloth...'

The woman had done enough for them already, they should not be taking more of her bounty. Turning quickly indoors, Saran put her feelings into words.

Taking the folded cloth the older woman smiled. 'What I give, heaven returns–' The rest never came for as her fingers touched briefly against Saran's she drew her breath sharply.

Having witnessed the reaction several times, Luke was impatient with the two; why not say what was seen, what it was given the older one to know? Maybe it would be for the good of each of them. In a few minutes it would be too late for they would have taken their leave. Resolute at the thought he asked, 'What is it you sees whenever you touches against Saran?'

Pushing the cloth into a drawer Harriet Dowen's mouth set in a firm line. 'That don't be for you to ask.'

'But last night you said it circled me, so it be only fair I should know what it is!' The sense of injustice lacing his reply carried over to his blue eyes, showing clearly in the look he now turned to Saran.

Was she being unfair to him? Uncomfortable with his stare she turned her back, pretending to busy herself with a last-minute smoothing of her skirts. It was true what he said, Harriet had told Luke that that which was shown her in those 'flashes' somehow included him, so maybe it was only right he should know. Facing the older woman as she came from the scullery, Saran forced away her apprehension, saying evenly, 'Harriet, would you tell me, please ... who or what are the moon dancers ... is Enoch Jacobs still living, and ... and will I find my mother and sister soon?'

'I can tell you of the dancers well enough, but to the rest I would needs tek your hand atwixt my own. If you wants to hear then sit you at the table.'

The first to take a seat, Luke held his breath. Could be he would be told to wait outside.

'This be your asking, will it be for your listening and for no other?'

The meaning was clear to Saran. With her word the lad would be banished from the room ... but he had not abandoned her when finding her trussed on the heath, he had released her and stayed with her when he could easily have sprinted away; he did not deserve to be closed out, what she heard he too would hear. Giving him the fleeting ghost of a smile she nodded at the woman settled at the table.

'The moon dancers,' Harriet began, 'waits for the unwary. Like golden will o' the wisps they flickers on the surface of the waters, their streams of light stretching and swaying, lifting and falling to a tune only the one that be called can hear, and once it be in the ears there can be no shutting it off ... any man or woman, any child caught by its melody be forced to dance; unable to resist, wanting only to be part of that shining reel, they steps into river or canal – where they drown.'

'Be they ghosts of dead folk ... folk who drowned afore them?' Luke's awestruck question breached the small silence.

'Who can tell,' Harriet shook her head slowly, 'be they spirits of folk dead or the spirits long believed to dwell in forest and water.'

'But such don't be real!' the lad answered, superior in his knowledge.

'Don't they!' Harriet swung him a quieting look. 'Neither do the dancers of the moon, but they comes and when their dance be over so does the life of some poor soul; so tek care, lad, think wise and well afore you lets the words from your mouth.'

'So it was a play of moonlight Enoch saw on the water, moonlight and cloud shadows. In his drunkenness he thought he was watching a troupe of dancers and when he tried to join them…'

'That was when his life were teken.' Spreading both of her hands on the well-scrubbed table, Harriet answered Saran's unfinished question. 'I doubts my words will prove untrue when I says the man you calls Enoch Jacobs be dead though his body will be long in the finding and then no man will know his face for it will have been eaten by life that swims in the waters.'

Life that swims in the waters? Luke shivered. He would take no more dips in the canal and the nearest he would come to covering his whole body with water would be a bowl filled from a kettle and a cloth to soak in it!

Harriet turned a blind eye to the lad's sudden loss of superiority, hiding her smile at the rapid disappearance of youthful swagger. 'Return you to that place if it be that is your purpose,' she said to Saran, 'but you'll not have the finding of the man you called stepfather. Ask about him, talk of him to the magistrate if that be your wish, but that path be strewn with the rocks of heartache and it gives no lead to that you truly yearns to find.'

There was a sureness in the voice, a quiet certainty in that disfigured face. Saran sat silent with her thoughts. Harriet Dowen had no reason to deceive her, nothing to gain by turning her from her intent and what would be gained by mistrusting the woman? The blood in her veins telling her it would be no gain but misery, Saran answered with a question.

'Leaving what is done to lie in the past, by not

returning to Willenhall but going on, will I find my mother and sister?'

'I'll answer first by telling what it is has already been shown me, then you can judge whether it be you wants to place your hand in mind.' Closing her eyes the woman breathed twice, long and slow, then, lifting her lids, she began.

'I saw a man with flaming hair, a man with a smile upon his face but with deceit and treachery in his heart. He takes the hand of a slight gentle woman whose own heart be heavy with the loss of a husband. He promises to cherish and take care of her and her daughters but with the marriage made he shows his true self – an evil drunken self that sells everything for ale, beats the three of them with a leather strap taken from his waist when they tell him there is no more to sell, and finally sets a bond around their neck, leading them to a tavern where the older be sold for half a crown while the child–'

'There is no need to go on.' Saran's words erupted on a sob. 'You have been shown true, the people you describe are my family, it is them I must search for. Please, Harriet, help me!'

Looking deeply into hazel eyes glinting with tears she knew the girl was fighting to hold back, Harriet Dowen turned her hands so the palms were upward.

'I gives no guarantee, I can ask for nothing to be shown, neither can I refuse what be sent. The powers be sometimes strong and at others they be scarce a flicker in the shadows of the mind, but whichever it should prove you have my word I will not tell it wrong.' Bowing her head, her words barely audible in the quietness of that tiny kitchen, she prayed, asking her power be governed by the spirit of the Lord and no presence of evil attend it. Then, looking again at Saran, she said softly, 'Ask the grace of heaven, child. Then place your hands in mine.'

'Why do you stay with me, Luke? You could go on, find shelter in one of those towns; it would be better if you did, I can make my way alone.'

Luke glanced sideways at the girl who had sat huddled with her face hidden on her knees near enough the whole of the day and who even now did not lift her head.

'I be in no hurry,' he answered, chewing on a blade of grass; 'as for shelter, this won't be the first night I've spent on the 'eath nor do I sees it as being the last and I reckons that so long as it sits well wi' you then we will travel together, a bit o' company be good for a soul.'

His soul or hers? Pressed into tear-dampened skirts, Saran's eyes remained closed. The lad had heard the words spoken across that table; his future locked with hers should they choose the same path from the crossroads, a future filled with toil and topped with sorrow. But he did not have to walk beside her, his could be a different future, one where heartbreak was not the mile-stones which marked the way. But they had not yet reached that branch in the road, when they did ... as they must ... she would speak again of his leaving her and following his own way. She had been selfish. A short distance from the home of Harriet Dowen she had given way to the fears in her heart; sinking to the ground she had wept, and when the tears were spent had continued to sit locked in her own despair, wallowing in self-misery, and all the time Luke had stayed with her. But her self-pity was over, she would not give way again. Lifting her head she watched the darkening skies of late afternoon become strewn with banners of purple, gold and scarlet as the setting sun flaunted its dying beauty.

*'Ask the grace of heaven, child.'*

The words Harriet Dowen had spoken that morning ... had she meant them only to be said before their hands were joined? No; Saran knew that was not so, the woman was giving her words to use when she herself was no longer present to help.

She had placed her own hands between the outstretched ones.

Overhead the glorious streamers merged and blended, stretching a brilliant canopy of luminous colour, irradiating the earth with a lambent burning glow. Lifting her face to it Saran felt the rest of what that woman had said flare with equal luminosity in the darkness of her mind. The moment their hands had met the woman's body had stiffened, her head held taut on her neck, and her glazed eyes had seemed to stare into a different world.

*'The way be not easy,'* she had muttered, *'the path which fate unrolls before you be pitted with grief and anguish, pocked with bitterness and misery ... but out of sorrow comes forth greatness, you will rise from the ashes of despair and as you walks you casts a great shadow, a shadow that covers many. Some be*

*grateful while others seek to throw it off. But there be one walks beside you, his future locked with yours. Give him your trust, for through him you find what it is you seek.'*

'We should go on.' She looked at the lad who had sat patiently those long hours while the emotions she had held in check so many days poured from her. 'Maybe we will reach the town before night.'

The smile that flashed in his blue eyes was not relief for himself but for her, that she had found the strength to face the grim future Harriet Dowen had predicted. Stretching a hand Luke helped her to her feet while his heart told him wherever fate led Saran Chandler he would be there at her side.

'We best keep to the track from now on for this heath most like be honeycombed wi' worked-out gin pits, same as be around Walsall; the miners took the coal an' left the holes gaping in the ground and they don't be easy seen, 'specially so when it be dark.'

'I often wondered why they did not fill them in before sinking another shaft.'

'Don't tek no wonderin'; like my father said, filling the pit afore movin' on brought no pay for the labour and if the men of Walsall couldn't earn then their families couldn't eat.'

That was the first time he had made mention of any family.

Reaching the track worn in the rough grass, Saran matched her step to his. Was his father dead, as hers was? Why would his mother let him go into the world on his own at such a young age?

'My family be all gone.'

His answer preceding her question, Saran walked on in silence.

'They died from the cholera; mother, father, brothers, sisters, all dead barring one. Her name were Emmeline but we all called her Emmie. Five year old her were when the cholera struck, three year below me. Why we didn't die only the Lord above can tell but it would have been better if we had...'

The young voice throbbed with a bitterness that caught at Saran. This lad had suffered far more than herself but she had been so tied up with her own sorrows she had not even thought he too could be hurting inside.

'We ... we was took into the poor 'ouse.' He was speaking quietly, his words spaced, swallowing on each sentence before he could get the next past his throat. 'Emmie was frightened, 'er were no more'n a babby but when 'er cried to be put wi' me the wardress slapped 'er face. Weren't allowed 'er said, males one side of the building females on the other. I seen Emmie just once a week after that, in the chapel on Sunday, but even then we was not allowed to speak. Then one Sunday I seen her little face so red and puffy I thought her'd been crying. I called her name but before I could reach 'er I was caught by the beadle and hauled away. The penalty for speaking when not asked was ten strokes of the cane and six days in the glory hole; that were a pit dug underneath the storeroom with no light of any sort but plenty o' company ... if you calls rats company. That were bad enough but worse waited my bein' brought out.' He swallowed hard, brushing the back of one hand across his cheeks.

'Emmie were dead and buried ... my sister had died and I hadn't been allowed out of that hole to see her laid to rest. I thought then my heart could take no more sorrow, but then some six months later I was called to the beadle's office. I was of an age to be indentured, sold into service until my twenty-first year, but I told him I would be no man's servant. At that he flew into one of his rages, spluttering and shouting as he reached for the cane kept hanging on the wall behind his desk. "You'll do as you be told, boy," he was shouting, "you'll do as I says or you'll die same way as that snivelling brat died, I'll kick you down the stairs same as Liza Jebbins kicked your sister!"'

It was some moments before Luke spoke again, moments in which Saran seemed to feel some of the agony emanating from him. But when at last he did speak the choking sobs were gone and in their place was a hard metallic anger.

'It seemed at that moment, there in that room, the world went dark; a darkness such as couldn't be related to the sun sinking below the horizon, a darkness no shadows of night could bring. It was a suffocating, drowning blackness such as had not come even with the deaths of the others of my family ... an eclipse, a darkening of the soul that shut out every feeling but hate. Emmie had not died of the sickness of the lungs as I had been told, but murdered, kicked down a flight of stairs by a wardress! The beadle saw my face, saw the torture his words produced and he laughed...'

Pausing in his stride Luke turned away, keeping his face from the light of the newly rising moon, hiding his pain from her. But it could not be hidden. Saran waited, wanting to hold him, to soothe his hurt as she had so often soothed Miriam's; but, afraid he would resent it, she stood unmoving beside him.

Speaking almost to himself, his words no more than a whisper, Luke went on.

'I saw that swine laughing ... laughing at the death of a little wench who couldn't defend herself; I snatched the stick from him, then slashed it hard across his head and he fell against the fireplace. I raised the stick but he didn't move, then I seen the blood trickling into the hearth. The beadle was dead, his skull cracked and I were glad. It took a second or two for me to realise nobody had heard and, my senses returning, I put the stick back in its place and took the glass he'd refilled wi' brandy while laughing and I tipped it over him afore setting the glass atwixt his fingers...'

He had caused the death of a man! Breath trapped in her throat Saran tried to comprehend the enormity of what she had heard. The penalty for manslaughter was death! Luke would know that. He would know that should he be caught he would go to the gallows, yet he had stayed beside her the entire day. The lad had risked his own life ... was risking it still ... and all to comfort her!

'I could 'ave gone then, over the wall and away while the rest of them warders was busy herding them inmates to the refectory for the evenin' meal, but instead I put myself into the glory hole.

I guessed the death would be seen as an accident for it were well known the beadle were overfond o' the brandy, and if anybody wondered as to me I 'oped it would be thought as I'd already been sent to my employment. Be my thinkin' right or wrong I kept me to that hole until it were my supposin' the inmates to be in their beds, leavin' the staff to their own pleasures.

'It took no time to slip into the females' wing and to find a door wi' the name of Jebbins painted on it. So I waited, watched from an alcove as the woman went into her room, waited again until I believed her to be sleeping afore I went in. I found her easy enough, her snores leading me to the bed. As I reached it the moon shone into the room and at that moment Liza Jebbins opened her eyes. P'raps her thought me to be the ghost of the child her had murdered for her didn't move; then, realisation dawning, her opened her mouth but I was quicker; I had the pillow from beneath her head, pressing it over her face afore a sound had left her throat; I held it there while I spoke close to her head. "You be goin' to die," I told her, "die the same way Emmie Hipton died." I held that pillow 'til her struggles stopped but not long enough to see the life gone from her. Making sure her were unconscious only I pulled her from the bed and to the top of stairs that led to the hall. There her regained her senses, and, helping her to stand, I wished her a safe journey to hell ... then, with my foot against her stomach, sent her on her way.'

# 5

Stood in the darkness, the lad held in her arms, Saran could still hear the sobs that had shaken him. He had told his story, released the tears, but the pain would go on, it would live with him to the end of his days. He had scrambled out through a high window in the wash-house, dropping to the ground below the wall surrounding the workhouse. Winded, he had lain there listening for sounds that said he had been discovered, then when none came had run.

Two years! Saran felt her own heartache diminish in the light of what Luke had told her. Two years of being ill-used, bullied and beaten by warders, but worse than that was the knowing that women and girls fared no differently to him; two years of being so close to his sister, of seeing the misery in her eyes whenever they were fortunate enough to glimpse each other in the chapel yet being unable to touch or speak to her. Saran's arms tightened protectively. She had known unhappiness but Luke had known a torture that had driven him to sending a woman to her death. That was his danger now; the search would be on to find him once the authorities learned he had not taken up his apprenticeship, that he had run away. They would put two and two together ... and that would lead Luke to the scaffold!

They had to go on, to put as much distance between himself and Walsall as could possibly be managed.

'Luke,' she spoke softly, 'Luke, we must not stand any longer ... the constables could be looking for you.'

Stepping free of her arms the lad cleared his tears with a swift wipe of the hand. 'We would 'ave heard had there been a hue and cry; them narrow boats as passed by on the cut, the bargees don't miss nothin' as happens in the places they passes through and they spreads it as they goes along; it travels mouth to mouth covering the country like fallin' rain. No, if we ain't got news then it means the happenin' is bein' seen as no more'n an accident, Liza Jebbins catched her foot in her nightgown when called to the privy and toppled headlong down the stairs, as for me goin' missing, the Board of Governors will see it as one less body dependent on the parish, one less mouth it might have to feed, so there be no chance they'll have a search party combing the streets of Walsall.'

'Even so, we should still move on.'

'No more tonight, a step or two from the track could see you in a pit shaft ... best we wait for daylight. Besides, you needs rest.'

'But I've rested too long already, we could have reached one or other of the towns Harriet spoke of if I hadn't sat the whole day nursing my own worries.'

'The day were given to easing the weight burdening your heart but there was no rest in that. We'll stay the night here.'

Once before she had heard that change in him, a quiet firmness in his voice, now she heard it again. In all but years Luke Hipton was already a man. Feeling the tension that held her body like a bowstring, Saran knew the boy was right, the hours of giving way to grief had left her weary. Making no further demur she sank to the ground.

Settling beside her Luke said apologetically, 'I wish I could mek a fire to warm you, p'raps I could find a few sticks...'

'No!' Saran's hand caught his arm, holding to it. 'You said yourself it isn't safe to walk the heath in darkness, and the night is free of frost so we won't freeze.'

'Saran...' Several minutes later Luke spoke again but this time his voice held none of that former note of authority. 'Saran, if it be acceptable to you p'raps we could sit close, it helps keep a body warm.'

Hidden by night shades, Saran's smile hovered about her mouth. He had the thought and speech of a man but in some measures Luke Hipton was still a boy. Placing an arm around his back, her smile faded as she felt him wince. The legacy of the beatings he had suffered ... cuts in his flesh left by the slash of a cane? Drawing him gently to her side, the coldness of new fears touched her nerves. His age, the fact he was still only a boy had made no difference to his masters... Miriam was younger still. Miriam too was no more than a child! Was the man who had bought her treating her as such or did he whip her as Enoch Jacobs had done? Curling her fingers so tightly they throbbed against her palms, Saran knew she had to find her family.

*'I can ask for nothing to be shown, neither can I refuse what be sent.'*

Harriet Dowen held a taper to the candle that would light her to bed. The wench had asked and had been told. But her had not bin told all! 'I adds naught to what be given me and I teks naught from it.' Those were the words she spoke to bodies who came asking for her help, asking her to use the gift heaven had given in place of an unblemished face, so why hadn't it bin that way with that wench?

Making her way to the tiny bedroom at the top of the narrow wooden stairs she set the candle beside her iron-framed bed.

*'I teks naught from it.'*

As she loosed the curls of her hair, braiding it into night plaits, her mind repeated the words; her eyes, staring beyond the candle flame, saw in the shadows of her room the same pictures she had seen when holding the hands of Saran Chandler, pictures she had not spoken of. It was the first time ... never before had she withheld what the powers of second sight disclosed.

'I took naught from it.'

Soft as the velvet darkness that played beyond the spill of candlelight, the whisper barely disturbed the silence yet it rang loud as the passing bell in Harriet's brain. She had told herself that same thing throughout the day, sought comfort from the words; but there had been no comfort. She had taken naught, disguised nothing ... but was withholding not tekin' away?

Dropping to her knees, she clasped her hands together. 'Lord,' she murmured, 'it be I've misused the powers trusted to me, that I knows, but the wench whose hands I took atwixt mine had a heart already overflowing with sorrow. I couldn't add more by tellin' her the rest of what I seen ... the cruelty, the deceit ... it'll be hard enough to bear when time comes, I couldn't give it to her to be borne the years between. I knows the pain of a broken heart for have I not carried the mark all these years? The blood-red flaw set across my face in my mother's womb, the disfigurement that turned men from marrying with me! The cause wouldn't have bin the same for Saran Chandler but the pain that lies afore her strikes as deep; that be a pain my not revealing all I seen will shield her from 'til it be time. It were against all the ways I've gone afore, ways I believed You would want me to tread. I asks no forgiveness, Lord, for I wouldn't be wanting to put You in the position of refusin', all I asks is understanding.'

Sealing her prayer with the sign of the cross she climbed into bed. Lying there, the same pictures playing again and again in her mind, Harriet knew that what had been shown to her would come to pass. Saran Chandler would know that pain, more than once she would feel her world reel and shatter about her, feel an agony of mind that would mark her soul as vividly as that which marked the face of Harriet Dowen.

A sound echoing in her ears, Saran woke with a start. All was still. Overhead a lacework of stars glittered against a sable sky, soundless and tranquil as the surrounding heath. Had it been a dream that had her so abruptly awake, her nerves quivering? A nightmare that had disappeared with the opening of her eyes? But dreams and nightmares left behind some fragment of their presence, some fraction of themselves in the mind, but there was nothing. Yet something had wakened her, a sound that had come out of the darkness, come from something that was still there, hidden by the colour of night.

'Did you hear that?'

Luke, too, was awake. Saran felt a childish relief that she was not alone in what she had heard, that it was no fantasy had her senses twanging.

'What d'you reckon it were?' Sitting up straight Luke stared into the moonlit expanse.

Had it been a fox or animals fighting over territory? That was what she wanted the sounds to have been, but as Luke got to his feet Saran recognised the improbability of such being the cause; the overall noise, the resounding echo! it was too loud ... yet in the centre of it had been a kind of scream.

'It were no creature ... they don't set up a commotion such as we just 'eard, not if they wants to survive, and it be no miners on their way to the shafts for it don't be light enough for working gin pits.'

'Perhaps it was imagination.'

Luke's derisive sniff only added to Saran's feeling of self-scorn that followed on the heels of her words.

'Two folk don't usually imagine the same thing

at the same moment!' he answered quietly, his gaze probing the velvet gloom. 'We both woke to the same noise so I says that noise were real and if the mekin' of it were no cause of creature nor of workmen, then what did mek it?'

'Could it be one of those shafts falling in on itself?'

For a moment Luke stood silent, musing on the question, then with the knowledge inherent in every child born into the grind of coal-mining that formed the lifeblood of the world he had known, he replied, 'A crownin' in? Could be, they occurs regular enough but they gives off no scream ... not less there be men workin' when the slide begins!'

'But you said they did not begin mining until it was light and there isn't a sign of dawn.'

'Miners don't be the only folk crosses the heath, travellers does the same thing. Granted they don't journey at night lessen they has to but there be times when there be no choice.'

He was saying he thought the sound that had awakened them had been made by people! Saran's blood slowed in her veins. People ... a scream ... an accident!

Already stepped on to the track they had settled beside, Luke turned and in the moonlight Saran saw the look of concern on his face. 'Wait you here,' he said, 'don't move from this spot. I'll go along the track a ways–'

'No!' Clutching his sleeve, Saran held on. 'If you go, I go with you.'

The silence was thick, settled like a blanket over the darkened world, yet the sound of that scream remained fixed in Saran's brain – a scream of pain, desperation and fear all mingled into one. Her hand closed in the boy's, Saran shivered as they walked on. Let it all have been a delusion, the deception of a tired brain, a misconstruction arising out of cold and hunger, let it be any or all of those things. But deep within herself she knew it would be none of them!

'Over there!'

Stopping so abruptly she walked into him, Saran stared the way Luke pointed. Peering into space dancing with moon shadows she could see nothing but, as she stared, one spot became more solid, an ebony patch silhouetted against the sky. Not an animal – screwing her eyes she strained to identify the unmoving shape – and no collapsing shaft heaped mounds on the surface of the ground...

'It be a wagon ... Lord above, it be a wagon!'

Even as the boy gasped the words, recognition of what she was seeing flooded over Saran and without a thought of safety she began to run. A wagon meant a man, maybe a woman, children, and that scream ... could be they were hurt!

'What d'you reckon this were doin' on the heath this time o' night?'

Having reached the vehicle Luke stared for a moment at the horse fastened to the shafts, shaking his head when the animal gave no response to his touch.

'It be no wagon,' he went on, 'this here be a carriage. The horse don't be movin'...'

'The driver ... what of the driver?'

Responding to the urgency of her question,

Luke moved to where the driver would have sat, but in the gloom she saw the shake of his head.

'There has to be someone!' Saran almost shouted. 'Carriages don't drive themselves.'

'Well, I can't see... Oh God!'

The exclamation lending reality to what she had prayed would not be, Saran moved to the boy's side, catching her breath as a sudden burst of brilliant moonlight bathed the scene. Trapped beneath the carriage which rested on its side, only his head and shoulders showing among the tangle of wreckage, a man lay. Unconscious or dead! Dropping to her knees Saran held her face close to the stricken man's, releasing her pent-up breath as she felt the light fan of his own against her cheek.

'He's alive.' She looked up at the boy watching her. 'Can we get him free?'

Bending beside her Luke looked closer. 'If we tries to drag him clear we could cause him more hurt, I says leave it 'til it be light enough to see better.'

Dawn could be hours away ... the man could die!

'William!'

It was a thin frightened cry followed almost at once by one of pain.

The carriage! Saran was on her feet and moving. They had not thought to look inside.

'Let me.' Shoving her aside as she made to climb on to the wheel, Luke sprang, agile as a monkey, holding with one hand while the other wrenched open the door.

The cry, it had sounded like a child! Below him

Saran waited, anxiety working her nerves like puppet strings.

'William!'

'It be a woman.' With moonlight streaming on his face, Luke looked at the girl stood staring up at him. 'I ... I think her be…'

'Not dead!' Clasping her hands together, Saran felt her throat close. That last cry had been faint. That last cry! Defying the thought she scrambled into the carriage. Light barely filtered inside and she could at first see nothing, then as her eyes adjusted she made out a figure lying slumped at the far side.

'William ... the baby...'

Baby! Was there a child here with the woman, was it crushed beneath her body?

'It be as I thought?' Luke's voice trailed in the darkness. 'Her's pregnant?'

Pregnant! Was that the child the half-unconscious figure had meant ... and the cry of pain ... had the shock of the accident sent her into labour?

Thoughts swirled in her brain but one stood out from the rest: the woman needed to be got out of the carriage.

'That be easier said than done, we be a yard or so from the ground and it don't be like we can ask her to jump.'

Ignoring the boy's blunt reply to her suggestion they try to move the woman, Saran leant towards her.

'Can you move?' She eased the slight shoulders carefully forward, comforting the groaning with a quiet assurance she herself did not feel, managing inch by slow inch to manoeuvre the woman to the door of the carriage.

Glancing towards the ground where Luke had jumped, she saw him raise his hands. This was something she had not thought of, how to lower the woman she now knew was in the throes of labour; yet it must be done.

'Please, I know you are in pain but to help you we have to get you to the ground. Do you understand?'

At a whispered 'Yes', Saran placed the woman's legs over the sill of the carriage; they reached halfway to the ground, surely they could lift her from there.

Touching a hand to the woman's arm, she gave a shake, she mustn't lose consciousness now! 'I'm going to climb down,' she told her. 'When I call, let yourself slide forward ... do you hear? Let yourself slide forward.

'I don't know whether she can do what I ask but it is the only way.'

Nodding at the breathless explanation, Luke lifted his hands once more. 'Then we best get it done afore her falls out.'

But it took a sharp slap to the woman's face. Getting no response from her calls, afraid the woman would slip into a dead faint, Saran clambered again on to the carriage wheel and from there delivered the stinging smack. It revived the flagging senses and, jumping quickly back to Luke's side, she helped catch the figure as it tumbled forward.

Breath returning to her lungs she covered the shaking figure with the rug Luke had recovered from the carriage; but that was not enough. The ground was damp with dew.

'We need a fire.' She glanced at Luke returning from checking the unconscious driver. 'She must be kept warm.'

'I have matches I took from the storeroom along of the workhouse but that be all. I can't mek a fire wi' just matches.'

Knelt beside the woman beginning to writhe with pain, Saran flung a hand towards the empty carriage. 'The seats, tear the stuffing from the seats.'

'What! I can't, I'll be–'

'Luke!' It was brusque, snapping from the tongue like icicles. 'Do it ... now!'

She would take the blame for the damage. The boy had been afraid of what would happen once it was discovered; a long term of imprisonment and likely several strokes with a cat o' nine tails. But that would not happen. Saran watched the flare of firelight leap into the gloom. She would see Luke was gone from here the moment the first light of day peeped above the horizon.

'The coachman, he be breathing stronger and from what I can mek out it be mostly the tangle of reins lyin' across his stomach, but his legs ... I fears for them.' Heaping sticks on the burning stuffing he caught Saran's glance. 'The box o' that carriage be smashed already so I thought we might as well use it to keep that woman warm. Be there anything more I can do?'

'How far are we from a town ... do you know the way?'

'I got no knowledge as to where we be,' Luke

shook his head, 'as for the way, that be puzzlin'. I ain't never been more 'n a spit from Rutter Street 'cept to be took to the work'ouse and the only time I got to see beyond that wall were when I done a runner, that were the night I met you.'

The woman needed a doctor. Maybe she could leave her long enough to find the town Harriet Dowen had spoken of, to find a house or someone who knew where a doctor could be found. Looking again at the woman, firelight showing a face contorted with pain, a body arching with agony, Saran remembered her own mother and knew the time for leaving was past ... the child was already entering the world.

# 6

The child had not cried.

Picking up handfuls of wadding Luke was throwing down from the overturned carriage and carrying them to where the woman lay, Saran packed it tightly around her; exhausted as she was she had to have warmth if pneumonia was to be kept away.

'That be the lot.' Luke jumped to the ground. 'D'you think her'll be all right ... I mean ... her don't be going to die, do her?'

Saran glanced at the lad she knew had tried his best to help, feeding pieces of shattered coachwork to the fire before wiping perspiration from the woman's brow with cloth torn from one of her fine lawn petticoats.

'No.' Saran smiled, the shake of her head visible in the pearling dawn. 'She won't die.'

'And ... and the babby ... what of the babby?'

Tucking a corner of the rug more closely about the tired figure Saran seemed to live again those brief dark hours. It had not been as long as it had been with her mother but the agonised cries had testified to the pain being no less. She had tried to remember all her mother had told her that night, of how to help the child into the world, how to care for it. Her hands had trembled as she supported that tiny head, then the fragile body. But it had not moved! She had given way then, allowing the fears that had steadily mounted in her to turn to panic ... it was her fault, two babies born dead ... two tiny lives sacrificed to her ineptitude ... she had done something wrong and because of it two innocent children had died before they lived! She had tried so hard ... prayed so hard! The feeling of hopelessness and despair that had swept her had been so strong she had screamed heaven's injustice ... why take infants who had been given no time in the world? Where was the mercy in that?

Her cries had brought Luke running. She had sent him away earlier, when she knew the final moments were near, trying her best to allow the woman privacy. He had stumbled across from the far side of the capsized vehicle, almost throwing himself beside her as he called her name. But she could make no reply, only stare at the child's still little body. It was in that same moment Luke had once more shed his youthful years. Taking the tiny form from her he had turned it on its head with one hand, bringing the other in a loud-sounding smack to its bottom.

Touching a hand gently to the tiny bundle wrapped against its mother's chest, Saran smiled. Heaven had shown its mercy.

'You did right not to move 'im, lad, the man 'as a broken leg as we can see, an' could be more we don't; it'll need a doctor for to tell that.'

The miners they had heard crossing the heath in the early hours of morning smiled approvingly at the lad who had run to ask their help.

'We've freed 'im from 'neath the shaft but there

be no doubt you did a damn sight more forrim than we, burrowing into that wreckage to strap his leg; if'n you 'adn't 'ad the sense o' mind to light a fire close beside 'im then I reckons cold on top o' shock would 'ave done for the bloke. And you, wench...' he turned to Saran, 'you should be gied a medal for your night's work, that there babby owes its life to you, ar, an' the mother an' all!'

'It was Luke saved the baby...'

'Well, don't go presenting me with no medal!' Luke took his jacket as another of the men wrapped his own about the wounded man.

Holding her baby close the woman reached a hand from the makeshift stretcher the miners had made from the seat of the carriage, her eyes warm with gratitude. 'I have no medal,' she murmured, 'but please take this, it is not valuable except in the thanks it carries.'

The workman brusquely interrupted Saran's attempts to return the brooch that had been dropped into her hand. 'Talk about it later, wench. The sooner we 'as these folk to a warm bed the better off they'll be; an' the pair of you come wi' we ... I've a feelin' it's more'n a bauble you'll be gettin' for what you've done.'

'It could be as that fella said ... could be as we'll be given more'n a medal for 'elping them folks.' Luke watched the figures walking quickly in front, the gap between them widening with every step.

She had urged him to run when the sun had risen, begged him to go, to leave her with the woman and the man who gained consciousness only to drift down almost at once into his silent world of darkness. But the lad had refused. 'We're in this together,' he had said, 'and we'll ride it out together ... only not in that carriage!' He had grinned, jerking his head towards the broken vehicle, but she had not smiled; she had felt only the worry she was feeling now, a worry that gnawed deep inside her. Once recovered, the man Luke had covered with his own worn jacket might well want to give them more than a medal, he might prefer to reward them with prosecution for damage to his carriage!

'I thinks we should keep up wi' them miners, seems they recognises the folk they be carryin' but we don't; if we loses sight...'

'We could be doing ourselves a good turn!' Coming to a halt Saran watched the receding men. 'Think about it, Luke, for all we know there might be no gratitude in that man; despite what we did for them he might only see the damage we did to his carriage.'

'But we only done it for their own good, ain't as though we done it aimless!'

No, what they did had not been done senselessly, Saran acknowledged silently, but would a magistrate see it that way?

'But the woman, 'er seemed grateful, mebbe 'er'll part wi' a bob or two cheerful enough.'

Was that really what the lad wanted ... had he cared for those people only for what he might get out of it ... did money mean so much to him? Almost as soon as the thought entered her mind, Saran swept it away. Luke was unworthy of such an idea, had he helped her, stayed with her in the hope of a reward! No, he had done those things out of the goodness of his heart, and his actions of the night barely passed had been born of that same kindness, it was shameful of her to harbour any thought which said different! Guilt at what had risen in her mind touching her cheeks with a colour that matched the rosy hue of the new day, she said quietly, 'Maybe we should go along to find out.'

''Old up!' Luke's hand was on her arm as she made to walk on. 'That carriage ... the damage we done to it, that be only one stick in your craw, only one o' the bones you be chokin' on, the other'n be thought o' tekin' money for summat you feels anybody who don't 'ave a stone for a 'eart would do glad ... wi' no askin' o' payment ... a body kinder than me.'

'There is nobody kinder than you, Luke, and no one more deserving of a reward.' Touching a hand to the fingers clutching her sleeve she pressed gently. 'Let's go before they are out of sight.'

'No.' Luke shook his head, his hand dropping from her sleeve. 'The reward I spoke of, that bob or two, it weren't for meself I wanted it ... it were for you. I can manage wi' what can be got from a hedge or a brook but you ... you needs a proper meal and a bed.'

She had been so very wrong! With guilt rising fresh inside her, Saran blinked against quick tears. How could she ever have had such dreadful thoughts! How could she have reasoned Luke capable of an act of callousness or greed?

'You don't want no payment, Saran, you thinks

to tek it would be wrong and it would! But I'd 'ave done it ... I'd 'ave done it for you.'

'Luke...' Her eyes bright with emotion, Saran looked into the face turned towards her. 'There is only one thing I want you to do for me, that is to make me a promise, vow to me now that you will never act against what your heart tells you is right, that you will not turn away from what you know to be true no matter who the person or what the reason. Promise me, Luke, promise you will stay true to yourself.'

He had made his choice. Lying face down Luke Hipton stared into the clear water of a stream, his fingers gently tickling a fish. They had paused at the crossroads Harriet Dowen had said they would reach, they had watched the miners out of sight before following the track in the opposite direction.

*...one whose future be locked with your own should you follow the same path from the crossroads...*

That was the gist of the words the woman had mumbled, words said to Saran Chandler but were meant as much for him. But how long would her life circle his? Flicking the fish on the bank he sat up, letting his glance wander to the girl adding sticks to the fire. Light brown hair gleamed in the daylight and though her face was hidden from him he saw it clear in his mind's eye. Her was pretty ... pretty as Emmie's doll, the one that had been snatched away as they had been entered into the workhouse. But Saran Chandler were no doll, her were a wench an' pretty wenches wed soonest. Catching a smile as she turned towards him, Luke felt a weight press heavy on his heart. Saran Chandler would be sure to wed soon and when that 'appened her would no longer want the company o' Luke Hipton.

The thought plagued the rest of that long trudge but as they neared the town that signpost had named as Wednesbury it was ousted by the sight spread out before them. Was there really a town at the bottom of this hill? Did the sky still exist somewhere above that thick dark cloud of smoke belching from a myriad of chimneys? Was this truly Wednesbury or had they stumbled on the gates of hell!

'We'll go back, go the other way.'

'And find what?' Saran shook her head. 'Didn't Harriet tell us there was little to choose between either town? Darlaston is probably just the same as here.'

His lips set stubbornly, Luke stared at the jumble of tiny houses cramped together along narrow streets despite the empty heath that stretched away on all sides.

'Harriet Dowen don't be knowin' everything!' he said, anger burning away disappointment.

'She knew enough to tell us the way would not be easy ... and that we would find a crossroad–'

'Don't tek no magician to tell that!' Luke's reply was mutinous. 'Even a five-year-old babby be wise enough to know there be bound to be a crossroad somewheres along any track!'

What had he thought to find? Saran's glance wandered over the tall-steepled church, its black walls standing sentinel over the small huddled town. Locked for years in the isolation of a workhouse, knowing only the cruelty of warders and the pain of separation from the sister he loved, had he built some myth for himself? When running away had he imagined a utopia where everything would be green and beautiful ... a place of welcome? She had not the gift of sight, the gift given Harriet Dowen, but she could have told him such dreams were a fallacy, that to lose oneself in their delusion was to lose touch with reality. That town was their reality. It was not green and beautiful, it was smoke-laden and grimy with the touch of soot, but while it was no dream it offered a hope.

'I says we try the other place ... it has to be better than this!'

The anger was still evident in his voice but now the hurt of finding a dearly held dream in pieces at his feet showed in that young face. It was not easy to lose a dream.

Gently, but without condescension, Saran spoke quietly. 'Luke, the town where I lived, Willenhall, was little different to the one we are looking at now. It too was dark with the smoke of chimneys and the forges that worked the brass for making locks. Its people toiled so long bent over the workbenches that their spines became misshapen. The area became known as Humpshire, there were so many men and women with this deformity. I remember asking my father why we stayed there, why not go live somewhere where the air was clean, not heavy with the dirt of coal-mining and metal-smelting; he told me then that all of our part of England bore the same blight, that men called it the Black Country, and within its circle no town fared differently to the other. We will go to Darlaston if that is what you wish but try not to be disappointed if what my father said proves to be true.'

'No.' Luke shook his head though the trace of disappointment lingered. 'Like as not Harriet Dowen and your father were right an' we'll find no better in that town.'

*'there be one walks beside you, his future locked with yours.'*

Descending into that smoke-wrapped town, Saran remembered. Luke Hipton had once again made his choice.

'It were all I could find, it were tek it or leave it, an' to leave it meant another night wi' naught but hunger pangs in the stomach.' Luke held out the strip of fat bacon that had been payment for helping a jagger sell coal from a cart. For nigh on ten hours he had hauled sacks, lifted sacks and, as tiredness weighted his limbs, he had dragged sacks to wherever customers said he should. 'It be a day's work,' the jagger had told him that morning. He had stood in the line along with others seeking a day's hire but only the coal jagger had looked at him. 'There'll be pay at the end of it, but regard me... I don't give what ain't bin earned, I deals in no charity!'

He should have said he dealt in no honesty! His limbs sore as after a beating from one of the workhouse warders, Luke tried to smile as he passed the bacon to Saran but his young heart was heavy. There would be no bacon tomorrow, maybe nothing at all, for much as he might be willing to accept the coalman's offer of work should it be made, maybe his aching arms and legs would not cooperate. P'raps if he prayed real 'ard. But 'adn't he done that every night, prayed 'til he couldn't think of another word to say? But it seemed the angels 'ad turned their backs on Luke Hipton!

'It will be better tomorrow, we will both get work.'

'We've said the same for more'n a week yet it ain't never showed sign 'o bein' different.' Disillusion tracing every word, Luke paused, resting his aching body against a wall. 'We stands the line every mornin' along of the High Bullen an' when we gets no offer traipses around every house an' shop yet the answer be always the same, "We 'as nothin' we wants the doin' of." It were wrong to come to this town, wrong o' me to talk you into followin', you should go your own way, Saran, you'd like to get a position in one o' them big places we've seen.'

'You did not talk me into anything, Luke Hipton!' Seeing a sharp tongue the quickest way to deal with self-recrimination, Saran applied it quickly. 'I have a mind of my own and I will use it in deciding what I should do. I will not leave this town or any other I might go to without first making sure there is not a single soul can tell me of my family.'

Luke straightened but could not keep from giving a quiet groan. He was too tied up with his own well-being, he should give more thought to that of the girl who was suffering torment of mind as well as of body.

'You d'ain't find nothin' out today?'

Afraid that to answer would bring the tears that had threatened all day, Saran shook her head. She had asked at every door she had knocked on but no one had heard of the buying of a woman and child, no one had seen two people matching the description she gave, and with every shake of a head the desolation in her heart had increased until she felt it must break.

'I asked an' all, but it were the same wi' me as wi' you, seems your folk ain't bin heard of in Wednesbury.'

He meant to be kind and it was kind, Luke had enough to handle in keeping himself alive without bothering his head on her account. Saran tried to fend off the extra unhappiness his words brought but as they walked on she felt the tears press harder. He was the one should go his own way, he had no reason that could hold him in any one place, neither did he owe her any loyalty; alone he could travel more quickly and a place for one to sleep was given more readily than for two.

'We came together, we stays together!' Luke answered adamantly after she had steeled herself to say what she thought. 'Only two things will see we separated, the first be when you tells me I ain't no longer wanted an' the second be if you asks me to turn to the parish. I can't knock the door o' that work'ouse I seen along o' Meeting Street, I … I can't face such again … I'd rather die than give meself over to that.'

He was saying that now but in the days ahead … if with time things got even worse … if one of them should get sick … but the workhouse! Dear

God, never let Luke go back to that!

Lost in the turmoil of her thoughts, Saran bumped the shoulder of a man bent under the weight of a heavy bundle slung across his back. Apologising for her clumsiness she heard the clink of metal as the bundle was lowered to the ground.

'Ain't no hurt done.' The man wiped a forearm across his forehead. 'I been promising meself a rest since leaving Brummajum.'

'Brummajum,' Luke echoed, 'be that another town ... be it bigger than this'n?'

Drawing breath then loosing it in a short loud puff, the man looked enquiringly at them. 'You be new come to Wednesbury?'

'A week gone,' Luke answered.

'Then my advice to you be to leave agen with the mornin' for there be naught but misery an' hunger to be found in these streets.'

'You reckon Brummajum be better?'

'Would be to mislead you, lad, should I tell you it were when truth be it ain't, not for the likes o' we; there be no part o' the Black Country be easy for a poor man, no matter what his trade an' that there Brummajum be no different.'

'Is it far?'

In the deepening dusk the man's rueful smile faded quickly. 'You'd think so, lad, if you 'ad to walk the ten mile there an' ten mile back every few days an' while you be walkin' you don' be earnin', which in turn means less bread for the bellies of children that be empty enough already.'

'Then why travel so far?'

'The answer to that be simple, that be the only

place I can sell the nails I meks.'

'And a place which pays least for them.'

Having bent to retrieve his pack the man let it lie, straightening to look at Saran. 'You be in the nailin'?'

'No.' Her reply was quiet. 'My father was a lock-maker, he often sent brass lock to Birmingham but the money paid was less than their true value.'

'*Was* a lock-maker?'

'He ... he died.'

'That be 'ard for you, wench ... you an' your brother, 'ave my sympathy...'

'Afore you go,' Luke spoke quickly, cutting Saran off before she could explain the mistake, 'might you be able to tell where we could find a place to get this bacon cooked?'

Grunting with the weight of the pack settling across his back, the man shuffled it into position, surprise in his voice when he answered, 'Bacon! You 'ave bacon? There be a treat my little 'uns don't know the tastin' of.'

Under cover of the gathering night Luke caught Saran's hand, squeezing her fingers hoping she would realise he wanted her to leave the rest of the conversation to him; soft-hearted as she was, she would let the man they were talking with finish up with the bacon and the both of them would know yet another hungry night.

'My missis'll let you 'ave the use of a pan an' there be a fire in the brewhouse you be welcome to the use of.'

'We have no money.'

Beneath the weight of his pack the man's head lifted. 'I d'ain't ask no payment neither would I tek any, ain't every man in Wednesbury be out to rob his neighbour!'

'Luke did not mean any offence,' Saran cut in quickly. The man's feelings had been hurt. 'He wanted only that you should know...'

'One thing I bets I already knows–' his tone softer the man gave a sad half smile '–that be you've toiled like a Trojan a full day for that there bacon, that some work master got his profits from your sweat; but, like I said, we ain't all the same so you brings your earning along of me. It be warm in the brewhouse, you can eat it in there wi' a bit more comfort than agen the church wall.'

Tuned to Saran's feelings, Luke knew the proposal sat uneasily. In the short time of their being together he had learned she was not a girl who took without thought of payment.

'Mister,' he said as the man turned away, 'one good turn deserves the same. Let me carry that pack.'

'Nay, lad,' the man hitched it higher, 'though if it be a good turn you be after doin' then p'raps when that bacon of your'n be cooked you'll let my little 'uns dip a slice from the loaf in the liquor it meks, that would be a feast for them.'

'They'll 'ave their bread dipped and a cut off the bacon to eat along of it.'

Feeling Luke's fingers tighten with his answer, Saran felt a smile warm her insides. The boy was once more the man.

# 7

It was even smaller than the home of Harriet Dowen and, unlike that, held no trace of prettiness or comfort, no touch of chintz to give colour, no oil lamp to light its dingy interior, only the glow of a small fire and one candle fought the cold shadows.

'You can sit, an' welcome.'

A thin woman in patched skirts, grey hair drawn back from her face, placed the solitary chair beside a rough table devoid of cloth. 'There be tea in the pot, I ... I be sorry we 'ave no sugar for the sweetenin' of it.'

Murmuring her thanks Saran glanced about the minute room, empty except for table, chair and three stools set close to the fireplace, yet even in the sparse light she could see they were white from daily scrubbing. Poverty was this woman's constant companion but pride too was an escort, it showed in the cleanliness of her home, in the well-washed faces of her children and in the obviously special cups she took from a wall cupboard.

'Be you passing through?'

Holding a small pottery jug in her hand a girl of around eight smiled shyly as she handed milk to Saran.

'Martha,' the woman's tone sharpened, 'you knows better than to ask questions, that nose of your'n be a mite overlong, don't I always be telling you so!'

'Beg pardon miss.' The child blushed, her bare feet patting on bare boards as she ran to her mother, holding her embarrassment in the ragged skirts.

'I should think so!' Smiling, the woman stroked a hand over the child's dark hair. 'Now, reach you the pan for to cook the bacon.' The girl moving to her task the woman, who had introduced herself as Livvy Elwell, took a half loaf of bread from the same cupboard. 'You be welcome to a slice, the both of you, it will make you a good supper.'

Yes, it would make herself and Luke a fine meal. Saran glanced at the bread. But give the children also a slice and what would this woman and her man have? Should that prove to be their own supper – and there was every possibility it was – then their kindness would mean they were the ones went hungry.

Taking the cast-iron frying pan from the still blushing Martha she glanced to where Luke stood watching and as their eyes met he gave a tiny, almost imperceptible, nod.

'You'll be wantin' the use of this.' Livvy was holding out the broad-bladed kitchen knife.

'Would you cut it, please?' Saran asked shyly. 'Luke and myself would be pleased if you would all share it with us.'

They had slept warm. Shivering against the sharp air of early morning, Saran drew her thin coat closer about her. Was her mother as cold, or

Miriam? Thank heaven she had given the shawl to her sister.

'That be the lot for today, I don't 'ave use for another pair of 'ands.'

The rough voice cutting into her reverie, Saran glanced up in time to see Luke brushed aside by a heavy-set man, his jowls half hidden by a woollen scarf tied about his ears.

'I'll tek the same wage as you paid the other day.'

'A wedge o' bacon!' A laugh, coarse as the voice, scraped the smoke-laden air. 'I ain't so flush wi' money I can throw it to any work-shy bugger as crosses my path, I expects a full day's labour and you d'ain't give it.'

Rage rising hotly to his face, Luke grabbed the man's sleeve. 'I be no work-shy bugger, mister!' he snapped. 'Ten hours I worked for you wi'out so much as a cup of water and instead of the shillin' you promised I got a wedge of bacon that were little more'n fat.'

'And that were more'n you deserved. Now get out of my way, you moanin' little scroat!'

His free arm already lifted to strike a blow, Saran stepped between them. 'Touch him and I'll–'

'You'll what? What is it you'll do?' Sly, degrading eyes trailed slowly from her face to her toes. 'I'll tell you what you can do an' I'll even pay you a tanner forrit, you only needs open your legs–'

He got no further. With every ounce of strength behind it, Saran's hand crashed against his face.

'You bloody bitch!' The enraged shout bounced from the few buildings skirting the High Bullen.

One swing sending Luke hurtling backward the coal-jagger shot one hand to Saran's throat, gripping with the hold of a fighting dog, the other hand curling to a fist. 'I'll teach you to slap your betters.'

'Not today, Turley!' Sharp and painful, a hand strong as the jagger's own chopped across his wrist, releasing the grip he had on Saran. 'We put up with a lot of things in this town but that don't stretch to the beating of a wench nor a lad when they have done nothing to merit the deserving of it. Now, you take my advice and be off about the robbery you call a business or I might just take that sixpenny you spoke of, buy a pig's head and stuff it, wide end on, right up your arse!'

Shaking from the encounter, clinging to a Luke who would chase after the departing jagger, Saran tried to stammer her thanks.

'Be no need of thanks,' the newcomer interrupted. 'It only pains that Turley made no move against me, I would 'ave enjoyed giving that no-good swine a leatherin', Lord knows somebody should; as for you pair, tek a tip from me and avoid him, the man be naught but vermin.'

Unable to still the trembling of her hands, Saran pushed them deep into the pockets of a coat she had outgrown and which fastened only with difficulty. The Elwells had given them a place for the night but that was all they must accept. She had known the goodness of heart in the couple's offer of their sleeping in the brewhouse, but that was their place of work, it housed the forge, anvil and workbench used to make the nails that scarce afforded them a living, it was where the man and his wife worked long into the night; that they would not do with Luke and herself sleeping there. So they had said their goodbyes. But where would they rest when this night fell?

As Luke called thanks to the man who had intervened, Saran watched the figure swing loosely away. Dressed as most men she had seen in this town, moleskin trousers, jacket and muffler, he seemed somehow different, a surety of self displayed in the way he walked, the way he held his head high.

'Wonder if that place would give me employment.' Luke too had watched the man until he disappeared into a long building running parallel with the edge of the High Bullen, tall painted letters proclaiming it to be the 'Coronet Tube Works'.

Reading the words to herself Saran could muster no feeling of optimism. Were there employment to be had would there be men standing the line each morning?

'I wouldn't set too much hope on it,' she said, not wanting to disillusion yet wishing to soften the blow refusal always gave, 'after all, you have no experience.'

Beside her Luke's mouth quirked in the cheeky grin she had come to love. 'I ain't got no experience o' bein' king neither but I be willin' to give the job a try if'n that new queen be fed up o' doin' it.'

The new queen. Victoria. Saran felt the pang of bitterness bite hard on her heart. There was little more than a year between her own age and that of the girl who sat on Britain's throne and until the coming of Enoch Jacobs there could have been no more happiness in one than the other. But all of her own happiness was gone, swept away with her mother's marriage. She had no envy of the queen, no envy of the lush comfort that must be that other girl's life, her only wish was that, like Victoria, she too had her loved ones close beside her.

'You thinks I oughtn't to try over there, then? An' it be no use to try many o' these for I've asked more'n several times already.' His grin faded as Luke cast a glance over his shoulder at the group of timbered buildings facing the newer tube works across the space that had not so long ago been used for the sport of bull-baiting. Waiting on an answer, a tingle of worry touched his nerves when none came. Saran became more disheartened as day followed on day with no word of her folks; soon it might be he could no longer joke away her misery, no longer bring a smile to her mouth.

'What say we tries that way? We ain't give that a go yet.' Giving no time for refusal Luke turned sharp right, avoiding having to pass Meeting Street and its dreaded workhouse. Taking an alley which led between a covey of closely packed houses, and crossing the wider street that led from the church, he walked quickly towards Little Hill.

What could he hope to find that he had not already found in this sad town? Saran's steps dragged as she followed. There was nothing here but poverty and heartache, she had seen it in every tiny house she had called at hoping for some word that might tell of her mother and sister; men, women and children, some not yet eight years old yet every hand busy with the business of nail-making. They had spoken kindly to her but their eyes – screwed in a nest of lines embedded by the glare of brilliant fire amidst the gloom of perpetual shadow in the windowless shack that served as wash-house and workplace – never lifted from their work, while their hands and feet not once ceased their monotonous jig. A mixture of fascination and horror holding her, she had watched the working of bellows, stoking of the red-hot fire, the turning of iron and the sparks as it was hammered on the anvil; brusque harassed movements, jerking as if the lash of some unseen whip, and all the time the smoke that bit into the lungs. How did those people bear it? How did they live such a life? Yet without the nailing there were many would have no life, starvation walked close to the poor of this town. And yet there was generosity here, people like the Elwells ever ready to share their last crust with a stranger. She would never be in a position to fully repay the kindness that family had shown, never be able to help them rise out of their poverty, only the will of heaven could do that.

With her hands still buried deep in the pockets of her coat, her fingers curled with the intensity of the prayer that whispered in her heart. Glancing to where the great black edifice that was the church of St Bartholomew stood proud against the smoke-shrouded sky the silent voice spoke inside her.

*Lord, You know how it is with me, You know I cannot ease the hardship of those people. I ask nothing for myself but please keep Livvy Elwell and her family from hunger, let Your clemency shine over them and Your compassion enfold them; help them, Lord, for I do not have the means.*

No, she could not help the Elwells nor ease the suffering of so many others like them. Fingers still curled into her palms though her prayer was done, Saran remembered the words she had whispered so many times in the days and nights of being parted from her family, words that echoed again and again in her troubled sleep.

*Lord, watch over my mother and sister, and help me find them.*

But they were words that suddenly seemed empty, a parroting of fruitless sterile phrases, useless and impotent, finding no listener except herself. Why should the Lord help the Elwells, why help one when He made no attempt to help the other!

Following behind Luke, seeing the play of daylight dart from light brown hair, Saran faced the truth. Her mother and sister were lost to her. She would never see them again.

They had found nothing over the crest of Little Hill. True, the houses gracing Brunswick Terrace and Squires Walk were larger than those of the cramped town. Set apart from each other, enhanced by spacious gardens, they blared the importance of the new industrial elite; the iron masters and owners of coal mines were rapidly overrunning the gin pits each worked by one or two men. But for all their loudly sung prosperity they offered neither work nor charity to the less fortunate who found the way to their door, and none gave the time to listen to enquiries of her family. Money and manners, why did one seem to leave the other behind? But that was unfair! Saran's slow footsteps came to a halt though the thoughts in her mind continued their parade. She had spoken only with servants, people possibly under much the same pressure of work as those in the minute brewhouses or coal pits; to be seen wasting a moment talking to her could have meant the likelihood of dismissal. Was it time and not manners had forced their brusqueness?

Luke had tried to find some cheer in the day but even he had fallen silent as, one after the other, kitchen doors closed on them.

She should not insist upon remaining in this town, Luke would not leave without her, he was only gone from her side when, as now, he had been given employment. Employment! Saran's thoughts became acid. A few hours unloading then reloading a carter's wagon, carrying heavy sacks and boxes for the promise of a sixpence! Yet he had taken it and gladly, happy that tonight they would eat, that twopence would buy them a bed in some hayloft. But she had found no work, she was bringing nothing to the partnership and nothing to Luke except worry. That could end now, though; instead of waiting here for him, as they had arranged, she could walk away, be gone before...

'You shouldn't think of going in there, the Turk's Head be busy on market day and not all of its customers are gentlemen.'

She had not realised she was stood across from a tavern. Breaking her stare, Saran felt a sweep of colour rush to her cheeks as she looked at the speaker, taller by a head than herself, his eyes rivetingly dark in a strong beardless face, a well-formed mouth smiling.

'I ... I wasn't thinking of going in...' she stammered. 'I was just watching.'

'Watching!' His mouth still curved in a smile, the man drew his brows together lending his dark eyes an amused inquisitive look. 'Now there's an occupation I haven't come across before, might I ask does it pay well?'

Catching the humour in almost coal-black eyes, Saran's initial nervousness at being addressed by a total stranger faded. 'It is not an occupation,' she returned, 'and it most definitely does not pay well; in fact, it doesn't pay at all.'

'In that case I won't take it up, making a living in Wednesbury is a hard enough task as it is, I won't add a thankless one to it.'

She should not stay here talking to a man she had never seen before, but if she never spoke to a stranger how would she ever hope to get news of her mother and sister? The last thought making sense, she quieted the niggling doubt resurfacing inside her; she would take any risk if it meant she might hear of her family ... and what risk could there be in speaking to a man in broad daylight in a market square filled with stalls and women hurrying about their shopping?

Gathering her courage she asked, 'Do you live here in Wednesbury?'

'For twenty-six years,' he answered with a rueful shrug of wide shoulders. 'And like to be more than a few yet to come for I live with my grandmother, she reared me from a small child and I won't ever leave her. So you see, my fate is sealed.'

Murmuring a word of apology to a woman whose way they blocked, Saran responded with a smile. Living in a place so many years he must know everybody, hear of anything unusual ... like a man purchasing another man's wife!

'But you,' he was speaking again, 'you are not from these parts, I would have seen you before this ... a face as pretty as yours a man doesn't forget easily.'

Only her father had ever called her pretty.

Enoch Jacobs had labelled her plain. *'Her looks,'* he had said, *'would never be of consequence, never bring men to 'er door, to do that 'er must learn to use what were atween 'er legs an' Enoch Jacobs be the man to teach 'er.'* And he had tried. From the first week of becoming master of her mother's house, he had found ways of keeping her behind when sending Miriam and their mother off on some errand, made excuses that resulted in her being alone with him. It had begun with a stroking of her hair, a finger trailing her cheek while his thick lips slobbered and his eyes glazed. She had said nothing of this to her mother, not wishing to cause her pain. Then the stroking and the trailing moved from her hair and face to her body, podgy hands fastened over her breasts, slid over her bottom, pulling her close into himself, and at the same time he began to mutter his threats, saying what he would do to her mother should their 'little secret' be spoken of. So she had suffered his hands. But that had not satisfied Enoch Jacobs. One night he had entered the bedroom she shared with Miriam. Stinking of drink, he had knelt beside the bed and she had felt his hand beneath the sheets, sliding under her nightgown and up over her thighs to touch between her legs. It had been over in a minute though it had seemed an eternity, then he had shuffled to his feet, weaving his way from the room, and she had cried herself to sleep.

She had wanted so very much to leave that house, to get away from the beast that lived in it but, young as she had been, she knew that if one daughter left he would prey on the other, satisfy his lust on an eight-year-old child. Then the fear that haunted her every hour became a reality, had come the one day it was no longer the elder girl had to stay behind but the younger one. She had not needed to ask, feeling that small figure sobbing in her sleep had told her ... her own release from the torture of those hands had become her sister's nightmare. How calm she had become then. Held in an anger so intense it kept her numb she had slipped from the bed, tiptoeing to the kitchen, and in the glow of a sleeping fire had found what she looked for. An hour later by the striking of the church clock, he had come. The door of the bedroom had opened. Less drunk than normal, he had not weaved but walked softly to the side of the sleeping child. Saran remembered the pause, a hesitation when she had known his eyes were on herself, ascertaining that she was asleep, then he had slid to his knees! The shudder of that thin figure, the frightened cry...

Stood there now in the street Saran experienced again the revulsion, the detestation, the hatred she had felt at that moment, but she had kept it fastened inside, held in bonds of silence. His head had been bent over the child whose nightgown he had lifted to her chin, his mouth pulling at breasts as yet no more than tiny buds, his hands shuffling with the buttons of his trousers. Totally immersed in his carnal pleasure he had not felt the slight movement of the bed as she had slid from it, so sunk in lecherous enjoyment he knew nothing else until his head was snatched back almost to his shoulders, the point of the sharp-bladed knife pressed against the vein pumping in his neck.

'*Touch my sister again,*' she had threatened against his ear, '*touch her one more time, come near either of us and I vow before every saint in heaven I'll sink the rest of this blade into your throat. You will never know when, whether by day or in the darkness of night, but have my promise, it* will *come.*'

The beatings had started the next day, the blows that sent her pregnant mother sprawling in the daytime, the unspeakable cruelty that had her cry out at night.

'What the–'

Saran did not hear the rest of the man's anxious enquiry. As a sob caught in her throat she was already lost in darkness.

# 8

'I couldn't get no more for 'em, all he would pay was sixpence ha'penny a thousand.'

'Sixpence ha'penny!' Livvy Elwell dropped heavily to her stool, her tired eyes filling with tears. 'But we can't live on that – two 'undred and twenty tacks for a penny – 'ow does a nail master expect folk to feed themselves?'

'Nail masters don't give no mind to 'ow,' Edward Elwell dropped his head into his hands, 'they don't give mind to anythin' other than their profit, to 'ow much more they can squeeze from a man.'

'Sixpence ha'penny!' Livvy stared sightlessly at the table she had scrubbed, though every bone of her screamed fatigue from carrying metal rods to and from the furnace, working the bellows, pounding the hammer on the anvil, chopping every one of the eight hundred tacks she had fashioned that day. 'We already laid four of our babbies in the churchyard,' she murmured half to herself. ''Twas cos they was clammed, so teken wi' hunger their poor bodies couldn't beat off the sickness, so starved of bread they 'ad no strength against the cough that wracked 'em, so death took 'em ... and it be waitin' in the shadows for to tek the others and we both along wi' 'em.'

'We 'as to manage.'

''Ow ... tell me 'ow!' Worry gave a sharp edge to

her voice as Livvy flung the words at the man hunched in the chair. 'Tell me 'ow we can live, four o' we, on what be left after we pays our way!'

'I tried, Livvy, I tried tellin' 'im...'

Her own misery shoved aside she was beside him as his explanation died on a sob, her arms about his thin frame, his face enfolded between her breasts.

'T'ain't your fault,' she murmured, her own tears spilling down lined cheeks, 'you 'ad to tek what you was give, you couldn't do no more. It be a bit 'ard but like you says we as to manage an' so we will.' Holding him, feeling the raw unhappiness surge from his chest in great dry sobs, Livvy felt the strength of desperation. This was her man, the one she had promised her life to and she wouldn't let him sink. The money paid for tacks had lowered so they would make more. But how? In the quietness of the tiny kitchen she was forced to face the truth. There was no way they could produce more than they already did!

'Lord, I feared you was dead, run down by a wagon or some such!'

Luke's tone conveyed the shock which had still not altogether left him.

'I seen you in that bloke's arms all limp and lifeless... I tells you, Saran, it fair put the wind up me.'

'I'm sorry, Luke, it was stupid of me to give way like that.'

'A faint ain't stoopid! Not if it be genuine, it ain't, an' from what I seen you wasn't doin' no gammitin'.'

No she had not been acting the fool. Saran took the pot the landlord of the Turk's Head had had filled with hot tea, pouring it into heavy pottery cups placed on the table by a harassed-looking woman. Offering one to the lad who even now seemed wary of moving from her side, she smiled assuringly.

'What 'appened?' Luke accepted the cup but not the assurance. 'Did that bloke ... did 'e touch you ... say anything 'e shouldn't?' Mistaking a frown that touched her brow for a sign of disapproval at so personal a question he stared self-consciously at the steaming cup in his hands. 'I shouldn't 'ave asked that, it were just–'

'That you were concerned for me.' Saran touched his hand gently. 'I'm grateful for that, Luke. As for the cause of my faint, it was nothing that man said or did.'

His head jerking up, Luke ran a swift worried glance over her face. 'Then what! Be you middlin'?'

From the corner of her eye Saran caught the quick turn of the serving woman's head. As with many towns she guessed this one also dreaded the cholera.

'No.' She shook her head quickly. 'I am not feeling unwell, it is no more than tiredness, it has been quite a journey from Willenhall.'

Across the large kitchen the woman's body visibly relaxed. Tiredness and hunger were no strangers to Wednesbury, they were ailments many suffered from; lethal, but not a sickness passed one to another, not the plague that smallpox or cholera proved.

‘Well, we won’t be journeyin’ nowheres tonight,’ Luke beamed, ‘you be goin’ to sleep in a bed. I be goin’ to ask the landlord right now for to give you a room all to yourself.’

A room to herself, how much would that cost? Luke had earned sixpence from the carter but after paying for broth the woman was dishing up to them, and paying for the tea ... a room would probably take more than he would have left, unless – a frisson of uncertainty licked the edges of her mind, a brush of doubt – had Luke reserved money from any other source, could he have accepted it from that man she had talked with?

‘Luke,’ she said as he tipped off the remainder of his tea, ‘sixpence won’t pay for a place for each of us.’

Setting his empty cup on the table with a satisfied thump, he grinned. ‘It don’t ’ave to, landlord said I can bed down in the stables, seems they ain’t used so much now that there new Holyhead Road has teken the coach trade away.’

Guilt replacing the doubt, Saran was glad of the opportunity to look away from that pleased grin. Had she learned nothing during the time they had spent together! Luke was young but his pride was old, innate; a quality born in him, the heritage of generations who had lived by the skill of their hands, by the strength of their bodies, and while there was strength in his he would take no charity.

Thanking the woman setting a bowl in front of her she picked up a spoon, holding it while she said, ‘I want no bedroom, Luke, and no argument;

a stable was good enough for the Holy Child, it should be good enough for me.'

'But–'

'No! No buts, the matter is settled.'

The meal finished, Luke shoved his bowl away. He had come from collecting his sixpence from the carter who was taking a tankard of ale inside the inn, he had seen Saran falling to the ground and a man move to catch her, a man whose eyes had shown more than sympathy as he held her.

*'it was nothing that man said or did.'*

Nodding to the woman collecting his empty dish, the words which had revolved in his mind while he ate spun another thread to their web.

Saran had answered quickly, but she had told only what was *not* said, she had given no word of what had passed between them. Had she spoken truly, was the feeling of mistrust niggling him justified? Or had the man insulted her and she was passing it off so as to cause no trouble?

'The wench might feel easier were her to leave by the back, there don't be no leerin' looks that way.' Having gathered the spoons along with Saran's bowl and deposited them in a large stone sink, the woman ran her hands over her long apron, nodding her head in the direction of the bar. 'There gets a few in there who don't be dummocked by a few pints o' porter with a toppin' o' Methodist's cream. They looks for summat else to satisfy their appetites along of rum and stout, summat like a young wench, an' they won't let a little 'un like yourself tek her from 'em, not like him who lifted her from the ground.'

A tavern was the last place she would have chosen to be, and she had no stomach at all for walking out past a host of men. Murmuring her thanks, Saran moved towards the kitchen door.

'I 'ave to pay for the meal.' Taking a coin from his pocket Luke glanced at the woman.

'I'll tek you through to the gaffer, an' while we be gone, wench, you might care to use the privy, you'll find it to the left of the stables.' Handing Saran a lantern, waiting until she left the kitchen, the woman spoke hurriedly. 'Tek a word from the wise and get that sister o' your'n away from this town, afore somebody else beats you to it.'

'What do that mean?'

'Listen, lad,' the woman lowered her voice, her look agitated as if afraid they may be overheard, 'it be wrong to judge a dog by its collar, appearances ain't always what they seems. The one that carried that wench in 'ere ... well ... just remember a clean shirt can hide a peck o' dirt!'

Having paid the landlord, Luke helped Saran into the hayloft but sat awake long after she had fallen asleep. His heart had dropped when he saw her fall and it had not lifted when the man she had been talking with insisted on carrying her into the tavern. There had been a look in those dark eyes, a look he had neither liked nor trusted. Jealousy, he had told himself, as the man had ordered she be taken somewhere quiet, away from the stares of market traders and carters, jealousy of someone saying and doing what he himself should be doing.

Resting his back against a bale of hay he stared into the darkness. That serving woman had no cause to feel jealously, her words had not been born of envy but of concern.

*'appearances ain't always what they seems ... just remember a clean shirt can hide a peck o' dirt.'*

For whatever reason the woman had a dislike of Saran's helper; more than that, she seemed to hold a positive mistrust of him.

Easing himself more comfortably into the soft hay, Luke knew the woman was not alone in her judgement.

Dusting wisps of hay from her skirts Saran's fingers touched against a small hard object nestled deep in her pocket. The brooch the young woman had given her ... she had completely forgotten it. Taking it out she cradled it in her palm. It was worth little the woman had said, but watching light from a chink in the roof glint from the stone that was its green heart Saran knew that for herself at least the fact that it was just a trinket with little value did not detract from it. It was pretty, and it had been given out of gratitude. At Luke's quiet call she returned it to her pocket, resting her hand over it for the few seconds her mind took to ask health and well-being for the couple they had helped that night on the heath, adding a quick prayer for the baby she had helped birth.

Beyond the stable the spring morning was cool causing her to draw her thin, badly fitting coat more tightly about her body.

'You be cold.' The last pennies of the sixpence he had earned were in Luke's hand no sooner he spoke. 'We'll go get you some breakfast.'

Following down the short ladder which gave access to the floor of the stable, Saran was quick to refuse. Take time to eat and they may lose the chance of a day's work.

'No,' she gave her skirts a final shake, 'let's go straight to the line; you never know, it might be our lucky day.'

It might be *her* lucky day. She walked silently beside the boy. Perhaps today she would learn the whereabouts of her family; the thought lay heavy, giving no trace of the lift the same thought had accorded her when they first arrived in the town.

Reaching the High Bullen they joined the small group of people already stood there; men with jacket collars raised against the sharp air, but more against the depression that sat heavily on their shoulders, men whose whole attitude told of poverty and despair; and the women, heads hidden by shawls, whose dejection showed as clear as that of their menfolk, mothers with barefoot children clinging to their skirts. It was all going to be so much better, the new queen would change everything, bring hope and prosperity to their lives, was that not what folk had said when rejoicing at her accession? But where was the prosperity for these people, where the improvement ... and, most of all, where was the hope?

'You here again, young 'un?'

The words directed at Luke brought an instant smile to the boy's face.

'Ar.' He nodded. 'Mebbe today I'll be given something.'

'But not with the jagger, eh?'

'No.' Luke's grin disappeared. 'Not wi' the jagger, a slice o' bacon be tasty on the tongue but it don't buy a bed for the night.'

'A bed! You and your sister are sleeping rough?'

A hint of concern evident in his question, the man who had threatened the coal-jagger only days before cast a quick glance to where Saran stood among the women.

'It don't be for long, we be leavin' Wednesbury in a day or so, movin' on.' Luke rubbed his hands against the early morning chill.

'Wednesbury not to your liking, then?'

It wasn't the town that was not to his liking. Luke had a swift mental vision of the man who had carried Saran into the tavern, of the look on his face. No, it wasn't Wednesbury town he had no liking for!

'It ain't the town so much,' he replied, 'but yer can't live wi'out money an' if it can't be earned then there be no sense in stoppin'.'

Across the space of the High Bullen a hooter sounded from the building that pronounced itself the Coronet Tube Works.

'That be the starting bull.' The tall figure glanced across the way then back to Luke. 'If you be averse to hard work, lad, then don't follow me across the street; if it be you are not, then I'll get you a place alongside me in that works.' Only then did he look directly at Saran, touching a hand to his brow as his eyes locked with hers. 'I'm sorry I can't do the same for you, miss, but unlike the coal mines the ironworks won't take women on.'

‘Saran...’ already trotting after that tall, loosely moving figure, Luke called back, ‘wait for me... I don’t know what time it’ll be but wait.’

‘The Turk’s Head?’

‘No!’ The reply was instant, its sharpness cutting off her words. ‘No, not there, don’t go you to the Turk’s Head, I ... I’ll come to you beside ... beside the Elwells’ ’ouse.’

Had it been imagination? Two hours later, all chance of being picked from the line gone with the last of the hirers, Saran walked slowly towards the town centre. Had it been no more than fancy she had seen that tall figure pause in its stride, the strong head turn to look at her when Luke mentioned the tavern? Had it been merely a trick of a mind subverted by cold and hunger?

But then why would he, a total stranger, have any mind where she waited? Don’t be fooled, Saran Chandler, she told herself grimly; apart from Luke there is not one other person in this town cares a jot where you are or what becomes of you!

He’d bought the woman and her brat, paid half a crown for one and ten shillin’ for the other and what had he got for ’is money! The day’s trading done, Zadok Minch closed the books that recorded every item of sale and expenditure – every item except the personal little concessions, the trifling gifts he made to himself every now and then, like the two he had bought in Walsall. The husband, the drunken lout who had dragged them into the tavern at the end of a rope, had vowed they would give good service. Vowed! Throwing the accounts books into the drawer of a heavy desk he locked it then tucked the key into his pocket. The man was a liar and so sure as Zadok Minch met with 'im again he'd kick that twelve shillin' and sixpence right out of 'im. The woman? He 'adn't cared overmuch for the money 'er 'ad cost; two scullery maids got rid of, replaced by one gettin' naught for 'er labours than a meal and a place to sleep. But the little 'un, that ten-bob trifle? Irritation rising, he kicked against the desk. No man laid out that kind o' money to see no pleasure forrit! Tonight he–

'I see Arthur Trow along of Wharfedale Street lowered his price by another tuppence a bundle.'

Tonight could wait! Zadok looked across to the tall figure who stepped without knocking into his private office.

He was handsome and shrewd, but he had a long way to run to catch up with Zadok Minch. 'But not the quality?' he barked. If this one or Arthur Trow thought they could pull a fast 'un, sell 'im dross in place o' quality iron, or try to squeeze an extra penny a thousand out of 'im, then they was in for a bloody sharp shock.

'Same as before.' The attractive mouth smiled. 'Trow understood it was the price he was to lower not the grade of metal.'

Tuppence a bundle. Zadok's brain clicked like the balls on an abacus. He had forty nailers on his books, forty men and most of their families supplying him with all types of nails, and at a shilling profit on every bundle of iron rod he sold them now becoming a shillin' and twopence, every twelve hundred nails counted as a thousand, plus twopence farthing when these were sold on at thirty per cent more than he paid for 'em ... he were seein' a return of summat near a shillin' an' sixpence the thousand.

His calculations finished he looked at the figure standing watching. If 'e thought to get a share then it were another shock 'e were storin' for 'imself. Taking his watch from his waistcoat he looked at it then flicked it back, saying as he did so, 'You can go, I 'ave no more business today.'

'Wait on!' Younger and more agile, the man stepped forward, his smile fading. 'This is the second time the price of iron has been reduced, the second time I've saved you money by telling nailers the rod costs the same though nails and tacks be fetching less, and this time I expects a share.'

'Oh you does!'

'Yes ... I do. It is no more than my due.'

This one was getting cocky. Zadok touched a hand to his crop of side whiskers. And what did you do when a trained dog got cocky? You kicked it in the crotch!

'I bin meanin' to get to that.' He met the stare of his visitor full on. 'I bin meanin' to tell you what your dues be ... they be what I decides they be, no more no less, an' you'll get no more'n you've bin gettin'; an' afore you meks complaint let me remind you it be a dangerous trade you follows. A fogger who creams a percentage, who pays a nailer tuppence a thousand less than the nails 'e buys be worth, not to mention sellin' 'em on to a nail master at yet another threepence over the odds, be liable under the Truck Act. Her Majesty's Commissioners would be more'n interested in 'ow you meks your livelihood, an' I don't 'ave to tell you they'll tek a pretty dim view of it.'

'A middleman has the right to make a living.'

'That be right enough,' it was Zadok's turn to smile, 'but the authorities 'olds no peace with a fogger that be robbin' the nailers blind.'

'Robbing them blind!' The younger man's fist came hard down on the desk. 'You are a right one to talk!'

'An' talk is what you won't never do if you knows which side o' your bread be buttered!' Zadok growled. 'I 'ave what I 'ave an' you keeps what you gets, so let that be the all o' it, lessen you *wants* a taste o' the cat and a 'oliday at 'er Majesty's pleasure.'

Leaving his hand to rest a moment on the desk, the young man breathed deeply before straightening. 'You promised me a share ... you gave your word.'

The pup had received his kick in the groin and was whimpering. Zadok enjoyed the quick flush of triumph. He wouldn't bark so quickly next time.

'My word was it?' He frowned, hiding the sweetness of victory. 'Well, now I be givin' you another. Tek what you will from the nailers you deals with but don't think to do the same wi' Zadok Minch, for he knows 'ow to deal wi' two-timers.'

Two-timers! His handsome face taut with anger the younger man drew himself upward. One day

Zadok Minch would learn the real meaning of double-crossing!

Leaning against a stone horse trough Saran dipped her hands in the water then held them to her mouth, swallowing the few drops that stayed in her palms. It had been six hours since she had left the High Bullen, nearly twice that number since she had eaten the bowl of broth Luke had bought for her at the Turk's Head.

'That might be good for horses but for you I would recommend something warmer.'

With her hands already immersed again in the trough Saran started, sending a shower of droplets cascading into the air as she spun round.

'Whoa!' The deep voice laughed. 'I was simply wanting to be sociable. Do you always try to drown folk giving you the time of day?'

'I ... I'm sorry; you startled me.'

Making to brush the droplets from a fine worsted coat, then realising her wet hands would only add to the damage she had caused, Saran let them fall to her side, colour rising rapidly to her cheeks.

As dark and riveting as she remembered, eyes filled with amusement regarded her as she was handed a large, perfectly laundered handkerchief. Her colour flamed even higher as a rush of pleasure rippled through her. Thanking the man she had talked to across the street from the tavern she dabbed at her fingers before returning the handkerchief.

'The fault was mine.' He smiled, cutting off her further attempt at apology.

Pressing her palms self-consciously against her skirts, Saran felt the small hard lump that was the brooch nestled in her pocket. 'No,' she stammered, 'you were–'

'I know...' the amusement lighting dark eyes became a smile curving an attractive mouth '...I was simply trying to be sociable, but if you are truly repentant for showering a man with water then perhaps you will take a cup of tea with your victim.'

Tea! Hot sweet tea! The very thought was pure ecstasy and for a moment she languished in it. But taking tea with a strange man, no matter how kind, was out of the question.

'Thank you, but–'

'Now you are not going to throw that "we are strangers" excuse at me, are you?' The smile widened. 'After all, I have held you in my arms.'

Her face scarlet, Saran dropped her glance. She had tried to remember, to live the moment again but with her senses awake.

'Allow me to present myself, Jairus Ensell.'

Saran watched the slight unaffected bow as he spoke. Unlike her stepfather he had made no attempt to touch her, he did not leer at her as had those men shouting to be shown her breasts; his manners were those of a gentleman. Reassured by what she saw she dropped a faint curtsy. 'Saran,' she murmured shyly, 'Saran Chandler.'

'How do you do, Saran Chandler,' he answered soberly. 'May I take the liberty of asking if would you take tea with me?'

What would be the greater wrong, to rebuff a man who had come to her assistance when she had fainted, to snub an offer he could only have made out of kindness, seeing her drink water that had been used by animals; or to accept, to walk alone with him into some tavern?

'There are tearooms in Union Street, I think perhaps they might prove more acceptable than an inn.'

He could have read her thoughts, seen what was in her mind as clearly as had Harriet Dowen.

'It is most kind of you but I must–'

'Whatever it is you "must" can be done better after a cup of tea ... and I promise I will not press you to stay a moment longer than it takes to drink it.'

His smile was open, and beyond their sparkle of laughter his eyes were honest. Her doubts calmed, Saran nodded and began to walk beside the man, who shortened his step to match her own. For all his good clothes and way of speech that was less rough than other men she had spoken to while looking for work or enquiring after her family, Jairus Ensell had not treated her like she was a beggar, a scavenger of the streets. He was polite, kind and thoughtful. He was a man she could trust.

# 9

Why had she told him so much of herself, how could she have let it all pour out the way she had? She had not meant to speak of her mother and sister, of their being sold like animals, or of Enoch Jacobs dancing with the moon and her meeting with Luke; she had meant to say nothing, yet the whole story had poured from her like water from a jug. She must have bored him terribly, only the politeness that was a natural part of him prevented him from showing it. Embarrassed by her own lack of tact, Saran fell silent.

'Your stepfather was scum, he got what he deserved and you should not spare him another thought.'

The hand that touched hers was clean, free of the calluses which covered those of the miners and nail-makers she had spoken to, a hand that was gentle ... a blush rising to her cheeks she drew away swiftly.

'You say you have enquired in every part of the town and no one knows anything of your family?'

Saran nodded, not yet able to meet those dark eyes. 'I've asked at the houses and workshops but each time...'

A tremble that warned of tears ending her explanation, Jairus Ensell watched the girl sat opposite him. Though her head was bowed, partly hiding her features, her face was etched clearly in his mind. Peaked with hunger, drawn from days walking the streets seeking work and a family who had been snatched from her, and from nights of trying to sleep on the heath and under hedges exposed to rain and cold, it was still ... attractive? No, it was more than that ... beautiful, then? Beautiful as the statue of that Greek goddess he had seen. No! He checked the thought. That had been false, a lifeless illusion of beauty, while what he saw in the girl that boy had freed from a yoke was, despite her sufferings, no misconception; when she smiled her mouth curved attractively while her eyes took on the sparkle of woods in autumn sunlight. Hers was no cold carved perfection, she was a warm living girl whose beauty was as yet sleeping. No, Saran Chandler was no illusion!

'Saran ... I shall use your first name for I feel we are friends.' His voice was deep, like dark music. Saran found herself listening, wanting it to go on. 'Wednesbury is a small town, almost all of its inhabitants are tied to a place of work and that means contact with the wider world is restricted. So it follows that they might well have heard nothing of the selling of a woman and child...'

'*Might* have heard nothing?' She looked up quickly, the hypnotism broken. 'Are you saying they could have lied?'

The dark eyes smiled at once. 'That was not what I meant, all I am saying is that with little movement from mine or workshop their circle of acquaintance is not as wide as, say, that of myself; I travel often to Birmingham and meet with people on a far wider scale, so perhaps you would allow me to enquire…'

He was trying to be kind, but to allow him to ask of her family would be taking advantage. And kindness, even his, must end somewhere; far better here and now.

'That will not be necessary,' Saran shook her head, 'you see, Luke and I have already decided we will leave Wednesbury tomorrow so I will be able to enquire further for myself.'

She was leaving! Jairus stirred cream into the coffee he had ordered for himself. That was bad luck on his part. He was interested in Saran Chandler ... very interested!

'Luke.' He sipped the hot liquid. 'Did you not say he was given work this morning?'

The tea was life giving. Saran swallowed, savouring its hot sweetness before nodding. 'Mmm, a day's labour at the tube works up on the High Bullen.'

'The Coronet Tube Works.' Jairus replaced the cup on its saucer. 'John Adams's place. But it isn't given to providing casual employment; men are not taken on for a day ... who was it said there would be work for him there?'

'I don't know the man, he called Luke from the line, telling him to follow into the works. He did not say his name.'

It would not be Adams, he did not walk the line himself ... nor was that tube factory short of labour! So who was it had taken the lad in, and why? Musing over the dilemma Jairus's wondering came to a halt as Saran described a tall fair-haired figure, one who had threatened the coal-jagger. Only one man would do that: Gideon Newell! Now where did his interest lie?

'...so you see we shall be moving on tomorrow.'

He hadn't really heard the last of what she had said. Catching the eye of the tearoom proprietress Jairus signalled for the bill. Outside in the street, his thoughts collected, he glanced at the girl whose gratitude for the tea brought an attractive tinge of colour to pale cheeks. Could she be Gideon Newell's interest?

'You told me employment had been difficult to find the whole way from Walsall.'

'Very difficult.' Saran nodded.

'And I have no doubt it will prove the same wherever you go in the Midlands, it certainly is between here and Birmingham; so should it be Luke has been found a permanent place in the tube factory will he be willing to give it up, to travel on with you?'

She had not thought of that. Faced with the sudden probability she halted, the irritated mumbles of passers-by whose way she blocked going unheard. If Luke were given permanent employment ... but he wouldn't be, he had no experience of tube-making ... yet even the most skilled of craftsmen had to start at the beginning ... thoughts tumbling like leaves on the wind Saran did not feel her arm being taken, her steps being guided along the street.

*'men are not taken on for a day.'*

The words returned loud to her mind, and with them her decision. She would not stand in Luke's way, not present him with the burden of choosing to stay here with the security of a job or throw it away to go with her; she would not wait for him beside the Elwells' house ... she would leave this town now.

'It be no good talkin', wench, there be no way I can feed my babbies an' keep a roof over their 'eads an' I won't see 'em laid in the ground as was the others born o' me; the workhouse be a hard place but at least they won't starve.'

The workhouse! Livvy was sending her children into the workhouse! Her heart wrenching with pity, Saran watched the lined face crumple into tears. She had decided on leaving Wednesbury but found she could not go without leaving some word for Luke so she had come to the place he would look for her; the Elwells would give him her message. But her own worries had flown as she had come face to face with the couple. Had the devils of hell confronted them they could not have looked any worse ... but then Luke professed there was no hell worse than a workhouse and these people were having to hand their children into it.

'There must be a way, Livvy.'

'You think we ain't looked?'

The cry was not meant to be admonishing, Livvy intended no rebuke; the sharpness of her cry was the pain of the knife slashing her own heart, the echoes of which found a place in Saran's.

'We've thought an' thought on it.' Livvy was speaking again but now her voice was quiet, heavy with despair. 'We talked the night long but it always come out the same way, it be impossible to live on what the nailin' brings.'

'But last week–'

'Last week nail master were payin' seven pence ha'penny a thousand for tacks,' Edward Elwell cut in. 'On that we could scrape through wi' the wife an' me not tekin' a meal every day, but now if we missed meals five days outta the seven we still couldn't manage. Sixpence ha'penny! You couldn't feed a dog on that.'

She did not know the true worth of the small flat-headed nails she had watched Livvy and her husband make but surely that amount for a thousand could not be right. Helpless to advise, Saran could only listen as Edward continued.

'I told 'im, I did, I told nail master we couldn't live on what he were offerin', that my babbies were near clammed as it was, but their starvin' med no odds wi' 'im; sixpence ha'penny were his price, tek it or go to the fogger.'

'Fogger ... is that a man would buy your tacks?'

'Oh he'd buy 'em, all right!' Glancing at Saran, Edward Elwell's red-rimmed eyes displayed contempt. 'A fogger be a go-between, he buys from a nailer and sells to the nail master. As for bein' a man! Huh... I'd rather 'ave dealin's wi' a snake any time. Foggers be worse thieves than any nail master, least he only teks his cut one way, but the thief of a fogger teks it every way. He charges more for a bundle of iron rod while payin' less for the finished article, then sells on, chargin' the master over the top.'

That was no less than robbery. Surely it could not be legal? Putting the thought into words Saran was answered with a short laugh.

'It ain't.' Edward's laugh held no humour. 'The government passed a new law forbiddin' any such practice. The Truck Act were meant to protect such as we, but since when did a fogger or any nail master pay mind to the law? They pays what pleases 'em while we ... well, a man can't feed his kin on iron nails.'

It needed no further explanation, Saran realised what he was saying. It was take the money or starve ... now they were starving.

'It be easy for the nail master to talk.' Dabbing her eyes on a black apron heavily scorched with burn marks from sparks flying from red-hot metal, Livvy took up as her husband choked on his words.

'I tried so 'ard, Saran, tried to find a way to keep my babbies wi' me but wi' nobbut ten shillin' an' fourpence a week... I don't be a magician ... folk wants payin' for the food they sells, they got no more than me to be givin' away.'

It could not have been so very different the night Livvy had taken Luke and herself in off the streets, the night she had shared the last of her bread with them. Guilt burned hot in Saran as she remembered. Had the following day been one of those on which this kind-natured couple had been forced to do without a meal? Had she and Luke taken the bread from their mouths? Oh Lord, why could she not have seen ... why hadn't she realised?

'Ten shillin' an' fourpence,' Livvy's swollen eyes glistened with new tears, 'that be what we got an' the lad helpin' in the workshop along o' me and his father while the little 'un, my little wench, sees to the preparin' o' the food ... that be when there be food... It be the outgoin's,' she went on after wiping her eyes yet again, 'they swallows most o' them shillin's, they be gone afore I gets to buy a loaf.'

Watching the woman's tear-stained face, Saran was stung by the memory of her mother, of the many times she had tried to stretch the odd pennies left to her by a drink-sodden Enoch Jacobs, juggling halfpennies, searching for the cheapest food then pleading for a farthing to be deducted from a stale loaf or a cut of meat fit only for a dog; she had seen Livvy's misery before ... seen it in her own mother.

'I set it all down afore Edward left for Brummajum.'

It was like a stream pouring from Livvy, the hopelessness, the pain; but its coming left no healing wake.

'Every penny it teks for to live I set to paper so it could be shown the nail master and not a farthing did I add as shouldn't 'ave bin there. Two shillin' and sixpence rent for house and workshop, breeze for firing the forge be a shillin' and sixpence, while there be another shillin' for repair of tools besides sixpence for use of anvil and bellows. Then after that comes three shillin' an' sixpence it costs to buy a bundle o' rod ... an' that you must 'ave if you be to work the next week. I set all o' that for nail master to see yet still he drops the price he pays. There be nothing for we 'cept the parish.'

Nine shillings! Saran counted silently. Nine shillings ... that left one shilling and fourpence to keep a family of four; no wonder Livvy was at her wits' end.

'I showed him what Livvy 'ad set down,' Edward caught his wife's hand, 'told 'im we worked all day an' three parts o' the night for to earn what we got, that we couldn't mek one more tack than we was mekin' already.'

'Did you tell him of the children?'

'He knowed about them, wench, this don't be the first time the price paid has bin lessened, that be a favourite pastime wi' all nail masters as I've knowed of; but it'll be the last time it 'appens to Edward Elwell.'

'You can't give up ... there has to be someone who will pay a decent price.'

'I d'ain't want to give up,' Edward's sad eyes lifted to Saran, 'but tack-mekin' 'as given me up.'

A slight frown speaking her confusion Saran looked from one resigned face to the other and it was Livvy who answered.

'What Edward be sayin' be this, the mekin' o' tacks by 'and be finished, nail master spoke o' some new-fangled machine that can mek 'em a 'undred times faster'n a man an' machines don't need to eat bread, neither does they tire.'

So their paltry living had been taken by a machine, profit had been placed above a man and his family! And this was the new England, the better life folk had sung of in the streets when the new queen had come to the throne.

Watching Edward enfold the sobbing Livvy in his arms, Saran felt a despair to match their own ... a despair born of the knowledge that she could do nothing to help.

She had intended to leave Wednesbury, had *wanted* to leave so Luke could be free to make his way without having to think of her. She had gone to the Elwells to ask them to tell Luke of her intent, but the misery she had met in that house had dictated otherwise: she must face her own decisions.

Stood on the rise of ground people of the town had told her proudly was once an iron-age fort thrown up under the instruction of Ethelfleda, daughter of Alfred the Great, Saran glanced across to the soot-lined church away to her right. She had been this way with Luke, both of them wondering who it was could live in the tall houses set back amid long stretches of neat gardens. Squires Walk ... so different to the rows of mean little back-to-back houses shoved tight together such a short distance away, houses that held so much poverty, so much misery. Livvy, Edward, the woman at the Turk's Head, the man who had taken Luke into that works and Jairus Ensell, they had all been kindness itself, but it was a kindness she couldn't repay.

Clear on the smoke-thickened air the church clock chimed seven. Was that the way Luke would come from the tube works, was he already stood waiting for her outside the Elwells' house? There was no way of knowing, but she could not go there herself, not before asking at each of these houses if would they give her work.

*There be nothing I could ask mistress to tek you on for ... we don't be short o' maids ... sorry, me wench, but there be no post for you to fill* ... the same replies she had met everywhere else she had been, met her again. They were kind enough, the housekeepers or cooks she spoke with, she could have a cup of tea, a slice of bread and dripping, but as for employment... She had thanked them for their hospitality, at the same time refusing it. The streets were already dark and she had to call at each house, even though her hopes of finding any kind of paid work were fading fast.

Dejection a mist over her senses as she left the last of the houses, Saran ran past the wide space of open ground into Walsall Street, unaware of the figure in her path until colliding with it.

'Try that with a wagon and you won't come off as light.'

'I beg your pardon.' Her hands pressed to her mouth to still the quiver of disappointment muffled the words.

The hand that had steadied her tightened sharply on her elbow and, though she did not lift her face, Saran felt the tension increase along the arm that held her and the head turn to sweep the street with a quick searching glance, and when the voice spoke again it held concern rather than rebuke.

'Are you all right ... has anyone frightened you?'

'No ... no one has frightened me, I ... I was careless, I'm sorry.' Pulling her elbow free she lowered her hands, and as they pressed against her skirts to pass the tall figure she felt the outline of the brooch in her pocket. Why hadn't she thought of that earlier! Eager to be gone she lifted her head, light from the lanterns fixed to the wall of the coach house close across the street illuminating her face.

'You are Luke's friend – the girl stood in the line up along the Bullen! He said he had to meet you outside of Edward Elwell's house.'

Her mind only half on what was said, Saran looked up, taking a moment before recognition brought the touch of a smile to her lips.

'And you are the man who said for him to follow you into the tube works. I did not know what time Luke would be...' She paused. Home? That would be a lie – they had no home.

'What time the shift finished.' He completed the sentence for her. 'That were half an hour ago.'

'Then I have to hurry, Luke will worry as to where I am. Thank you again, Mr...'

'Gideon Newell, and you don't have to tell me your name, Luke has done that already.'

'Then we will say goodnight, Mr Newell.'

'I'll walk with you.'

It was not an offer, it was a statement. Holding her skirt with one hand she felt the small hard lump that nestled in her pocket. How could she tell this man without being rude? Tell him she would rather go on her way alone.

'Thank you,' the words came at last, 'but I must not detain you.'

She had a softness of words, a way of speaking... Gideon Newell pulled himself up sharply. He had let his mind play on Luke Hipton's friend too long during the day, he must not allow it to career in that direction again.

'You won't be detaining me.'

It held a clipped ring to it, a brusqueness that

seemed almost to deny the note of concern she had heard earlier. Following as he turned back the way he had come, she strove to think of some way to have him leave her.

'Really there is no need for you to go out of your way, the Elwells do not live far from here.'

It was weak, especially seeing there were several beerhouses to pass before she reached Russell Street and any girl would welcome an escort past such places.

'I know where Edward Elwell lives and it isn't that way.' Having walked with her along Springhead, Gideon paused as she turned in the direction of the market square.

It would be of no benefit to lie; but to tell? As blood rose to her face Saran wrestled with a pride she should no longer have. After all that had happened to her, owning to pawning a brooch should hold no embarrassment; yet it did, it seemed she placed no value on an act of friendship and she did not want this man to think that of her.

'I was intending to call at Kilvert's shop,' she blushed more deeply, feeling his eyes on her. 'I have been for going there several times, I thought maybe Mr Kilvert would know if my brooch is worth a few pennies.'

'Would that be the brooch given by a woman you delivered of a child?'

Just how much had Luke told of her ... was delivering that woman all he had confided or had he told a perfect stranger of her mother and sister being sold for beer money, of Enoch Jacobs?

'I see you need no informing as to where my

brooch came from or the reason of its giving, so why not see it for yourself!' Annoyance staining every word she held the brooch on the flat of her hand.

'*Your* brooch!' A hardness emphasising his words, Gideon did not look at the bauble. 'Did Luke play no part in saving that couple? He may not have helped the child from its mother but it was he as much as you kept all three from possible death ... unless what he told me was lies and I do not judge Luke Hipton a liar. So the way I look at it is this, the lad played his part therefore the reward were not just *yours*, Miss Chandler, half of it be rightly his, as is freedom to speak of it. However, I can see it has caused you vexation and for that I apologise ... the fault is mine for listening to him. But I have warned strongly against his telling anyone else of that trinket and I give you the same advice. Wednesbury has its villains, as does any other town, and though that brooch be worth little or nothing there are those would take it from you.'

The words had shot at her, each stinging like a pebble thrown at her face, but Gideon Newell had spoken only the truth. The brooch had of course been a gift to both Luke and herself, the woman who gave it must have meant for it to be sold and the few coppers it fetched shared equally between them. But she had not intended to share ... she had not meant for Luke to have a penny.

# 10

‘I wondered where you was, I was becomin’ feared...’

‘I’m sorry, Luke, I called at so many houses that the time had gone before I realised.’

‘Be all right now you’re ’ere.’ Luke Hipton breathed a sigh of relief as Saran came up to him. ‘I was about to go look for you, I thought p’raps you ’adn’t ’eard my call as I crossed to them tube works.’

‘I heard–’ She got no further, Luke’s words cutting her off.

‘It weren’t so ’ard as Gideon ’ad me think, though to be fair I reckon that were more his doin’ than not; kept me close alongside all day, he did, and what be more I’ve bin told I can work again tomorrow. I bin given another day in them tube works, ain’t that bostin’, Saran? Ain’t that just bostin’!’

Yes it was wonderful. Saran stayed silent. Gideon Newell had been kind to Luke ... just as he had tried to be kind to her. For a brief moment she saw again the look touching his face before he turned away leaving her alone in the street, a look of disillusionment, a sadness that seemed akin to regret, a look that seemed to say he had not expected selfishness. She had not meant what she said to sound that way but he had strode away before she could explain; it had been obvious Gideon Newell wanted no explanation. But why had not giving it been so painful ... why was it painful still?

'...so if I works real 'ard chance be I might get given another day in the tube works.' Ending suddenly, Luke let the silence lie undisturbed between them. Saran was not usually this way, just the opposite, she listened when he told her of his day, showed interest in all he'd done and seen; something had happened, something that hurt! The thought sent a tingle along his spine; the man who'd carried her into that tavern, the man the serving woman showed no liking for ... was he somehow responsible? Or had she heard bad news of her family? Reaching for her hand he held it tight in his own. About her family he could do nothing, but if that man or any other hurt her then he would kill them!

'Saran.' With the thoughts still filling his mind he spoke slowly. 'If it should be as anybody – any man – causes you grief, you will tell me, won't you?'

'Yes, but–'

'You *will* tell me, promise me, Saran, promise me!'

There was so much feeling in the words: anger, sorrow, protection and love ... yes, there was love for her mixed in that demand. Squeezing the fingers that held hers, Saran answered softly, 'I promise I will never keep anything from you, Luke.'

But she had meant to keep one thing from him, she had been bent on selling the brooch to the pawnbrokers without telling Luke, had intended to take the money she got and say nothing of it. But she had not wanted it for herself! Almost a cry for forgiveness, the thought rang in her heart as a picture of that disillusioned face rose to her mind; Gideon Newell had judged her selfish and deceitful and, given the circumstances, he could not be blamed.

'I got this today.' Releasing her hand Luke delved into a pocket of the trousers which, like his jacket, had fitted years ago but now rose above his worn-through boots. Palm outstretched he displayed several coins. 'A day's pay, that means you get a warm meal, an' Gideon told me of a place ... a friend of 'is mother who'll find you a bed.'

Find *her* a bed, provide *her* with a warm meal; he did not speak of himself. How could she have been so thoughtless of him? Reproach staring at her from the face in her mind, she shook her head and turned away. Luke had shared ... was still prepared to share everything with her ... and she had not given a thought to sharing with him.

Clinking the coins together Luke snapped his fingers shut. 'Saran,' he stepped closer, 'there be summat as don't be right with you, don't tell me there ain't cos I knows that will be a lie; is it ... is it your kin, 'ave you 'eard bad?'

It was there again, that concern, the compassion. Choked by the emotion it evoked in her, Saran took a moment to answer. 'No, I have heard no news of my family.'

'Then what? Did summat 'appen at one o' them houses you called at, did some stuck-up body say something that 'urt ... threaten you wi' the dogs?'

She could not leave it like that, Luke had the right to know what had been in her mind to do; and if telling him meant him turning his back on her, walking away as that tall figure had done, then it would be no more than she deserved.

A fast-rising moon illuminated the thin face drawn with fresh concern, stirring the pangs of guilt as she turned to him. She was the cause of much of this boy's worry, part of the burden resting on his young shoulders, and telling him of how she had been about to cheat him would only add to that burden. She had promised herself she would quit this town without his knowing. Her hand closing over the brooch, she drew a deep breath. It was a promise she would keep.

Had it been embarrassment or had it been shame? Gideon Newell turned towards a small cottage stood some way past the oak-timbered Oakeswell Hall. Which was it he had seen on the face of Saran Chandler? The lad had laughed when she had been called his sister, but they were friends, he had said, good friends.

Good friends! His hand resting on the low gate which led into a tiny garden he stared into moonlit shadows. The lad was certainly that, but the girl ... could anyone so prepared to deceive be called a friend! In what else had she duped the lad? Was her story of a family sold for gain true or a tissue of lies? She had been bound with a rope when Luke had come across her in the dawn hours ... but what did that prove, that she was a victim of her stepfather? Or had she been tied to prevent waywardness ... was it that she was the shame of the family? No! Instinctively he rejected the idea. He had felt a little angry when speaking of that brooch, disappointed at the possibility of her not deciding things with the lad who so obviously thought her special – but a woman of the streets? No, he could not think that of her. So why think of her at all?

Pushing the gate open he stepped through it. Making no move towards the cottage he continued to stare vacantly into the shadow-enfolded garden. Hadn't he asked himself the same question while heaving ingots of iron into red-hot crucibles, while drawing it into tubes which, when cooled, would be soldered end to end? He had watched her in that line, a thin coat pulled close against the bite of early morning, seen the way its light gleamed on her hair sending tiny sherry-coloured darts dancing from it with every movement, darts he had seen again with each showering of sparks as he poured molten iron. Why think of her at all? Loosing a long silent breath he stared hard at the golden moon. It might be simpler to ask himself why he could not stop!

The dirt of the factory scrubbed from him, the rust of iron dust beaten from trousers and jacket that were now laid as usual across the rickety chair in his bedroom, Gideon lifted his face for the kiss that was more welcome than the kidney pudding his mother set before him on a table scrubbed 'til it squeaked. But as her lips brushed against his brow his thoughts were of another, far younger, mouth. Would its kiss taste as sweet, would it calm him as his mother's always had, or would it tug, pull his heart, as thoughts of that gleaming hair and gentle-looking face had torn at it all day?

'Has it bin a hard day?'

It was a question his mother often asked, holding a little of the ache he knew she always felt for him, worry that the iron-filled crucible might fall, killing him as the coal that had fallen in the deep seam of the mine had killed his father, trapping him behind it, so far behind that rescuers had never found him. He had been four years old when that disaster had struck taking several of the men of Wednesbury to their death, and his mother had reared him alone, taking no other man in her husband's place. It had not been easy ... it was not easy for her now. Touching the hand resting on his shoulder he looked up. No matter how hard the work in the tubes it could be no more than she had toiled for him.

'No more than usual,' he smiled, 'and what of your day? I hope you took notice of what I told you and rested.'

Smiling as she reached a cream enamel teapot from the hob, Charity Newell offered the silent prayer of thanks she always offered when hearing that nothing untoward had marred her son's day. 'I needs no rest,' she said pouring tea into a thick mug, 'but I did sit an' talk some while I was along at the Hall.'

Taking up knife and fork Gideon cut into the savoury pudding. There had been no need of his mother working since he had been fourteen; somehow or other he had always found a day's work, a day's money to keep them in bread and coal, and then the tube works had taken him on permanently. But his mother had kept her post at Oakeswell Hall, assisting the cook. 'That way I 'ave a body to talk with during the long hours o' the day' was all she would say whenever he had suggested she no longer work.

'Were a bit of excitement up there today, seems the master's bin invited to stand as godfather to the child of William Salisbury along of Darlaston. Will be quite a do, I reckon, seein' the standing the man has in that town, mind the ceremony can't be for a time yet for the mother still be lying in. Poor wench, it be naught but a miracle of heaven they all be alive an' well what with that accident an' then that babby delivered on the open 'eath...'

Accident ... baby! Two words stood clear of the rest, pushing everything else from Gideon's mind. He had not thought Luke a liar but young lads were sometimes given to adding to the truth here and there, and as he had listened to him talk while they worked, suspicion had reared its head; he had wondered if the lily was being gilded just a little.

He remembered his mother relating the news gleaned from her usual source, but pretending otherwise would bring a repeat without his seeming interested. Keeping his glance on his plate he said, 'Accident ... has there been an accident?'

'Gideon Newell!' Charity's exasperated stare followed her words. 'I wonders why I bothers to bring 'ome any sort o' news at all for I doubt you ever listens! I told you some time gone, William

Salisbury were drivin' his wife to be with her mother – well, that be understood, any young wench about to give birth to her first wants her mother alongside o' her, be only natural – any road up, like I was sayin', he were drivin' the carriage 'imself not leavin' it to no coachman, and that were a mistake for the whole lot tipped over and 'im unconscious beneath it; had it not bin that a wench and a young lad found 'em I dreads to think what would 'ave followed.'

Keeping his glance lowered and his tone even, Gideon kept up the pretence of not remembering. 'Mmm,' he swallowed a mouthful of kidney pudding, 'lucky for William Salisbury.'

'Lucky for 'im!' His mother's snort was one of deep disapproval. 'It be lucky for 'im he be no son o' mine ... whatever give 'im such a crack-brained idea o' drivin' for 'imself in the dark and with a wife near nine months' gone? Yes, he be lucky all right, lucky that babby weren't dead afore ever it breathed God's air. I don't know who the wench were as brought it into the world but I reckons her saved the life o' that child.'

His meal finished Gideon moved to the chair drawn to the fire. His mother did not know who had brought that child into the world but he did. It was a young girl with sherry-coloured hair, a young girl whose face smiled in his heart.

Stood close against the wall of the tiny house that was the Elwell home, Saran's fingers closed about the brooch. It was a trivial piece, the woman who gave it had told her, worth very little. But that was of no matter ... what was of consequence was Luke's knowing she had thought of selling it without asking his opinion. Leaving this town without telling him was one thing, the selling of the brooch was entirely different.

'Luke,' she began hesitantly, 'there is something–'

'Tell me later, first let's get you to the woman Gideon told of.'

Pulling her hand from her pocket she held out the brooch, and the words she so dreaded saying poured out of her. 'I ... I was going to take this to the pawnbroker, to his shop in Union Street. I meant to sell it ... I would have told you, really I would but–'

'Why tell me? It be your trinket, given to you by that woman.'

'Given to *us*, Luke, given to *us*.' The answer was almost a cry. 'That is what is so wrong ... this brooch belongs as much to you as it does to me, I have no right to sell it–'

'You 'ave as much right as need be.' Luke's quick reply cut short her self-recrimination. 'After all, I'd look a right pansy seen wearing that, what would Gideon Newell think o' me then!'

Gideon Newell! Saran's teeth closed on her lip. Why did that man figure so much in her thoughts and, it seemed, in Luke's?

'I don't want that thing,' Luke laughed, 'you do what you wants wi' it, though it would look right pretty pinned to a Sunday frock.'

But she had no Sunday frock and Livvy's children would soon be put to the workhouse;

even if this trinket fetched no more than pence that money would delay their parting for another day.

Catching her hand Luke held it so the light from the moon glistened on the stone's green centre.

'It do be pretty the way the light sparkles from that bit o' glass.' He looked at her, smiling as he folded her fingers over the bauble. 'Try askin' Kilvert will he swap that for a coat somebody's pawned an' never had money enough to retrieve.'

'I don't want a coat, neither do I want the money... But it was almost dishonest of me to even think of acting without first asking you.' It was not the thought of Luke's eyes upon her brought the blush as she bowed her head but the memory of those others, the hardness that had glittered in them as Gideon Newell had turned from her.

'T'ain't that I would call dishonest,' Luke answered as she finished speaking. 'Nor will it give me any heartache. You was acting for the good o' others an' that be as I would want. But Saran...' he caught the hand she had withdrawn as she had talked, 'one thing I would tek 'ard, that be if you should leave me wi'out a word.'

Saran heard her own swift intake of breath. She had said nothing of that part of her intention ... had he guessed ... did he already know her so well? The heat in her cheeks intensified and her own words drowned in the emotion that welled up in her. Luke had spoken with more than his voice: he had spoken with his heart.

'You will tell me, won't you?' Luke went on

though his throat was husky. 'You'll tell me when you get fed up o' my bein' with you, you won't just turn your back, leave wi'out a word?'

Swallowing hard against the lump in her throat, Saran drew him close. 'I won't ever not want you with me, Luke,' she whispered, 'remember what you once said to me ... we be together, we stays together.'

That was not what she had told herself minutes ago! Returning the brooch to her pocket, the promise she had made, and had been so determined to keep, echoed again in her mind, she would quit this town without his knowing ... but as she looked at Luke now, saw his young face smiling in the moonlight, she knew she could never go through with it.

'Ain't doin' no good to stand 'ere witterin', all we'll get from that is like to be a grievance o' the lungs, let's get you along to the place Gideon spoke of.'

The night air was still treacherous, the chill of winter apt to return a sting to it at a moment's notice, bringing a cough to those forced to stand in it; but even recognising the common sense of the lad's words, Saran hesitated. She did not want to seem ungrateful yet the pain of what she had seen earlier in that cramped little house overrode all else.

'Luke,' she asked as he turned away, 'will you be taking a bed at this house you speak of?'

'Ain't no need, I can climb into a hayloft somewheres, there be plenty of 'em along of the taverns.'

What he really meant was the money he spent

on himself could be kept against another night's lodging for her.

'I can climb into haylofts every bit as easily as you can.' She tried to sound amused but the words were tight, sharp almost, and when Luke swung quickly to face her she dropped her glance.

'There be more to this than that brooch, you bin actin' strange since gettin' 'ere. What be goin' on!'

He was bemused but at the same time adamant. Luke was not going to be consistently put off hearing what still bothered her. Swallowing hard, screwing together her courage, she lifted her glance to a face now devoid of its smile. She could only say what she felt, only hope he too might be of the same mind.

'Luke,' she began quietly, 'I know what it is you are doing for me, I've known that ever since our first meeting and I appreciate it, truly I do–'

'But?'

It seemed a world of sadness was reflected in that one word, a fear that all he held dear was crumbling away before him.

'It … it isn't that…'

Taking her hand as she stumbled over the words Luke was once again the man, older in mind, wiser in heart. 'Saran, there ain't nothing you can't say to me, nothing you needs hide; we be friends, don't that be enough?'

Yes, it was enough. Her fingers curling about his own she felt the awkwardness leave her. Luke would understand. Quietly, uninterrupted by a lad who watched moon shadows dance across her face, Saran told of Edward Elwell's job being taken over by machines, of Livvy's heartbreak when telling of taking her children to the parish, and finally her own idea of giving any money she could get for the brooch to the couple, to tide them over if only for a little while.

Over on the hill rising black over the night-shrouded town the church clock rang again, elaborating the silence that followed as she finished, then, as the last chime died, Luke laughed.

'Why d' ain't you say all o' this in the first place, you 'ad me thinkin' all sorts when there be no need to worry.'

No need for worry! In the shadows Saran's brows drew together. The Elwells had been so kind to them, how could Luke not worry for them now?

'Look,' he chuckled again, releasing her hand, 'you says you can climb into a loft easy as me so why don't we do just that and give this to the Elwells?'

With tears pricking her eyelids Saran looked at the coins once more offered to her on an open palm.

# 11

Luke had given every penny of his day's wage to the Elwells. The couple had not wanted to take it but the lad had said he had hoped they could all take a meal together, and himself and Saran sleep beside the fire that fed the forge, except there had been no fire. Livvy had guessed the real reason behind their asking to stay the night in the workshop and her mouth had trembled as she took the money and hurried off to buy sausages and bread; and the next morning Luke had left the remainder of his wage on the table, asking for lodging for the coming night. He had smiled as they had walked to the High Bullen together, saying it was the best possible way he could spend his money seeing she herself refused to be settled in the house Gideon Newell had spoken of.

Gideon Newell! Saran watched the tall fair-haired figure who had called to Luke then strode into the tube works without a look or word for her. He thought her deceitful, a fair-weather friend ready to rob a boy of his dues. But it didn't matter what he thought of her.

'Nuthin' again today, pity I weren't young an' pretty, then my old man might 'ave sold me.'

Her mind on her own thoughts, Saran was only vaguely aware of the mumblings of a woman stood in the line beside her. 'Sorry,' she answered apologetically.

'Me an' all!' the woman replied dourly. 'Sorry I ain't about ten year old an' as sweet-faced ... could be I'd 'ave fetched a price in some tavern, it'd be a better life than this'n.'

'Fetched a price?' Saran frowned. 'I don't understand.'

'That be cos like as not you ain't 'eard,' the woman sniffed. 'Seemed a woman an' daughter were sold over Walsall way a week or two gone, sold in a tavern, so my old man were told ... huh! I reckons they was lucky.'

*A woman and daughter ... sold ... a tavern over Walsall way* ... Saran's heart leapt. Her mother ... Miriam ... it had to be them!

'Wait, please,' she called to the woman already making her way towards the market square. 'The woman and her daughter ... who were they, did they live in Wednesbury or in Walsall?'

'T'weren't Wednesbury.' The woman shook her head as Saran caught up to her. 'That much I be sure on, as for them bein' Walsall folk, that I couldn't rightly say.'

'But you know–'

'I only knows what my old man told me an' no more, he 'eard it from a carter, they gets to 'ear most things but whether they be all truth ... well, you meks your own mind up about that.'

It had to be the truth. Please, God, let it be the truth. The prayer silent on her lips, Saran caught the woman's arm. 'Please, what carter would that be?'

'Could 'ave bin one of a number, but why should you be in a lather?'

'I...' She released the woman's arm. 'I have to

find that carter.'

'Then I reckons you best begin at the Turk's 'Ead, all them carters puts up there, but chance be they'll be well on their ways be now.'

Her words of thanks streaming behind her, Saran flew the rest of the way along High Street, not stopping until she reached the tavern.

'Be you lookin' for the lad?' Crossing the rear yard the woman who cooked and served food caught sight of Saran looking into each of the stables. ''E ain't here; I ain't had sight of him since the night you was brought into the kitchen.'

Glancing into the last of the stables Saran turned a desperate look to the woman. 'I'm looking for a carter.'

'A carter?' Tired eyes in a worn face regarded Saran. 'Well, wench, you be a bit late o' catchin' one o' them, the last one left some twenty minutes since. Was you wantin' to buy summat?'

Saran felt a scream of desperation rise inside her. This was the first breath of news she had heard of her mother and sister since Enoch Jacobs had sold them and now the man who might tell her more was gone!

'There'll be morc traders along during the day...'

'No!' The cry rang across the cobbled yard. 'It has to be that one!'

'Steady, wench!' The woman's voice was kindly. 'If'n one o' them 'as done you down, teken more from you than he should, then you tell his looks to me an' when he comes again...'

Tears she was finding ever more difficult to hold back sparkling in her eyes Saran shook her head. 'This carter, the one I am looking for, he spoke of a sale...'

'They always be doing that.'

'But this was a special sale, he said he'd heard of a woman and young girl having been sold in a beerhouse in Walsall.'

'A woman and a young wench!' The woman's brows drew together. 'Them carters deals in all sorts o' goods but ain't never one o' 'em traded for folk ... not to my knowing, they ain't, and I gets to hear most of what they does sooner or later; but s'posin' what you thinks be so, then the pair you speaks of, be they kin to you?'

Struggling with the emotion that was rapidly overwhelming her, Saran whispered, 'They are my mother and sister. My stepfather sold them for–'

'Say no more, wench.' The woman's voice was brittle with disgust. 'It be high time summat were done about that practice, men can treat their womenfolk like they wouldn't treat 'orses and naught the constables care, even though I hear tell it be against the–'

Her mother had taught that it was ill-mannered to interrupt an adult but Saran was too wound up to worry over her manners. 'Please!' she blurted. 'Can you help me find which carter it was?'

'You wait you there.' Her mouth set determinedly, the woman walked quickly into the tavern, emerging several minutes later. Keeping her voice low, she glanced from side to side as if anxious not to be seen talking. 'The one you seeks be gone to Darlaston. Tek the Bilston Road from the Bullen, if you hurries you'll catch up wi' him, and God speed you, wench.'

At last! Thanks gleaming through her tears, Saran ran back the way she had come. At last she would find her mother and her sister.

The lad had been given permanent employment. 'He keeps the job so long as he works hard and keeps his nose out of trouble, that I expect you to see to.' John Adams had smiled as he said the words but Gideon knew him too well to believe there was one of them that wasn't meant. Luke had been lucky to be taken on at all and it had been done only as a favour to Gideon Newell. Watching the boy move quickly and surely, taking finished tubes to the stacking place, Gideon's qualm was not Luke but the girl he had thought to be sister to him. Employment might hold the lad in Wednesbury but she ... would Saran Chandler remain in this town? And if she did not, would it matter? Setting a block of red-hot iron on the bed of rollers, Gideon stared at it for several moments, the question riding his mind. Would it matter if Saran Chandler left Wednesbury? Drawing the iron through the swages until the required thickness of flat iron was reached, he felt the answer in the tilt of his heart; it would matter to him. But why should it? It wasn't as if he had known her long enough to experience that feeling, he had spoken with her no more than once and then they had parted company on sharp words. If this was a passing fancy with him then the quicker it was passed for good the better! The thought was meant to help, to ease the ache of uncertainty inside him, but as the hours wore on the questions persisted and with them a stronger feeling, almost a desolation he could not curb and one he knew would grow should Saran Chandler leave Wednesbury.

'I knows you spoke for me an' I thanks you for it.' The day finished, Luke looked at the man walking beside him. 'I knows Saran will want to thank you an' all.'

Would she? Gideon Newell kept the query to himself. Or would she think he was once more overstepping the mark? She had not taken it kindly when he had pointed out that the brooch she had been given belonged as much to Luke as to herself, she had seen his words as an interference; would she see his getting the lad a job in the same light?

'I wouldn't 'ave been given work at all were it not for you.'

'Well, just see you listen to what you are told and do only that, don't go trying to do things off your own bat, for molten iron is a dangerous thing.'

'I learned that already.' Luke lifted his hands, staring at them through the evening shadow. 'Them sparks sting like the prod o' the devil's fork.'

Catching Luke by the shoulders Gideon stared hard into the thin face which lifted to him. 'And a tipped crucible can burn a man to a cinder quick as the fires of hell; remember that, and stay clear of them. The shout be given once only ... there is no second chance. Men running with a crucible filled with molten metal don't stop for anything nor anybody daft enough to stand in their way, just make sure it isn't you!' A small shake adding emphasis to his words he stared a moment longer, then smiled. 'Now get you off to wherever it is you be going to meet your friend.'

Calling goodnight, Luke ran along Springhead and had reached Russell Street before remembering. Gideon had called him from the line that morning and he had been so hopeful it meant another day's work he had run to the tube works without arranging where to meet with Saran once the day was over. But she would know where to be, she would surely guess he would have said to meet where they had last night, outside the Elwell home. But they could not expect to stay there. Luke's fingers touched against his empty pocket. 'You be one of the regular workmen now,' the owner of the works had told him, 'and as such you'll get your tin once a week, same as they do.' That meant he had nothing to offer the Elwells in exchange for a night beside their forge ... and fired or not it would have proved better for Saran than a night under a hedge; but why a hedge? He grinned to himself. Hadn't her said her could climb into a hayloft easy as he could? But that wouldn't feed 'em ... they would needs to eat. Held by the complexity of the situation, Luke stared at the shadowed market place, the last few of its traders packing their boxes on hand carts prior to leaving making no impression on his troubled mind. He could manage without food, he'd done it before when he'd been locked away for days in the glory hole, that unlit cellar in the workhouse, the warders not bothering or not wanting to bring him a meal; but Saran, he could not see her go hungrier than they already were.

'Hey up there, how were Bilston then?'

The loud call jolting his mind clear, Luke glanced towards a market trader pausing in his work to shout a greeting, grinning at the carter who replied, 'Same as Wednesbury ... thick with smoke and soot.'

'Be that right!' The market trader lifted another box on a handcart. 'Reckon I'll go there to trade then, for they says where there be muck there be money.'

'Oh ar,' the other man laughed, 'well, it be the same there as it be 'ere, folk keep diggin' in the muck but they never comes up wi' the money, seems you bin listenin' to fairy tales.'

The laughter of both men rested on the evening as Luke set off behind the rumbling wagon. If he had a pound he would bet it against a penny the wagon would stop at the Turk's Head and, if luck were on his side, maybe the man would pay him a couple of coppers to unharness the horse and take it to the stables; tuppence would get Saran a sandwich from the cookshop.

An hour later, carrying slices of pork with bread dipped in the meat juices, bought not from the cookshop but from the serving woman who had answered his knock on the kitchen door of the tavern, Luke turned his steps towards Russell Street. He had insisted the serving woman take the tuppence in return for the bread and meat, and she in turn had given him enough to share with Edward and his family.

*'Tek it.'* The woman had shoved it at him through the half-closed door, her voice a hurried whisper. *'What the gaffer don't see his 'eart won't grieve over ... tek it an' tell that wench o' your'n I be askin' after 'er.'*

It was not a slice o' bacon – Luke held the warm package close to his chest – but a bite o' hot pork would taste as sweet to the Elwell kids.

'You told me you'd get it!' His ice-cold eyes contrasting violently with the angry red of his face, Zadok Minch brought a clenched fist heavily down on the brass inlaid desk.

Standing the other side of it the tall figure of a man watched the steadily rising temper stain cheeks and forehead a deeper shade of scarlet. A little more and Minch would drop dead of a heart attack ... now wouldn't that be nice!

'I thought I would.' He spoke calmly, knowing the irritating effect it would have on the older, heavier man.

'Thought!' Zadok roared. 'Thought! Seems that be all you do is think, what bloody good does you expect thinkin' to do!'

Perhaps a mite more than bawling. A smile not quite revealing what touched his mind, the tall figure shrugged. 'I can always try again.'

His breath exploding between thick lips, Zadok dropped heavily into a captain's chair set next to the desk.

'Try again,' he fumed. 'Try again! How many times do yer think yer can grab the wench afore you be seen, you don't be playin' ring a ring o' bloody roses!'

He was not playing any game, not with the girl and certainly not with Minch. The man had the idea he would get the goods for nothing ... now that *was* a thought set to do no good.

'How was I supposed to know she would be empty handed?' Calm as before the question attracted the required effect.

Zadok's colour deepened, his lips shining with spittle. 'You be supposed to know! You reckons you 'ave a brain so why not use it once in a while ... for I tells you, lose me what it be you told me of and all business atwixt me and you be ended, you can find some other way of robbin' folk, for you'll be no fogger as deals wi' Zadok Minch.'

With eyes clear and sharp, a razor-tipped mind cool and collected, Zadok's visitor regarded him evenly. 'Supposing next time proves more fruitful. Supposing the brooch proves to be worthless, what then? I don't take risks for no reward, not even for Zadok Minch.'

'Worthless?' Pulling his brows together, Zadok glared.

'That was how the girl described it.'

'An' you think that be the truth?' Zadok growled. 'Can you see William Salisbury, the richest man in Darlaston, presentin' a wife he be daft over wi' a worthless trinket! Believe that an' you'll believe shit be chocolate; I tells you that there lover's bauble be worth more'n a guinea or two.'

'So what if it is already in Kilvert's pawnshop?'

His teeth ground together with a spasm of fresh rage as Zadok glared at the figure watching him calmly. Christ, what kind of slow-witted fool did

Wednesbury spawn!

'The wench had no money, you said so yourself.' Every word spoken slowly, enunciated clearly, he waited for each to be absorbed before continuing. 'Don't that tell you ... don't it point clear to the fact her couldn't have teken the brooch, couldn't have pawned it or the money her got would have bin in her pocket. To me that says the brooch be still about her somewheres so find her; strip her, do anythin' you wants with her but bring me what the wife o' William Salisbury give her the night her birthed that babby!'

He would find Saran Chandler. Turning his back on the nail master the tall figure strode from the house stood in its own wide grounds. He would find the girl whose face never left his mind for long, the girl he thought of constantly, thought might fill his heart. But hearts could be filled by other women and pretty faces bought on almost any street if a man had money, and that brooch would bring money ... only not to Zadok Minch!

# 12

The bread and meat, wrapped in a piece of cloth, was warm against his chest, and Luke's mouth watered at the thought of the feast to come. Gideon had been away from the works for a part of the morning and on his return had shared the bread and cheese that was his dinner. Luke remembered the sweet taste of the cheese in his mouth. He had tried to refuse it saying he wasn't hungry, but Gideon had insisted; he must have recognised the lie. Hugging his precious package Luke turned along Russell Street. Gideon Newell was a good man to have as a friend.

The Elwell house was in darkness. Luke paused as he emerged from the narrow entry into the small yard shared by houses built in blocks of four. That was no surprise, for paraffin cost money and so did the candles Livvy did not light until putting her daughter to bed, the fire of the small forge providing illumination in the workshop where the others spent most of the night hammering out nails. But there was no glow of flame from the tiny window; as last night, the forge was cold. But that alone should not account for the sudden weight that hit his stomach. The day's wage Livvy had so tearfully accepted last night wouldn't stretch to buying coal, that much he realised, but surely one candle...

The elation of buying supper draining from

him, Luke stared, oblivious of the sounds of hammer on anvil coming from other people working half the night. The church clock had struck eight as he had run through the deserted Shambles, its butchers' stalls bare and empty, the only movement that of dogs scavenging for forgotten scraps. Eight o'clock! The weight in his stomach grew. Saran should be here, she wouldn't wait for him anywhere else. Apprehension a finger touching his spine, he moved towards the shrouded house.

Saran was not there! His eyes, used to the long hours spent alone in the workhouse, had quickly adjusted to the darkness and he had found no difficulty in going through those tiny rooms. Stood once more in the communal yard, Luke tried to think. Edward Elwell could be looking for work, p'raps he had walked to Brummajum, gone to see the nail master he sold to, gone to ask if would he let 'im have a load of iron on tick ... not that there was much likelihood o' that by what Edward had said last night – nail masters allowed no credit; maybe Livvy had found summat, some cleanin' job or the like and teken the little 'uns with her... But that didn't tell why Saran weren't here.

'Ain't bin nobody in that 'ouse since the mornin'.'

Covered from chest to ankle by a scorch-marked black cotton apron, a hessian sack tied with rope about her middle, a gaunt-faced woman shook her head at the lad who had knocked on her brewhouse door.

'The bums come round early and turned 'em

into the street, said the 'ouse were needed for a family as could pay, d'ain't give 'em no time to pack anythin' ... not that them poor souls 'ad anythin' to pack.'

The bailiffs had chucked the Elwells out! Luke tasted a sourness in his throat. No matter they hadn't nowheres else to go, they'd been put on to the streets.

''As a young wench called since the Elwells were put out?'

'You means the one as left along o' yourself this morning?' The woman shoved an inquisitive toddler behind her. 'No, 'er ain't bin back, not as I've seen.'

Saran had not been at the house since early morning. Luke walked slowly back along the Shambles and into the market square. There was nothing to be teken from that, her walked the streets all day askin' for work an' enquirin' after her family, but each evenin' her had been alongside o' that house waitin' of him comin'. So why not tonight ... why was Saran not there ... where was 'er?

Questions tumbling his mind like acrobats he watched a heavy cart rumble past. The Turk's Head! Had Saran gone there, for all he'd asked 'er not to? That was unfair. He pushed the thought away. 'Er wouldn't never do anythin' 'er promised otherwise; besides the woman in the kitchen would 'ave told 'im.

So what else to do ... who to ask if they had seen 'er? Suddenly conscious of the lumbering wagon, one possible answer leapt at him. Carters passed lots o' folk, mebbe that one might remember seein' a young wench on 'er own.

Sprinting after the cart, Luke called his question.

'Young wench, you says...' Pulling on the reins, a bewhiskered man looked down from the driver's box. 'Could 'er be the one laid in the back there, one I found as I passed along the Bilston Road?'

He had made a bargain and it would be kept. The chatter of his mother going over his head, Gideon Newell stared into the fire. The delivery would be made and he would be given the reward spoken of. Young Luke Hipton's look had been full of curiosity, the youngster had longed to ask where it was he had been those hours he had been gone from the tube works, but they had parted company for the night with the lad being none the wiser. What he did not know he could not prattle about. Gideon watched the sparks from settling coal shoot into the black vacuum of the chimney. Gideon Newell's business was his own and he meant to keep it that way. News of what he had been about earlier in the day would be abroad soon enough.

'I'll be off, then, to take a cup of tea with Ginny Trotter but I'll be back afore it be time for bed.'

'No need to rush.' Gideon rose to his feet, smiling at his mother throwing a shawl about her head. 'I know well my way to upstairs and I've long since stopped being feared of monsters lurking underneath my bed.'

Her own smile fond, his mother tied the shawl beneath her breasts. 'Ar, you be a man growed an' like your father – God rest 'is soul – you be feared o' nothin', and honest as the day. Gideon Newell be a son any mother could be proud of.'

Settled once more in his chair Gideon returned his gaze to the crimson heart of the fire. Charity Newell knew her son, but even she did not know his dreams, the hopes of a future that would take him out of this cramped little house. *'Get it for me, bring me what I ask and you'll not go unrecognised.'* Those had been the words said to him, the promise he was given.

The bargain had been made. Leaning back in the chair Gideon closed his eyes. The first attempt had borne no fruit, but that did not mean the tree was bare. He would try again, soon!

Saran was dead! Numb with shock, Luke stared with empty eyes at the cloth-wrapped package clutched forgotten in his hands. He 'ad thought 'er careless wi' time and all the while 'er 'ad been lyin' in that wagon covered by the driver's coat! Saran, the wench 'e had come to love, Saran was dead!

'Give them to me, lad, I'll warm a couple in the oven and set the rest in the cupboard for mornin'.'

Hardly aware of the words, Luke offered no resistance to the sandwiches being taken from his grasp.

'Go wait you in the loft ... the landlord'll 'ave no knowledge o' your bein' there, my Ben'll see to that; I'll fetch your bread an' meat across to you soon as I gets a minute.'

The carter had driven into the yard of the

Turk's Head tavern and, at the request of the serving woman, Ben the ostler and the carter had between them carried the limp form up into the hayloft.

The woman who had asked no question slipped quickly into a side room, emerging with a blanket. 'Best tek this,' she said, hustling him from the kitchen. 'The carter'll be wantin' 'is coat so cover the wench wi' this an' then wi' straw, my Ben'll 'elp you do it.'

Luke was blind and deaf to all but that one horrifying thought, and his fingers refused to hold the blanket until a sharp slap caught against his cheek.

'Sorry, lad...' the woman whispered, thrusting the blanket at him, 'but this be no time to stand gawkin', the landlord could be out 'ere any minute and if 'e finds that wench then we'll all be forrit.'

This woman had shown them kindness before and she was showing the same again, but what good would a blanket do? The slap having brought him to his senses Luke kept to the shadows, slipping soundlessly across the cobbled yard. What good was a blanket to a dead girl!

Huddled into a corner of the loft Luke listened to the sounds of night dying on the street. Men leaving the tavern calling raucous goodnights, feet rapping on the footpath and occasional carriage wheels rattling on the cobbled road, and all the time the figure beneath the blanket was still and silent.

*'knocked about ... bruised summat bad...'* He had heard the muffled whispers of the carter as he

had helped carry Saran into the stable. But who would do such a thing ... who would want to hurt a wench who had never harmed so much as a fly? Resting his head on his knees Luke let the tears flow. He had vowed he would never love anyone again after his mother had died, vowed never to let anything mean so much that losing it would break his heart a second time ... but he loved Saran Chandler, and losing her was breaking his heart.

'You promised,' he sobbed quietly, 'you promised not to leave wi'out sayin' ... you promised, Saran ... you promised.'

'Her ain't broke no promise, lad.'

As a hand touched his shoulder Luke lifted his head, meeting the sympathetic eyes of the ostler, a small candle lantern held above his head.

'You be wrong if'n you be thinkin' the wench be dead, her be unconscious an', for all I knows, 'urt worse than them there bruises shows but her ain't dead.'

'Saran ain't ... her ain't...'

'No, lad.' The hand on his shoulder gripping more tightly held Luke back as he made to scramble to the side of the still figure. 'Leave the wench lie 'til we be sure no bones be broke, but as for bein' dead then 'er ain't; so you eat what the wife 'anded to me an' there be a cup o' summat to wash it down. I'll leave the lantern, the tavern be all but bedded for the night so nobody will be usin' the stables afore mornin' and a light little as that won't be seen across the yard.'

Saran was alive. The ostler gone, Luke moved

carefully to her side, the lantern's weak flame lighting a pale face, one cheek marked with a dark bruise.

*'knocked about ... bruised summat bad...'*

The words returned clearly to his mind but this time no horror followed in their wake. Hanging the lantern on a nail protruding from a beam he lay beside the sleeping girl, touching one hand gently to the blanket. Cuts healed and bruises faded... He smiled a prayer of thanks already on his lips. Saran was alive ... she was alive!

'You go to your work, lad, you be goin' to need the coppers you earn.' It had been a battle between himself and the ostler's wife, she saying Saran would be safe with Ben and herself, while Luke wanted to stay by her side.

'There be naught you can do,' the woman persisted. 'Be foolish to lose a job you've only just got.' She had smiled then, her voice softening. 'Go you on, lad, the wench'll be well cared for, you 'ave my word.'

'I be waitin' on that one ... wake up, lad, this be no place for daydreamin'!'

The irate shout rang above the hiss of spitting crucibles and clang of tubes being hoisted into piles. Jerked back to the present Luke grabbed a lump of iron but not before he caught the rapid turn of Gideon Newell's head and the immediate alert glittering in his sharp eyes.

Running with a wheelbarrow filled with iron ore Luke fed it into the red-hot crucible, turning still at a run to fetch more. They had not spoken with each other this morning. With the hooter already sounding he had dashed into the works, going to his place with only a brief nod to Gideon; and in the half hour given for the midday meal he had sat alone, his thoughts with the injured girl lying in that hayloft.

She had murmured several times during the small hours. He had held her head, offering her the milk Ben's wife had sent from the kitchen, but she had turned away each time with a cry of fear ... and the name she had murmured...

'What be wrong wi' you, lad ... be you moonin' after some wench? If you be wantin' to see 'er agen you'd best keep your wits about you. Remember, tekin' advice *after* trouble be like tekin' medicine after death, it don't be a lot o' use!'

Garnishing his words with a cuff to the head, the workman muttered on angrily about 'kids ... useful as a boil on the arse!' before nodding to a second man, the two of them grabbing the carrying poles holding a second crucible and taking it to the moulds, filling each with molten iron.

Somehow the day had ended. Luke breathed a sigh of relief at the blare of the hooter indicating the finish of his shift. Grabbing a piece of rag he rubbed it over his hands, removing some of the dirt before reaching for his jacket. One worry was over but the next had already taken its place. 'Ad the landlord of the tavern discovered the wench in his hayloft ... where was her gone if'n 'e had ... and more than that, 'ow could Saran be fed wi'out money? The woman at the Turk's Head couldn't go on smugglin' stuff out to that barn wi'out somebody gettin' suspicious.

Enmeshed by the strings of thought twisting and winding about his brain Luke was unaware of the tall figure stood watching him until it spoke.

'Is something wrong, Luke?' Gideon Newell eased his own jacket over powerful shoulders.

'Should there be?' The answer incisive, Luke turned away.

Men hurrying past – each tired face telling they also were relieved to have reached the end of the working day – called their goodnights, Gideon replying in kind.

'I don't know,' he said as the last man stepped through the wide doors into the yard. 'I'm asking you ... is something wrong?'

Was something wrong! The cold tip of anger which had pricked in the dark hours when Saran had cried out, stung again. Gideon Newell could ask that, knowing what he did!

'Nothing!' he answered savagely. 'There be nothing wrong.'

'Then why the frost ... why no word the whole day?'

Leaving the works, crossing the yard to the street, Luke knew he must control the feelings inside him until Saran was well enough to talk, to tell him if the anger bubbling like the molten iron in those crucibles was justified.

'I ... I just be tired, that's all.' It was not a total lie; afraid Saran might need him he had tried not to sleep.

'I know you didn't go to the house we spoke of

... did you spend the night with the Elwells?'

Why had he asked that? Luke's lips firmed together. What did it matter where the night had been spent?

'Luke!' Receiving no answer Gideon reached for him, spinning him about. 'Luke, what the hell is wrong with you ... or is it Sa– Miss Chandler? Is she ill? Tell me, Luke, is there anything I can do?'

Twisting free of the restraining hand, Luke looked into the strong face. Had he been fooled by this man, was his friendship a sham, a means to an end?

'No,' he answered quietly. 'Saran be fine and so do I. We can manage without help ... from anybody.'

Feet drumming on the cobbles, he raced away along the High Street.

*'knocked about ... bruised summat bad...'*

The words matched the rhythm of his feet but those Saran had cried in the night hammered in his heart.

*'I don't have it ... I don't have it, Gideon.'*

# 13

He had told Gideon Newell of that night out on the heath. As Luke ran the length of the High Street low-fronted shops still hoping for customers spilled light in pale pools while wagons and men pushing handcarts moved busily along the road, winding up their own day's business. Mindless of irate protests as he dashed past, Luke let the thoughts he had fought all day run wild and free in his mind. He had told Gideon of that accident with a coach, of the man trapped beneath it, of the woman whose child Saran had helped birth and the brooch ... he had told him of the brooch. What a fool he had been, what a stupid, stupid fool!

His breath painful in his chest he slowed, passing the George Hotel at a walk. That place was where Saran should be, in a warm comfortable room, not holed up in a stable loft like some criminal hiding from the law. Saran had committed no crime, that was him, Luke Hipton was the guilty one; he had let his feelings run away with him, he had taken a liking to Gideon Newell, had told him everything ... had trusted him...

A peal of laughter catching his ear, Luke glanced at the couple emerging from the columned entrance of the hotel. One day Saran would dress like that. She would wear silk gowns and fur-trimmed capes and be accompanied by toffs in fancy waistcoats, with cape and top hat and gloves.

Watching them climb into a waiting carriage then drive away, the harshness of reality closed around him like a winding sheet stifling tomorrow with today. Why had he let his tongue run on like a bolting horse; if he had held it still Saran wouldn't be lying injured ... wouldn't have been attacked. It must have been the brooch – but why, when the thing was practically worthless? Every thought giving rise to another he walked slowly across the fast-emptying market place. Then a thing worth only pennies was a treasure to somebody who had nothing, somebody who was starving. But Gideon Newell was far from starving!

Yes, Gideon Newell! Lifting his head, as if only now recognising that one thought which had hovered the whole day on the verge of reason, he stared into the evening greyness. He it was had been told all, he it was had been absent from the tube works yesterday for an hour or more, he it was knew Saran kept the brooch, and he had seen her in the line, had seen her standing there beside himself, so Gideon Newell would recognise her! What more evidence was needed! The tip of anger burying itself more deeply, Luke turned into the yard of the Turk's Head tavern, the truth blinding him with its clarity. Gideon Newell was the culprit, Gideon Newell had attacked and beaten Saran!

She had not seen her attacker, not known anyone

was near until a hand had closed over her mouth from behind and she had been forced to the ground. She had run as far as breath would allow, following the way she thought the carter to have taken. Leading out from Wednesbury the Bilston Road had become no more than a trackway threading between fields of high-sprouted corn, a trackway that held no sign of a carter's wagon. The day had been so bright. Eyes closed, Saran remembered... So bright and still, the fields devoid of workers making it seem the world was empty. But it had not been empty. A man had lain hidden among the corn ... waiting.

*'Hand it over.'*

Words more painful than the bruises marking her body played for the thousandth time in her mind.

*'I know you haven't pawned it.'*

Fear had kept recognition of what it was the man was demanding from registering, and as he pressed her harder on the ground she had tried to tell him she had no money. He had struck her then, a heavy blow to the head sending her senses reeling.

*'It isn't money ... I want what you be taking to William Salisbury, that which his wife gave you; now where is it, you bitch! Where do you have that brooch hidden?'*

Another blow knocking any words from her, she had been twisted on her back, a hand viciously gripping her chin.

*'I mean to have it, even supposing I have to rip it from you.'*

It seemed the words were being spoken again,

the eyes above the scarf tied about the lower half of the face glittering maliciously above her own, and her lips moved with the cry she had tried to utter then, *'I don't have the brooch.'*

Her jaw was held so tightly the words could not have been intelligible yet somehow her attacker must have gathered the meaning for he had rained several blows to her face before savagely tearing at her clothes. A fruitless search building frustration into anger he had snatched her to her feet, shaking her so her head had snapped on her neck, then a closed fist had sent her sprawling into merciful blackness.

A movement in the shadows beside her setting her nerves flaring, Saran caught her breath, releasing it with a relieved gasp when Luke's voice whispered to her. Ignoring the bite of bruised ribs she pushed to a sitting position, reaching for the boy's hand.

'I just feel a little shaky,' she answered his question, hoping the lie did not show through. 'I'm not hurt in any way and it's over now so let's forget it.'

Forget it! Luke's fingers tightened. He would never forget it and should fate ever offer him the chance to repay what had been done then he would grab the opportunity and wring every last drop from it.

'There be a couple o' dray carts pullin' into the yard.' The wife of the ostler peered over the top of the short ladder. 'I knows you been workin' at that toob place the 'ole day, lad, but my Ben thinks you might like the chance o' earning a copper or two by helping with the unloadin'.

Them draymen will willingly give a tanner apiece if it means they 'ave an hour in the tap room wi' a tankard or two for company.'

Sixpence apiece ... a shilling would see Saran more comfortable, it would bridge the gap 'til pay day. Luke was on his feet, scrambling down the ladder and thanking the woman already in the yard.

He could take her to the house Gideon had mentioned. No! Rejection arising as swiftly as the idea, Luke clenched both fists. He wanted no more of Gideon Newell.

'You be sure that be as you wants it?' With the casks of beer unloaded into the cellar and the two silver coins in his hand, Luke sat beside Saran.

'I think it would be best.'

'But why?' he asked. 'T'ain't as if that landlord knows we be 'ere, why pay for summat 'e don't know nuthin' about so can't 'ave the missin' of?'

'*We* know, Luke,' Saran answered softly. 'We also know that Ben and his wife are putting their livelihood on the line by hiding us here, by bringing us food we haven't paid for. Should they be discovered they would be put on the streets.'

Same as the Elwells 'ad been chucked out. A picture of that darkened house flitting across his inner vision, Luke knew that what Saran suggested was right, they must pay the landlord for lodging in his barn and for the food they took; but sixpence? It was half of what they had!

'You done right, lad.' The woman's smile showed in the light of the candle lantern carried by her husband. 'Pay your way whensoever you can, for an honest hand meks a light spirit.'

It also meks a light pocket! Keeping the thought to himself, Luke took the broth she handed him. That landlord wouldn't never have knowed...

'It took no noticing earlier that the clothes you be left with don't have enough o' themselves to hold together.' The woman's glance rested on Saran. 'That bein' so I brought these ... they don't be no Sunday walking outfit but I reckon they'll fit an' you be welcome to 'em if it be you ain't above tekin' 'em.'

Touching a hand to the clothing the man laid on the straw at her feet, emotion filling her throat, Saran murmured her gratitude. One day, she prayed silently, please Lord, let me one day be able to repay the kindness of these people.

'I come across this afternoon after the midday rush for meals slackened off.' The woman spoke again. 'I don't expect you remembers much about it, wench, you bein' as sleepy as you was, but I was feared you could 'ave bones broken. Now my Ben be no doctor, not even one o' they animal kind, his business be lookin' after 'osses and 'e knows a broken bone when he feels one. Well, bones be bones and I reckoned animal or 'uman they'd be not much different so I had Ben run his hands over you. I stayed close at your side so you need 'ave no fear for your modesty once I told you of it; you 'ave my word my Ben put no finger where it were not needed. I 'ope the liberty I took don't raise too much offence.'

'I take no offence, especially not for an action aimed at my own well-being, I only wish I could return the kindness you both have shown Luke and myself.'

'Heaven repays a bad turn.' The woman got to her feet. 'It also repays a good 'un. I be glad to leave what we do in the hands o' the Lord for He has the knowin' of how best to give reward.'

How best to give reward? Spooning the broth, Luke was silent. Would the swine who had attacked Saran, leaving her half dead in that cornfield, get his reward ... would he be given what was warranted?

Laying aside her bowl Saran glanced at the thin face wreathed by candlelight. From their first meeting this boy had earned what money they had, he had worked to provide her with food and shelter while she had contributed nothing. It was not for the want of trying she had not gained work but that did not detract from the fact it was Luke's shoulders bearing the burden, a burden that was as heavy as it was unfair.

'Luke,' she spoke quietly, 'you have employment at the tube works, I don't know how much it will pay but it should be enough to provide food and lodging somewhere clean. I want you to do that, I'm grateful for all you have done for me, but now–'

'If you be going to say what I thinks you be going to say, then don't say nothin'!' Luke's spoon dropped noisily into his bowl. 'We've talked on this before an' things be the same now as they was then; if'n you feel you 'ave to move on then we goes together an' that tube works can keep its job.'

'But, Luke–'

'I don't want to hear no more!' Luke broke in fiercely. 'I've said me piece and that be the top and bottom of it. We can move on or we can stop 'ere in Wednesbury ... but either way we does it together!'

What good turn had she done that heaven should reward her with such a friend as Luke? Listening to the sounds of him scrambling down the ladder, Saran's flush of happiness was chilled by a sudden thought following hard on the heels of the first. What bad turn had Miriam and their mother done ... what harm had they committed that they be sold like cattle, that their life be exchanged for the price of beer! Was that the judgement of heaven?

'Saran.' The bowls returned to the kitchen Luke stretched out, wriggling his body into the warm comfort of the straw. 'Can I ask what brought you on the Bilston Road?'

He must think she had gone back on her word, that for all her promise she was leaving without saying anything of it to him. Guilt, repentance or a touch of both brought a tinge of colour to her cheeks. She could only tell him the truth, whether he believed her or not he himself must decide.

'I was told a carter had talked of a sale he had heard of taking place in Walsall, the sale of a woman and her daughter.' Speaking quietly she related all of what she remembered to a silent Luke.

'This fella who jumped on you,' he asked as she finished, 'did you recognise 'im, can you say who it were?'

'I told you, most of his face was hidden by a

scarf or a handkerchief.'

'The voice, then!' Luke persisted. 'Can you place the voice?'

Somewhere in the dark unreachable field of memory something flickered, a word ... a tone? Saran tried to grasp it, to draw its flimsy shadow to the forefront of her mind but, like a dream on waking, it was gone.

Despite the anger that still chilled him, Luke could not totally banish the slight niggle of relief that brushed its edges when she shook her head. Surely she would have recognised that voice ... but her not doing so didn't mean it wasn't the one he thought it was. Logic battling with judgement, he closed his eyes. It didn't mean her attacker wasn't Gideon Newell.

'I ... I can't say...' Saran felt blindly for that promise of something remembered, something known yet unknown. 'It happened so quickly and the scarf covering the mouth ... but it's over and whoever it was is long gone by now so we must put it behind us.'

Long gone! Luke stared at shadows challenging the light of the lantern. Was he? Or was he sitting in a house along of Oakeswell End? Was Gideon Newell planning how to try again to take that brooch?

Dressed in the clothes Ben's wife had given her, Saran hurried the short distance from the tavern to Union Street. She had wanted to stand the line, to go along to the High Bullen in the hope of a day's employment but Luke had been adamant. The last of his shilling had been spent on a breakfast they had shared and he had gone to the tube works with no sandwich for his dinner. Seeing him smile, knowing that beneath it he was hungry, she had made up her mind. Asking Ben to set her ruined clothes on a bonfire he had burning on the open ground that bordered the rear of the tavern, blushing as she saw him glance at the torn bloomers, she had walked quickly from the yard, the old woollen shawl drawn low over her face.

*'You stay close alongside Ben and his wife, her says you can sit in the kitchen, her'll tell the landlord you be 'elping out for a day or so.'*

Stood outside the pawnshop Saran tried not to hear the words playing in her mind or think of the promise she had given and had already broken. Luke could not go on as he had, working thirteen hours at that factory then a couple or so more loading and unloading carts; she had to do something to help and this was the one sure way she knew.

'Wait there an' don't you let go of his 'and or I'll tan your arse when I comes out.'

Her hand on the latch of the shop door Saran glanced at a harassed-looking figure detaching fingers clutching at her patched skirts, thrusting their owner towards a child not much older than itself. Handing the older boy the string by which she had pulled a box fastened to odd-sized wheels she gathered several bundles from it before issuing a second warning. 'Mark what I says now, keep an 'old o' the little 'un and don't let 'im go near no carts or it'll be a lamping for you.'

'Ta, miss...' A face Saran guessed was young

behind worry lines nodded as she opened the door, standing aside for the woman to pass. '...but I mustn't podge ... er ... push in front, you was 'ere first so you 'ave to be first served.'

Having assured the woman she was in no hurry to enter the shop Saran had turned her attention to a window filled with bric-a-brac.

'You be lookin' for summat special? You should ask old Kilvert ... he don't put everythin' that be brought to 'im in that there winder.'

'I'm not looking for anything special.'

'Strewth!' Brown eyes, wide beneath a mop of rust-coloured curls, looked at Saran as she turned towards the older boy. 'I bet you d'ain't look for that black eye neither but you copped it just the same. Reckon it be your old man done it, me father gets the same way sometime but he's always sorry after, an' mother...' he flicked a sideways nod at the pawnshop door, ''er often be threatenin' me with a hiding same as you've just 'eard but it don't never come to nothing; it be the clock got her riled this mornin'.'

Another pair of brown eyes stared up at Saran from the younger boy, several inches shorter than his brother and half hidden behind him.

Changing his grip from hand to collar as the younger child turned its attention to a passing cart, the older boy talked on, undeterred by the fact his listener had asked no question. 'The clock be Mother's pride an' joy. It were given as a wedding present by the nobs along of Oakeswell Hall, give her the clock together with the sack they did, said they couldn't 'ave no maid who were liable to go getting herself tied up with children. So it were a case of here's a clock now tek your hook! Now her won't even 'ave that, for once things such as that be popped into old Kilvert's place they don't be like to be fetched out again. Mother don't never 'ave money to spare for that but her does always buy the little 'un a ha'p'orth of jelly babies out of the pennies the neighbours pays for her fetching their stuff to the pawnshop, saves them leaving the nailing to come 'ere so they pays a penny a bundle ... but I sees you ain't got no bundle ... be you goin' to buy summat?'

'I've told you afore about botherin' folk! One day you'll 'ave somebody answer with a smack to the 'ead and serve you right if they does!' Dumping the younger child unceremoniously into the rickety box and snatching the string into her own hand, the woman turned, her eyes darkening sympathetically as she saw the bruises on Saran's face. 'I apologises for my lad, he don't mean no harm, miss, it just be he don't think ... though Lord knows I've warned him about lettin' his tongue run away with 'im, but his head be harder than nail-rod. I swears nothing goes into it.'

Threats of informing the boy's father of his 'bothering a wench' drifting behind her, the woman hurried away. Another family it seemed the trade of nail-maker was insufficient to support; another family which probably worked all day and half the night only to see their earning snatched from them by the greed of a nail master, as did the Elwells.

Luke had not had the time to visit them.

Pushing open the door of the shop, Saran remembered how he had passed over her enquiry of the family; it had been quick, almost guilty, but he should not feel that way, the Elwells would hold no resentment once they learned of his hurrying from the tube works in the hope of a chance to earn a few pence unloading carters' wagons or filling them with fresh goods ready for an early start the next morning. And she? She would finish her business with the pawnbroker and then she would call on Livvy.

# 14

The man had thought her a thief! Pulling the shawl low over her brow, Saran almost ran from the shop, stopping only when she reached the market place. He had thought the brooch was stolen ... that she must have stolen it!

The pawnbroker had looked keenly at her, his eyes piercingly bright despite the gloom of the shop's musty, damp-smelling interior, his tone holding a note of accusation as he had asked how she came by the brooch.

He had held the trinket in his hand, twisting and turning his palm the better to catch what little light dared filter its way through the dusty window.

'*A gift you says.*' That had been when he had stared at her. Saran clutched the shawl, drawing it closer about her, wanting to shut out that sharp accusing look. '*And what sort of man gives a trinket like this to–*'

He had broken off, making a display of taking a magnifying glass to the brooch, but she had known the words he had bitten back: *what sort of man gives a trinket like this to a whore?* But she was no whore. She had wanted to shout that at him, to snatch back her belongings and leave; but the pawnshop was her one real hope of getting money, the only way she could be sure of helping Luke and herself, so she had swallowed the hurt, standing silent as the man had inspected the brooch.

He had taken a long time in the inspection, carrying the brooch to the open door, holding it to the sky, peering intently through the green glass that was its centre.

*'Did you want to pledge it or to pawn it?'*

He had returned to stand behind the high counter and as he placed the brooch on its surface she had thought his hand trembled slightly.

*'I do not really want to part with it for good,'* she had answered truthfully, taking the brooch in her hand and looking at it ruefully.

*'You realises there be a three-month time limit on goods pledged, that if you don't redeem them afore that limit be passed then they becomes my property ... mine be the legal right whatever it be folk pledges.'*

Three months! Could she honestly tell herself she would be able to retrieve the brooch in that time ... honestly say she would have the money? As she had weighed the possibility in her mind the pawnbroker's voice had become little more than a whisper, then the door was shoved open and a woman carrying a large bundle on her hip had pushed her way between shelves lined with similar parcels, dropping her own heavily on the counter.

*'I be serving!'* John Kilvert had snapped. *'You'll have to wait outside.'*

*'Oh ar!'* the woman had snapped every bit as sharply as she grabbed the bundle back to her hip. *'And you can wait for me coming back to this fleapit, Kilvert, only don't wait outside for I fears them chestnuts you calls balls will freeze to the ground*

*afore you sees me!'*

*'You'll strike a better bargain by selling that there trinket, I can pay more for a sale than I can let you have as a pledge.'*

He had ignored the woman's irate outburst, his eyes on the brooch Saran had picked up as that cloth-wrapped bundle had slapped down on the counter.

*'You won't get no better deal than that which John Kilvert offers.'*

It had been said quickly and for some inexplicable reason her fingers had closed firmly over the brooch as the man's tongue had flicked across his lips.

*'I'll give you ten pounds...'* he had reached for the brooch, *'ten pounds. That be a sum you won't be offered in no other pawnshop.'*

Ten pounds! Even now the amount had her gasping. It was an undreamed-of offer, that much money would keep herself and Luke for a year! So why had she not taken it? Her refusal of the offer had surprised her as much as it had the pawnbroker. He had called after her as she had turned for the door, had shouted that maybe he could raise his offer a few shillings to show goodwill. But she had not looked back. Leaning against the wall of a herbalist shop she sucked in a deep breath, trying to still the flutter in her stomach. The woman she had helped that night on the heath had said the brooch was of no value, it was a trinket worth just a few pence ... but ten pounds was not just a few pence. Drawing in another long breath Saran touched against the small hard lump nestling in a pocket of her skirt.

The pawnbroker had thought her at best to be a thief, and that was what she would think of herself in keeping this brooch, what she would think every time she looked at it.

'Saran?'

At the sound of a woman's voice calling her name sending waves of happiness cascading over her, Saran pushed away from the wall.

'I thought it were you ... but what in the world has 'appened, wench, you be black and blue.'

She had thought ... for one wild joyful moment had believed– Hiding her disappointment Saran smiled at Livvy Elwell's next-door neighbour.

'An accident,' she lied, 'I wasn't watching where I was going and a cart...'

'Eh, wench! You 'ave to be careful ... there be folk about who 'ave no care for others, they'd run you down as lief look at you. Them bruises be the only 'urt, I hopes, you don't 'ave no bones broke?'

'None.' Saran shook her head, then before the woman could speak again said quickly, 'I am going to call on Livvy later, perhaps you would be kind enough to tell her...'

Beneath the shawl the woman's head shook and her eyes took on a different question. 'You mean you ain't 'eard? But I told that lad that was with you in that 'ouse, told 'im meself, I did.'

Breath still ragged from her dash along Union Street, Saran trembled slightly. What had she told ... was this what she had waited to hear, prayed to hear every day? Did this woman have news of her family ... had Luke thought her too ill to be told, was that the reason he had said nothing, knowing she would have gone to them no matter how ill she felt?

Her heart drumming painfully she forced the questions away.

'He come to see the Elwells, same as you be goin' to do, but like him you won't see 'em. They be gone.'

'Gone!' Her brows drawing together, Saran stared at the woman. 'Gone where?'

'Who knows.' A ragged shawl lifted as the thin shoulders shrugged. 'All I be knowing is the bums throwed 'em out ... the lad seen for 'imself the house were empty, I'd 'ave thought he would 'ave spoken of it.'

Livvy and her family evicted by the bailiff! Stunned by what she heard, Saran stared after the figure hurrying between stalls dotted about the market place. Luke had known, yet even this morning he had said nothing!

'This must be my lucky day.'

Pleasant with the trace of a laugh, a voice at her elbow spoke again.

'Please, Miss Chandler ... Saran ... don't say you have forgotten me already.'

'I ... no ... I...'

'For God's sake, girl, what happened to you! Those bruises...'

Struggling against the shock of what she had just been told, Saran looked at the man staring at her, his handsome face drawn with concern.

'An accident ... it's nothing.'

'Nothing! Lord, girl, you look ready to faint.'

'Not again, Mr Ensell.' Saran pulled the shawl

across her cheek. 'I would not cause that trouble again, it was unforgivable the first time. Please excuse me, I have an errand...'

'You are not going to get five yards judging by the look of you. The errand can wait at least the time it takes for you to drink some tea.'

'No, I can't, I–'

Catching her hand, Jairus Ensell's tone was firm. 'I'm not taking "no" for an answer, so unless you want me to carry you into that tea house you will agree to my suggestion.'

He looked as though he would carry the threat through. Saran looked into the eyes regarding her challengingly. A few minutes, she would stay a few minutes then make her excuses.

In the cosy room, tea set on the table, Jairus Ensell watched the girl sat opposite. Purpling bruises dark against a creamy skin and a mouth still a little swollen from the cut visible beside it, disguised but did not hide a certain prettiness. A flower waiting to bloom ... Saran Chandler was all of that.

'Better?' He smiled as her glance lifted to him.

'Tea is a wonderful medicine,' she nodded, 'I do feel much better.'

'Enough to tell me what really gave you those bruises? You did not bump into any door, that much I'm sure of. Saran, if any man has raised his hand to you I swear he'll pay.'

For a moment the eyes looking into hers glittered with unspoken threat, and far in the reaches of her mind something stirred. What was it? Saran strove to remember, then she knew. She had seen that look before ... seen it in the eyes of

Enoch Jacobs!

'You can't tell me.' The threat gone from his eyes he smiled briefly. 'It was arrogant of me to think otherwise, a man you scarcely know ... how could I expect you to confide in me? Please forget I was rude enough to ask.'

Was that the way her mother would want her to appear, thankless of this man's solicitude? Pink tingeing beneath the bruises she lowered her glance.

'I do not think you arrogant,' she murmured, 'you are one of the kindest people I have ever met.'

'Then let me help, let me deal with whoever hurt you ... with what is still troubling you.'

'Whoever it was attacked me…'

'Attacked you!' Jairus Ensell's fist clenched on the table. 'You say some swine deliberately did that to you?'

'It happened two days ago...' Speaking in hushed tones she related the whole of the event.

'As you say, the rogue will be long gone,' Jairus said after listening. 'He won't stay in the area if he knows what is good for him and, though it is small consolation, he did not get what he was after.'

'The brooch ... no, I had left that with Luke.'

'And Luke has it still?'

Shaking her head Saran drew the trinket from her pocket. Laid on the white tablecloth, its glass heart gleamed like wet grass in sunlight. 'Luke gave it back to me before he left for the tube works this morning. I took it to the pawnbroker.'

'Kilvert?'

A nod her answer, Saran watched him pick up the brooch and hold it to the light as the pawnbroker had done.

'It would be a pity to hide so pretty an ornament away in a pawnshop when it should be worn and enjoyed; but why did Kilvert refuse you a pledge ... is the brooch so very cheap he was afraid you would not bother to redeem it?'

'Quite the opposite, he seemed anxious I should sell it to him, he was willing to offer ten pounds or a little more for what he called goodwill.'

Bringing the glass centre closer to his eye, Jairus smiled through it.

'Ten pounds ... and you did not take it, why ever not? It is a pretty piece, I own, but ten pounds would buy you a hundred, and each as pretty as this.'

Why *had* she not taken that money ... why had she refused the offer that pawnbroker had made? Only now, watching another man twist the brooch to the light, did she admit the answer.

'I could not accept the money.' Holding her hand for the brooch, she smiled. 'The woman I helped said it was worth almost nothing, obviously she made a mistake. It is probably worth even more than Mr Kilvert offered, therefore I must return it to her.'

'Good for you.' Handing back the trinket, Jairus's fingers closed over those receiving it and his dark eyes glowed their approval. 'But you must not go alone ... would you allow me to take you?'

Pulling her hand free Saran felt the colour

deepen in her face. 'I don't know the name of the people... I only know the men who carried them took the Darlaston Road.'

'Then I will take you to Darlaston now.'

Returning the trinket to her pocket, Saran stood up. 'Thank you, but I can't go now, I promised Luke I would go with him later.'

'And you do not break a promise.' Dropping a silver coin on the table, Jairus smiled at the waitress bobbing him a brief curtsy.

That was not the promise she had made to Luke. Leaving the tearoom Saran wondered why she had told yet another lie ... and why she felt no urge to retract it.

'Did Livvy say where they might go?'

Saran had stared at the house the Elwells had lived in, at the workshop where they had tried so hard to make a living. But despite the hours they put in, despite the toil, they had failed. Stood now in a tiny brewhouse that was workshop and washhouse to the woman she had talked with earlier, she watched the same routine that was the nail-maker's life, the endless movement between forge and anvil, the constant hammering of red-hot iron, stoking the forge and working the bellows with no pause even to wipe perspiration from the face.

''Er said only as there was nothing left, that the nail master had teken the lot, including tools which 'ad been paid for by the Elwells, said as they would go against what were owed...' The woman pressed a treadle with her foot to bring the Oliver down viciously on the almost completed nail, the weight of the heavy hammer flattening the iron to form the head. 'Though saying them folk owed so much as a farthing be a lie by my reckoning, nail masters don't allow no credit, not even a farthing.'

Flinching at the clang of hammer on iron, Saran watched the finished nail eject from the bore, the woman returning immediately to the tiny forge for the next piece of redhot rod.

'Did they have relatives, someone they could turn to?' The shouted question mixed with the ringing clamour of hammer blows, so Saran was unsure it had been heard, but the woman shook her head.

'Nobody I knows of, ain't no visitors, other than yourself and the lad which come with you, been to the 'ouse; but that don't be surprisin' for nail-making leaves no time for visiting.'

Her presence in the stifling, dusty workshop was an intrusion, an interruption to work she knew meant the difference between a slice of bread or no meal at all, yet still she had to ask, had to find out all she could.

'The children,' she called again over the resounding clang of the heavy Oliver, 'what of the children?'

Hands and feet working in rhythm, the woman did not lift her eyes from the work in hand, only the timbre of her voice changed to one of pity as she called her answer.

'Broken-'earted were Livvy, God 'elp 'er, broken-'earted when her took them poor mites.'

'Took them where? Where did she take them?'

Wanting to snatch the hammer from her hand, to push her foot from the treadle operating the

Oliver, to silence the bellows and make the woman stand and answer, Saran could only watch the repetitive, soul-destroying cycle.

'Where else do you tek babbies when they be near enough starving!' The woman brought the hammer viciously to the narrow iron strip. 'Where else when you no longer 'ave a crust to put in their 'ungry bellies? 'Er took 'em to the place where we all find ourselves afore long, 'er took 'em to the parish.'

The workhouse! Like the pounding of the hammer, the words struck against Saran's brain. Livvy had been forced to put her children into the workhouse! Stood in the tiny shared yard she stared through tear-filled eyes at the house whose door had been so readily opened to herself and Luke, her heart aching for the woman who had shared her last bread with total strangers. Livvy was suffering as she herself suffered, Livvy was feeling the pain that would never lessen, the pain of being torn from her family; the tears she shed were the same tears, the heartbreak the same heartbreak, the hopelessness, the desolation, they were all the same and they would go on for Livvy as they went on for her.

The choking in her throat thickening, she walked slowly to the street. Livvy and Edward had done all they could for her and she, what had she done in return? She could have helped them, could have prevented the taking of those children to the workhouse. But she had done nothing. It would have been so simple. Head bowed she retraced her steps, the noise of the carts and wagons rumbling past, the calls of traders in the market square making no headway against the sting of guilt pressing on her heart. It would have been so easy to sell that brooch, to take the money and share it with that family, and now it was too late, the Elwells were gone!

Had Luke known they were to be evicted or, like herself, had he found out only after they had already left? It had to be the latter; Luke was as grateful to that couple as she was herself, had he suspected they would be turned so soon on to the streets he would have found a way to prevent it; sold the brooch ... anything ... he would have helped them. She had come so close. Her hand closed over the trinket in her pocket.

So close to saving that family. Pressed into her palm the brooch dug into the soft flesh. It was hers and Luke's, given to them, the woman would not have parted with it had she not wanted them to have it; the brooch was theirs to do with as they thought fit and Luke would see things as she saw them. Drawing the shawl closer she walked on.

It was too late to help the Elwells.

# 15

'You still don't 'ave it! All this time and you still ain't got it!' Heavy jowls quivering beneath long side whiskers, small eyes wreathed with lines that deepened now as his podgy face screwed in anger, Zadok Minch glared at his tall visitor. 'All this time and you waltzes in here with nothing to show forrit!'

'I told you what happened.'

'Oh you told me right enough!' Zadok's temper snapped. 'You told me ... but telling don't be what I wants, that bauble be what I wants. William Salisbury's mother were a granddaughter of the Davenports of West Bromwich ... the granddaughter of an earl ... that tells me that any jewellery her left behind won't be no rubbish and who would that jewellery got to but her son and it would be his wife would 'ave the wearing of it.' Pausing for breath he slapped a hand noisily on the desk, setting quilled pens rattling on their crystal stand. 'It be my belief that brooch be part of what were bequeathed, that what that wench thinks be no more than a trifle be a jewel of value. Now you get it afore her teks it into her head to be rid of it.'

'And how do you suggest I do that?'

The smoothness of voice, the mouth curving in a half smile, was fuel to Zadok's fury. 'I ain't yer mother!' he exploded. 'I don't wipe your arse for you ... I don't care how you do it so long as it's done!'

And so long as *you* get the brooch. Hidden behind cool eyes the thought played gently. Zadok Minch was prepared to leave the risks but ready to grab the prize with both of those fat greedy hands. But that brooch was one prize he would not get.

'You had the wench once, beat her senseless if what reached my ears be fact,' Zadok ranted on, 'then like a fool you left her, 'stead of holding on to her. That kid her be tagging along with, he'd have spoken up quick enough if he knew her were being held for exchanging with that bauble, he knows no more of its likely value than do the wench herself, he would have found where her had it hid and handed it over soon as asked, so set yourself to finding the girl and one way or the other you'll 'ave found the brooch. That be easy enough even for a fool like you to understand, and now it be said you can leave, our business be done 'til you brings what I asks.'

There were fools and there were bigger fools. Easing his frame in the restrictively narrow chair kept for visitors to the office located above the floor of a large warehouse, his own anger curbed behind a cool smile, the younger man watched the other push away from the desk. Then there were fools the size of Zadok Minch!

'Not quite done,' he said as Zadok turned towards a bureau, fishing a key from the pocket of his waistcoat, 'we have not yet agreed payment for the consignment delivered last night.'

'I ain't had time to reckon that.'

'But you have had time no doubt to sample it.' The younger man rose. Tall and well muscled beneath a tweed jacket he towered over the thickset nail master. 'A debt settled can be a debt forgotten, by both you and me, so I suggest we settle this one now.'

There had been no room for misunderstanding. With several banknotes in his pocket Zadok's visitor strolled easily from the warehouse. Should Minch want more deliveries of that he was greedy for, he would pay ... and next time the price would be higher.

What was wrong with the lad? The newspaper his mother was always given once the owner of Oakeswell Hall had finished with it lying forgotten on his knee, Gideon Newell stared into the fire. Luke Hipton had been such a friendly youngster, but now ... it was like he could not bear to look ... whenever spoken to he turned his back. He had felt like grabbing the lad, shaking the reason for his surliness out of him; but that would do no good, a man could lead a horse to water but he couldn't make it drink, and Luke Hipton was a stubborn character, he wouldn't be forced into anything.

Something had hurt him. Gideon watched blue-tipped flames flicker cautiously into the black emptiness of the chimney before being snatched into the dark void. He had asked, but Luke had turned away. Whatever was riding the lad must have happened during the time he, Gideon, had been away from the tube works; but then why no evidence of displeasure on his return, why wait until the following day? It didn't make sense. But then a lot of things in life appeared to make no sense, such as the task he had been set that day, the same task he had been about today.

The newspaper slipping from his knee he retrieved it, folding it in half, his mind on other things. Questioning eyes had followed him as he had walked from the works, and those of the lad had been among them; but where the glances of the men had been open, that of the lad had been dark and hostile, and behind that had been anger and accusation. But allowances had to be made, a lad went through all kinds of moods and fancies while becoming a man, hadn't he himself suffered the same?

*'Folk be like the caterpillar...'*

Gideon smiled as he remembered the comforting words his mother had often spoken those times emotions had got the better of him.

'*...they be all wrapped in a shroud of their own mekin' until one day the wrapping splits and they comes out changed ... they be given a new start.*'

A new start! That was what he himself would have now the bargain he had made was fulfilled. The reward would see Gideon Newell walking a different path.

*'Get it for me, bring me what I ask and you'll not go unrecognised.'*

Those had been the words, the words that promised a fresh start, a better life; and today he had delivered what was asked for.

'You say her ain't been 'ere all day?'

'That be right, lad, that be what I'm sayin'.'

'But I told her afore I left, I told her to stay close alongside yourself and your wife.'

A pitchfork in his hand, the ostler paused from loading hay into a byre set on the stable wall. Wiping a sleeve over his moist face he looked at the lad hovering like a mayfly at his side.

'I've no doubt you did, Luke, but women be women and there be some among 'em as can't tek a telling.'

'But you says her's been gone all day!'

'Ain't been back to my knowledge.'

'But that ain't like her.'

Lifting his cap Ben ran the back of his hand over corn-stubble hair.

'Well, you knows the wench better'n I does, but the fact don't alter for all that; her went from 'ere this mornin' and her ain't been back since. You go speak to the wife and her will tell you the same thing, we ain't seen hide nor hair of the wench and that be the truth of it.'

Saran had gone. She had waited for him to go to his work then she had left. She had broken her promise. A lump solid in his throat, Luke walked from the stable. He would never have thought ... never have believed she would go back on her word. Saran was not that kind of girl. Yet she was not here!

What did it matter who earned the bread! Ashamed of the tears stinging his eyes he turned face to the wall, kicking savagely at the glazed brickwork adorning the front of the tavern. He was happy to share and he could keep them both, so why couldn't that have been enough for Saran?

'Be you lookin' for an hour's work, lad?'

Keeping his face turned away, Luke shook his head. What did he need with tuppence if Saran were not there to share it!

The howl of a dog coming to him from the darkness Luke stared about him. He didn't remember walking from the Turk's Head, hadn't noticed the direction he had taken. So where was he? His glance swept the dark silhouette of buildings, each low roof huddling against its neighbour and none showing a lighted window. Yet there were lights, small pinpricks too anaemic to cast a glow beyond a few inches and each pale sickly gleam coming from the rear of houses.

The howl of the dog becoming a sharp challenging bark, Luke stared into the thick darkness. Those dots of light could only be workshops, nailers' workshops. He had come to Russell Street. Could one of these people tell him of Saran ... could one of them have seen her?

It had been like trying to mine coal with a needle; it had brought no results. Each door he had knocked on had been opened to him and, though the rise and fall of hammers had not ceased, his questions had been answered, but none of those answers had been the one he hoped to hear.

'What do you be about, standin' looking at folks' houses? Be off afore I lets the dog to you!'

Turning quickly Luke's glance found the woman, a lighted candle in the jar held in her hand.

'I seen you.' Her voice accusing, she held the jar higher. 'I seen you from the privy; skulking about looking to steal, I shouldn't wonder, but you'll get more'n you bargained for when my man–'

'No ... no, I ain't come to steal,' Luke answered quickly. 'I be come to ask about Saran ... my name be Luke Hipton.'

A breeze sweeping the yard the candle spluttered as the woman held it closer to Luke.

'Well, so it is, but why stand in the yard, lad; come you inside.'

'I've already talked with your husband, I asked had Saran – you know, the girl with me when we come to the Elwells – I asked had her called today but he said as her 'adn't.'

'He were away to the fogger's.' She led the way into the workshop, setting the jar next to a cracked jug placed on a shelf. 'The wench made a visit, 'sides which I seen 'er earlier on. I talked with her in the town this very mornin'. But why be you 'ere askin' after her?'

Outlining his story briefly Luke watched the woman heat a narrow iron rod, hammer it into a point at one end and a flat head at the other before a final blow severed the finished nail and the process began again.

'Well, lad, I can tell you what were said atwixt her and me, that be easy enough. I told her same as I told you, the Elwells had been throwed out on the streets.'

'Could her 'ave gone to look for 'em, do you think?'

Selecting a fresh length of rod from a bundle on the floor the woman pushed one end into the glowing forge, sparing a moment to glance at Luke.

'A nailer don't 'ave time to think.' She twisted the iron in the fire. 'I told you what passed between the wench and meself, though what were said atwixt her and the man–'

'Man!' Sharp as the ring of hammer on metal, Luke's retort followed the woman carrying the red-hot strip to the anvil. 'What man were this?'

Her concentration on her onerous task the woman replied, her words keeping to the rhythm of quick hammer blows. 'I only seen him from across the market square. I turned to mek sure the wench were all right ... her had seemed upset on hearing of the Elwells, and with that there accident her had suffered ... I were thinking to go back when I seen him come up to her so I went on me way; as for who he were I couldn't say certain, but he were tall and broad in the shoulder.'

*tall and broad in the shoulder*

His boots clattering on the cobbles Luke raced across the empty market place and on up Spring Head towards Walsall Street.

*tall and broad in the shoulder*

He needed no more description ... the man Saran had talked with was Gideon Newell.

Today he had found what had been asked for. Settling deeper into his chair Gideon watched the play of flames, their brilliant orange, blue and violet radiant against the black of coal. Both parties had been satisfied with the deal, a deal that would see him and his mother gone from Oakeswell End; a week or two more and–

The thoughts ripped from his mind, he jerked

to his feet and was across the room when a second violent knocking sounded on the door ... his mother...! Lord, had anything happened to his mother?

'Gideon Newell!'

As a voice shouted his name, Gideon almost leapt the last few feet. Snatching open the door he stared, forcing his vision to accustom to the night shadows.

'Where is her ... what 'ave you done wi' her?' Strident with anger the words lashed with the speed of a striking snake.

His mind still vibrating with anxiety for his mother, Gideon looked at the lad stood at the door. 'Luke, is something wrong?'

'Don't pretend you don't know ... now where is her?'

This was nothing to do with his mother. Gideon felt the anxiety drain from him.

'It be you!' Luke flung the accusation. 'You was the one 'alf killed her, you, Gideon Newell, so don't go pretendin'...'

Allowances had to be made ... lads went through all kinds of moods... Thoughts which had played in his mind an hour before returned, but were pushed aside; allowances ... well, this lad had used all he was going to get! With one hand fastening about the collar and lifting Luke clear off his feet, Gideon snatched him into the house, one foot closing the door at his back.

'Now, young 'un,' he gritted, 'no man goes accusing Gideon Newell, not even one that be only half grown. You've had something in your craw long enough, my advice be to spit it out afore I shake it out of you!'

Eyes catching the lamplight glittered unafraid against the threat. 'Like you shook her ... like you shook Saran afore you 'alf killed her...'

'Saran!' Gideon was suddenly tense. 'Has something happened to Miss Chandler?'

He was trying to mek out he knew nothing about it! Luke glared at the man he wanted only to kill. 'It won't work!' he spat furiously. 'I knows it were you done it that day, same as I knows–'

'Done what!' With anger threading dangerously through his veins, Gideon spent some of it crashing a fist on the table. 'What is it you think you know?'

He had flinched at the strength displayed in that blow, a strength he knew was still tightly curbed, yet Luke did not back down. Saran had no one other than himself to fight for her and he wouldn't stop 'til he was dead.

'Think!' His lips curling in disgust he let the words flow in a torrent. 'I don't need to think, I be sure–'

'That isn't enough!' Gideon cut the flow short. 'You need to be more than sure, you need to be absolutely positive. I like you, Luke, but that doesn't mean I'll take anything you throw; whatever you come here to say best be said now.'

There was no mistaking the meaning, the ice-cold warning gleamed from hard eyes but, drowning in his own anger, Luke failed to read it.

'Then I'll say it,' he answered through clenched teeth, 'not as you needs to be told, but I'll say it anyway. It be you I told about that brooch, you and no other. It were you went absent from the works the day Saran were attacked and left in the hedge along of Bilston Road, and you again today who left the works and was seen talkin' to her, and now her be missing. But you knows where her be. You couldn't get that trinket the first time cos Saran 'adn't carried it with her so you tried again today–'

'Stop there, Luke ... stop right there!' It was almost a whisper, ominous, quiet yet screaming caution. 'Are you saying I tried to steal that brooch, that I attacked Saran Chandler in an attempt to rob her?'

A few feet from the figure head and shoulders taller than himself, Luke felt the first tremor of apprehension shiver along taut nerves. Gideon Newell had strength born of years of manual labour and it would be no hardship for him to break a lad's neck.

'Who else?' Luke refused to be deterred. 'Who else but you; ain't nobody 'cept the Elwells knowed of our 'elping that woman on the 'eath and they wouldn't never harm Saran.'

His fingers curling into fists, Gideon looked at the lad glaring defiance. 'But you think I would ... you think me capable of such an act.'

'What I thinks of a man sneakin' from his work to go trackin' down a wench he's already beaten black and blue don't bear the speakin' of, so just tell me where I can find her ... lessen you wants to talk to the constables.'

'There's going to be talk all right.' Reaching for the jacket hung on a peg behind the door, Gideon slipped it on. 'But this I'll tell you now, I'm no thief, Luke, regardless of what you might think and I know nothing of any attack made on your friend, nor do I know of her whereabouts. If she hasn't turned up by the time we get back then we will talk to the constable.'

'Get back from where?'

With a firm grip on the boy's shoulder Gideon propelled him from the house, his answer tight as his grasp.

'From showing you what a young fool you are!'

# 16

*'Where be we going?'*

His shoulder still caught in Gideon's grip, Luke had asked the question several times but the man who literally frogmarched him along had made no answer. Gideon Newell was going to show him what a fool he'd been. Luke's anger sat chokingly in his throat. Yes, he'd been a fool, a fool to go knockin' on Newell's door instead of going to speak with the constable. He'd given the man the opportunity he needed, the chance to get shot of the only one who could point the finger, the chance to get rid of him as he'd gotten rid of Saran.

Leaving Oakeswell End and making their way to Wood Green, speaking not a word, they had strode through what could have been an empty world. Fields Luke knew were filled with waving corn hid their faces beneath a veil of deep shadow. Stretching away into blackness it seemed they shrank from a road devoid now of the carts and wagons of daytime; afraid of the silence of night.

Wood Green had been where they were headed. Recognising a large house set between dark stretches of ground, windows winking like great yellow stars, Luke tried to twist free but the grip which held him was strong as the iron it worked. Surely this was not where Saran had been brought ... whatever Newell had done with her he wouldn't dare 'ide it here, Wood Green was home to the richest folk in Wednesbury; the men at the tube works had said that even John Adams lived along here!

But Gideon had turned between tall pillared gates, marching not to the rear but to the front entrance of the imposing three-storeyed building.

*'Tell John Adams it be Gideon Newell asks to speak with him.'*

Luke remembered the indignant splutter of the black-coated butler who opened the door; as he looked down his nose the rebuke had died on his lips when Gideon had repeated the request in a cutting 'don't play with me!' tone of voice.

They had waited only moments in that high square entrance hall, but Luke knew that the gleam of polished wood beneath the glitter of a chandelier, whose crystal droppers sparkled like gigantic raindrops, the graceful curve of a staircase winding upward towards a landing which separated into two diverging corridors from whose walls painted portraits stared down at them, would never be forgotten. It had been as if he had entered heaven, but a heaven that improved as they were shown into what the long-nosed butler described as the small sitting room. Entering that room, fitted with sofas and chairs with long elegant legs, pretty tables with prettier ornaments, tall pointed windows with drapes that fell in sweeps to a floor almost lost beneath a carpet wide as a small field, he had held his breath. Were this room small then what paradise constituted a big one?

*'Gideon!'* John Adams had risen as they were shown in. *'Is something amiss at the works?'*

*'No, there be naught amiss there.'*

*'Then what?'* The man had frowned.

*'You have my apology for disturbing you in your home, sir.'*

John Adams had waved away the apology. *'There is no need for that, Gideon, I well know you wouldn't do it were it not important; but would it have to do with the lad you have by the scruff of the neck?'*

Releasing his hold of Luke's shoulder, Gideon had nodded.

John Adams had stared hard at Luke, but behind it had lurked a half smile. *'So, the young lion has found its roar, and what particular flea do you have in your mane?'*

Luke had opened his mouth to reply but Gideon was quicker. *'If you have no objection, sir, I would ask you answer a question of mine afore being given answer to your own.'*

The smile fading, John Adams had transferred his gaze. *'Very well, Gideon, ask your question, though I must first ask why come here tonight when questions can be asked just as well tomorrow at the works?'*

*'I realise that, Mr Adams,'* Gideon had replied with a short glance at Luke, whose saucer eyes were staring at everything in sight. *'I also realised it could be thought I'd had a word with you before that, a word the lad here had not been privy to, so with your leave I ask it now. Would you please tell where it was I went when leaving the works not only*

*today but earlier in the week?'*

*'That be nobody's business ... much less that of a boy. What on earth are you thinking of, asking a question like that!'*

It was sharp, anger raising dull red to the man's cheeks and Luke had felt like taking to his heels, but the thought of Saran hurt and possibly dead held him fast.

His fascination with the room suddenly disappearing, taking with it the tingle of fear, Luke's head had lifted and the look he gave his employer held none of its previous awe.

*'It be my business!'* he had said calmly. *'It be my business when Saran be knocked 'alf dead one day and gone completely the next, and Gideon Newell being the only one with reason to do it.'*

Had John Adams seen the pain Luke could not keep from entering his eyes or heard the slight quiver that trembled on the last words? Thinking of it now, as he walked in silence beside Gideon, he could not be sure but the man had glanced once at Gideon before saying, *'On both occasions I had Gideon go to Monway Field, there to inspect a piece of land I am thinking to purchase; I know the making of tubes, but a man born to Wednesbury knows better the attributes of the land. I trusted Gideon Newell to inspect and tell me truthfully of its worth or otherwise in the use I envisage for it. Should he have had business elsewhere then it cannot have been carried out during either of those absences for I also make it my business to know how long it takes a man to walk from the High Bullen to Monway Field and, given a half-hour to walk the ground I wish to purchase, he took no longer than that. Does my explanation take the bone from the young lion's throat or is he still choking?'*

It had been logical. The night of finding Saran in that carter's wagon, he and Gideon had left the works together; time would not allow Gideon to have gone halfway to Bilston, found Saran somewhere in the darkness and beaten her senseless... But then if not Gideon ... who?

He had apologised to John Adams but the man had not left it there, he had demanded to be told the reason Gideon had been the source of suspicion, and when given the all of it had immediately offered the help of his staff to search for the missing girl. But Gideon had suggested that they return to enquire for her at the Turk's Head before mounting a full-scale search.

But Saran had not returned to the tavern. Luke felt the despair which had settled on him then weighing even more heavily now. If not Gideon, then who? The same thought plagued him as he strove to keep pace with the wider stride of the man who had brushed aside all apology. They would walk the length of the Bilston Road, Gideon had said, they could have that done in the time it would take to organise men with lanterns and dogs, and if they did not find her then he would accept John Adams's offer and begin again with the dawn.

He could so easily have agreed to the proposal of the owner of the tube works, that Luke be dismissed from his job, so easily have turned his back, leaving further searching for Saran to Luke himself, but Gideon had done neither. He had taken things into his own hands and, walking beside him now with the silence and the blackness of fields all around him, Luke had to admit the relief of it. Gideon had refused to listen to any contrition on his part, saying only he would have thought the same were he in Luke Hipton's shoes, but that did not lift the guilt from his heart. He had practically accused the man of murder.

'Gideon, about what I said–'

The words were hardly out when a sharp hiss had the rest silent on his tongue, the hackles on the back of his neck stiff and hard.

'Listen!' The whisper barely loud enough to hear, steel-like fingers fastened on his shoulder warning him not to move.

What was it ... what had Gideon heard coming from the surrounding darkness? Straining his ears but hearing nothing, he turned his head to speak but the fingers pressed harder, repeating their own unspoken warning. It was then he heard it, softly at first it came on the silence, a tap ... a crunch on the hard ground. His breath held in his throat, blood freezing in his veins, Luke listened. Footsteps ... footsteps coming towards them out of the night ... someone else was walking the Bilston Road!

She had not meant to leave Wednesbury, not meant to go any place without first talking with Luke, without giving him an explanation. She had promised ... promised him she would not think of doing such a thing; and that was the trouble ... she had not thought! She had let her own wants come first, allowed her emotions to get the better of her. Huddled in the worn-through shawl Saran shivered as much against a world darkened by shadows as against the sharp nip of night air.

She had excused herself from the company of Jairus Ensell as quickly as good manners allowed. He had walked with her to the edge of the market place and for a moment she had thought he would insist upon accompanying her further but he had smiled at her refusal and turned away. Why had she refused? The thought had risen more than once and each time she had no answer, just as she could have no real answer for breaking her word to Luke; no answer other than a heart breaking for the Elwells, for the children sent into the workhouse, the driving guilt of not helping them when she had the chance. That had been her reason, her only reason, for doing what she had.

She had known she ought to have taken the time to return to the tavern, ought to have told Ben and his wife of her intention, to have left word for Luke, but instead she had taken the road to Bilston. There had been no carter's wagon to give her a ride and her legs already ached as she had reached the small octagonal toll-house that stood at the boundary of Moxley.

*'Darlaston, you says.'* The toll-keeper had smiled kindly. *'Well, I reckons if you takes the track through them there cornfields you'll save yourself a lot o' walkin' for it'll tek you direct to that town, though you needs 'ave a care when them fields end for there be a mess o' gin pits, they pocks the ground an' some of 'em grown over with grass so a body don't know they be*

*there, so keep you to the track. You'll come to the Lodge Holes colliery along near the top, folk there will be able to direct you should you need 'elp with finding the rest o' your way.'*

But she hadn't known the rest of her way, hadn't known which direction to ask for or even the name of the woman she hoped to find. All she had was the desire to be rid of that brooch.

Ahead, the sound of footsteps echoed in the darkness, sounding and fading, returning to tease her ears like moon-touched shadows. Whoever was there would let her walk with them, surely they would not refuse. Forcing her tired limbs to hurry she paused as a figure emerged from the gloom, a tall figure whose hands reached for her.

'Please!' she gasped, pain lancing fresh along bruised arms as the hands gripped her. 'Please not again ... Gideon!'

'I'm sorry, Luke, the last thing in the world I wanted was to cause you concern yet that is what I did ... I didn't stop to think about consequences.'

'No need to go on about it, I just be glad it were Gideon an' me come across you on that road, it could so easy 'ave been...'

The rest too awful even to contemplate, Luke let it fade. By what John Adams had said, it was not Gideon Newell who had attacked Saran, but the name that had come from her in the darkness had been his. Why ... why that name if he had not been the culprit?

'Was Mr Newell very angry hearing you say all those things?'

'Well, he weren't pleased. I thought when he shoved me out of the 'ouse that I were in for a lathering.'

'He would have been judged within his rights if he had given you a hiding.' Saran glanced at the boy walking beside her. 'I must thank him for not doing so.'

'I thanked him already,' Luke grinned, 'said I was grateful he 'adn't left me in pieces.'

Many a man would have done just that having been accused of assault. Walking on in silence Saran went over Luke's story in her mind. He had thought that Gideon Newell had beaten her then left her on the edge of a cornfield ... that the man had wished to rob her of the brooch ... and yet he had insisted on accompanying Luke in his search for her. Did anyone who wished you harm do such a thing? That question had stayed in her mind, for she had known Luke's sharp brain would have come up with a dozen reasons for just such an action. But it had remained unasked, not simply because of that... With a faint hint of pink rising to her cheeks Saran felt the real reason beat hard in her chest. She did not wish to hear anything that would place a shadow of guilt against a man who had shown them both kindness.

'You be ready for a rest.' Luke had spotted the faint blush of colour and was concerned. 'I said it were too soon yet for you to be walking any distance.' Taking off the jacket whose sleeves hung well clear of his wrists, he laid it on the rough grass, hovering over her and insisting she sat on it. He was so thoughtful of her and she ...

she had acted without a thought for him, of the worry she would put him through. If hearts could sigh Saran knew hers did then, knew that even though Luke had forgiven her she could never fully forgive herself.

Stretched out beside her on the wide empty heath, his eyes closed against the bright afternoon sky, Luke chewed on a blade of grass as he spoke.

'It took courage doin' what you did, I ain't sure I could 'ave done the same thing. Tekin' that brooch and givin' it back after being offered ten pound ... I ain't sure I could 'ave done that at all.'

The one doubt she had had made itself felt again. Half of that ten pounds would have belonged to Luke, but she had given him no opportunity of accepting or refusing money that would have helped him make a start in life; she had robbed him as surely as that attacker along the Bilston Road had wanted to rob her.

'Luke.' She glanced at the lad. 'Luke, it's not too late... I could go back, ask to be given–'

'You ain't going back nowhere.' With his eyes springing open, Luke sat up. 'I knows what be eating you, though you ain't said it. You thinks you took my dues from me when you refused to take that ten pound; well, they was dues I wanted none of; I'd told you to do as you would wi' that trinket and if you had throwed it in the brook then that would 'ave been all right wi' me. I tell you one more time, *you* be all that matters, *you*, Saran, and not some brooch whatever it be worth; money buys a lot of things but it don't buy a quiet heart and it don't buy happiness. I've got both in our friendship.'

Smiling against the tears the words brought to her throat Saran watched as he settled once more on the springy turf. Luke could be happy with so little but she could never be really happy until she had her mother and sister with her again. She had asked in that town, in Darlaston. Some of the women she had spoken to had frowned and hurried on their way, too taken with their own troubles to be bothered with hers; some had stood and listened, but none had known of a woman and young girl having been bought. '*It would 'ave been the talk of the town*,' they had said, '*we would 'ave heard. No, wench, ain't nothing like that happened in these parts*.' But it had happened and only a few miles away; somebody somewhere must know of it.

There had been no such problem tracing the couple she and Luke had found that night lying injured on the heath. It seemed all of Darlaston knew of the birth of the child, of the injury to the father, all of them speaking of the miracle of their being found, and if any of them wondered why a stranger spoke of it they did not question, they simply enjoyed the relating of a tale, the like of which seemed to have been a miracle of heaven.

Darlaston House had stood a short distance from the nucleus of tiny shops and several taverns that was the heart of the smoke-laden town. Set in wide flower-bordered grounds, the red-brick building rose square and imposing, windows glinting like crystal, tall chimneys lifting to the sky; it had been so grand she had almost turned away, run back to the more familiar background of workshops and hammers beating out iron on a hundred anvils. Only the touch of that stone against her fingers had kept courage from deserting her, but the thought of climbing the wide curved steps which reached up to a heavy door had been too much; her nerve failing, she had gone quickly to the rear whose beautifully kept lawns and rose beds complemented the house in the same way as the front.

*'You should speak wi' Mrs Clews,'* a stable hand had told her, *'her be the housekeeper and will answer to you.'*

The woman had come to the kitchen. The spring sun warm on her face, Saran stared into the distance to where the black spire of Wednesbury parish church pierced the blue like a dark needle. The master could not possibly be disturbed, he was not yet fully recovered from his accident ... and no, she would not bother the mistress with some passing beggar!

It had not been embarrassment she had felt when the kitchen maid had sniggered, nor anger at the woman's tart snub, but almost a sympathy, a regret for manners so lacking as to permit a reply of blatant rudeness to a simple enquiry; but then had she not met with that at other houses ... been answered in like fashion by those who felt little charity for folk placed less well than themselves?

*'Passing, yes, ma'am, but a beggar, no. I came here not to ask anything of your mistress but to return this. If I cannot be allowed to do so myself then, ma'am, perhaps you would do so in my stead.'*

The quiet dignity with which she had spoken had carried the effects of a thunderbolt. It had spread a wave about the large kitchen swallowing in its wake the smirks of maid and cook alike, leaving the housekeeper gasping at sight of the brooch gleaming like green fire in the palm of Saran's hand.

The woman had been gone only a few moments then she had returned, her tone chastened as she had invited Saran to follow her to the mistress's sitting room.

Across the open heath a tree pipit in love with spring clung to a clump of gorse, its canary-like song serenading the afternoon while beside her Luke sighed, for a time at least in a heaven of his own.

Dressed in the palest of lemon voile, raven hair caught high on her head, the woman whose face she remembered so well had welcomed her into the elegant room, her smile one of genuine pleasure. But the smile had faded when Saran had refused to accept back the brooch.

*'But it was a gift!'* Ann Salisbury had insisted. *'A mark of my gratitude. William, will you not tell her?'*

His left leg heavily bandaged between two slats of wood, William Salisbury smiled at his wife as he was brought into the room, his wheelchair drawn close beside the couch on which she sat.

*'My housekeeper tells me you were our angel of the night, Miss...'*

*'Chandler, sir.'* Saran had blushed as she bobbed a curtsy but her glance had not strayed from the man's face, *'My name is Saran Chandler.'*

*'Well, Miss Chandler, before I agree to my wife's request to say what it is she would have me tell you, allow me to voice my own most heartfelt thanks for*

*your assistance that night. The men who carried us home tell me that had it not been for your intervention, my wife and my son may well not have survived, for that part of the heath is not well travelled by miners, the coal once worked there being as good as exhausted. But am I not correct in thinking you had a young man, a brother perhaps, with you, one who fastened bits of my broken coach to my leg?'*

*'Luke was not to blame for ripping up the seats of your carriage nor for the burning of parts of it, that was my doing and I will take the blame for it.'*

*'Blame!'* William Salisbury had laughed, but there had been an open admiration on his face. *'There can be no blame except it be mine for attempting to drive across that heath at night ... but we need have no discussion of that, my lesson is well and truly learned.'*

*'We tried to find where you lived,'* Ann Salisbury had said then, *'we made so many enquiries but it appeared no one in Darlaston knew of you. My husband and I wished so much to thank you for all you did but our efforts at tracing you came to naught, my only consolation was your accepting that worthless trinket.'*

*'The trinket is not worthless, ma'am, it is worth ten pounds and that is why I cannot accept it!'*

William Salisbury's smile had died at the quick outburst, his eyes showing a trace of disappointment. *'You have had the trinket valued and obviously do not hold it worthy of the assistance you and your brother gave my wife and myself. In that case, Miss Chandler, be good enough to state your own price, just what is the reward you came here to claim!'*

# 17

*'I am not here to claim any reward, either for myself or for the boy you call my brother.'*

Sat in the warm sunshine, a tree pipit singing its aria, Saran remembered the swift flood of indignation that had the colour deepen in her cheeks as she had answered what literally was an accusation of attempting to elicit a larger sum.

*'Luke is my friend and I have his full approval in returning that brooch to your wife. I had thought to sell it, that I admit, but when the pawnbroker told me the amount he was willing to pay I knew that not only could I not take it but that there was a likely possibility of the trinket being worth even more; that being so Luke and I agreed it must be returned.'* She had drawn a deep breath, sending her glance to the woman watching from the couch. *'What little both of us did for you, ma'am, was done with a glad heart; your child being delivered safe into the world is all the reward we ask. I thank you for seeing me.'*

*'Wait!'* William Salisbury had reached out a hand as she had dropped a brief curtsy to his wife. *'I would see this trinket you have returned.'*

He had taken it from his wife. Saran watched the small bird lift from its perch to skim across the heath. They had both watched in silence as he stared at the brooch, turning it several times before asking, *'This is the trinket my wife gave you, and you say your friend Luke is in agreement that it be returned. Then the bruises to your face have nothing to do with this?'*

Tossing the brooch into the air and catching it in his palm, he had asked the question then listened in silence to her explanation, touching his wife's hand as the woman caught her breath in horror.

*'Yet you ran the same risks in coming here today with no companion; was that wise?'*

*'Possibly losing the brooch was also a risk,'* she had answered, *'one neither Luke nor I were willing to take.'*

*'He knew its worth?'*

She could have told the answer, said she had not spoken with Luke, said that it was not the returning of that gift had seen her on the Bilston Road that day, but she made no answer.

*'My wife made you a gift out of gratitude, I now offer you that same gift. Whatever its value it is yours with our thanks.'*

He had held the brooch towards her. Saran remembered the sudden shaft of sunlight slanting in at the window, how it had caught the large stone, causing it seemingly to erupt into a thousand tiny shards, each a glittering spear of green tipped with gold and silver.

The tinge of guilt at not answering his last question truthfully pricking her conscience she had faced him squarely.

*'I thank you for myself and for Luke but the answer is the same; we want no reward other than knowing you and your child took no serious harm from your accident.'*

He had made one further effort to detain her

then had his wife ring for a servant to show her out.

She had refused to accept both the brooch and the money that had been William Salisbury's last offer. Why, when it would have meant food and a roof over their heads? That too had been unfair on Luke, he must have felt some sort of disapproval even though he admitted to none. Looking at the thin figure lying beside her, trousers and jacket ragged and far too small, boots with barely a sole, she blamed herself as she had done on the way back from Darlaston, blamed her silly pride!

Opening his eyes Luke smiled up at her. 'Shall we try further on?'

Could she take any more disappointment, hear any more people say they had not seen or heard of her family without bursting into tears? And what would her weeping do other than add to the concern she knew this young lad held for her? Climbing to her feet she held a hand to him, groaning at the pretended strain of hauling him up. Tears would wait.

The girl had been terrified, her whole body was shaking as he caught her ... and she had cried his name!

Watching his mother tie her best Sunday bonnet, Gideon's thoughts strayed to the scene he had played over and over in his mind. Luke and himself had passed no one after leaving the High Bullen to follow Trouse Lane then on to the Bilston Road, the latter being so empty of movement it seemed they alone were the only people left on earth.

'You should come, lad, come pay the Lord His dues, you'll feel the better for it.'

'The Lord knows He gives nothing I don't thank Him for,' Gideon smiled as he answered, 'but I'll thank Him in my own room, not kneeling on the ground in yonder church.'

Her bonnet tied, Charity Newell looked at the tall strong figure that was her son and could not prevent a rush of pride. He was a fine upstanding man, one any mother would hold dear, and, though his views were not always in keeping with her own, the code he lived by were a fine one; do a man a good turn but be beholden to none.

Pulling the shawl about her shoulders she lifted her face for his kiss. Yes, Gideon Newell were a good son and one day, God willing, he would make a good husband.

Pay the Lord his dues. Returning the door to the latch Gideon resumed his seat beside the hearth. Hadn't he done that, thanked Him over and again that they had found the girl when they did, that nothing untoward had happened to her? Staring at marionette flames prancing as to the pull of a string, a small disparaging laugh locked in his throat. Heaven must have been heartily sick of Gideon Newell that night!

She had cried out as she caught sight of them in the shadows, he had felt the frightened thump of her heart those few moments he had held her close, a figure so light and fragile he could have broken it with ease; but he had held her as a king might hold a crown, respecting, revering ... but it had been more than that, he had held Saran

Chandler with love.

He had tried to deny it. Called himself all kinds of a fool as he had lain awake listening to her voice return on the silence of the night hours, watched her smile at him from enticing moonlit shadow. But still the fact had remained, that what he felt for that girl was more than respect, more than admiration. Yet her feeling for him was nothing other than fear; like Luke, she believed him guilty of attacking her, of trying to rob her of some paltry brooch. It had shown on her face as he had stepped towards her, sounded in that cry: *please not again ... Gideon.* His name! Coals falling in on themselves sent a shower of rainbow sparks over the hearth but they died unnoticed against the thoughts plaguing Gideon's mind. It was his name had fallen from her lips, his name brought the fear that had her crumple to the floor, his the figure that had terrified her.

Luke would have told her by now. The glowing heart of the fire held his gaze. Yes, he could believe that; the lad had been scourging in his accusations but his apology had matched that forcefulness. Yes, he would have told the girl what had been said by John Adams, that he, Gideon, was at Monway Field at the time she had been attacked. But would what seemingly had satisfied Luke Hipton satisfy Saran Chandler, or would she still believe it was he had struck those blows?

But why did she believe he had ... who had she seen to think it was him returning to hurt her again? And she obviously had thought just that or else why cry his name?

*'I told only you.'*

Luke's bitterly spoken words resounded in Gideon's brain and, swift on their silent heels, a question. Had Luke overlooked talking to someone else ... had he spoken elsewhere of the gift made by William Salisbury's wife? There had been so many opportunities; men at the tube works, the Turk's Head tavern where he said they had slept, carters whose wagons he helped load or unload. The list was long. Gideon drew a deep breath, his glance following the dance of fire. But it was one he must go through if he were to clear his name.

The bells of the distant church were ringing evening service. With Luke silent beside her, she rode the sound back into childhood. They had never missed church on Sunday. Herself and Miriam dressed alike in pretty cotton dresses with wide sashes, ribbons catching long ringlets beneath bonnets adorned with bows; and their mother, in her best blue taffeta dress, its slightly funnel-shaped skirt set off with a buckled belt and high white fichu gathered about the neck with a matching blue ribbon, looking regal beneath a wide-brimmed bonnet decorated with pink satin bows and tiny silk roses. Her father had been so proud of his little family and they had loved seeing him dressed in his single-breasted dark frock coat and striped satin waistcoat, all set off by his best Sunday top hat.

She smiled, the peal of the bells awaking memories she had long hidden. Sunday had been a special day, going to church together, the walk home with her father carrying their small white prayer books thus freeing tiny hands for picking flowers from the wayside; but even more special had been summer evenings when the last service was over, those precious few hours when their father had walked them through the meadows or along by the stream, pointing out a bird or a flower, laughing with them when either Miriam or herself could not pronounce the Latin name then telling them its common one. Those days had been magical and she had thought they would never end ... but they had, her lovely secure world had been snatched away with the death of her father and in its place…

'Saran.' Halting his step with the last peal of the bell Luke looked at her, then switched his gaze quickly to the horizon. 'Saran, there be something I ain't told you ... something as you should know.'

'There is something I have not told either, something I meant to say but each time–'

'If it be more to do with that brooch–' He turned quickly.

'Not that itself,' she shook her head, 'I had hoped ... intended to take a reward…'

'But you said you d'ain't want nothing!'

Hearing the bewilderment in his voice she forced herself to meet his gaze. 'I know what I said and in its way it was the truth. I did not want money for myself and ... please understand this, Luke ... I did not wish it for you.'

'Then what?' Luke's blue eyes showed confusion. 'If not for either of we then what did you want it for?'

'For the Elwells,' she answered quietly, 'I wanted it for the Elwells.'

‘But they were–’

A smile tender as her eyes touched Saran’s lips as Luke shifted his gaze. ‘I know, they were gone, the woman in the market place told me of their eviction... No,’ she shook her head as he made to answer, ‘you don’t need to explain why you said nothing yourself, you thought I had all I could contend with that night and, truthfully, perhaps I had.’

‘But if you knowed they was gone then how did you expect to give them money you might ’ave got from Salisbury? Lord, Saran! They could be anywheres.’

‘Yes, Livvy and Edward could be anywhere but not their children ... they are still in Wednesbury ... in that workhouse. I wanted money for them, Luke, to get them out of that place, but I failed them as I’ve failed my mother and sister, as I have failed you.’

‘You ain’t failed...’

‘Yes, Luke, I have! I refused money that would have helped me in the search for my family, that would have bought them back once I found them.’

‘Why then ... why did you refuse?’ The boy in Luke had vanished, leaving the man she had glimpsed before, one now demanding she face a truth behind her action. ‘All of what you’ve just said was knowed by you afore you went to Darlaston, you knowed what you speak of now would need money, yet you turned down ten pounds from Kilvert and who knows how much from Salisbury. Ask yourself what truly made you act so, for you’ll ’ave no peace until you does!’

She did not need to ask, she already knew, had known all along; only the turmoil of her own emotions had kept her from admitting it. To take money for giving aid, for an act of charity, went against all her parents had taught. *Help folk where you can and count it a blessing.* That had been the principle by which they had lived, to have gone against their teaching would have been to break faith with them ... to have followed the path of Enoch Jacobs.

Having listened to what troubled Saran, Luke resumed the way to Wednesbury. She had confessed to what lay heavy on her conscience, but could he do the same? She relied on him, depended on him to be sensible, to look at things and not let emotions get in the way. He hadn't done that, though; he had let his heart rule his head. It wouldn't be so bad if the repercussions of what he had done rebounded only on himself; he could take it and willingly. But his rashness meant Saran must suffer, she would bear the brunt of his stupidity.

Zadok Minch had set his mind to owning that brooch. The door closing quietly behind him as he was shown from the nail master's fine house, Zadok's visitor smiled to himself. The heavy jowls had reddened, the small eyes receding into enveloping folds of flesh as he had listened, the twitch of short thick fingers drumming his growing anger.

'You lost it!' he had almost screamed. 'Worth a bloody king's ransom and you lost it! I could kick your arse so 'ard it would be Christmas afore you put it on a chair again; get rid of you once an' for all!'

He could ... but he hadn't! Taking his carriage from the attentive groom he flicked the reins, leaving the horse to trot along the curved drive. Clear of the house he allowed the smile he had suppressed to touch his mouth. True, there were plenty of men ready to take his place as a fogger, a go-between who bought from the nail-makers at a price acceptable to Minch; yes, there were those would do that ... but the other? Not so many were willing to involve themselves in that trade. And Minch knew it, he also knew the consequence to his standing in society and the world of commerce should a careless tongue give word of it. There were many liked to play but none cared to be found out, and if Minch were brought into the open, so would several more be; that ... for all the nail master's chagrin ... could not be risked.

He thought his reasons were not known. The smile on the handsome mouth widened. Minch believed the truth behind his wanting that brooch so badly had not been guessed at. Well, in a way, perhaps that was right for he himself had not guessed ... he knew. He had known from the moment Minch had first asked him to steal it from that girl. With that trinket in his possession the sly little nail master could bring about the social ruin of William Salisbury. By paying a whore to swear that brooch had been given for 'extra' services a scandal could be created that would drive the man from Darlaston, leaving his copper and iron foundries to be bought for a song ... and Zadok Minch was quite a tenor!

Zadok did not have the brooch but neither did he. Servants were always ready with gossip and those of Salisbury proved no different. A carter paid to keep his ears open and his mouth shut had brought the news. A wench had asked to see Ann Salisbury and when refused had requested a brooch with a green heart be taken to her. Gloved hands flicked the reins, urging the horse on. His own desire for that bauble matched that of Minch, only the reason for having it differed. It had belonged to a countess, a member of the aristocracy, and that meant it would be no worthless trifle; Minch had realised that and so had he. The money it would have fetched would have bought him a new life, a life far from the smoke and grime of Wednesbury. But the wench had robbed him of that, she had given back the brooch and so snatched away his dream.

The smile was dead but in the gathering dusk dark eyes glinted like black ice.

But all was not lost. The wench was still in Wednesbury.

He had not thought the lad to ask his help. They had gone together to search for the girl, to bring her back to that makeshift bed in the hayloft of the Turk's Head tavern and Luke Hipton had been genuine in his thanks. Yet the feeling had remained that the lad had come to him only in rage, only to accuse, and as he had walked home after seeing them both safe Gideon had held the conviction that real friendship between them had ended. After all, the lad too had heard the name which had fallen from Saran Chandler's lips, heard the fear in it, so how could he expect real trust from him again?

Yet he had come. Early that next morning he had come and the question he had asked had left Gideon open-mouthed. Where had he got the idea, how could he hope to carry it through?

Restless as his own thoughts, Gideon reached for the jacket his mother preferred he wear on Sundays; the Lord's day must be respected.

*'I'd do it on my own without botherin' you, 'cept I knows they wouldn't listen.'*

Letting himself from the house Gideon remembered the look in those bright blue eyes. Compassion, sympathy, pity? No, they had held more than that, beneath it all had gleamed something else: Luke Hipton's eyes had burned with horror!

The lad had certainly been correct in his thinking, they *wouldn't* listen. But who could say there was wrong in that? A lad no more than twelve years old...

'Evenin' there, Gideon, 'ow be your mother, lad?'

Touching his brow, Gideon showed his respect for the elderly man who spoke as he drew near.

'She is well, I thank you, Ben.'

'The Lord shows His mercy.' A gapped smile showed as the bent figure tapped a finger to brow and chest in the sign all had been taught in their turn.

Spending a few minutes with the old man, minutes which proved a struggle to hold his mind to, Gideon nodded at the supposition he was making for the church from where he would walk his mother home. That had not been his intention, but then what had?

Pushing his hands into his pockets Gideon refused to accept the answer in his heart.

A lad no more than twelve years old, Luke had stood at the door of the house, his look saying should Gideon refuse him then he would find some other way ... and find it he would; Luke Hipton was quite a lad and one day he was going to be quite a man!

To go from one to another in Wednesbury asking their assistance in what he planned would only serve to prolong the boy's heartache, feed the anguish darkening his eyes, for there was none would agree to what they were asked.

Then why had he agreed? Unmindful of direction Gideon turned downhill along Springhead. Was it a young lad's biting pain, the mental suffering that had his hands clenching and unclenching, the urgency behind his plea? Yes, it was all of that and he would have given his help had Luke refused the terms he had laid down in exchange ... terms which involved Saran Chandler.

# 18

She would bear the brunt of what he had done! Guilt and worry swirling thoughts into a whirlpool in his mind, Luke walked in silence. Saran had told what troubled her, had spoken of what she had withheld from him ... but he couldn't be as open, he couldn't tell what it was he and Gideon Newell had agreed between them.

'Luke, what I told you just now, if ... if it has offended you–'

'Why should you say that?' Luke saw the shadow flick across the bruised face. His retort had been too quick, Saran had caught the undercurrent of disquiet, the unease which gripped him; now that the time when she must find out was near, his anxieties could not remain hidden.

'I wouldn't hurt you...'

'Nor would I 'urt you...' catching her hand Luke brought them both to a standstill, 'not for all the world I wouldn't, but...'

'But what?' Saran frowned.

His head lowered so she could not see his face, his voice aching with regret, Luke answered, 'I 'ad to do it, Saran, Gideon wouldn't never 'ave consented 'ad I refused ... and there were nobody else I could ask...'

Gideon! Saran's nerves quickened. What was he to do with Luke's distress?

'So I said yes,' Luke rushed on, 'I said yes

without askin' you, without givin' you the chance to say no... I weren't thinking proper, the only thing in my mind were how to get it done, I give no thought to you 'aving to pay; I be sorry ... I be truly sorry. I'll ask him, Saran, I'll ask him to overlook the promise–'

'Luke, stop!' Her hand gentle beneath his chin she lifted his face. 'What are you sorry for, what is it I must pay for, what promise have you made to Gid– to Mr Newell?'

'I didn't want to spoil the day by tellin' you.'

'I have had a lovely day and nothing you say will spoil it, so long as we are together.'

'That be it...' Jerking his head free Luke turned away. 'We won't be together once this day be over.'

'Won't be together... Luke, what are you talking about? Haven't we both given our word?'

'Yes, I know what were promised but my word proved to be like meself ... no good.'

'Now you stop that!' Grasping his shoulders tightly Saran shook the thin figure. 'I won't have you say such. You are the one good thing in my life. Now we'll sit down again and I won't move until you have told me everything ... everything, Luke! Let there be no half measures between us.'

Settled on the warm turf Luke hesitated. No half measures; yes, they had come too far together for that, but once she heard...

The smile playing on Saran's mouth was tender. Poor Luke, one moment so very much the man and the next still so very much the boy. But Gideon Newell was no boy! The smile fading quickly she felt her nerves jar again. Unlike Luke,

Gideon Newell was a man full grown, his was the mind of a man used to dealing with the world; so what had that mind dreamed up, what could he want from her now he knew the brooch was beyond his reach and that she had accepted nothing in its place?

'It were while you was sleeping, I couldn't clear my head of it.' As Luke began to speak Saran forced away her thoughts. 'It played there the whole night, fading a bit from time to time but never goin' completely and every time it come back it were stronger and stronger 'til it got so I couldn't stand it no longer...'

She could make him stop, tell him to organise his thoughts, but that might fluster him more; far better to let him speak them as they came.

'I d'ain't go with the idea of bringing you into it ... of mekin' no bargain but I ... I couldn't help meself, Saran, on God's honour I couldn't help meself!'

Lifting his face he looked at her, the pale light of early evening sparkling on tears glinting in his blue eyes, and in that moment she was twelve years old again comforting a younger sister who had fallen and grazed her knee.

'It's all right.' She drew him against her as she had drawn another child. 'It's all right,' she whispered now as she had whispered then. The memories so powerful they had her trembling as she pressed the tousled head close to her chest, her lips touching a kiss to it as they had kissed her sister's. '*We will make it better, Saran will take the pain away*.' Words and pictures dancing in the theatre of her mind showed her tying two small handkerchiefs into a bandage, smiling into a small tear-stained face as she fastened it about Miriam's knee.

The pictures fading as Luke sat upright she stifled the sob rising to her throat. No bandage would salve Luke's hurt, no story of fairies would take his mind from the pain; she could not kiss him better as she had a four-year-old ... she could only listen.

'I suppose that while I was so worried as to you ... where you'd gone and was you all right,' Luke sniffed, 'I kept the thoughts to the back of my mind, but once I seen you was safe, that no harm had come to you then I couldn't hold 'em back no longer ... they come and they come giving no rest 'til I thought I'd go mad. That were when I knowed I had to do it so I slipped away while you slept. I went to the house of Gideon Newell, I asked him would he go with me to the workhouse, would he ask for the release of the Elwell kids, for the authorities wouldn't give 'em over to me cause of my not being of age.'

'The Elwell children!' Saran could not hold back the gasp. 'You asked for the Elwell children?'

'What I told you were the truth.' Blue eyes pleaded for understanding. 'Thought of them being in that place, of that little wench being slapped and treated like dirt under the feet of them wardresses, of the lad mebbe locked in a glory hole and left alone same as I was. Oh, I'd talked to men at the tube works, men who knowed folk as was sent to that place and it were no better than the one I was in, it were the devil's own house they told me, a place folk would choose to die on the road sooner than go to and I couldn't bear the thought of the Elwell kids being there so I asked Gideon Newell to help me get them out.'

She could understand his feelings for those children, hadn't she felt the same herself, hadn't wanting to help them been the reason for her almost selling that brooch; but where she had only thought about taking those two children from that institution, Luke had actually tried. But even had he succeeded where would he put them? He had no place...

'Gideon asked the same.' Luke answered the question she had not realised had left her lips. 'But I'd sorted that. I went first to the neighbour of the Elwells to ask would they let the two little 'uns stay with them so long as I paid for their keep ... I told 'em the little wench wouldn't need much and if they let the lad work in the nailing as he had with his own father and mother then they could keep whatever he earned on top of what I paid 'em...' He paused, the plea for understanding dying from his eyes. 'I give the rest no thought,' he continued dully, 'I give no mind to the fact it would be you who suffered for what I done, you who would bear the brunt of my giving half of my wage every week, you who would have no place to live or sleep 'cept in a hayloft...'

'Is that what has been worrying you ... was that the awful news you have kept from me?' Saran's laugh rang across the empty heath. 'Luke, it is the most wonderful thing I ever heard, to offer what you did; but maybe God will be good and I will find work and a place for us to live, that being so perhaps the children will be released.'

'You don't understand.' Luke shook his head. 'They already be taken from that place, Gideon agreed...'

The Elwell children were no longer in that workhouse! Thanks to Luke, the children of the couple who had been so kind were no longer locked away, but all he worried about was herself being deprived of the comfort of a bed. Lord! Her heart shouted. She would sleep on stone and thank heaven for the privilege. 'They are with Livvy's neighbour?' The words grazed past the lump filling her throat and she smiled at him. 'Luke, I'm so proud of you.'

'No ... don't say that!' He jumped to his feet, his strangled cry full of heartbreak. 'You ain't heard it all, I ain't told it was too late, that the Elwell lad were already gone, teken by a man the day before!'

She had risen to stand beside him yet somehow she was alone in the world, her senses stilled by the shock of those words. The Elwell boy was already gone from the workhouse, taken by a man. But the man would not be Edward Elwell, he would not reclaim one child without the other, not take his son yet leave his daughter.

'I were too late! That lad be gone and it's my fault!'

The pain and self-accusation contained in the words reached into the void that had so suddenly surrounded Saran, returning her to reality.

'How can you say that?' she said gently. 'You tried your best and I'm proud of you.'

'No!' He brushed away a hand that would have touched him. 'I've done nothin' to be proud of, I left it too late to help that little 'un, as well as going back on my word ... you see, it ain't just yourself breaks a promise.'

Startled by the vehemence of the cry a rabbit ran past their feet, its white tail bobbing as it rushed headlong for the security of its burrow. Watching it Saran wanted only to emulate its action, to hide away from the world and its ills, but that could only be done in dreams.

'Luke.' She did not touch him, only spoke quietly. 'Whatever promise you have broken I know it was not done for yourself but for the Elwell children; surely you must see I would happily have done the same.'

'Would you, Saran?' He turned sharply and in the purpling dusk she saw his eyes held a depth of grief. 'Would you agree to go with Gideon Newell ... for that was the bargain I made.'

Luke had agreed she would go with Gideon Newell! Blood surged in one wild gush through Saran's veins. How could he have struck such a bargain ... how could he have thought...? But it was not Luke's action she questioned, she had known the horror he held for any workhouse; had she not listened to the anguish as he had talked of it those first nights on the heath, heard it cry from him as he had slept? His agreeing to such a demand had been made on the strength of that same torment being visited upon the Elwell children, given at a moment when his strength of mind had been at its lowest. Gideon Newell had seen that and taken advantage of it. But for what reason, what motive could he have for taking her away from Luke ... did he want a whore, a sixpenny girl to be got without paying the sixpence? Or was it that he saw profit of a different kind, the sort her stepfather had indulged in ... was Gideon Newell another Enoch Jacobs?

His confession almost over Luke choked with tears. 'I'll go see Gideon, tell him it be off between us, that I won't–'

'No, Luke,' she interrupted quickly. 'If you go back on things then so can he. He can tell the Board of Governors that after all he finds he has no use for Livvy's daughter, and she could be taken back to the workhouse. I couldn't face up to being responsible for that.'

'But I can tell them I be paying for the little 'un, for her keep.'

Much as she wanted to accept that, Saran knew she could not. There were too many flaws, flaws a man who could strike such a deal would, without question, take advantage of.

She tried to explain without too much hurt. 'Luke, you said the authorities would not give the child into your care because of your being under age... I too am under age, don't you think Gideon Newell would use that against us?'

It took several more long minutes to convince Luke that she was right, that they could not chance that little girl, already deprived of her family, being deprived a second time, being taken away from the only friends she knew. But in the end he had nodded, consenting that she should appeal to the man's sense of right and wrong.

But did Gideon Newell care for any difference?

Luke fell silent as they came to the town, lost in a world she guessed was filled with raised fists and sneering faces, a world he would willingly have given not half but all of his earnings from the tube works to save Livvy's children from ... except for her! Always her. She had been a bind on the boy from the time of his finding her tied to a tree and she was still a drag on him. It was she he worried over, she who should have a bed and a roof over her head. Well, that problem had been resolved; her going to wherever it was Gideon Newell planned to house his acquisition would relieve Luke of the burden.

'Saran ... Saran, be you sure?'

It was Luke who first caught sight of the tall figure standing opposite the tavern, his features just beyond the pale glow of its lanterns.

She could not go through the process of assuring him again, repeat the pretence she was willing to sacrifice herself when in reality it appalled her, but the horror of having one child dragged screaming from her filled her soul, there was no room for another.

Gripping the boy's chin she forced him to look at her. Praying her voice would stay firm, she said quietly, 'Go find Ben, ask him to let his wife know we are back safely. No, Luke...' she shook her head, preventing the interruption leaving his lips, 'we must stick to what was agreed. Do what I ask ... you have my word I won't go from here without telling you first.'

The sound of running feet rapping the cobblestoned yard died away yet still the figure she knew watched her from its island of shadow did not move. Did he want her to walk to him, was her subjection to begin from this very moment ... was he so eager to prove his mastery over her? But wasn't that exactly what he was now, her master? No money had changed hands yet he had bought her ... bought her as some man in a Walsall beerhouse had bought her mother and sister and now he had come to claim his purchase.

A flame of anger searing her throat she drew a long breath. He could force her to lie with him but never to smile or speak a civil word. Gideon Newell's bargain would prove no real conquest.

As instinct fought defiance, Saran stepped backwards, her breath releasing itself as the figure crossed the street with an easy stride.

'Miss Chandler, how nice to see you again.'

Desperately trying to control senses that were suddenly careering like a runaway carriage, colour sweeping her cheeks, Saran looked into the handsome face smiling down at her.

'Mr...' she stammered, 'Mr...'

'No, not mister.' His eyes reflected the gleam of the tavern lanterns as he reached a hand towards her. 'We have an agreement, remember; there is to be no more miss or mister between us, only Saran and Jairus.'

Five minutes later, trying to analyse her feelings, Saran watched the tall figure stride away towards the Five Ways, the crossroads which were the main arteries of the small town. Relief, yet in some vague way disappointment, had flooded over her as Jairus Ensell had stepped clear of the shadows. Relief – yes, she could understand that, it had been the immediate assuaging of mortification throbbing in her veins; the loathsome meeting she had expected not now taking place had brought the lift of spirits. But what was accountable for the disappointment, the dejection which was with her still? Watching the figure merge with the darkening evening she sifted each thought, rejecting first one then another, but always the knowledge remained that she had not imagined that feeling. It had been there, a quick stab in her heart, a rapid lurching in her veins which had left behind an emptiness, a feeling almost of loss. But that was ridiculous! Impatient with herself she pushed the idea away. All she had felt was apprehension. She had not been freed of the necessity to face up to the bargain Luke had made, she had accepted it; the moment was only delayed, therefore the bitterness of it remained, and it was that and no more which was responsible for her state of mind. Telling herself to think no more about it she turned towards the entrance to the tavern yard.

He had been passing when he caught sight of her and of course could not go on without wishing her good evening. Jairus Ensell's explanation had been given with a smile, his voice soft and pleasant. She had smiled in return but could muster no warmth to accompany it. *'I was passing...'* Yet she had seen him standing masked in shadow, knowing he watched her. Had his words been a deliberate lie? But then why should he be untruthful, what had he to gain from that?

Hesitating before the wide entrance that gave access to carts and wagons, Saran remonstrated with herself. She was being unfair to the man allowing even a hint of mistrust to enter her mind. He was merely being polite, showing her the same courtesy and respect he had shown before.

Had she news of her mother and sister? Would Luke agree to his driving them both to Darlaston, thus avoiding a tiring walk? Every point of their conversation had been one of his trying to help, of offering assistance while putting no pressure upon her at being refused, only repeating that should she change her mind then please to send word to the George Hotel and the owner would contact him. That way might suit her better than visiting him at his home. He had smiled when saying that, adding that for such a small town Wednesbury had an exceeding long tongue, one which did not always savour truth, preferring the taste of scandal, no matter it was groundless.

Jairus Ensell had spoken and acted like the gentleman he was. Saran pulled her shawl close with a determined movement. He would make no bargain behind a woman's back, he was a man she could trust. So why was that dullness, that feeling of having something snatched from her, still weighing heavily inside?

'Miss Chandler!'

One step into the cobbled yard Saran halted, every nerve suddenly tingling, vitally alive.

'I believe we have an arrangement!'

The world about her fading into the background she turned to face Gideon Newell.

# 19

‘*We*, Mr Newell ... *we* have an arrangement?’

Her voice cold and hard as hailstones, one word chipping against the other, Saran turned to face the man who had spoken.

‘Would you not say it was yourself has an arrangement? One made with a boy too unhappy to think straight. It didn’t satisfy you simply to take advantage of me, you had to do the same with Luke, a boy willing to do anything, to agree to anything in order to help a friend; but that is what you call yourself, isn’t it, a friend? Then I pray God Luke never makes another friend like you!’

Light spilling over his features showed them set like granite, eyes glistening dark as jet. ‘Miss Chandler–’

He got no further. The anger that had brewed in her a short while before bubbled over and she swept a hand sideways through the air. ‘I know why you are here and you need have no worry I will not keep to what you so carefully hatched. I need a moment to say goodnight to Luke then you may claim your reward.’

‘Reward, Miss Chandler?’ Gideon’s hiss scraped the night. ‘What on earth are you talking about?’

‘You ask that!’ Saran’s temper flared. ‘You who make your sly bargain behind your victim’s back, a man who uses a boy in order to get himself a whore–’

'Stop that!'

Gideon's hand grasped her wrist, jerking her towards him, but in her passion Saran was unaware of the ice suddenly crackling in his voice.

'I won't stop!' she flung back. 'I am not quite your sixpenny girl yet.'

'Listen to me, you little fool!'

Jerked against him, the anger behind the movement almost driving the breath from her body, Saran refused to be silenced. From tonight she may never have another chance to express her disgust for this man. Forcing enough space between them to enable her to look into his face she snapped, 'No, you listen to me! I will go with you for, like Luke, I cannot face the prospect of Livvy's daughter being returned to the workhouse; I will be what you want, a girl you can buy off the streets for sixpence, but I vow–'

'You don't need vow anything.' His tone like the ring of hard steel Gideon flung her away. 'Is that what Luke told you?'

Stumbling against the wall which enclosed the stable yard Saran struggled to keep her balance. 'He didn't have to, I guessed that much for myself! That you agreed to go with him to the workhouse is what he told me, that you would have the child released to you. But there was a proviso, wasn't there? You would do that but in return something must be done for you, Luke had to agree or the child stayed where she was. Does that make you feel proud, Mr Newell ... does bartering the freedom of a little girl make you more of a man? Not from where I stand. It gives no credit in my eyes, only pity; you and Enoch Jacobs, only two such men would stoop so low.'

Her outburst done it seemed the silence that fell between them would go on for ever yet it was only a moment before Gideon spoke. Each word was crusted with frost as he stared at her.

'You believe that? You believe I would be part of such an agreement, use a child ... trick Luke ... and all for the great prize of a whore? A girl you yourself have said could be got from any backstreet for sixpence!'

'Yes!' With her head thrown back Saran glared her disdain. 'Yes, I believe that.'

'A sixpenny girl!' The steel was gone and in its place a quiet scorn seemed to touch Saran's face. 'You guessed correctly, Miss Chandler; that is all you are worth!'

Light from the kitchen at his back gilding his thin figure, Ben Mason hurried across the stable yard, calling softly to Saran.

'Eh, wench, there be a man asking after you, been 'ere half an hour an' more.'

Still shaking from the anger of moments ago Saran nodded. 'I've already spoken with Mr Newell.'

Lamplight spilling after him in the semi-darkness showed the ostler's frown. 'With who? Newell don't be the name he give to the landlord; said 'is name were Thomas.'

Only a fragment of her mind on what the man said Saran gave no reply.

'There were no mistake,' he cast a quick glance

towards the kitchen, 'I 'eard him say your name clear as I says it meself, he spoke it when askin' the gaffer did he have a room kept for them 'aving private business; Miss Saran Chandler were his very words, did the landlord know of a young woman of that name and where it was her might be found.'

Her attention caught by Luke running to join them, Saran tried to recall the name. Had she and Luke met with anyone called Thomas?

'Ain't nobody as I've seen in the tavern afore,' Ben went on, 'an' if it be somebody you prefers not talkin' with then I advises you both to tek off, give it an hour or two before you come back, chance be he'll be gone by then.'

'But who is he?' Her question, directed more at Luke than at the ostler, met with a shrug of the lad's shoulders.

'Beats me,' he said, 'I ain't never heard of no Thomas.'

Could he be an officer of the parish, one sent to look into Luke's part in the business of Livvy's daughter ... had Gideon Newell told? But of course not, there was no way he could have seen anyone in the few seconds since her leaving him.

Denying the relief her realisation brought she looked at Luke. 'Wait for me in the barn ... no, Luke – no argument, I will speak with this man; far better we find out who he is and what he wants than have to look over our shoulder everywhere we go.'

'Saran,' Luke watched the ostler hurry away towards a hansom stopped at the tavern entrance, 'Saran, do you trust me?'

Already turned towards the kitchen Saran spun round to face the question. A few yards away in the street the sound of laughter drifted on the grey dimness as customers dismounted from the carriage, their voices drifting after them into the tavern; but it was the quiet voice of Luke stayed with her. There was something in the tone, an uncertainty, a doubt she had not heard before.

'Trust you?' She frowned. 'You know I do, Luke.'

His head coming up he seemed to grow before her eyes and when he answered his voice held a new strength. 'Then show it ... show your trust as I've shown mine in you, trust me in all things or none at all, for this way be no good.'

'This way? Luke, I don't understand.'

Luke the boy faded and for a moment all signs of the man he would become were there in its place.

'Don't you?' he asked. 'You don't understand? I thought we were real friends from the start ... but real friends don't shut the other one out.'

That was what she had done with the business of the brooch. She had gone alone to the pawnbroker; hers alone had been the decision not to accept his offer. She had not consulted Luke before haring off to Darlaston and she had not asked would he wish to take advantage of William Salisbury's reward. She had explained it away, telling herself and Luke that she had acted on the spur of the moment and he had said he understood, that it did not matter; yet all the time he was hurting inside ... all the time she had shut him out.

'This way don't be no good,' Luke repeated, his glance steady on her face. 'I be only a lad, that be true, an' if it be you thinks me not old enough to share your business then you needs only to say; but whatever you decides, I be your true friend, Saran, and I won't let nothing nor nobody 'urt you so long as I breathes.'

Emotion riding high in her throat, Saran nodded. 'You are young, Luke, but you have a strength of heart not born of years, and a character which does not owe itself to days. You are my truest and most trusted friend and no matter what lies in the future I want it to be as these past few weeks have been, faced with you at my side; there will never be any business of mine that is not equally business of yours.'

She had meant what she said and now, facing the sharp-eyed man sat in a small windowless room of the Turk's Head tavern, her hand in Luke's, Saran was thankful for the boy's presence, taking strength from his confidence.

'You are Saran Chandler and the er ... young man with you is Master Luke Hipton?'

'That be just plain Luke Hipton, mister, I ain't master of nobody.'

He had hesitated to use the term boy; now seeing the quick spark in those bright blue eyes, the man who had introduced himself as Alfred Thomas was glad he had not. The lad had a defiance best not provoked.

'Quite.' He smiled thinly, pointing to chairs placed at the opposite side of the table still set with the remains of his supper.

'Mr Thomas...'

A brief shake of his grey head halting Saran he rang a small, well-polished brass bell set beside his right hand, remaining silent while Ben's wife collected the dishes. The door closed once more, he lifted a leather bag on the table, releasing its metal clasp.

Behind small square spectacles clinging precariously to his large nose, he looked at Saran. 'You were about to say?'

Watching the hand slide into the bag, seeing the sheaf of papers being withdrawn, the fear that had ridden her outside in the street raced again, bringing every nerve to a painful quiver. She had been mistaken in thinking the figure in the shadows to have been a representative of the Parish Board sent to reclaim Livvy's child, but this man ... she was not mistaken a second time!

'Mr Thomas,' the words tumbled out, 'the Elwells' daughter ... Luke should not ... she will be well cared for, you have my word, please ... please tell the Governors...'

'I am sure what you are saying is true.' A thin-fingered hand spread the sheaf of papers. 'However–'

It was not given him to say the child could remain with them. Under cover of the cloth-covered table Saran's hand tightened over Luke's. The man had been sent to take her back to the workhouse!

'Mister!' Where her voice had trembled Luke's was firm. 'What were done were done by me, Saran played no part in it; her knowed nothin' of my asking Gideon Newell to tek that little wench from the hell folks calls the poor house, nor can that man be blamed, for it were kindness alone had him agree. I told him arrangements were already med for the little 'un, that lodgings and keep had been paid and would be so long as were needed. That it were to be from Saran and me the money would come was the only thing kept from the Board's knowing and that deception be mine only...'

'Luke Hipton.' There was no sarcasm behind the use of the name, the sharp eyes screwed behind the spectacles held more than a hint of admiration. 'As with Miss Chandler, I have no doubt of what you say, however I have no knowledge of the matter you speak of and I most certainly am not here by request of the parish.'

'You ain't?' Luke's frown knitted his brows together. 'You ain't come from that work'ouse?'

'Not in any wise.'

'Then who do you be sent by?'

A further spreading of elegantly written papers preceding his answer, the man glanced once at the door, satisfying himself it was firmly shut. 'I am acting on behalf of Mr William Salisbury.'

The chill of losing Livvy's daughter giving way to a new, equally frightening, fear, Saran leaned forward. 'I returned that brooch ... it was the real one...'

'Miss Chandler, at the danger of repeating myself, I have to say again there is no doubting you. Please...' he raised a hand as Luke made to speak, 'let me explain. I am Mr Salisbury's solicitor. He has given me instructions to act on his behalf, to place a proposal before you both, one he hopes you, Miss Chandler, might be disposed to accept.'

William Salisbury did not doubt the brooch she had returned was the same one his wife had taken from her gown the night of the accident. The ice in Saran's veins melted but her nerves still quivered.

'But I told him ... I told the two of them I wanted nothing, the well-being of themselves and their baby was enough.'

'For you, perhaps, but Luke Hipton was not present.'

'What Saran said went for me an' all!' Luke broke in quickly. 'I would 'ave been there to say it for meself except I were at work; but I tells you now so you can pass it to William Salisbury, I looked for no reward for what I done that night, it were little enough and needs no recognisin' except for a thank you.'

A finger pushed the spectacles from where they had slipped to the end of his nose as the solicitor smiled his thin smile.

'Well said, and of course your instruction will be followed to the letter, I shall tell it to William Salisbury myself. However, as I hope you appreciate, my brief is to pass his word ... all of his word ... to yourselves. May I have your permission to proceed?

'Following your visit last week,' he peered at Saran over rimless spectacles, 'Mr Salisbury had me draw up the papers you see on the table, but before I read their contents he and Mrs Salisbury requested I speak of their own feelings. They are, of course, understanding of yours but at the same time would ask you consider theirs. The proposal I am about to set before you is one they realise you are at liberty to refuse; but I am to tell you it would indeed give them great happiness would you accept. This,' he pointed to one of the papers, 'is the deed to a small property once owned by Mrs Salisbury's nurse. It has been made over to yourself, Miss Chandler, to share with Luke. Should you refuse it then it is offered solely to Luke; should he also refuse it will be bound in trust until he reaches the age of twenty-one when once more he will be asked to accept. Twenty pounds as payment for renovation goes with the deed.'

Catching the immediate shake of her head the solicitor again held up a hand. 'I know your answer, and though I was not instructed to tell you of the result it would bring, nevertheless I will. Refute it, give the answer I see in your eyes, and the property remains empty until the second time of its offering many years from now. Think of it, Miss Chandler, pride ... admirable but, nevertheless, pride ... will keep you from a home which I see from your being in this place would be a haven for you and for Luke Hipton; add to that it would also provide a home for a certain child newly released from the workhouse ... do I make my point?'

'You makes it to me, mister.' Luke grinned then looked at Saran. 'It meks sense, a place that were your own, the Board couldn't say no, they'd be bound to let that little 'un live in it with you.'

A home for the child of Livvy and Edward, a place where she would be loved, cared for until the return of her parents ... and Gideon Newell – she would no longer be obliged to do his bidding! It was a miracle she would never had dared pray for but to accept would keep her here in this town, bring responsibilities that would prevent her searching further afield for Miriam and their mother.

'I ... I appreciate the kindness of Mr Salisbury and his wife but–'

'Wait!' Hidden by the drape of heavy chenille Luke's fingers gripped tight. 'Not wanting anything from the Salisburys be one thing, but indulging your own pleasure at the cost of other folk be summat else again. Accepting what they asks be a trouble to your conscience but think what refusing can do. That couple has to feel satisfied as you does, they needs to have an easy conscience same as you, and this be the only way they can see of getting that; send back their offer and it will be as a slap to the face. What will that do for your peace of mind!'

So much deep thinking while still a boy, what would Luke Hipton be like as a man? One she wanted always as a friend.

'Mr Thomas,' Saran smiled, 'Luke and I will be very happy to accept the Salisburys' gift.'

He had not been there. The agreement made, the solicitor had left the Turk's Head and she had almost skipped across the stable yard. She would tell Gideon Newell his threat no longer carried weight, that Livvy's child was safe from the workhouse and Saran Chandler was safe from him. But he had not been there, the gateway and the street had been empty of people.

As she stood now outside the tavern, the rumble of wagons and calls of people setting out their stalls in the market square made no impression on Saran's mind.

Gideon Newell had left. Had that meant he no longer wished to barter for her, had changed his mind and would renege on the bargain he had struck with Luke? But that would bring him no satisfaction now there was a means of keeping that child herself... so where was the satisfaction she should be feeling? She had expected to experience pleasure in telling him his assistance was no longer necessary, that she and Luke had no need of him. But the taste she thought was joy in her mouth had turned sour even before she had reached the street, had stayed with her through the sleepless hours of the night ... was with her still! What she had thought would be pleasure had turned to emptiness, what she had expected to be contentment almost a regret. But how could it be regret? Irritated by a state of mind she did not understand she pushed the money the solicitor had given her into the pocket of her skirt. Her mother had had a word for the emotion which plagued her now, for the swift falling away of excitement that left a dejection which could not be explained; '*Anti-climax*,' was what her mother would say, '*you be feeling naught but anti-climax, give it a few hours and it will be gone.*' But she had felt this way for more than a few hours ... and it was still as strong as ever.

'Be you sure you can find the way by yourself?' Leaving his work for a moment the ostler came to stand beside her.

'You explained very clearly, Ben.' Saran smiled.

Lifting his cap the man ran leathery fingers through his hair. 'Listenin' be one thing, wench, doin' be another altogether. Don't you think it might be better to wait of that lad finishing his day along of the tube works, go together to Lea Brook? The place be empty except for Brook Cottage.'

'I will be perfectly all right, Ben. Luke agreed I go out there this morning to air the house and I promised to stay put until he comes to me this evening.'

Settling his cap into place the ostler shook his head. 'Oh well, you'll go your own ways in the end, young 'uns always does these days; but if it be you feels things don't be right, if you be uneasy out there on your own you comes straight back to Ada and me.'

'Thank you, Ben.' Saran kissed the bewhiskered cheek. 'I don't know what Luke or myself would have done without your help.'

'It were no more than heaven would want, wench, it don't hurt no man to hold a helping hand to them in need. My Ada and me just hopes you be happy in that house for it be no more'n you deserves.'

Hugging the man's words, feeling the warmth of them in her heart, Saran walked quickly towards the Shambles.

Harriet Dowen, the Elwells, Ben and Ada Mason and the Salisburys, they had all been so kind ... so different from Enoch Jacobs. Was that man truly gone from her life ... could it be true what Harriet had said of moon dancers, that beautiful ballet of flickering beams which beckoned the unwary to their death? Or would Enoch Jacobs one day return to blight her existence as he had done before? Her mind screamed against the possibility while her heart cried for it to happen, for only that man could tell her where to find her family.

'You been talkin' to the fairies?' Flipping the coin Saran gave to pay for sausages and a fillet of pork bought from the first of a line of stalls which graced the Shambles the butcher caught it expertly.

'Fairies?' Only half listening Saran frowned as the man fumbled in a leather bag fastened about his waist.

'Ar, wench, fairies ... seems they must 'ave pointed you to the gold they be supposed to 'ave at the end of the rainbow for you to be paying with a sovereign, t'ain't many of them I sees in a day.'

'I did them a good turn.' Saran smiled as he counted coins into her hand, adding their value aloud.

'Well, next time they calls you just point them little folk in the direction of my stall ... a few sovereigns wouldn't come amiss.'

Fairies were only real in stories. Clutching her purchases she felt the smile she had shared nestle in her heart. But, fairies or not, there was something, some benign influence touched her and Luke and she thanked God for it.

*'the way be not easy'*

Harriet Dowen's words floated on the edge of

her mind. They had not been empty words, she and Luke had known suffering, but now that was all over; from today the hardship was gone and she could really begin the search for Miriam and her mother. But first she must take this food to Livvy's neighbour, ask the woman to care for the child a little longer, until the property William Salisbury had given was ready to live in.

The clang of hammer on anvil ringing in her ears, Saran stared at the group of people who not for a moment ceased their work.

'The little wench,' Livvy's neighbour brought her hammer swinging on the narrow strip of metal held between large tongs, ''er don't be here.'

'But, Luke ... he said he brought her to you ... that he had arranged to pay for her keep.'

'Ar, he done that, brought the little wench like he said,' hammer striking iron kept rhythm with every word, 'and a Godsend it would 'ave been, not just for that babby but for mine an' all, for the money would provide a bit extra for we all to eat.'

Watching the woman return the iron strip to the fire holding it with one hand, the other working the bellows, Saran tried to sort the confusion in her mind. She said the money Luke had promised to pay would be more than useful, that she was willing to take the child in, to have her live with her own family, so why now was the woman saying she was not there?

'I would 'ave cared for that babby as I cares for me own even if no money were paid.' The hammer rose and fell, the woman's tired eyes never shifting from the strike. 'Livvy Elwell and meself 'ad a friendship from the day of our being born, a friendship that would 'ave seen her little 'uns living alongside of my own but Livvy knowed that way would only bring nearer the day my family be forced to tread the path her own trod, so her and her man took 'em to the poor house.'

'But the younger one – the girl – Luke said he had brought her to you, so why is she not here? I don't understand!'

As a finished nail was clipped free of the strip, falling into a bucket almost filled with the same, the woman began to shape another, her hammer ringing relentlessly on the anvil.

'What be to understand,' she called above the noise, 'the wench were teken from the poor house and last night her were teken back. I begged for her to be left with me, said as it saved the parish the cost of keeping her but that man would 'ave none of it; said the little 'un were to go back and that were the end of the matter.'

The clatter of the tiny workshop rang in Saran's head, but the noise of it was nothing to the clamour of her brain.

*'the little 'un were to go back'*

Every syllable burned like a brand on her heart.

*'the little 'un were to go back'*

Only one man could do that. Only one man had reason. Only one would take such vengeance... Gideon Newell!

# 20

This was where Gideon Newell in his spite had returned a helpless child.

A heavy oak door closing behind her, shutting off the meagre amount of daylight venturing into a small dank-smelling vestibule, Saran could not repress a shiver. Luke had once said he would rather die than go back to the workhouse and now she understood a little more the reason why. Bare stone walls lined with mildew stared blank and unpitying on two women, their heads shrouded in cotton bonnets, long dark aprons covering drab dun-coloured dresses, bare forearms red and blistered by hot water which was heavily laced with soda but which had little effect on the overriding smell of damp and decay.

'Mind your business!'

The sharp command sang like a whip, the whine of it echoing into the shadows; a groan following as the boot of the grey-uniformed wardress sank into the side of the inmate who had dared to look away from her task.

'Governor's office be this way.' Hands held imperiously across her stomach, boots tapping on the wet floor, the wardress led the way along a corridor so dark, its feel so malevolent, Saran wanted to turn and run out into the daylight. But that she would not do, not until she had that child safe in her own keeping.

Announcing her name with a deprecating smirk the wardress stood, hands crossed, her sharp features lengthening when the man seated behind a well-polished desk waved a dismissal.

He did not ask her to sit. Unease tickling her spine, Saran glanced towards the door as it closed.

'Well now, Miss Chandler, what is it you want us to do for you?'

'I ... I came to ask...'

'No cause to be shy; times are hard in Wednesbury, many of its people need the help of the parish and we are here to help.'

There was something about the man, something in the way his eyes suddenly gleamed and the tip of his tongue ran swiftly over his lower lip, something about the smile which, despite itself, revealed more menace than kindness.

'You are needful of a place in this institution?' Keeping his eyes fixed to her face he moved around the desk, the serpentine tongue flicking twice, the gleam in close-set eyes already a smoulder.

She had seen that same look on men's faces, knew the evil which lay behind it. She had seen it in that beerhouse where she had been paraded for the amusement of would-be buyers, known the evil that had brought Enoch Jacobs to a child's bedroom. Panic that the memory always brought clawed her throat, danced along her veins, swirled in her head. Saran instinctively drew the shawl closer.

'No!' The cry as much a castigation of her thoughts as it was a denial of the man's belief in her reason for being here, she stepped away from the hand reaching towards her. 'No, I am not asking for a place in the institution.'

'Then why come?'

Her stepping away had not halted him. Saran's back came up against a cupboard. Breathing deeply, fear still throbbing in her chest, she stammered, 'I ... am looking for a child ... a little girl, I think she is here.'

Inches from her, the insidious smile slid further over the slack mouth while the eyes took on a dark heat, a calculating, purposeful fervour.

'A sister?' The hot eyes slithered over her face then down towards breasts hidden beneath the shawl.

Fear and disgust imprisoning words, Saran shook her head.

'Not a sister?' The smile widened, a sly satisfied gratification.

'Her name is Elwell, Martha Elwell; she was admitted some days ago along with her brother Joseph, they are the children of a friend. Joseph, I believe, is no longer in the care of the parish but Martha, she ... she was returned.'

'Returned!' Heat-filled eyes lifted, boring deep into hers. 'The child is no kin to you but is the daughter of a friend.'

Caught between his body and the cupboard, fighting hard against the returning panic, Saran tried to answer calmly.

'Yes. Edward and Livvy Elwell are friends of mine and I would like to give their daughter a home.'

'Like.' He took half a step closer. 'We all have our likes, Miss Chandler, some can be satisfied free of charge while others must be paid for.'

'I can pay, I have money.'

As her hand dropped to her pocket the worn shawl fell open and as though drawn by a magnet those glittering snake-like eyes fastened on the small mounds pushing against the blouse Ada Mason had given her.

'Money does not always purchase what we want.' Cool and deliberate he touched the topmost button. 'You want my help ... it is there for the giving.'

*'the tits, show we the tits...'*

Suddenly she was back in that beerhouse, the bawdy shouts ringing in her ears, Enoch Jacobs's touch burning her flesh. Her eyes tight shut against the horror of it, she moaned, 'The money ... in my pocket ... take it, take it all.'

A laugh, hoarse and thick, sounded as he brought his wet mouth against her throat, fingers snatching the buttons free, clutching fingers closing over her breasts, squeezing and crushing. 'Keep your money ... I prefer these.'

Lips sliding wetly downward closed over her nipple, sending a shudder of revulsion stinging from head to foot, driving fear before it. Fastening her fingers in the thinning grey hair Saran snatched hard. With his head back almost to his shoulder blades, a gurgle rattled in the governor's throat then turned to a gasp as, all her strength behind it, she pushed, sending him sprawling across the desk. Following with an equally swift move she flung open the door to the wardress, who every sense told her had been listening.

'I have come for the Elwell girl,' she gasped, her

fingers trembling as she fastened her blouse.

'The Elwell girl, she–'

'Get out!' Scarlet with fury the governor roared at the wardress's attempt to reply.

'The girl, sir?' the woman asked, averting her eyes from the man scrambling to his feet.

'The girl stays where her be! And you...' he glared at Saran stood close to the door as the wardress clicked away down the gloomy corridor, 'you will regret your little display of modesty, false as it was, for you won't ever see the child you asked for and the child won't ever see the outside of these walls ... many folk die in a workhouse, one more won't never be noticed!'

She had come here to help, to take a child from the suffering and heartbreak life in the workhouse was said to be, to take her and keep her safe for the sake of those two kind people, but all she had done was condemn the child to a possible life of torment.

'Please,' she took the coins from her pocket, 'there are almost ten sovereigns.'

'Keep it!' The close-set eyes gleamed their pleasure as he stood straight. 'You keep your sovereigns ... I will keep the girl. Now get out or I'll have the Watch take you out!'

It would do Martha no good to argue, the man was incensed and in this place, where he was accountable to no one, that fury might well be visited upon a helpless child. Turning away she shuddered at the crash of the door being kicked shut. Like Enoch Jacobs, the workhouse governor would grab at any weapon to fight with when denied what he desired, and his particular weapon was the holding of Livvy's daughter.

'It be a palace!' Luke repeated the phrase he had breathed on entering each of the rooms of Brook Cottage but Saran could make no answer. This house with its three bedrooms and small front parlour needed no renovation, it had been carefully prepared to receive herself and Luke; the pretence that repairs were necessary had been a way to ensure they accept the twenty pounds. Saran followed the excited lad back to the comfortable kitchen filled with the warmth of a glowing fire and appetising aroma of roast lamb. She had left the workhouse, running from Meeting Street, but though her breath was gone on reaching the Market Square every moment of the minutes spent with the governor remained strong. Why did fate give a man such as he a position whereby he could ruin other people's lives, make their days a misery?

'What's up Saran?'

Luke had asked the question twice since returning to the kitchen but she had not heard. Now he put it again, catching her hand as she reached for plates.

'Don't tell me there be nothing for I knows you ain't listened to a word. Be it the house ... be there summat about it as you don't be easy with?'

The note of regret behind the obvious concern reached where no words had. 'The house...' she forced her thoughts to come together, 'the house is perfect, everything we could need is here.'

''Cept your heart.'

'What?' Surprised by the quiet interruption she

stared at the troubled young face.

Letting her hand fall Luke turned his face to the fire. 'It's been obvious since my comin',' he said quietly, 'you've been looking for a way to say it but you don't 'ave to for I knows what be troublin' you; it ain't proper for a lad and a wench who don't be no kin to live together in the same house.'

'Luke ... Luke, what are you saying?'

He did not turn but his shoulders in their too-small jacket drooped. 'I be saying you have no cause to feel uneasy ... I be leavin'.'

When was she ever going to see past her own misery! Again she had failed to recognise the pain she was causing a lad who had no objective other than to give her comfort.

'Luke.' She touched a hand to him. 'The only proper thing left in my life, the one thing giving me any sort of solace is you. You are the one person in the world I turn to for hope, without you my last joy would be gone, you are the rod which supports me ... without you I don't want to go on.'

Relief glinting in blue eyes dewy with desperately fought tears Luke turned.

'If it don't be as I thought then what do it be, Saran? For you've scarce spoke a word and heard far less.'

She had to tell him the whole of the day's story, Luke was too shrewd to accept anything other than all of it.

'I set away from the tavern with the intention of coming straight to Brook Cottage.' Drawing the reluctant Luke after her Saran settled them both in chairs she had earlier drawn to the fire. 'But I got to thinking of Livvy's neighbour, the one you asked to care for Martha. I wanted to thank her for sparing time to speak with me the other day and for trying to talk the man from the parish into allowing the child to stay with them in Russell Street...'

'Talk the man into ... what man?'

Luke was on the edge of his chair, his eyes turning to blue fire as Saran recounted the day's happenings, how Livvy's friend had not known the identity of the man come to reclaim Martha, of her visit to the workhouse – leaving out the governor's attack on her – and about how, after standing some time outside the Coronet Tube Works, she had come here to Brook Cottage.

'I wanted to face him there, where every man he works with would know the kind of man he is! To shame him into telling me where he has taken Martha.'

'Who?' Luke's hands clenched about the curved arms of his chair. 'Who were it you wanted to shame?'

'I wanted to let them all know what he did, how he could take his revenge on a child, but then I realised that to cause a fuss would rebound on you ... you could be sacked; but I won't let him get away with what he has done.'

His voice cracking with the first deep notes of manhood Luke leaned forward, grabbing her hand and shaking it until she looked at him.

'Let who get away? Saran, who be it you wanted to shame?'

Trembling with the emotion which had ripped through her, the answer came raggedly. 'Gideon

Newell ... it was Gideon Newell I wished to shame.'

'Gideon Newell!' The blue fires died, Luke's hand released its grip. 'You wished ... but why!' He shook his head. 'Why Gideon?'

A furnace of anger, which had burned in her since discovering the child had been removed from the house of her parents' friends, glowed still in the bitterness of Saran's answer.

'Why? Because his sordid little scheme failed ... because with William Salisbury's gift I no longer have to lie with him, be the sixpenny girl he had no need to pay for!'

Brows drawn together in confusion Luke took a moment to answer and when he did it was with a blend of disbelief.

'Gideon asked that of you ... asked you to...'

'Why else do you think he forced that agreement on you, one that gave me in exchange for taking Martha out of that terrible place? He knew it was the only way.'

'Saran, I didn't–'

'I'm not blaming you, Luke,' she cut in swiftly. 'Like myself, you were willing to accept anything in order to gain that child's release, and Gideon Newell ... he was willing to do anything to get his revenge.'

Hanging above the fire the kettle steamed, setting its lid rattling. Understanding having its birth quietly in his mind, Luke reached across and shoved the bracket back against the cast-iron fireplace.

'We did 'ave an agreement, Gideon and me,' he said slowly, 'it was one which involved you.'

'Luke, you don't have to...'

'Explain?' He smiled. 'One of we has to and I doubts that will be Gideon. What you thinks don't be the understanding I had with Gideon Newell. True, he placed a price on what he were asked to do and that price were you, Saran, but not to be his ... his whore; what he demanded were that to get his help I had to agree to your takin' a room at the house of his mother's friend ... that were all, as God be my judge he asked no more.'

He had asked no more! Stunned by Luke's words, Saran stared into the fire. She had accused Gideon Newell of using Livvy's daughter as a means to his own ends! Had accused him...

Covering her face with her hands she tried to shut out the rest, to silence the words screaming in her mind.

*'A sixpenny girl! You guessed correctly, Miss Chandler; that is all you are worth!'*

He had bought the nails cheaply. Telling those families to take the price he offered or to try to sell their products elsewhere had paid off. *'No other fogger would buy from you,'* he had said, *'try any other middleman, you will only hear the same answer, "I'm buying no more nails or tacks, there be a glut of them."'*

Folding several five-pound notes, a tall dark-haired man placed them carefully into a pigskin wallet. Doing business his way was proving quite a financial success and one that would go on into the future. It be too much! Climbing into a small carriage he smiled, remembering the wince of Zadok Minch as that man had heard the asking price of this latest shipment, but he had paid.

A satisfied smile touching a handsome mouth he took the reins between strong hands. Yes, Minch had paid ... and he would go on paying. The man had requirements not all foggers could fulfil, the goods he asked for needed special skills, the touch of an expert, to produce and not every man had such skills, in fact – he flicked the reins, setting the horse to a steady trot – he knew of none other than himself, and Minch knew that also; hence, unwilling as the man might be to do so, he would continue to part with his money. And should the day come when he would not? Cloaked by night shadows the handsome mouth smiled again. That bridge would be crossed when reached and until that time he would enjoy the proceeds a shrewd mind and a clever tongue brought.

It was almost too easy. The seller and the buyer both eager to do business and there was plenty of that to be done so long as men like Zadok Minch existed.

But too much too soon jaded the appetite. The goods acquired solely for one nail master would be held back for a while; it could be they might be said to have been offered for by another ... the market proved nothing worked so well as competition, and Zadok was not a man to lose a monopoly!

To say that special product was sought after elsewhere ... that would be excellent play, a mark of the true connoisseur! The clap of hooves the drumming of applause in his ears, Zadok's handsome visitor drove into the night.

# 21

It had been several days since apologising to Gideon Newell but the embarrassment of it was as fresh as though it had been done not an hour ago. He had been gracious enough in accepting what she had believed as being a mistake, saying it was one any woman as worried as herself might make, but his handsome mouth had quivered while dark eyes had openly smiled.

Mixing yeast with warm water Saran covered it with a cloth then set it aside to rise. Luke said the matter had not been spoken of between himself and Gideon Newell but for her, in the long hours of the night, the conversation ran again and again.

She had told him of Luke's exact words, it was nothing he had said had caused her to think as she had, it was all her own constructing. That was when she had seen the smile in those dark eyes, watched the fine mouth quirk.

Spooning flour and salt into a bowl she added lard, rubbing them vigorously together until they were the texture of breadcrumbs.

He had not laughed nor had he rebuked her.

Adding milk to the bowl she blended the whole to a soft pastry. Shaping it on a board she lifted it into a greased tin then added potato and mutton she had diced, finishing the dish with a pastry lid.

*'You were frightened, Miss Chandler. Under such*

*circumstances it is understandable you could misinterpret my intentions.'*

Brushing the pie with a little of the milk she carried it to the oven, the words of Gideon Newell clear in her mind.

She had been afraid ... afraid and upset.

Reaching for the large crock bowl in which a quantity of flour had been put to warm, she tipped the bubbling yeast into it then, with a little tepid salt water, mixed the ingredients to a stiff dough.

Why could the man not have been angry?

Placing a clean cloth over the bowl she stood it in a corner of the hearth where the warmth of the fire would help the bread to rise.

Anger she could have understood!

Scooping up the utensils of her cooking she scrubbed each of them in the shallow brown-stone sink.

Anger would have been easier to deal with than the shadow of a smile. A show of indignation, animosity or even downright hostility she could have coped with.

Snatching a cloth from a line strung across the scullery she dried each piece in turn, mortification adding a briskness to her fingers.

His giving vent to the anger he must feel would not have made for a pleasant meeting but at least it would not colour her every waking hour as that quiet smile had done.

The dishes finished and put away, she lifted the pie from the oven.

Why was the memory haunting her, why were those dark eyes watching from the depths of her, why would the scene of that meeting not fade from her mind?

She had arranged with Luke to be waiting just beyond the gates of the tube works; that way, to inquisitive eyes, it would seem she was waiting to walk home with him.

Fingers holding the shawl were shaking as the tall dark-eyed man, the boy at his side, had come towards her.

*'Luke said you wish to speak with me.'*

The quiet evenness of those few words, the complete absence of displeasure or resentment had thrown the practised apology from her mind and she had stammered awkwardly.

*'I ... it was wrong ... I should not...'*

*'There is no need–'*

*'Yes!'* she had interrupted. If he did not listen to her now he might never listen. *'Yes, there is. I should not have acted the way I did, I might at least have given you a chance to speak.'*

That had been the moment those dusky eyes had smiled and his head had given the briefest nod.

*'I agree. But what is done is done and it is over. Please pay no more mind to it. You were frightened, Miss Chandler. Under such circumstances it is understandable you could misinterpret my intentions. You made a mistake any woman in your situation could have made. Forget it, Miss Chandler. I have.'*

Raising a hand to Luke stood a little apart from them he had turned and walked away.

Stood in the bright sunlit kitchen Saran tried now as she had tried then, tried to stifle the thought that had played in her mind as that tall figure had turned from her. He had made no mention of the child, not once spoken of what had been at the very centre of that accusation. Had that been deliberate, had he consciously avoided the issue, turned from her before word of it was raised?

Unsettled by the questions, appalled by the answer her mind kept repeating, Saran took a still-warm loaf, wrapping it in a cloth. The dough sat in the hearth would take some hours to rise. Throwing her shawl about her shoulders, the loaf in a basket she had earlier filled with bits and pieces from the larder, she left the house. But as she walked towards the town the thought she feared most beat in rhythm with her steps.

Gideon Newell had refrained from addressing the cause of her anger, had ended their conversation abruptly thereby evading speaking of Martha, though he must have known she had discovered the child's being returned to that dreadful place. Her glance lifting to the black spire of the hilltop church which touched its tip to the blue of the sky, Saran felt her heart trip. The man had accepted her apology, but had that apology been justified or had Gideon Newell's silence hidden a terrible truth – the truth of taking the girl from the house of her mother's friend, the truth of returning Livvy's daughter to the workhouse!

*'the child won't ever see the outside of these walls'*

Each remembered word a whiplash across the heart, Saran had left the stifling workhouse. The air of Russell Street, though laden with the acrid stench of dozens of closely packed, identical nailshops with their forges belching heat, felt infinitely pleasant and cool in comparison to that miniature hell.

*'many folk die in a workhouse, one more won't never be noticed'*

Relentless as the swing of those hammers, the words rang on the anvil of her mind. She had come to Russell Street hoping that somehow the child was back with Livvy's friend, that some miracle had caused Gideon Newell to forget his revenge for what, after all, was no fault of the girl. But miracles didn't happen for Saran Chandler. The one begged for nightly in her prayers went unheeded while, daily, all enquiries of her mother and sister met with blank faces and shaking heads.

What had become of them? Had the man who had paid his money to Enoch Jacobs kept them? Were they being subjected to the same abuse the governor of the workhouse had tried to inflict upon herself? Was that the reason for their purchase?

The horror of it choking her throat, she walked on, all around her the sound of hammers mixing with the harassed voices of women hurrying to buy from the market stalls. Every moment of their absence from the workshops, a few less nails were made, meaning fewer pennies to buy their next meal.

Livvy's friend wept on seeing the contents of the basket, her tears leaving pale tracks along dust-covered cheeks.

'I ain't 'eard no more o' the little 'un,' she

sobbed, stacking the precious food into a locker fixed to the wall of the poky room which must serve as kitchen and living room, insisting Saran share a pot of tea. 'That man who fetched her away … I 'ave no knowledge as to who he were but he had to 'ave come from the parish for he were dressed as no nailer would be nor any workman as I knows of, they don't make the kind of money it takes to buy clothes such as he were wearing.'

She would have recognised Gideon Newell, the town was small, its occupants all familiar with one another, yet the woman had said she had no knowledge of the man who had come to her house. The thought brought an instant lift to Saran's spirits only for them to crash with the next. Gideon Newell was no fool. It would have been a simple matter for him to pay someone else to fetch Martha away, some corrupt official, a man without feeling. That had to have been his action. He would not want the people of Wednesbury knowing him for what he was, a man so given to vengeance he would rob a helpless child of its life, so he had paid another to act in his stead; and now that governor would never release Martha to her or anyone else. Luke was blind to the truth, he trusted Gideon, believed him; and she almost had.

'It seems we are destined to always meet this way, Miss Chandler, though I admit any way of meeting with you would afford me great pleasure.' Crossing the market square after leaving Russell Street she almost collided with a tall smiling figure.

Struggling with the confusion of conflicting thoughts Saran blushed. 'Mr Ensell, how ... how very nice to see you.'

'If you meant that you would smile.'

'I ... I'm sorry ... I was deep in thought.'

'But not so deep now, so where is that smile I have had so much difficulty in forgetting?'

She really didn't want to talk, she wanted only to go home to sit and sort the chaos that swirled in her brain; but to brush this man aside would be bad manners.

'Is something wrong, Saran?' Jairus Ensell's own smile slipped away. 'Is there something I might help with?'

The whole thing suddenly too much to bear she lowered her gaze.

'There is something!' Firm and steady as his voice, his hand closed on her elbow and he guided her quickly from the market square. Settled in the tearooms he said quietly, 'What is it, Saran? Please don't deny something is upsetting you, for a girl as sensible as yourself does not cry over nothing.'

'I ... I had bad news–'

'Your family?' he interjected quickly but Saran shook her head.

'No, not my family, the daughter of a friend, a young girl. We had hoped to have her with us to live at Brook Cottage.'

'Ah yes, Brook Cottage...' he nodded, 'news travels fast in a small town and none so fast as in Wednesbury. I heard of William Salisbury's gift and agree with the man, honesty such as yours deserves no less. So why is this young girl not with you?'

'Leaving the tea untouched in her cup Saran drew a long breath, using it against tears welling in her throat.

'The ... the workhouse has refused to release her. I told the governor there was a good home waiting and there would be money to keep her, I even offered reimbursement for the days she had been supported by the parish but the answer was the same, Martha would not be released.'

Across the table the handsome face darkened with anger. 'What!' he ground. 'They refused to release the child, for what reason?'

Her eyes raised to his glistened with moisture, her pale features suddenly turning scarlet.

'You need not answer, Saran,' he said, 'your colour answers for you! But we will see what reply that governor gives to a man. Tell me the name of the girl and of any family she might have, and with your permission I will call upon you at Brook Cottage this evening when Luke can be with you.'

He had left her then, saying that to accompany her home, to where it was known she would be alone at that time of day, would induce gossip he would not have her subjected to.

Recognising the kindness and courtesy she was grateful but had been equally thankful at being left to walk home alone.

Taking the risen bread dough from the hearth she tipped it on a floured board, kneading it for several minutes, minutes filled with the same questions, the same confusion that had twisted and turned in her mind since leaving Russell Street.

Gideon Newell had looked her squarely in the face all the while they had talked, had listened to her apology with not the merest flicker of an eyelid to say it was not justified; Livvy's neighbour had said the man come to her home was not Gideon Newell and Luke, too, was absolutely convinced he had played no part in returning the child to the workhouse, yet the doubt refused to be dismissed.

Setting the dough aside to rise a little longer she stared with sightless eyes into the red heart of the fire.

In spite of his coming with Luke to find her that night, in spite of his not having made the proviso she had thought for taking Martha from the institution, in spite of the regret she had detected behind his telling her that what was done was done, that it was over, in spite of all this still that dreadful suspicion hovered like a black cloud.

But why was it a suspicion she had not divulged to Jairus Ensell? She had told him of her own visit to the workhouse, told him most of what had passed between the governor and herself, but not once had she mentioned the name Gideon Newell. Why?

Flames leaping into the dark chimney matched those burning the question into her heart. Why, when all the evidence pointed away from it, did she still believe Gideon Newell was the man responsible for destroying a little girl's life?

The Elwell children were no longer at the workhouse. Covering the inside of a large basket with a freshly laundered cloth, Saran packed it with loaves and dainty finger-sized rolls she had spent most of the night baking.

Jairus Ensell had kept his word, calling at Brook Cottage that same evening. He had spoken with the governor, seen the register of residents containing the names Joseph and Martha Elwell – destitutes. The date of their entry into the institution had been penned beside the names as well as the date of their being withdrawn, but as to who had taken them only the description 'gentleman' was written.

Covering the deliciously smelling bread with another spotless cloth she carried the basket to the yard, setting it on a hand cart Gideon Newell had helped make.

Gentleman! Grasping the handles of the cart she pushed it towards the town. There had been nothing more, Jairus Ensell had been certain of that, nothing that would give a clue as to where those children had been taken. Like her mother and sister, it seemed they had vanished from the face of the earth. But they had to be *somewhere*.

Luke had listened then shook hands politely when Jairus had left but she had been aware of an underlying current of ... what? Bringing the cart to a halt outside the malthouse, the first stop on a round of deliveries that had begun so quickly, she let the question dwell for a few seconds before acknowledging what she knew to be the answer. There had been an undercurrent of dislike between Luke and Jairus; in fact, Luke made no secret of the fact that on his part it was not simply dislike, it was mistrust. For some reason he could not or would not explain, he did not trust Jairus Ensell.

'Eh up, wench! That there bread be nice enough to eat!'

His red face wreathed in smiles, the maltster came from a doorway set at the top of a short flight of stairs.

Reaching for a fat, round, batch loaf, Saran's own smile greeted his. 'I'll believe that when you order another of these.'

'Then believe it, wench, for I be doin' that now and sayin' along of it you can bring me one o' these every day, for I've tasted none so good since my Bessie were teken ... God rest her.'

Hands coated with the fine mealy dust of wheat rubbed against the apron reaching to the man's feet as he extracted a coin from his pocket and exchanged it for the loaf, which he held close to his whiskered face, breathing deeply the warm aroma.

'I hope you enjoy it!' Saran said as he smiled appreciatively.

'Enjoy it, I'll say I do, wench, that and a bit o' cheese be satisfyin' to any man; why wi' a glass o' wheat wine the queen in her palace could ask no better.'

'My grandfather liked wheat wine, he used sometimes to let me watch him brew.' The delight of memory was shining in her eyes as Saran dropped the coin into her pocket.

'Then your gran'father had good sense as well as good taste, it were smart o' him passing skills to a young 'un; ain't many as wants to learn the old ways since them there toob works an' nailin' shops comes to the town.' His smile gone the old man shook his head sadly. 'Seems no lad be interested ... they all wants this modern way o' earnin' their livin' ... coal an' iron be their god, but one day they'll learn, one day when their insides be rotted by the black dust and their lungs seared from the fires o' the forge or the scorching blast o' iron furnaces, they'll realise just how 'ard a god that be; but you, wench, you seems to 'ave teken the guidance of a mother's hand that showed the mekin' o' good bread, an' if it be you fancies addin' to that the skills o' your gran'father then come you to Ezekiel Millward, I'll gladly teach you all I knows and you'll find no better wheat in all of the country.'

She liked Ezekiel. Pushing the cart along Dudley Street and on through the market square Saran answered the smiles and greetings that came from all sides. The people here had accepted her and the knowledge held comfort, yet at the same time left her unsettled. Each day the order for her dainty rolls and small loaves increased as the cooks in the houses of the town's wealthiest residents saw the purchase of them as a method of reducing their own daily chores and it was proving a way for her to earn her own living, being no longer a burden on Luke; but it also tied her to Wednesbury, prevented her holding to that self-made promise to move on, to widen her search for her mother and Miriam.

She had asked her question so many times. The last of the dozen rolls having been closely inspected by a sharp-eyed cook, Saran took her money and left the large house, hauling her cart aside as a shining black carriage passed along the drive. So many enquiries but only ever one answer, 'I ain't heard o' no woman being bought.' The large house being the last but one of her deliveries she pushed the cart to the High Bullen.

'Eh, wench, that be right good o' you bringin' an old man a bite o' bread an' bacon.'

Stood beside the open gateway of the Coronet Tube Works a man with a wooden stump strapped below the knee of his right leg smiled as Saran bent over the cart and reached for the sandwich she brought each day.

'You be a good wench,' the man beamed his gratitude. 'I tells that young Luke Hipton to hurry and grow so as to marry you afore somebody else do ... he won't know what he's lost 'til some man teks you from him.'

'I don't think Luke need have any thought of that, no man is interested in me.'

Straightening she turned, placing the sandwich in eager hands and as it was taken she lifted her glance. For a moment her eyes locked on a pair which seemed to penetrate to her very soul; then Gideon Newell strode away.

His look had not been that of a guilty man nor an angry one. Pushing the empty cart Saran let her thoughts once more race free. Gideon Newell had given no indication that he had lied about Livvy's daughter, shown no sign of the gratification he must be feeling.

*A man's smile can hide evil in his heart, but the truth of the soul shines in his eyes.*

How many times had she heard her father say those words and how often had she seen the truth of Enoch Jacobs's black soul reflected in that man's narrow eyes as he had watched herself and Miriam?

But there had been nothing remotely resembling that in Gideon Newell's gaze, not once in any of their meetings had she caught the faintest glimpse of anything but truth, so why could she not accept what Luke had? Why could she still not bring herself to believe his innocence?

Catching her foot on a stone she stumbled against the cart, and as she regained her balance she upbraided herself for allowing her attention to wander. Turning her steps along Meeting Street she was calculating the week's requirement of flour when her breath caught in her throat.

It had to be! Transfixed, she stared at the figure sunk to the ground beside the closed door of the workhouse. The patched skirts, the faded shawl, the body curled in upon itself as if waiting for the next blow to fall.

'Mother!' she whispered. 'Oh Lord, thank you ... thank you!'

# 22

'Mother!'

The cart forgotten in the mad leap of joy that surged through every vein, Saran ran the few yards separating her from the figure crouched before the heavy closed door. Miriam must have gone inside, gone to ask for them both to be taken in. But that would not be necessary now, they would not need a place in the workhouse, they were with her ... at last, she had her loved ones safe; they would have a home, food and above all they would never be subjected to the cruelty of Enoch Jacobs ever again. Her mother and her sister, God had given them back to her! Her eyes blinded by tears of pure joy, Saran sank to her knees, gathering the huddled figure in her arms, her lips pressed to the shawl-covered head.

'Mother...' The word trembled from lips caressing the bowed head. 'I tried so hard to find you ... after Enoch Jacobs... Oh, Mother, thank God, thank God you came here!'

Cradled against her chest the woman whose body felt so thin and frail shook with the sobs that wracked one after the other through her wasted frame, but Saran felt only the wild happiness of reunion. A few weeks of loving care and her mother would be well again, and the roses that had faded from her sister's cheeks would bloom with new life. She would care for them, she would never again let them from her sight; they were together at last and no power on earth would separate them a second time!

'It's all over,' she murmured softly against the worn shawl. 'You are safe now, you and Miriam both. You have no need to ask the welfare of the parish, you both have a home waiting for you. Give me a moment to fetch Miriam and I will take you there...'

'No.' The sobbing woman pushed free of the arms holding her, covering her face in the patched shawl. 'The home you speaks of don't be no home for me; as for my girl her don't be inside that workhouse...'

Miriam was not in there! A touch of fear, cold against her heart, killing some of the joy, Saran glanced at the heavy oak door, her heart jerking as the sobbed words were repeated.

They had been sold at the same time. Enoch Jacobs had auctioned them off in that tavern and she had watched them being led away by the man who had purchased them, yet Miriam was no longer with their mother. Had her sister been sold yet again, passed into the hands of some other man simply for money? Thoughts careered more rapidly than Saran's brain could handle, one flying into the next before it could be logically answered. How long ago had that been, had her mother been rejected, given her freedom for whatever reason? No! Though her mind reeled beneath the onslaught of questions that one was repudiated, quashed even as it touched the fringe of recognition. That type of creature, one who paid money for the pleasure of owning a fellow human being, did not grant them freedom. Yet her mother was here, it could only be that she had escaped the man's clutches, that she had seen the chance for freedom and had taken it; but to run from a place – however vile her life had become there – to escape whilst leaving her daughter behind, a child she had ever tried to protect! The idea was preposterous, unthinkable! Rebecca Chandler loved her children too much ever to turn her back on either one of them and that protective love had continued though she had married the lecherous Enoch Jacobs. So why was Miriam not with her? If her sister were not inside that workhouse then where was she ... and who was she with?

Forcing her mind under control she placed both hands on the woman's heaving shoulders while keeping her touch and voice gentle.

'Mother,' she asked quietly, 'where is Miriam?'

A series of stifled sobs hindering the reply, Saran felt the touch of fear close like a block of ice about her heart.

'I ... I don't be knowing...'

So it had come at last. Choked with tears the one sentence Saran dreaded hearing more than any other fought its way past the woman's grief. The long-prayed-for miracle had only been half granted; her mother was restored to her but her sister was still lost. But she would find her. Gathering the weeping woman once more in her arms Saran gazed at the dreaded door through tear-glazed eyes. Yes, given God's help she would find her sister.

'It was lucky I saw you, it's not often I find myself that way but I was visiting an elderly cousin of my mother and Meeting Street was the shorter route back to the town.'

'I'm very grateful to you, I don't know how I could have managed on my own.'

'And I am grateful fate gave me an extra opportunity to be with you, Saran ... albeit for a little while.'

The name slipped easily from Jairus Ensell's tongue, the smile curving his handsome mouth matching its smoothness; and as he took her hand, raising it to his mouth, his voice became soft.

'I pray that same fate might smile upon me daily.'

'That would be an incursion on your time and I would not be responsible for that.' Saran blushed.

Smoky eyes lifted to hers, fingers tightening on the hand she shyly tried to pull away. 'My time is yours,' he said quietly, 'I want you to take every minute of it ... I want–'

'That tea be wanted now!'

Framed in the doorway that gave on to the stairs Luke glared at the scene being played. He could guess what Ensell were at, the same game so many of the likes of him played: win a girl's gratitude and you'd won your way into her bed. But Jairus Ensell were not going to find his prey in this house, nor out of it, if Luke Hipton had any say in the matter. His stare unrelenting he watched their visitor take up his tall hat. There were no need for him to come to Brook Cottage; true, he had helped Saran bring home a woman too overcome with grief to walk unaided, and what with the hand cart and all! But that didn't mean Ensell had to call again tonight!

Seeing Saran's smile, hearing her soft acquiescent reply to his request for permission to call again, Luke felt the animosity to the man build into a wall. Why couldn't Saran smile at Gideon Newell in that way, why couldn't her words to him be sweetly said as they were to Ensell, why did her favour that one above Gideon? Women! He swallowed hard. They had little sense while they was babbies and it seemed they had none at all when they was growed!

He waited for the door to close on Jairus Ensell before reaching for the tray stood alongside an ancient wooden dresser, its shelves filled now with pretty plates, cups and dishes Saran had bought from a potter whose house stood at the end of the lane which had taken the name from the trade once prevalent there. 'I'll tek this upstairs,' he said as Saran returned to the kitchen. 'You set yourself by the fire and rest.'

'You are a sweetheart and I love you.' Dropping a kiss on his cheek Saran smiled as he rubbed a hand ferociously over the spot. 'But you have done enough already and after a day in the tube works you are the one should rest.'

Busying himself setting cups on the tray Luke thought of the man just left. Had Saran fallen in love with him? If she must have a sweetheart, why not Gideon Newell, a man worthy of her? P'raps telling her, telling her Jairus Ensell were no man to trust her life to ... but it were no business of his what Saran did or who her gave her heart to; he was just Luke Hipton, a runaway from the workhouse, a lad who, purposefully or not, had caused the death of a wardress. A murderer! Luke felt the hairs on the back of his neck rise. That is what the law would call him should it ever suspect the part he had played in that drama. But, like the drowning of Saran's stepfather, the death of that hateful woman had never been reported in any newspaper or any Watch station he had dared to look at; but still in his worst nightmares he felt the heavy hand of the Night Watch fasten on his shoulder and heard the words, 'taken to a place of execution'.

Bringing the teapot from the hob Saran caught the look on Luke's face, a look that perfectly portrayed the feelings she sometimes still woke to in the depths of the night when imagination mingled with the darkness, bringing again the horror of those hands touching beneath the bedcovers, the loathsome mouth whispering its sick lies in her ear, when her whole body stiffened with the nauseating fear that had been Enoch Jacobs; that was the look she saw now, Luke was afraid as she once had been.

Setting the prettily painted teapot on the table she went quickly to him and this time he made no effort to rub away the touch of her face against his cheek.

'What is it, Luke?' she asked quietly.

For a moment Luke wallowed in the luxury of being held, allowing memory to replace Saran's arms with those of his mother, letting her lips become the ones that had so many times kissed him and Emmie goodnight; but it wasn't his mother, it was Saran, and she must not think him a cry baby. Breaking away he kept his face averted, using the excuse of fetching milk from the scullery in order to dash away the tears rising to his eyes.

Taking the milk jug from him, adding a little to each cup then filling them with tea, Saran understood the defiant pride of the lad and, respecting it, asked no more questions, instinct telling her it was old memories had painted the look of fear on the young face. But Luke need fear no more institutions, they had a home and, whatever else may happen, she would defy heaven itself to keep it.

'Her be woke now.' Luke gave a sideways nod towards the stairs door. 'Her said yes when I asked would her like a nice cup o' tea but lessen you gets a move on I reckons her'll be asleep again without ever 'avin' a taste of it.'

He was chiding her in order to take her attention from himself. Smiling to herself Saran picked up the stout wooden tray. Luke Hipton *was* a sweetheart but he wasn't quite as smart as he would have himself think.

*'my girl don't be inside that workhouse'*

Carrying the tray slowly up the narrow staircase, Saran let her mind return yet again to the scene in Meeting Street. She had literally thrown the hand cart aside, running to that thin figure whose skirts spread like a dark cloud as it crouched beside that closed door, drawing it into her arms, pressing kisses to the shawl-covered head, her heart leaping with a wild singing joy.

Her mother was returned to her; heaven had, after all, heard the prayer of a broken heart. At first she had not believed her sister was not in that squat austere building begging the charity of the parish, it was only after the words were repeated that the horror of them hit her. Halfway up the stairs she paused, wanting the rest of her thoughts to go away, thoughts in which she had almost believed her mother had managed to escape while leaving Miriam to her fate. How could she have imagined such! Guilt tripped her senses as she forced herself to go on, each step of the stair a mountain it took all of her determination to climb.

*'Where is Miriam?'*

In the silence the words rang in her mind as clearly as if spoken aloud, and the answer followed close behind. *'I don't be knowing!'*

She had held the thin quivering figure in her arms while her brain had reeled from the blow; Miriam was still lost to them.

Stood on the small landing Saran breathed deeply, trying to still the shaking of her hand which had the cups rattling on the tray. There was enough sadness in that small bedroom, she must not add to it.

Tapping at the door with the toe of one boot she waited until it opened. Stepping inside she lay the tray on a small table set to one side of the bed then, straightening, smiled at the figure lying there in a white cambric nightgown, grey hair, combed and braided, lying over each shoulder and highlighting the pale sad face.

'I thought you might appreciate some tea,' she

said, holding a cup for the trembling hand to take.

'Saran, wench, this be right good of you.'

Looking at the figure in the bed, Saran shook her head. 'It is no more than Edward and you did for Luke and myself, Livvy, I am only glad I was in time to prevent you signing the both of you into the workhouse.'

How was it she had made such a mistake ... how could she not have known the figure she held in her arms was not that of her mother?

Having sponged and dried her body, Saran slipped a plain cotton nightgown over her head.

Why had she not recognised the voice as being different, had she not heard that of her mother all the sixteen years of her life?

Taking her hairbrush from the small dressing table she had bought from a second-hand shop she drew it slowly through her hair.

But she had not stopped to think or to ask how. She had seen the crouched figure and suddenly all reason had flown on the wind; it was her mother ... it had to be her mother. And there was the reason for the mistake! She had wanted that reunion so badly, prayed for it so many times, a need in her driving so hard, that rhyme or reason had found no place in her thinking on seeing what her heart had so long desired.

Laying the brush aside, unmindful of the paler streaks the sunlight had painted in her light brown hair, she weaved the heavy strands between her fingers, twining them expertly into plaits on the ends of which she fastened narrow white ribbons.

Longing had made her blind and deaf to all except what she wanted to see and hear, and longing had played her false! Her toilet finished she knelt beside the bed, resting her forehead on clasped hands. It was not her mother and sister she had been reunited with today, but heaven had demonstrated its mercy and thanks must be given. Murmuring her prayers she ended with the words said so many times before, 'Lord, watch over my family, keep them from harm and, if it be Thy will, send them back to me.'

Settled in her bed, the candle blown out, Saran's brain refused to rest. In the shadows cast by a silver moon phantom figures moved, playing out the rest of what had happened outside the workhouse.

*'My girl, my little wench, they say her don't be in there but her has to be, I took her there meself along of her brother.'*

Held close against her shoulder the woman had spoken, but her words, muffled and interspersed with sobs, had failed at first to make any impression on Saran's consciousness. Then, like a stone splashing into water, it had struck, ripples of understanding spreading and widening, forcing itself to the forefront of her mind.

*'along of her brother'*

Each word had been the clang of a bell, leaving her brain reverberating, sounding and resounding until at last she had taken the frail shoulders again in her hands, forcing the woman to look into her face.

What had she felt then! Saran's eyes closed

tight and, though the silvered shadows were cut off, the pictures still played across her eyelids. Her agony had shown! The look on Livvy's face and her strangled cry, *'I be sorry,'* had proved that. It had taken minutes for the shock to fade and the disappointment to become thankfulness that at least Livvy was returned to her home. But then the woman had sobbed out her story. Edward and she had found no work, they had tried in towns and villages but everywhere was the same, no hands were wanted. So Livvy had no home.

*'I 'ad to come back.'*

The sobbed words seemed to echo in the silence of the night, and as Saran's eyes opened the woman's stricken face stared at her from the shadows.

*'I 'ad to see my babbies, hold 'em once more afore I die ... but they don't be 'ere; them inside says they be took out...'*

It had become too much for Livvy then and she had slumped forward, her slight weight pressing Saran back on her heels. She had been struggling to lift the sobbing Livvy to her feet when two strong hands had taken the limp figure, lifting it easily then supporting it with a strong arm while Saran herself clambered upright. Lying in her bed she remembered the rush of relief she had felt at seeing the tall man, a quizzical anxiety marking his handsome face as he reached his free hand to help her to stand.

*'What is happening here?'*

Jairus Ensell had kept hold of her hand while asking the question and now, in the darkness of her room, her cheeks burned with the pleasure of his touch.

At that moment Edward had stepped back into the street and she had pulled quickly free but her nerves had trembled from the knowledge that Jairus Ensell looked only at her.

*'They says as they 'ave no name for the man that took our children!'*

He had looked helplessly at his wife who collapsed against Jairus, her cries pitiful to hear. Jairus! In the soft intimacy of shadow a smile curved Saran's lips. He had been so kind, offering to pay for lodgings for the Elwells, then when she had said they must come to Brook Cottage he had half carried the weeping Livvy the whole of the way, giving no heed to the dried mud brushing from her skirts on his costly clothes; and reaching the house he had drawn water from the well, tipping it into the brick boiler built into the brewhouse then lighting a fire beneath it so Livvy and Edward could both take a warm bath.

So much care for others and for herself – the blush returned, hot and disturbing – those deep eyes had never been far from her face, those hands always there to help; brushing against her own, touching yet not touching. And this evening he had returned with clothing he said was no longer required by his aunt or himself, waving away the thanks of a grateful Edward who had carried them upstairs to his wife.

There had been no onus upon Jairus to give assistance, no responsibility, yet he had done so willingly just as he had several times previously;

he had also repeated his promise to continue to search for the whereabouts of her family and now those of Livvy's children. He had shown nothing but consideration from their very first meeting, wanting no more than friendship; but was that all *she* wanted or had the touch of those fingers, the warmth in those dusky sensual eyes aroused a deeper feeling?

Restless with the emotions churning inside her she climbed from the narrow bed, going to stand at the window that looked out over heathland flirting with dancing beams of silver moonlight.

Had she read too much into what was meant to be no more than a helping hand ... was she allowing herself to see what was not really there?

*'My time is yours.'*

The intoxication of the softly whispered words quickened the flow of blood along her veins, fanning the embers of the fires they had lit, but they had meant nothing! Saran rested her forehead on the window-pane, seeking its coolness.

*'I want you to take every minute of it... I want–'*

What was it he would have said had not Luke interrupted? What was it Jairus Ensell wanted?

Lifting her face from the cool glass she stared out over the moonlit emptiness, a heavier and more pressing question in her heart.

What was it Saran Chandler wanted?

# 23

That bloody cheat of a fogger had tried his tricks again! Zadok Minch fondled the slender-limbed body lying beside him on the wide bed. The price had had to be raised in accordance with the difficulty of obtaining specialised goods. Had to be raised! Irritation tightened his fingers on tender flesh, causing his companion to protest. The price, though, hadn't been all of what was raised; his temper had not merely kept pace with inflation, it had exceeded it. The fogger had shrugged elegantly coated shoulders, saying he could always sell elsewhere, and yes, there were others in Brummajum would pay. But that avaricious swine knew that to keep the price he must keep the circle of buyers small ... too wide and goods lost their intrinsic value.

Smart! Zadok stroked the white thigh. But not as smart as Zadok Minch; he had told that fogger what to do with what he had for sale, though the following of such advice would mean the man being unable to sit down for a very long while.

'What are you smiling about?'

An attractive face lifted from its place on his shoulder as Zadok chuckled.

'Nothing that need bother you, my love.'

At the answer violet eyes darkened, a full-lipped mouth tightening.

'You promised, Zadok,' the husky voice had an edge of pique, 'you promised me there would be no more!'

'And I've kept me word.' Zadok hid the irritation prickling his skin. How many more bloody times would he say that before it became one time too many!

'There is only me, isn't there, Zadok?'

For the present! Zadok kept the thought cloistered in his mind; this one gave the sort of pleasure he wanted, but pleasure could be offset if the giver became too demanding, and there was always another strumpet to be found.

'There be only you,' he lied, trailing a hand over a flat stomach. 'I were smiling at thought of the fogger that were here a while since. He were trying to raise the price of some special nails I were wanting but he reckoned without Zadok Minch, I pay no man over the odds, I told him he couldn't raise nothing with me.'

'Unlike myself!' The attractive face smiled as the slender body lifted, bending its head to touch full lips to Zadok's navel, the tip of a tongue sliding wetly downward. 'I can raise you every time ... all it takes is this.'

As the tongue caressed the tip of his flaring column of flesh Zadok jerked like a marionette.

'You like that, don't you?' Violet eyes teased.

Gasping through clenched teeth, Zadok closed his eyes against the intensity of the rabid fire that leapt in his groin. This was the reason he put up with the whore's possessiveness; this seething passion that had his balls like iron, the pulsing thrill that sent blood rushing like a torrent in his veins, the feverish excitement that had him hard as a stallion.

'You like my tongue, Zadok? But I know you like this more...'

As he felt the body slide away from the bed Zadok's eyes flew open, his dry lips parting with the force of need driving through him, desire beating like a sledgehammer in his brain.

'I'm right, aren't I?' Violet eyes stared provocatively. 'You like this more, so why not take it?'

Yes, he liked that more. Both hands grabbing the slender hips, Zadok drew the tantalising body towards him, burying his face in the tussock of dark-brown hair nestled at the base of the stomach, kissing the warm triangle before snatching the exultant figure down on the bed and rolling it beneath his own inflamed body.

*'We can help the Elwells wi'out Jairus Ensell!'*

Setting a new batch of bread dough to rise in the corner of the hearth, Saran washed the utensils in the scullery, Luke's argument of the evening before running in her mind.

*'Don't take no thinkin' out to see they needs a roof over their 'eads and work for their 'ands!'*

*'But Jairus...'* She had blushed at the way the name slipped from her tongue and Luke too had caught the familiarity.

*'Jairus!'* he had said, irritation giving the name a razor edge of contempt. *'That man ain't the be-all and end-all the way you seems to think!'*

The various dishes and spoons washed she carried them back to the kitchen, putting each in its place. Luke made no secret of his dislike of Jairus Ensell ... but the man could help Livvy and Edward, surely Luke could see that.

*'There be no rush so far as the Elwells be concerned,'* Luke had continued obstinately. *'They don't neither of 'em be fit enough yet for work and 'til it be otherwise they can stay here, and as to their board and keep I'll pay that meself.'*

His words had stung and though she realised they were said in the heat of the moment tears had prickled her eyes. Seeing them, Luke had been beside her in a moment, words of apology tumbling from his lips.

*'It don't be the way it sounded... I didn't mean... Saran, honest... I knows it were not the money you was thinkin' of.'*

*'We are both tired.'* She had smiled immediately at the lad who was as dear as any brother could have been. *'Why don't we talk of this tomorrow?'*

But they had not talked of it. Luke had risen as usual at the last moment, leaving just enough time to wash beneath the pump in the yard and swallow two gulped mouthfuls of tea before dashing off to the tube works. Spooning tea into the pot Saran covered it with water bubbling in the heavy iron kettle. Luke was content with his lot and she too should be content, fate had been kind, it had given them Brook Cottage, and Wednesbury was providing them with the means of earning a living. But true contentment could never be hers until her mother and sister were here with her.

At a knock on the rear door of the house Saran looked up and Edward Elwell stepped through the scullery into the kitchen, the clothes Jairus Ensell had left for him hanging loose on his thin frame.

'Be my Livvy all right?'

Her heart twisted as the desperate fear locked in every word and highlighted in panic-stricken eyes chased thoughts of her own unhappiness from her mind. Setting the kettle back over the fire she smiled reassuringly.

'Livvy is resting. I was just making some tea, perhaps you could take some to her.'

'That be more'n kind, Saran wench, but me and Livvy will be takin' no more of what we 'ave no means of payin' for. With your permission I'll go fetch her and we'll be on our way.'

'To where?'

Confronted by a strength which gave the question the impetus of a demand Edward Elwell shook his head.

'Where don't matter no more, since we don't 'ave our children it meks no odds where we go.'

'It does to me!' Saran snapped. 'And it does to Luke, we are both of the same mind. You and Livvy must remain here at Brook Cottage until you can get a place of your own.'

Slumping into a chair Edward lowered his head into his hands. 'That won't never be,' he murmured, 'I've asked at every place in Wednesbury but I would 'ave had more luck had I been asking for the moon. There don't be nothing, not even collectin' night soil.'

'But you have a skill, you are a nail-maker and nails will always be wanted.'

Edward's head shook without lifting. 'Ar,

there'll always be a call for nails but not them as be med by hand, they are being turned away; nail masters be buyin' cheaper, machines be doing a man's work and tekin' the bread from his mouth. There be others in the town as be near following the path Livvy and me was forced to tread but, like me, they'll find the world 'as no heart.'

She had once thought as Edward did now, but some power had guided her steps and brought her to the heath where she had helped a woman give birth, brought her to Wednesbury and to this house ... and Luke, it had brought her Luke, the most cherished gift of all.

'Edward.' Calmness replacing the twitch of impatience that moments ago had made her words hard, she waited until the man's head lifted and his hopeless gaze fastened on her. 'Edward, please don't say any of this to Livvy, not yet; I fear she might not have the strength to face another setback.'

Saran smiled at the man stood in her pretty parlour, sunlight from the window creating a blue crown on jet-black hair. 'It is a wonderful offer, Mr Ensell, and so kind of you.'

'No, not kind, Saran...' he stepped close, eyes dark as his hair looking deeply into her own, 'selfish ... my offer is made on purely selfish grounds. It provided me with an excuse to call upon you.'

Mesmerised by the intense look which seemed to drive into her deepest parts she tried to answer, but when none came the handsome face took on a slight frown.

'My bad manners, my illiberality at calling without invitation is unforgivable...'

Reaching a hand to his sleeve as he took up his hat she blushed as it was caught between strong fingers. 'Your coming here is nothing if not kindness, to think of Livvy–'

'It is not for the Elwells I came,' he interrupted, his eyes boring into hers. 'True, the offer of a place with my grandmother provided the opportunity but the real cause was you. You have come to mean a great deal to me, Saran; since the moment of my first seeing you, of catching you in my arms as you fainted, I have thought of little but you. I love you ... I know I should not say it but I must or burst from want of doing so. I love you, Saran, and I ask you to become my wife.'

She was to become another man's wife! Stood behind the small cottage that had been his home from birth Gideon Newell stared across the wide pastureland and crop fields that belonged to Oakeswell Hall. Luke had broken the news, repugnance staining his every word.

*'Ensell be in love with 'er.'*

The memory twisted like a knife blade in the chest.

*'He asked would 'er marry him and her said yes.'*

It had cut deep, taking the breath from his body, but in his hatred of the idea Luke had not noticed the pain lance across his face, a pain that burned now as it had that morning.

*'Why?'*

The talk had resumed while they had sat together in the yard of the tube works, Luke eating the fresh bread and cheese Saran had left for him when giving the old gatekeeper the sandwich it had become a habit to save for him.

*'Why would Ensell want to marry Saran? I would never have placed him as a man to marry beneath him, seems too much the dandy for that.'*

The lad had ranted on until a short blast of a steam whistle recalled them to the noise and heat of the tube works. But the silence Gideon had kept had been only in his mouth while the whole of the rest of the day his insides yelled the turmoil in his brain.

To have shared his suppositions with the lad would have added fuel to the flame of young judgement and done no more than anger a young woman who already held no liking for Gideon Newell and would rightly see any words of his as having no business in her life.

Nor had he any rights and, for that matter, neither had Luke, they were no kin to Saran Chandler, they were simply friends. No, no, that was wrong... Luke Hipton was a friend, Gideon Newell could not even claim that. But what was Jairus Ensell claiming? More than friendship; but love? Rain clouds gathered force, besieging the moon, threatening its golden beauty with an all-encompassing darkness which matched the turgid shadows in his heart.

That was the doubt that had played in his mind since Luke had divulged the man's asking Saran to marry him; was Jairus Ensell truly in love with her or did he see what she owned as more desirable? Saran Chandler had no fortune but was Ensell aware of that or did he think William

Salisbury had given a great deal more than he had, so seeing that reward as a way of paying for a few more years of fancy living?

The first few drops of rain touching like tears against his face, he turned towards the house. That was Jairus Ensell's first and only love, that much he would stake his life on; a fogger who thought nothing of taking the last penny from a man and leaving him to starve while the fruits of those labours were dedicated to upholding his own lifestyle. Like a leech Ensell clung to a man's back, and like a leech he sucked until there was no more left to drain; would he do the same to Saran Chandler? There was no doubt of it! Bypassing the cottage Gideon strode into the fast-gathering storm. The only question was whether he would take the true prize he had set his sights on before or after becoming Saran Chandler's husband?

'It be good o' the man mekin' the offer he has, but the missus, her don't want to go live Wolverhampton way.'

Edward Elwell looked apologetically at the two people sat with himself and Livvy in the lantern-lit kitchen of Brook Cottage.

'It ain't like I don't be grateful...' Livvy held a scrap of cotton cloth to her trembling mouth, 'I am, wench, truly so; but my babbies ... I can't leave 'em again, not a second time.'

A glance at Luke telling her he understood the woman's mental attitude, her complete refusal to admit to herself her children were lost to her, Saran touched a sympathetic hand to those clutching the makeshift handkerchief.

'I understand,' she said pityingly, 'and so will Mr Ensell.'

'We wouldn't want him thinking as we had throwed that offer back at him ... but with Livvy ... the way things be...'

'Mr Ensell will not think any such thing, Edward, he knows how broken-hearted you both are and, believe me, he will continue to search for the children as he will search for my family.'

Ensell could think what the hell he liked! Luke kept his jubilation well hidden as Saran poured tea they all hoped would soothe Livvy. At least the Elwells would be free of him if they accepted the proposal he had talked over with Gideon during the day. Talked over! That was hardly an accurate description, getting Gideon to say anything at all had been harder than drawing iron.

'Forgive the question, Edward, but do you understand figures?'

The tea poured and cups passed to each, Saran resumed her seat as she asked the question.

'Ar, wench, some.' Edward nodded. 'Me father taught me to read and to write and to know me numbers though I be no scholar.'

'Then, given the opportunity, you could weigh and record a delivery of nails?'

'I could do that easy, wench, and tell the true price, unlike the foggers and nail masters that has this town by the throat.'

'And the iron strip necessary for the making of nails, could you take on the responsibility of ordering that?'

Where would all this lead? A frisson of apprehension tickled along Luke's spine. It was one thing for him to throw his money away, but for Saran to do the same! Opening his mouth he closed it, saying nothing; he had argued ... he had tried reasoning, but Saran was adamant.

'I knows the nailing well,' Edward Elwell was replying, 'I was born to it as were many a man in Wednesbury, I don't think there be any part o' the trade be unknown to me though, to tell it honest, I ain't had no experience of the part you be speakin' of.'

'No matter. There is, however, one more question I would have you answer but before I ask it there is something Luke would like to say.'

Edward Elwell took his wife's hand, holding it between his own.

'You don't need to say it, lad, me and the missus we knows it be time we was on our way.'

'T'ain't what I were about to say at all, Mr Edward.' Luke used the respect he had adopted when speaking to the man. 'I were going to say that you and Mrs Livvy ... well, if you goes tomorrow and finds a house, a little 'un like, then ... then the money be here for the renting.'

'Oh lad!' Edward's choked words followed his wife's cry. 'Oh lad... God bless you... God bless you.'

Her own feelings reflecting in her eyes, Saran smiled at an embarrassed Luke. How many in today's world had so generous a heart?

'You will overlook my Livvy not givin' her own thanks straightaway, but her still be heartbroke...'

The rest choked in the man's throat and he

turned his head, not wanting his own tears to be seen.

'I think Mrs Livvy and yourself should both listen to the next question Saran be goin' to ask.'

A quick glance telling her to speak on before he as well as the Elwells would give way to tears, Saran nodded.

Edward's smile glistened in moist eyes. 'Ask whatever you will, Saran wench, you can be sure Edward Elwell will answer truthful.'

There was still time for her to change her mind, to say different to what she had outlined to him. Watching the girl he had come to love as a sister, Luke mentally urged the words to remain unsaid.

'Before I do,' Saran spoke quietly, 'Luke and I both want it clearly understood that whatever you and Livvy choose to do has our complete support. I wanted you to hear Luke's suggestion before I made one of my own, that suggestion being you act for me, become a manager.' Seeing the utter surprise come to the man's face, she wondered for one fleeting moment whether what she had thought on the whole day was really the best for all concerned; if it went wrong she would lose everything, which was the very reason she had resisted every argument of Luke's that he should be involved. What money he had he must keep against his own work being taken from him.

'Me ... a manager...!'

Edward Elwell was almost tongue-tied with the unexpectedness of it.

'You have what it takes, you said it was a job you could do.'

'Ar, so it be, but a manager...'

'If you have no liking for my suggestion then take the offer Luke has made. I will buy the necessary equipment and iron for you to start and will purchase the nails you produce.'

Saran was mad, she was out of her mind! Luke swallowed the protest rising in his throat. She knew absolutely nothing about the making of nails and even less about the selling of 'em!

'You ... a nail master ... eh, wench, you 'ave no idea what it is you'd be tekin' on.'

'Which is why I need you.'

His head swinging slowly from side to side, Edward Elwell looked into the young face. The wench had gone through some hard times but her had no idea of what becoming a nail master would hold, her would have to fight tooth and nail with the roughest.

'A nail master can't mek a livin' from just one nailer...'

'I know that, Edward. But wasn't it you said nail masters have this town by the throat, that they are choking the life from its families? Then help me, work with me to break that stranglehold.'

'It be easy to talk, wench.'

Determination tightening her mouth, Saran sat upright in her chair. 'Yes,' she said, 'it is easy to talk and easy to back down; which will you do, Edward?'

# 24

'It don't do for me to tell you your business, Saran wench, but renting a warehouse be costly.'

'But we will need somewhere to weigh and store nails and the brewhouse isn't big enough, and I wouldn't want this kitchen turned into a storeroom.' Saran looked at the man whose delight in accepting her offer to act as middleman had been obvious.

'I knows that as well as you does,' Edward Elwell nodded, 'but where be the sense in payin' out good money...'

'So what be your way?' Luke asked.

'Well, lad,' releasing his wife's hand the older man leaned forward, tracing a finger over the spotless tablecloth as he spoke. 'This 'ere be the canal an' these be the buildings standin' close alongside.'

'They don't be warehouses!'

'No, lad, they don't, but that there biggest could be. Don't you see,' he looked at Saran, 'by usin' one o' your own outbuildings you cuts the cost down considerable, the only outlay you would 'ave would be the buyin' of a pair o' weighing scales and a man took on to keep the accounts.'

An accountant! That would be unnecessary for it was a job she could do herself, taught as her father had taught her; but offsetting the cost of a warehouse was something well worth the considering.

'Saran.' Livvy Elwell's sad eyes watched the slender figure reach a black-bound volume from a drawer of the dresser and bring it to the table. 'Saran, I 'opes you don't mind ... my Edward 'e were only thinkin' to 'elp.'

'And he has, Livvy.' Her smile reassuring, Saran resumed her seat. 'Edward,' she looked at the man dressed slightly incongruously in the clothes given by Jairus Ensell, clothes no nail-maker could ever have afforded, 'the barn stood nearest to the canal, could that make a suitable warehouse?'

'I 'ad a look at it yesterday – beggin' your pardon for not askin'–' Edward paused until a wave of Saran's hand told him he had caused no offence. 'Seems there couldn't be a better place, not to my mind; it 'as plenty o' space and within 'alf a dozen yards them nails can be on a narrow boat and off to anywheres you've a mind to send 'em.'

'And the nailers, would they be willing to bring their nails here to Brook Cottage?' The question was Luke's.

Despite the heaviness weighting his heart since the loss of his children, he smiled. 'Edward Elwell weren't the only man to carry a sixty-pound load of iron strip from Brummajum and almost the same weight back again in the form o' tacks or nails, and neither is 'e the only one will be happy to do business wi' a nail master who will deal fair wi' him.'

'You said *almost* the same weight of iron is returned.'

'That be right, lad.' Edward nodded. 'Account 'as to be teken o' waste, the iron rod be worked until the last piece be too little to handle, that be waste; and every man reckons it to be fourteen out of every sixty pound.'

'Does the nail master absorb the cost of wasted iron?'

'You'd see the stars shine in the daytime sooner than you'd see that! No, wench,' he answered Saran, 'each worker stands his own loss, though some of 'em welds together the fag ends o' the iron rods so as to offset some o' the loss, but the work involved teks valooable time and them nails as is made from welded bits 'ave to be sold as sub-standards, for which the nail master pays no more'n a quarter of the price.'

'But there is always some left unused ... what becomes of that?'

'The fogger teks it, reckons 'e be doin' a man a favour, and it be a case of letting it be carted away or 'ave it pile up around the feet, and nail-shops be small enough places to work in wi'out piles o' rusting iron clogging every corner.'

'And the fogger ... the middleman, what does 'e do with it?'

Saran listened to the question she had not thought to ask. The man was once more showing in the boy.

'Teks it to the nearest iron foundry and sells it, scrap iron can be melted down and reworked.'

A double gain. Saran's glance dropped to the book lying closed beneath her hand. Was it any wonder nail-making was profitable for all except the nailer himself! Looking again to Edward she said, 'Any man who brings his waste iron to us will have the weight recorded and suitable payment given.'

'With respect, wench, I must point out summat it seems you ain't thought on. Every man I spoke with was in favour o' bringing his work to you but each one as does will lose his forge and his bellows for they be the property o' his nail master and wi' them took from him a man can't work.'

Maybe the owner would sell, and if not...? She would cross that particular bridge when she came to it.

'The warehouse near the canal...' she switched the conversation back to the staffing point, 'there is another building close beside it, one I think – given a little work – would become a comfortable house.'

'Ar,' Edward nodded, 'it'd be comfortable enough forra prince.'

'Oh I wouldn't dream of offering it to a prince,' Saran smiled, 'but I am offering it to you and Livvy.'

Watching the man later, his arm supporting his wife as he helped her to the stairs, Saran remembered the words she had brushed aside: *'each one as does will lose his forge and his bellows'*

Bridges were sometimes rickety and sometimes they collapsed beneath the feet!

*'The world is changing and we must change with it or go under.'*

Only part of his mind was on what his employer had told him as Gideon nodded goodnight to Luke, watching the lad sprint through the works' gate eager to be home.

'Be you off an' all, Gideon lad?'

'Not yet, there's a job I want to finish.' Gideon smiled at the gatekeeper stood sentinel at the works' entrance.

'You does more'n your share in that there works, but then John Adams don't be a bad 'un to work for, he'll see you right, I don't doubt. Let me know when you be done.' The gatekeeper limped away, his wooden leg stomping heavily on the ground.

Yes, John Adams would pay him for the extra hours. Gideon turned back into the empty factory. Unlike so many of the mine owners or nail masters who saw extra hours given to a job as no more than their rights. Would Saran Chandler develop the same attitude? Saran Chandler a nail master ... it was preposterous, the whole idea was ludicrous! Whoever heard of a woman becoming a nail master, let alone one as young as she was; she had no knowledge of the trade and none of the world of business; it was a cut-throat world and the men in it would eat her alive. Hadn't he tried to prevent such stupidity ... tried to talk sense into the girl? Luke had grinned at the questions, answering, *'It be a waste o' breath. When Saran decides summat, it be decided.'*

Like she had decided to marry Jairus Ensell! Despite having told himself that was one decision made absolutely no difference to him, Gideon felt his heart twist. Taking the strip of red-hot iron from the forge he picked up a heavy hammer. Saran Chandler had made her choice, now he must make his.

The door to the works closed behind him, Gideon glanced at the tiny hut that provided shelter for the old watchman. There was no need to disturb him, he would see the gate closed when he roused from his nap and realise the job had been finished and he, Gideon, had gone home.

His boots making virtually no sound on the hard-packed earth that was the works' yard he was almost to the gate when a sound had him standing still. A feral cat? There were plenty of them running wild on the heath. But that was no cat! He listened, muscles tensed, nerves alert. Cats could scramble over iron tubes and make no sound. Motionless, silent except for the throb of a pulse beating in his throat, he glanced about the yard. Blanketed beneath the night it lay still. He must have been mistaken. A day of never-ending hammers striking iron could play tricks with the hearing. He was half turned again towards the gate when, breaking free of cloud, the moon bathed the yard in a brilliant glow, gilding the pile of tubes stacked ready for collection, and on the crest of them a figure.

'Hey!' Even as he shouted, Gideon was running across the yard.

Balanced on the tubes the figure twisted its head then both arms lifted as the metal beneath its feet moved.

'Jump!' The danger immediately obvious to him Gideon yelled, 'Jump, you fool!'

But the instruction was lost amid the clang of tubes moving and rolling, shifting beneath the figure which, losing its balance, fell backward beneath the tumbling mass of iron.

'What the 'ell!' Blinking sleep from his eyes the crippled gatekeeper stumbled from his hut. 'What be gooin' on, Gideon lad?'

'A thief.' Gideon was already tearing at the heap of fallen tubes, throwing them aside in his haste to reach a figure that might already be crushed beyond help.

'A thief!' The old man shuffled clear of flying iron. 'But there be nowt 'ere for the tekin' 'cept toobs or ironstrip and a bloke can't carry enough o' them on 'is back to mek 'em worth the trouble o' sellin'.'

'Well, that was what he was taking.' Gideon straightened as he lifted the last tube. 'Look for yourself ... in his hand.'

Stepping forward, the brilliant moon making it easy to see, the gatekeeper blew through gapped teeth. 'Christ, Gideon lad ... it be naught but a babby!'

A little more than that but only just. What in the flicker of moonlight he had taken to be a crouching man was just a boy, probably younger than Luke.

'Is he ... is he dead?'

The question trembled in Gideon's mind as it had trembled on the other man's lips. Was the lad dead ... killed for a strip of iron! Lifting the boy carefully he carried him to the small hut, laying him on the makeshift table which almost filled the narrow space.

Bringing his lantern closer the old man held it over a face streaked with blood, catching his breath as he looked. 'I knows that lad,' he said, 'I've knowed 'im from the minute of his bein' born and I knows he wouldn't never thieve nuthin'.'

'You know him?'

'Course I does, and so will you. Look closer, Gideon lad, look past the cuts an' the bruises then tell me what you sees.'

Smoothing back the hair plastered to brow and cheeks, Gideon took the lantern, holding it closer to the small face.

'Oh my God,' he breathed. 'Oh Lord, it's...'

'That be right,' the older man nodded, 'that there be Edward Elwell's son.'

'You bloody fool!' Zadok Minch hurled the whip he had been holding against the wall, the leather of it leaving a blood-stained trail across its surface. 'Why the hell did you let her bring it up?'

'I ... I'm sorry...'

'Sorry!' It rang around the elegant room. 'Sorry be buggered, where the hell were you?'

'I ... I was cooking ... my hands were covered in pastry when you rang.'

'You be lucky your whole body don't be covered in blood!' Glaring at the woman who had been his wife for ten years Zadok tasted the sour dislike he had known since making her his bride, though for the first few months of marriage her father's money had sweetened his tastebuds. It had set him up, paving a way which had led to his becoming, among other things, a nail master, a business which paid for his little excesses.

'God Almighty!' He kicked against a delicate spindle-legged table sending it tumbling to the floor, a dainty Staffordshire figurine it held crashing into pieces. 'How many times...? How many times have I said it? Never let nobody 'cept yourself bring it up. Don't that be plain enough for you ... be you so bloody stupid you can't understand a simple order such as that!'

'Zadok, I ... I have apologised...'

His small eyes seeming to recede even further into puffy sockets, long side-whiskers quivering from anger working the heavy jaw, Zadok swept a hand along the ornate mantelshelf, smashing porcelain into the stone hearth.

'Apologies!' he bellowed. 'What bloody good be they, will they repay the cost of what be lost? Goods such as that don't grow on trees, they costs a man money!'

And what do they cost a wife? Trembling in fear of the whip lying against the wall, the terrified woman gave no voice to the thought. She had long ago learned it was for her own good to keep silent about many things.

'Gone!' He ranted on. 'Twenty-five pounds gone and all on account of you not tekin' note of what I says! God in Heaven, I ought to bloody well have you committed.'

And take who in my place? The woman stood silent while the room reverberated to the sounds of breaking china and falling furniture. Who but a wife, a woman condemned by the laws of marriage to become no more than a man's chattel, bound by the laws of the land which said she must obey without question, while it allowed him to take every penny which had once been hers. To be committed to an institution would be infinitely preferable to the life she was forced to live here in this house, having to aid a husband she detested and to stand by whilst he had a life she hated even more. But Zadok would never have her put away, beneath his ranting and raving, beneath his cruelty, lay the one thing which stayed him from signing her into total obscurity, the assurance her presence in this house provided, assurance that pronounced before the outside world that Zadok Minch was a caring, upright man faithful to his wife. A God-fearing man bent only on the business of a nail master.

'Do you want me to...'

'What!' Zadok's clenched fist drove heavily down on a sideboard setting bottles rattling in their silver holders. 'What could I possibly want you to do, you whose brain has no competition with that of a corpse? Just see this place cleaned up afore I come home!'

Caught by the heavy frame pushing her aside Zadok's wife fell, striking her head against the carved oak sideboard. Pausing only to look he strode from the house.

Edward Elwell's son! Gideon looked at the pale blood-streaked face, its eyes closed. What on earth was he doing here, hadn't that governor said the Elwell children were no longer inmates of the workhouse?

'Do he be dead?'

The old man's question chasing his thoughts,

Gideon brought his cheek closer to the still lips. 'No.' He straightened, handing back the lantern. 'He's breathing though it be shallow.'

'Thank the Almighty.' The gatekeeper crossed his chest with a forefinger of one hand. 'But there be bound to be bones broke, that were a might o' iron tumbled about 'im. I don't think he should be moved 'til the parish doctor 'as teken a look at 'im.'

And reported his whereabouts to the Board of Governors who, if the lad had indeed been given over to some businessman, would simply hand him back. Rejecting the idea, Gideon ran a hand gently over the boy's limbs. He had worked many years in the tube trade and witnessed more than one accident where men had been injured by falling tubes or red-hot iron, and he had learned how to recognise broken bones.

'There's no sign of anything broken.' He turned to the man watching him. 'Maybe we should wait before disturbing the doctor.'

'You thinks that be wisest?'

'I do.' Gideon nodded, hoping the older man would raise no objection. 'But should the lad not be conscious in a few minutes then I'll run along to Holyhead House and bring the doctor here.'

Was his decision the right one? Gideon watched the old gatekeeper fetch a blackened kettle from the brazier which burned outside the door of the hut and pour hot water into an enamelled basin. Taking the piece of wet cloth the man handed him he gently wiped the blood from the boy's face, his mouth tightening as purple bruises showed dark against the skin.

These were not the marks of a newly occurred accident, bruises took time before they showed like these.

Beneath the gentle sponging the small body stirred and the eyelids flickered open.

'It's all right, lad, you're quite safe but you had a bit of a mishap so just stay still a while.'

Fear, stark and desperate, flared in the swollen eyes and for a moment it seemed the boy would try leaping from the table.

'Gideon be right, you needs lie still, Joseph lad.'

'Gran'father... Gran'father Bates...'

'Ar, lad,' the old man took the trembling hand, patting it gently, 'it be Gran'father Bates. You be 'ome, son.'

Brewing tea beside the open brazier Gideon and the gatekeeper talked quietly.

''E don't be kin to me,' the older man said, his voice low, 'but I been friends wi' his folk and there'n afore 'em, that be the reason of both Livvy's little 'uns calling me gran'father.'

It seemed the workhouse did let the boy go but what of his sister ... was she also taken, as Ensell was told, or was she still there, as Saran was told? Gideon glanced through the open door to where the young boy still rested. There was something not right in all this ... something not right at all!

'I don't think he is seriously hurt.' Gideon returned his glance to the older man who handed him a tin mug filled with hot sweet tea.

'Me neither, though it be a miracle what wi' all that iron tumblin' round 'im.'

'Some of the tubes crossed each other, preventing most of them actually landing on the boy, but nevertheless it is a miracle.'

A crutch under one arm his crudely fashioned leg resounding on the wooden floor, the old man entered the hut, asking as he went, 'Be you awake, Joseph lad?'

'I ... I want me mother!'

'An' you shall go to 'er but first tek you a sup o' tea, it'll 'ave you feelin' better.'

Obediently, the boy reached for the cup held to him, a cry of pain becoming a groan of agony as Gideon's helping arm passed around his back. Handing the cup to the gatekeeper he bent over the boy.

'Joseph, the pain, show me where you feel pain.'

The small face glistened with moisture. 'Me back ... it be me back.'

The fingers and toes moved, arms, legs, neck all moved independently, which indicated no serious harm to the spine. Gideon breathed a sigh of relief.

'I be sorry to cause you trouble.' Clenching his teeth against the effort, the boy sat up. 'You ... you won't tell me mother I were stealin'? I ... I just wanted a piece of iron rod and I would 'ave brought it back, honest I would.'

'You have caused no trouble.' Gideon smiled kindly. 'But why do you want an iron rod?'

'Ar, Joseph lad, why steal a bit of iron rod?'

Tears welling on to his cheeks the boy answered, 'I ... I wanted to do to 'im as he done to me ... no, no, Gran'father Bates that don't be true ... I wanted to do more'n that, I wanted to kill 'im!'

'Kill!' The old man looked aghast. 'Who be it

you wanted to kill, lad?'

Whimpering as he removed a tattered shirt Edward Elwell's son slid to his feet. 'The man who done this,' he muttered, 'I wanted to kill the one that done this.'

# 25

'I was not expecting you.'

'I don't need make no bloody appointment!' Zadok Minch glared at the attractive face, its painted mouth pouting affectedly.

In a voice soft, melodious and above all careful, the slender figure dressed in a deep-violet taffeta housecoat caught with lilac ribbon over a matching silk nightgown answered, 'No, my dearest, of course you need make no appointment, it is simply that I could have prepared something...'

'This be my house, paid for by me, same as everything in it ... and that includes you!'

Throwing his coat aside Zadok stormed up a curving staircase.

As you are making perfectly plain! The thought adding no smile to generous lips, the attractive figure followed him, heavily ringed hands lifting taffeta skirts and revealing beaded satin slippers.

'Brandy!' Slumped in a winged armchair Zadok bellowed the order.

'Would you care for a bite of supper?'

'Tcha!' Zadok swallowed the golden amber liquid in one gulp, thrusting the glass forward for more.

It was rare for Zadok to come here, usually the boot was on a very different foot, with an invitation coming via his wife so meetings took place in his own house, with no trace of suspicion adhering to them; why then was tonight different? Handing over the brandy the rouged mouth smiled but asked no question.

'Bloody woman!' Zadok snatched at the glass. 'Why the hell do I put up with her? Never let nobody but yourself do it...'

Do what? Lowered eyelids hid the interest flaring in violet depths.

'...but did her take notice?' Brandy tipped into his mouth choked the words. 'Like bloody hell her did!'

He was speaking of his wife, that drab mousy woman he treated like a slave. Emerald following diamond, each ring was slipped from long fingers and laid carelessly on a side table, but beneath a seeming indifference Zadok's companion listened intently.

'Was baking, her said...' the empty glass shot forward, 'hands covered wi' pastry, her said, so her sends the other one.'

The lovely mouth smiled sympathetically as the heavily chased glass was filled, a little more added to it than before. 'Was that really so bad, she was cooking something especially delicious for you, I'm sure.'

Half the drink swallowed, Zadok's eyes shrank into folds of fat.

'Cooking! I don't bloody keep her to cook, I keeps her to do as I say, but seems that be too much for her pathetic brain to comprehend! But things'll be altered from now on...'

Words dredging up from the bottom of the glass sent a shiver through the slender body.

'...things'll be altered now her's seen what be

done when Zadok Minch be crossed!'

'I'm sure they will. Now relax while I pour us both a drink.'

Helped to feet already unsteady from the effects of brandy, Zadok weaved his way across the tastefully furnished room, dropping heavily on a cream-silk-covered bed.

'Twenty-five poundsh,' he slurred, accepting his refilled glass, 'twenty-five poundsh gone ... gone ... all the fault of that shtupid bloody woman!'

Sliding free several pins, shaking the luxurious folds of thick brown hair to tumble over shapely shoulders, the elegant figure smiled while keeping a distance from the grabbing hands. Zadok Minch would soon be in a deep alcoholic sleep but before he was…

'Twenty-five pounds is a lot of money ... did your wife lose it?'

'Shent the other one ... let her bring it.'

That was no answer and soon the man would be incapable of any answer, and tomorrow... Zadok Minch would be sober tomorrow.

Fingers toying with each lilac ribbon, sliding them seductively one by long slow one, dusky violet eyes giving their specific invitation, the housecoat whispered to the floor, settling like a pool on the cream carpet.

'She should not have done that.' The silk gown rustled downward, Zadok's eyes devouring the slender figure remaining just beyond his reach.

Smoky with pretended desire, violet eyes stroked the whiskered face, long fingers sliding enticingly over prettily rounded hips.

'Poor Zadok,' the mouth pouted, full and

luscious as ripe fruit, 'what can I do to make you forget how much you have lost?'

It would take only moments. Hair shimmering in the light of candles, hips swaying seductively, the smiling figure glided one step nearer, a slow voluptuous movement that had Zadok groaning for its promised rapture. But he would not get it yet, first he must fume a little more over his lost money.

'Losht ... twenty-five poundsh...' Podgy fingers clutched as the reached-for temptation was denied him and Zadok allowed himself to be pressed back on the pillows.

Bent over the alcohol-dazed man, thick folds of intoxicatingly perfumed hair brushing his face, long-fingered hands worked quickly, stripping the heavy figure of its clothing, while all the time the bewitching music of whispered words added to Zadok's self-pity.

'So much money, could your wife have taken...'

'Not her!' Zadok's hands reached out, the desire robbing him of his senses. 'That bloody fogger took my poundsh ... brought me a lad ... a sweet young...'

The rest was lost as Zadok buried his mouth in the glistening mound, but his words were not needed.

*'a lad ... sweet ... young'*

They burned in the mind. There were to be no more ... he had vowed he wanted only one lover, only one to share his games... So much for promises. Thoughts like acid flowed hot in every beautiful inch. Zadok Minch could lie to a fogger, he could cheat the nailers and beat his mousy downtrodden wife ... he could also miscalculate! He thought himself believed when saying there were no others...

*'sweet ... young'*

The words scorched like a brand. But that was a lie. All pretence gone from the violet eyes they stared cold and deadly as a cobra at the nuzzling head. But Zadok Minch had reckoned himself short. As fingers reached for the hardened flesh throbbing against the nail master's paunch, Zadok's lover smiled viciously. He had played his old game again, that was a mistake!

Hands to each side of the rotund face lifted it, the lovely eyes gleaming hard as Zadok's passion. Then, a smile still playing on the full lips, the slender body rolled beneath the one stretched on the bed. Zadok liked his games but he could find himself playing with more than soft flesh and a willing body!

His whole body tense with rage and disgust Gideon looked at the boy's back. Long red weals curved across it, open and bloody ... the marks of a whip. The lad had been horsewhipped!

'Lord, Gideon ... who could 'ave done such a thing ... an' to nobbut a lad?'

'Heaven knows,' Gideon breathed his answer. 'But not all of its angels will prevent my killing the swine should I find out.'

Helping the boy back into his shirt the gatekeeper's hands were gentle but his voice was firm. 'That can wait, first them wounds need tending afore they turns bad ways.'

Gideon acknowledged the advice. Rust from

the iron tubes and dirt from the ground the lad had fallen on would soon have those cuts infected, blood poisoning was too dangerous to take chances with.

'I'll get the doctor...'

In the uncertain light of the lantern the old man's head shook. 'No, lad, there be no better salve for any lad's wounds than a mother's love; he needs to be wi' Livvy. Take 'im to where her be, her'll know what to do.'

'Don't let 'im take me back ... please, Gran'father Bates, don't let 'im take me back to that 'ouse!'

''Ave no fear, young 'un,' the old man smiled at the small cringing figure, 'Gideon Newell won't give you to none saving your own mother, an' if I be any judge her'll fight the devil 'isself afore ever her lets you go again.'

Draping his own jacket carefully over the lacerated shoulders, Gideon echoed the older man. 'You have my word, Joseph, I will hand you to your parents and no one else.'

The frightened eyes had looked again to the gatekeeper before finally accepting the words as truth. Careful not to cause the lad more pain than he had to, Gideon carried him, his footsteps slow. Who was it the lad dreaded being given to ... and the other one, Livvy's daughter, was she in the same hands?

'This don't be the way to my 'ouse!'

Pausing, the small body shivering in his arms, Gideon looked directly into the frightened face lit now only by moonlight. 'Joseph,' he said quietly, 'what was said back there at the tube works was the truth, you need be in no fear of me, but if you wish I will return you to Mr Bates and fetch your mother and father to you there.'

For a moment the silence of the heath was Gideon's only answer, then the boy shook his head. 'I trusts you, mister. Gran'father Bates says you be all right so that's enough for me.'

Away in the darkness a pinprick of light marked Brook Cottage.

Watching it as they drew steadily nearer Gideon's mouth tightened. The lad trusted him, took his word as truth, but not so Saran Chandler!

Sat beside the bed Luke had willingly given for her son to sleep in, Livvy's tears ran fast down her gaunt cheeks. 'Who could 'ave done this to my lad, who could 'ave beaten 'im so hard that a mother's arms be too much forrim to bear?'

'He'll heal.' Edward's own tears glistened. 'We must thank the Lord we 'ave 'im safe.'

'I does thank the Lord but still I asks Him why ... why did He let my lad suffer so, and what of my little wench, why is her not sent back ... what good can it do heaven to 'ave children treated so, to see them whipped like animals!'

'Shhh, wench.' Edward tried to comfort the distraught woman. 'It ain't for we to question the ways o' the Lord.'

Livvy's head turned to face her husband and behind the tears shimmered an anger so strong it caught at his throat.

'That be what has been shoved at me since I were no age, drilled into me by priest and parent!

"Place no question afore the Lord, seek not the manner of His doings." Well, this I do question and condemn; if God can allow the innocent to be done by as my lad has been done by, then He no longer be God to me!'

Downstairs Saran caught the sound of Livvy's distress. 'It is understandable,' she murmured, 'what woman would not decry heaven, seeing her son beaten half to death.'

'Whoever did that to a boy deserves the hangman's noose.' Jairus Ensell caught her hands. 'Should he say who it was took him from the workhouse or remember where it was he went, you will let me know? Scum like that have no right to walk the earth, and if I find who it is they will not walk free another day.'

'Of course I will tell you.'

'And you, my love,' he lifted her hands to his mouth, kissing each in turn, 'try not to worry about the other child, I'm sure she is safe somewhere, and given time she will be found. I know I will never give up the search until she also is reunited with her parents.'

'Thank you, Jairus, I know Livvy and Edward are grateful for what you do. It helps them bear their pain having you search for Martha.'

'Anything, my dearest,' he kissed her hands again, 'anything at all I might help with, then please ask.'

The scullery door opening, Saran drew her hands free, her cheeks reddening as Luke walked into the kitchen.

'I've brought enough coals in for the night.' He addressed Saran while the very briefest of nods acknowledged Jairus Ensell's presence.

'I will be going, my dear. Please give my regards to the Elwells.'

'Would you care to see Joseph? He may be awake.'

'No,' Jairus answered quickly. 'Better not to disturb the boy ... though some other time...'

Conscious of Luke's presence, Saran took a step towards the door, embarrassed by the likelihood of Jairus taking her hands again.

'Of course,' she smiled, 'Livvy and her family will be happy for you to visit.'

Smiling down at her Jairus Ensell's eyes gleamed. 'And you, my love, will you be happy for me to visit?'

Smarmy bastard! Luke stood staring into the fire. He had helped Edward Elwell size up the barn intended for a warehouse and they had walked together through the rooms of the adjacent house. It all fitted so well ... except for Luke Hipton! There would be no place for him where Jairus Ensell was; he must look for another home!

Her prayers said, Saran lay with her eyes wide to the darkness. Beyond the house the cry of a barn owl punctured the silence. She had answered the knock that had sounded on the door earlier in the evening, she was the one who had opened it. It had seemed an age that Gideon Newell had stared into her eyes, his own burning deep into her, but in reality it could only have been seconds, then he had asked if Livvy and Edward were still at Brook Cottage. Nodding her answer she had stood aside for him to enter, feeling every fibre of her tingle as his arm touched against hers. Then her own wild churning had been brushed aside as Livvy had cried out.

He had been so gentle. Turning her face to the moon-silvered window, she allowed the image of those strong features to float in her mind, her heart tripping at what she saw in the deeply blue eyes. He had held the boy in his arms while the near-fainting Livvy was supported by an equally emotional husband.

The boy had come to the Coronet Tube Works probably to ask Grandfather Bates where he could find his parents. That was all the explanation Gideon had given. Staring into the shadows veiling her room she remembered the quick leap of her own senses, the innate feeling that he was not saying all he knew, that he would leave it for the boy himself to tell; but the tattered bloodstained shirt revealed when Edward gently removed Gideon Newell's jacket from his son's shoulders spoke eloquently enough.

The memory of Livvy's scream as she saw the open weals criss-crossing the boy's back seemed to spring live from the shadowed walls and Saran relived that moment of horror.

She had moved to take the coat from Edward meaning to hand it, together with her thanks, to the man stood beside her in the kitchen but as her glance fell on the raw, still-bleeding flesh she had heard herself gasp while the world had become a whirling vortex threatening to suck her into its wild black heart. Then she had been in Gideon Newell's arms, held so close against his chest the beat of his heart thumped above the noise in her head; but through it had run a whisper – like a thread holding everything together it had woven into her consciousness – *'My love, my love...'*

Then Luke had come from the scullery. Sensible, level-headed Luke, whose command of the situation marked him for the man he would become. It was he had reached a bowl from the dresser, he had filled it with water from the kettle, while she...? Beneath the covering darkness a flush rose to her cheeks; she had not wanted to move, not wanted to leave the comfort of those arms, to break from the hold which seemed to say it would protect her from anything life could throw at her. And Luke? He had smiled.

A smile for Gideon Newell holding her, a frown for Jairus Ensell kissing her hands! What was it caused so wide a difference in his feelings for those men? There had been no harsh words on Jairus's part yet Luke's animosity towards him was almost tangible.

Jairus was to be her husband. How would Luke react once her wedding was performed? He loved her too, loved her as much as Jairus, but did he love her enough to stay on at Brook Cottage?

Her eyelids lowering, Saran knew in her heart the answer was no. Where would he go? As sleep claimed her she saw in the mirror of her mind the boy smile at a tall clean-shaven man whose vivid eyes stared directly at her; the eyes of Gideon Newell.

She had cleaned the room. The wife of Zadok

Minch plaited her grey hair, securing the ends with a thin ribbon. She had gathered the broken pieces of her beloved Staffordshire figurines, the only things of her mother's that Zadok had allowed her to keep, her tears adding a sheen to the beautiful colours. They were beyond repair, smashed almost beyond recognition by his stamping foot. They had been the only things left which she loved; the only things in this entire house which held any meaning for her, and now they were gone.

Lowering slowly to her knees beside a bed Zadok had not come to since the first week of their marriage she clasped her hands, palms together.

'Forgive me, Lord,' she murmured softly, 'I know what sits in my heart is wrong, that I must come to stand before Your throne and account for it, but I cannot...' Choking on a sob she tightened her hands as from a room along the corridor the deep rumbling laugh of her husband, followed by a higher-pitched giggle of the prostitute she had been forced to invite to her home, came uncaringly to her ears. 'It is too much,' she whispered into her fingers, 'I cannot go on ... it is too much... Vengeance belongs to You but I shall take it... I shall repay what he has done. I want no forgiveness, Lord...'

As laughter floated again on the stillness she rose from her knees.

'One day,' she murmured as the laughter rippled again into the room, 'one day you will pay the price, Zadok!'

# 26

'That there be a drop o' good wheat wine, good as any I've ever tasted and I've supped a few tankards in me time.' Ezekiel Millward smiled at the young woman handing him a loaf of bread. 'Should you be serving that at them there celebrations there'll be one or two sore heads the next day.'

The crowning of the new queen! She had given no thought to that.

Hearing her say as much the old maltster smiled. 'I knows it seems a mighty way off as yet but time be in the habit o' passin' an' afore you knows it be gone. I tell you, wench, there'll be folk dancin' in the streets on that day an' every one of 'em will be wantin' to drink the 'ealth of her set to reign over the land. If an old man can give advice then mine be this, them butts we've filled ... set 'em aside 'til the time be near then tek one an' give a taste to the landlords of the George and the White Horse; be my reckoning they'll buy the rest an' pay the price you asks.'

'Sell the wheat wine?'

'Don't be surprised, wench, old Ezekiel would tell you nowt but truth. That there wine be good enough for any rich man's cellar, though it be over-strong for womenfolk.'

'You really think it would sell?'

Breathing in the appetising smell of the warm

loaf the old man nodded. 'Them folk o' your'n learned you well, you 'ave the touch with the wine as you 'ave with the bread ... use it, wench, for it'll bring you a good livin'.'

'If the wine is good then it is your doing, you taught me as much as my grandfather ... but why have you never sold any?'

The old man's smile died and it was several moments before his answer came. 'When the good Lord took my wife He took my 'eart. I did my work for I had to, but I knew no pleasure in it so would do no more than I must, then you come along; you, wench, 'ave lightened the sorrow I thought would never leave, you 'ave put a smile back in my life an' for that I blesses you and says take what me and your grandfather 'ave given in the way o' skill and build yourself a life that will take you from the smoke and grime o' this town.'

Following the day's route the words repeated often in Saran's brain.

*'build yourself a life that will take you from the smoke and grime o' this town'*

A few weeks ago it was all she wanted, to leave Wednesbury and search for her mother and Miriam, but how could she do that now ... how could she turn her back on Jairus who loved her, on the Elwells who already depended upon her ... and Luke, how could she see him give up the job he so evidently enjoyed, for he would leave it, he would not let her go from the town alone.

Brook Cottage, her bread round, the Elwells, Jairus and old Ezekiel. One by one they had fastened about her life, shackling her will, holding her ever more tightly to Wednesbury.

Her final call being the Coronet Tube Works she handed the gatekeeper the sandwich she always made for him, asking he pass another to Luke for his midday meal. Bent over the small cart, straightening the spotless white cover, she added, 'Would you be kind enough to pass a message to Mr Newell?'

'Tell 'im yourself, wench, since he be 'ere watchin' you as he does every mornin' you comes.'

Limping off towards the wide entrance to the factory the gatekeeper grinned at Gideon.

'You have a message for me?'

Why did the presence of this man always hinder her breathing? Saran fussed a little longer with the cover of the cart.

She had to stop behaving like a child, he was no different to Jairus or any other man; this breathless feeling, the rapid thumping of her heart was all her own doing ... apprehension of yet another quarrel was the only reason her nerves jarred whenever he looked at her.

'Yes...' she forced herself to stand upright but her glance stayed on the cart, 'yes, I do. Livvy and Edward would like you to call, they wish to thank you for helping Joseph.'

She had not looked at him! Gideon's mouth tightened. Brook Cottage was her home, it was not necessary for him to meet the Elwells there, she made it plain any visit of his was an intrusion.

'Thank you for delivering the message,' he said abruptly, 'I will ask Luke to bring my reply.'

His boot crunching on the hard earth brought Saran's glance darting upward.

'Can't I take it?'

Already several yards from the gate Gideon paused then turned, his eyes hard as his mouth.

'I would not put you to the trouble, Miss Chandler!'

Didn't he trust her, did he think she would distort his words? Angry both at the thought and at the silly churning of her insides, Saran glared at the handsome face.

'I can deliver a message!' she answered sharply. 'I am no fool!'

'Neither am I, and I can read the message you send each time we meet, a message which says I am not welcome. Therefore I will meet with the Elwells at some other place.'

What had happened to her heart? Saran felt the kick of it travel to her throat, robbing her of her breath, leaving a sick trail throbbing in her chest.

'Joseph,' she pushed the word out as he turned away a second time, 'Joseph, he ... he too would like to see you, but he ... he is not yet well enough to leave his bed.'

What had rushed those words from her as if her life depended on them being said, why had she lied about Joseph when the boy was already up and about?

'But you, Miss Chandler...' tall and straight as a young oak, his glance never wavering, Gideon Newell stared back at her, 'do you want me to visit Brook Cottage?'

Did she? Did she want a repeat of the turmoil going on deep within her, did she want to feel the breath stolen from her, the nerves of her whole body leaping as they were now? Lowering her glance she nodded.

'Then say it!' Hard as granite his words struck the space separating them. 'Look at me and say it!'

With a swift flush burning her cheeks Saran lifted her head, her gaze reaching to the vivid eyes resting on her. 'Yes,' she whispered, 'I want you to come.'

It was inconceivable! It wasn't true ... it couldn't be! But the boy would not lie. Scarcely knowing where her steps led, Saran ran along Lower High Street towards the White Horse inn. *'The London coach don't call 'ere no more, not since they built that there new 'Olyhead Road,'* Ada Mason had told her as she had burst into the kitchen of the Turk's Head. *'You wants to go to Brummajum then you 'as to board the coach there, though were it me, wench, I would–'*

Whatever it was Ada had intended to add had not been heard for Saran was already half across the wide cobbled yard, running for the street.

*'A woman ... it were a woman, said her 'ad been bought from a man.'*

Her heart, already thumping painfully with the effort of running, twisted again as Joseph's words blazed in her mind. She had returned to Brook Cottage when her bread delivery round was finished. The kitchen had been filled with sunlight streaming through its small windows, the aroma of yeast and newly baking bread delicious on the warm air. She had thought for several moments the house was empty, then, hardly disturbing the silence, the quiet voice of the Elwell boy had sounded. She had smiled to herself while washing her hands in the scullery prior to beginning the mixing of another batch of bread. The Elwells had settled into the house alongside the large barn and already several nailers brought their week's work to sell to Edward, while Livvy had proved invaluable in helping with the bread ... if only their little girl and her own family–

The thoughts had stopped there. Breathing in short rapid gasps Saran leaned for a moment against a wall of the Quaker Meeting House. The thoughts had stopped as Livvy's agonised cry rang through the bedroom and down to the scullery.

'You all right there, missy?'

'What...?' Flinching at the touch of a hand she stared vacantly at the kindly face.

'I asks if you be all right ... you seemed about to faint.'

'No...' Saran straightened though her brain whirled, causing her to be unsteady on her feet, 'I am quite well ... just a little out of breath running for the coach.'

'Well ain't no need to run the rest o' the way, the coach be standin' and likely to be for a minute or two yet if I be any judge o' that driver ... likes his tankard, do old Jem.'

'Thank you.' Saran's gaze followed the road to where a coach stood, dark-green paintwork almost lost beneath a thick film of grey dust.

'You be goin' to London?'

The question floated unattended on the surface of Saran's mind; only when the man's apology for asking it began did it register.

Free of a shawl her fair hair caught the gold of sunlight, trapping it among silken folds, while hazel eyes, still dark with the horror of minutes ago, turned again to the kindly face.

'No,' Saran shook her head, 'I'm going to Birmingham.'

'By yourself!' Eyes bright with interest swept the street behind Saran. 'If you don't mind a piece o' advice, missy, that don't be altogether the safest thing these days ... you never knows who you might come up against on the road.'

'The coaches are safe–'

'Oh ar, they be safe enough.' The bright eyes fastened on her with the quick interruption. 'But that ain't always so with the folk as rides 'em; cutpurses, kidnappers ... I tells you it don't be safe for a young woman to travel alone.'

The advice was probably sound and definitely well intended but she had to get to Birmingham.

'I be going to that town meself.' Raising a tall hat, the slightly corpulent figure smiled. 'Should you care for it to look as if we be travelling together then nobody will bother you.'

Wedged against her self-appointed companion Saran felt the press of his thigh against her own and a brief moment of unease tickled her nerves. Enoch Jacobs had pressed himself against her in just such a way whenever opportunity presented itself. But this was different, she glanced at the other occupants of the coach, each person squeezed tightly against the next; the man whose body was hot against her own was most likely as uncomfortable as herself. Soothed by the realisation, Saran released her mind and immediately it flew to Livvy.

The woman's cry, filled with pain, had rung through Brook Cottage and she had dropped the cloth on which she had been drying her hands and raced upstairs. Livvy had stood in the centre of the small room which Luke had allowed her son to sleep in; her fingers pressed to her mouth she had been staring at the boy who talked softly on.

*''E had sent for me times afore...'*

Held by a quiet magnetism, Saran had remained in the doorway of the small sun-filled bedroom.

'*...always to ask did I like what I see ... did I want to stay? And always the woman would giggle; the woman were worse'n 'im, 'er goaded 'im on in all he done, even the whip...*'

Livvy's stifled cry had wafted to the open doorway but held by unbreakable bonds Saran had stood motionless.

'*...liked the whip, he did,*' Joseph had gone on, '*liked to hear it crack, to see the way folk jumped when it sang along of their ear, to hear 'em scream when it cut into their flesh. It were late that night when the scullery woman come to the cellar to say I were wanted upstairs, her said her were to tek me herself cos the other were busy wi' the baking. My eyes wouldn't properly show me the way after days locked in darkness and the scullery woman, 'er helped me up them stairs...*'

Caught by the words echoing in her mind, Saran was barely aware of the driver calling West Bromwich and the people disembarking at the town.

'*They was there, together on the bed, the man who*

*said I'd been bought and paid for, him lying there naked, the woman nearly the same 'cept for the paint on 'er face...'*

Bought and paid for?

The nerves in her body had pricked like knives yet still she had been powerless to break the spell the boy's voice had thrown over her.

Bought and paid for as her mother and sister had been!

'*...told the scullery woman to get out 'e did.*' Binding in its quietness the boy's voice had gone on. '*'Er looked at me, seeming unwilling to leave me but then the whip ... it cracked, catchin' 'er about the shoulders. I don't blame 'er for goin', I would 'ave done the same meself.*' He had taken a long breath then, his small frame juddering at the pictures which must have been etched on his brain. '*"Come close," he said, "come see what lads who do as they be told gets to play with." When I made no move the woman giggled and said p'raps they should show me what it was. The man laughed and stood up, pulling her up along of him, then one by one took her clothes away...*'

Livvy had gasped at that but her son had talked on, as if saying what he did was the cure for both body and mind.

'*...that were when I seen, all but for the painted face, there were no difference atween the two, both had the same atwixt their legs as any man. "Come and share," the older one said, "come and share this." That were when he dropped to his knees, kissing the other man's stomach, tekin' 'im into his mouth.*'

'*No more! For God's sake, no more!*'

Livvy's tear-filled eyes had pleaded with her

son but the cry of her heart went unheeded.

*'The painted one laughed telling him he was a naughty boy behavin' that way, yet made no move to stop it and when the other got to his feet again said he should let me suck. The old 'un said I was to do it, and when I said no he grabbed me about the neck, forcing me to kneel, holding my head up while the other 'un pushed hisself into my face, pressed so 'ard I couldn't breathe 'til I opened my mouth...'*

Livvy's sobs had bubbled into the room, her worn face twisting with the horror of what she was hearing.

*'...I were forced to open my mouth, that were when they both laughed, the painted one touching my lips with...'*

Livvy's cry had rung out but the boy went on.

*'...I opened my mouth and while he laughed I bit... I bit hard and listened to his screams. It were worth what 'appened after that, worth bein' tied to the bedposts while that whip laced across my back. I belonged to Zadok Minch was what were shouted with every lash; I would do as he said. I don't know 'ow many times that leather cut into my back, I were near unconscious when the bonds about my wrists and ankles were cut and the scullery woman were tellin' me to run. When I thought later, mekin' my way 'ome, I remembered Minch staggering against a table wi' blood running down his bare flesh and a knife in the scullery woman's hand, but the painted man bein' no longer in the room.'*

Zadok Minch! The name! She had heard that name before! Watching Livvy gather her son into her arms, Saran had been snatched back to a heath wreathed in darkness, to a bush growing beside a canal glittering molten gold in the moonlight, to herself yoked by the neck, her hands and feet bound by the same rope.

*''E'll find 'ishelf another Zadok Minch.'*

The hated voice had slurred in her memory, the picture of a drunken Enoch Jacobs filling her inner vision.

Zadok Minch was the name Enoch had in his stupor let slide from his mouth, the name of a man who had bought her mother and sister.

*'bought and paid for'*

The words danced in her brain.

*'I puts another shillin' on my offer ... ye'll get no more from the men as teks their ale in the Navigation.'*

*'bought and paid for'*

*'bought and paid for'*

It rolled again and again in her mind. Could the man in that tavern, the one who had offered five shillings for her be the same one who somehow had bought Livvy's son? The question danced in her brain, weaving itself with another, one which had set the world tipping around her. Could this same Zadok Minch possibly be the man who had earlier purchased her mother and sister in that tavern in Walsall?

From downstairs had come the call of her name, spinning her back to the moment. Edward Elwell had called to speak with her of the day's business with the nail-makers.

'Zadok Minch.' He had frowned on hearing the question she had flung at him. 'Ar, I knows Zadok Minch, so does many another nailer in Wednesbury; he buys from them at a lower price and sells them the next batch of iron strip at a 'igher one. Be a man it be in the best interests not to know, but folk ain't never had the chance until you set up as nail master...'

'But do you know where it is he lives?' The abruptness of her second question and the sharpness of her tone had deepened the frown settled between greying eyebrows, and Edward had answered quickly.

'Brummajum... Zadok Minch belongs at Brummajum.'

'That be better, now we can be a bit more sociable can't we, my dear.'

His breath fanning warm against her cheek and a hand turning her face drove the pictures from Saran's mind. The coach was empty of all passengers apart from herself and the man who had spoken to her beside the Quaker Meeting House.

'You knowed which coach to take, the one old Jem drives; turns a blind eye, do Jem.'

She frowned, not yet entirely free of the thoughts that had held her. Why was this man touching her face, had she been so absorbed she had travelled beyond her destination?

'Have we reached Birmingham?' She edged along the leather-covered seat, her spine resting against its lacquered frame.

The face that had looked so kind while in Wednesbury now showed an altogether different side. Eyes that had smiled now gleamed with a light she had seen before, the mouth which had seemed so gentle now stretched in that same lascivious grin, the lips wetted by the lick of a tongue.

'Not yet.' The answer was husky, the hand that had touched her face snatching at her shawl, fastening over the tight breast beneath. 'We still have time to conduct a little business.'

The fear she had experienced whenever Enoch Jacobs had looked at her in the way this man was looking at her swept over Saran. 'Please...' She pulled at the hand holding so possessively to her breast.

'Manners pretty as the face, I likes that.' Glistening lips fastened like leeches to Saran's mouth while the hand moved to her skirts, dragging them up over her thigh.

'Lie you down.' His strength belying the mark of age he had appeared to carry, he dragged Saran down until she lay beneath him. 'Lie you down and spread your legs...'

'Let go!' Her mouth freed of the clinging lips, Saran tried to twist from beneath the weight holding her to the seat, her effort answered by a thick laugh.

*'turns a blind eye, do Jem'*

Fear turned momentarily to panic as Saran remembered the words. These two were obviously in league with each other; one took his pleasure, the other his payment. It would do no good to scream, for no help would come from the driver.

She must help herself. Holding to that one thought she forced her panicking mind to still. Maybe if she agreed...

'You are so heavy...' she smiled at the heavily flushed face still so close to her own, 'I can't remove my underwear unless you allow me to move.'

She must be careful, there would be no second chance. Keeping the smile on her lips, holding those hot eyes with her own, Saran slid to her feet as he moved aside. One chance ... it beat in her brain ... one chance and no more.

As her fingers released the button of her skirt she hid the disgust the sight of his naked throbbing flesh evoked.

One chance! Holding tight to the waistband of her skirt she raised one foot, jabbing a boot hard into the pulsing crotch.

# 27

'The decision has to be your own for were it otherwise your heart would not be rested.'

The decision had to be his! Gideon Newell stared into the fire that warmed the tiny cottage. But the promise had been his also, the promise to take his mother from this house, to make her life more comfortable, yet...

'I knows it don't be all for yourself you wants to step higher in the world and not for all that world would I stand in your way.' A folded tablecloth in her hands, Charity Newell looked lovingly at her son.

'I wanted it for so long, worked so hard for it.'

'To work hard be in your nature, it be the legacy of your father's blood, but now I tells you to think, son, think hard as ever you've worked, for only once will the opportunity be given, only once will the chance be held out to you, so be sure of your choosing.'

'I had it all worked out,' Gideon stared into the fire, 'I had it set so firm in my mind; I would accept the job of overseer in John Adams's new tube works, take you to the house that goes with it, give you a new life...'

The cloth put away in a drawer, Charity rested her hand on the old well-worn dresser. This house had seen her happiness and her sorrows, the birth of her son, the loss of her husband; it had known her dreams and her hopes, then watched them die, fade as life must have faded from the man she loved trapped in that coal mine, slowly, heartbreakingly.

'Your happiness is everything to me.' She spoke quietly, her hand stroking the surface of the dresser. 'But this house be the place your father brought me on our wedding day, it saw the love that gave you life and the pain which gave you birth, it was here I lived with him, lived a life such as I wanted from no other man, and it was here I raised you, and you, Gideon, give me cause for nothing but thanks to the Almighty; so I tell you, make your choice on John Adams's offer, for no workman he has deserves the job more, decide on what it be you wants and my blessing be given along with it. But though I knows it be my comfort drives your ambition, don't ask me to leave the place where my heart lives: this house be what holds your father for me, not some dark coal pit, here is where I feel his love, here is where he will be when my own call comes, waiting to take my hand as he took it that day before the altar. I love you, Gideon, you are my heart and I would gladly lay down my life for you, my son; but your father was my soul and I ask you again, do not part me from it.'

She had guided him wisely every day of his life. His mother held in his arms, Gideon stared over her head. And though she had not spoken the words, she had guided him now; he had stood at a crossroads and it had taken his mother to point the way.

John Adams had accepted his decision. Needing time to sort his feelings Gideon bypassed the cottage and the timbered Oakeswell Hall, walking on towards the High Bullen. It seemed a foolish thing to refuse such a post, his employer had said after listening, but if that was his decision then there was no more to be said.

It could have all been over, done! He crossed the wide square where once bulls had been baited for sport. He could have gone to Moxley, started a new life there.

*'don't ask me to leave the place where my heart lives'*

His mother's words, the words which had guided his decision. He could leave Wednesbury, take up a new life elsewhere, but he would leave his heart behind, the heart which Saran Chandler held. But what would happen to that heart when she became another man's wife? It would shatter as his mother's heart had shattered on receiving news of that pit fall; but, unlike his mother, he had shared no love with Saran Chandler, he would have nothing on which to build memories, nothing but empty dreams.

She had come to her senses where he had left her unconscious from the blow to her head. Zadok's wife touched the swollen lips of the scullery maid with a wet cloth. He had treated this woman worse than any other brought to serve in his house and this time he had almost killed her. It was her fault! Bridget Minch felt her heart twist. This woman, and all the others brought here by her husband, she should have done something, anything to prevent his treatment of them ... but what? She looked at the white face blotched with purple bruises. What could she do against a man capable of such cruelty?

Twenty-five pounds! She dipped the cloth in a bowl of cool water, sponging it gently over bruised flesh. Zadok had all but killed the woman for the sake of twenty-five pounds ... the money spent on the buying of a boy, and only half of what he hoped for the selling. The use of the whip on such young flesh would have reduced the profit but that alone did not account for the insane rage that had gripped Zadok, that had been caused by the child's escape. It must have put a fear in him such as he had never felt before: who might the boy tell of the goings-on in the house of Zadok Minch? And, even more perturbing, who might believe him?

Hearing a knock on the kitchen door, Bridget rose. Closing off the small storeroom adjacent to the pantry she waited a moment, listening for any sound uttered by the woman. The kitchen was one place Zadok never came and that tiny room where she had managed to half drag the scullery maid was a place he probably did not know existed. Silence saying the sick woman was sleeping or once more unconscious, she smoothed her apron, checking no tell-tale sign of blood having stained its virgin whiteness.

'Is this the house of Zadok Minch?'

'He does no business at night.'

Anger at her near-rape in that coach, at the insults and insinuations flung at her whenever she asked directions to this house, sat firmly in

Saran's chest. 'He will conduct business with me,' she said firmly.

'He won't see–'

Bridget Minch got no further. Pushing her way into the kitchen Saran stared at the drab, thin woman. 'Then I will see his wife, please tell her.'

The tired eyes flickered but as quickly they resumed the empty expression while bruised lips smiled a thin hopeless smile. 'I am his wife,' she said tonelessly, 'and I tell you he will not see you.'

This poor-looking woman was the wife of Zadok Minch ... the most prosperous nail master in the Black Country! Saran could not hide her surprise.

'I beg your pardon,' she said awkwardly, 'I had no wish to be rude.'

'Eyes will always speak true no matter what the brain might want,' Bridget answered quietly. 'I take it not as rudeness.'

'Then will you tell your husband I am here, that I wish to discuss the business of a young boy of the name Joseph Elwell.'

Pale as her face was it paled even further as Bridget heard the name. Who was this young woman demanding to see Zadok, was it that lad's sister, had he managed to find his way home?

'It'll do no good–'

Snatching a quick breath Saran's interruption was firm as it was sharp. 'Mrs Minch, please tell your husband he will speak with me or with the magistrate, I leave the choice to him.'

Was this what she prayed for every night ... was this the end for Zadok Minch and his evil practices? Hugging the hope to her, Bridget led the way to the upstairs sitting room.

This woman was wife to Zadok Minch, the mistress of this house, yet she had the mien and attitude which might be expected of some ill-used servant. Saran had noted the slow tread up the staircase and now a light, almost trembling tap to the door and the clenched hands as she waited for permission to enter.

'Bugger off!'

Seeing the definite flinch of the other woman's shoulders, Saran knew she was not mistaken: Zadok Minch was a bully.

'I told you... I said he would not see anyone.'

Frightened eyes turned quickly to Saran and for one fleeting moment she saw her own mother's terrified eyes, her body cringing before the vicious fist of Enoch Jacobs. Jacobs had joined with the moon dancers, but her mother ... maybe the man inside that room could tell where she and Miriam were.

'You will have to leave.'

Bridget Minch's whisper had barely left her thin lips when Saran flung open the door.

'Zadok Minch?' Her heart pounding, Saran stared defiantly. She had come to find her mother and no man on earth would stop her.

'What the bloody hell...?' Minch glared at his wife.

'I ... I apologise, Zadok...' she pressed backward, away from the anger already turning the heavily jowled face red, 'she ... she would not leave.'

'Would not!' He seemed to relax, his corpulent frame leaning into the wide armchair, one hand stroking the thigh of an attractive woman seated on his lap. 'The Night Watch will change that!'

Drawing her courage about her like a shield Saran lifted her head, a gesture which said she was in no fear of his threat. 'I would welcome them, and I think the magistrate would be more than interested in hearing the testimony of Joseph Elwell, the young boy you whipped almost to death.'

Seated on his lap the wide-eyed figure tensed, then reached a long-fingered hand to touch gleaming brown hair piled high on a well-shaped head, soft wisps of curls framing an expertly made-up face.

Aware of the movement and of the tension it covered, Zadok barked again at his wife. 'Get the Night Watch!'

'Wait, my dear, let us hear what…'

'Saran Chandler.'

'…what Saran Chandler is accusing you of… I would like to know what it is she thinks you guilty of.'

Inquisitive eyes had fastened on Saran, yet somehow she got the impression it was not what she might have to say interested this attractive woman but rather what the man fondling her body might have to say.

'What you be saying be pigshit!' Zadok glared at Saran. 'Remember, wench, thistles grow well in pigshit and them as sows 'em gets pricked!'

'But pull them out and you are left with clean earth, that is what I want, Mr Minch, clean earth.'

'Meaning?'

'The truth. I want the truth. The truth regarding not only Joseph Elwell but also my mother and sister, who were sold to a Zadok Minch by Enoch Jacobs in an inn in Walsall town.'

It was a wild gamble, a guess she could not authenticate, but as she flung the words Saran caught the quick glance directed at Bridget Minch and her heart leapt. It had not been an empty guess.

'Get out!' A snarl laced with venom had his wife stepping quickly from the room, closing the door as she went.

'First a boy and now a woman and her daughter.' The attractive figure laughed lightly. 'Really, Zadok my love, how do you answer such an accusation?'

Meeting the lips that bent over his, Zadok ran his hand from hip to stomach, pressing his fingers where skirts covered its base.

'The best way,' he answered as the generous mouth released his, 'the way I always settles a grumble.'

Pushing the figure from his lap he rose. Reaching behind the chair he lifted a thick, plaited leather whip.

'This be something folk don't argue with for long.'

'Is that the same whip you used on a young boy because he refused to play your filthy games!'

'Games?' The question was meant to sound amused but, caught by the light of several lamps, the wide eyes of his paramour glittered a virulent displeasure not lost on Zadok.

'Look at her!' Reaching out with the whip he

flicked Saran's faded skirts. 'Look at the clothes, they tell you why her be here; dream up some cock-and-bull story then come into a man's home and accuse him of it and he'll pay just to get her out. Well, this be one man won't be blackmailed by no bloody tramp!'

Anger overriding fear as the whip cracked close to her side, Saran stood her ground. Were Zadok Minch innocent he would not threaten, he would simply have had her taken by the Watch.

Silken skirts rustled as the slender figure moved to stand before a white marble fireplace, the perfume of violets wafting with each step. There Zadok's companion turned, a smile curving a painted mouth.

'Of course you will not allow yourself to be blackmailed, my darling, but let the girl speak, I find her amusing. This boy,' she said as Zadok made to refuse, 'what game was it you claim Zadok would have him play?'

'It was no game,' Saran answered coldly. 'It was something no decent human being would force another to do...'

'Enough!' His face swollen with rage Zadok cracked the whip, the force of it lifting strands of Saran's hair.

'I agree, my dear.' Taking a silk wrap thrown across a chair the elegantly dressed figure draped it about bare shoulders. 'I no longer find the evening entertaining, therefore I shall take my leave.'

The door closing behind the perfumed figure, Zadok let the full force of his fury show.

'You'll be sorry for ever coming to my house,

sorry you ever heard the name Zadok Minch.'

Saran watched the whip rise. The man was dangerous, incensed, but still she must know.

'The same as my mother and sister were sorry for hearing it?' she asked, more quietly than she thought possible. 'The same as Joseph Elwell must have been sorry. Did you do with my family what you wanted to do with that boy ... did you force them to fall in with your filthy ways and did you whip them half to death when they refused?'

For interminable seconds the whip stayed in the air, then, a smile curving Zadok's mouth, he lowered it, resting the handle across the palm of his free hand. 'The boy was of no consequence except for the loss of the money I could have got forrim, they pay well in the East for young boys.' He paused, small eyes glittering cruelty from puffy sockets. 'As for the others, the woman I purchased in that tavern objected to my ... games ... she objected to my taking what my money had bought, namely her daughter. I have no liking for old worn-out flesh so the woman was bought only as a servant in my kitchen, but the young one ... her flesh tasted sweet.'

'You swine ... you filthy...!'

A lightning strike of the whip lancing across her shoulders checked Saran as she launched herself at him.

'Maybe.' He laughed, a short grating laugh. 'But even a swine enjoys rutting with a younger one, and I did. I took what was mine right there on that heath while her mother watched.'

'No!' Saran shook her head. 'My mother would never stand by while you raped Miriam!'

'No more her did!' He laughed again. 'Her couldn't stand, not after this here whip had done its work, but her could watch. Oh yes, her could watch and I med sure her seen it all.'

He wasn't a man, no man would do what he claimed to have done. Yet as Saran stared into those cruel eyes she knew it was no lie. Zadok Minch had whipped her mother until she couldn't stand, then had raped Miriam before her eyes.

'Where are they?' she whispered. 'Where are my mother and sister? Give them back to me; here–' she fumbled in her pocket, withdrawing the money she had grabbed before leaving Brook Cottage '–this is more than you paid, take it and let me take my family.'

'Five pounds!' Podgy fingers closed over the white banknote. 'Now where would a tramp get five pounds from, unless it be from lying on your back with your legs spread.'

'I am not a prostitute.' Saran threw the words at the whiskered face. 'I earned that money selling bread.'

'Bread, was it?' Zadok sniggered. 'Well, it won't be no loaf you'll be giving Zadok Minch. If you wants your family you have to give him what lies atwixt your legs.'

Loathing rising like gall, Saran felt her stomach heave. He was asking ... he wanted...

'The choice be your'n.' Zadok's cruel eyes echoed the laugh grating in his throat. 'This be a game I won't force you into, but if you want your folk, you'll play it.'

If she wanted her folk! The words rang like a

bell in her brain. She wanted them more than anything in the world ... but to lie with this man!

'I have paid you far more than you gave Enoch Jacobs,' she said desperately, 'five pounds should–'

'Five pounds don't be enough!' he rasped, anger returning the dull-red sheen to his face. 'I've told you the cost, now pay it or go.'

The cost! How could she pay it ... how could she give herself to this man, feel his flesh against hers' his body entering hers? The very thought revolted her ... but not to pay it, to leave Miriam and their mother at the mercy of a man who hadn't the faintest notion of the meaning of the word! How could she do that?

Struggling against the nausea of what she had to endure, her tears blurring the heavy-jowled face, she let the worn shawl slip to the floor, her fingers slowly releasing the buttons of her blouse.

'You be older than the other one but Zadok Minch don't be a man to deny a wench pleasure on account of a few years; now your mother were a different kettle of fish altogether, her'd been rode that many times–'

'Stop!' Her cry only a whisper, Saran stared at the leering face.

'Stop?' Zadok Minch laughed. 'Why stop doing what you enjoy ... and I be enjoying this.'

'Please ... please, tell me where they are.'

Thick-fingered hands dropping the whip, the leer dying on wet lips, eyes dilating with lust the plea seemed to add to the fires sweeping through the nail master. Grabbing for her he snatched at her blouse and chemise, ripping them apart.

'Never pay for goods 'til them goods have been sampled.' Close against her throat his tongue licked every slurred word across trembling flesh.

Let it be over soon, please, God, let it be over soon! Unable to prevent sobs leaving her lips as she was pressed to the floor, Saran tried to hold fast to the one thing preventing her from screaming: once this man had taken what he wanted he would tell her where her family was ... she would have them back.

'The other one sobbed.' Her underwear was snatched away, and, his trousers removed, the heavy figure straddling her laughed again. 'Yes, 'er sobbed, but only 'til this were pushed into 'er, this...' he knelt upright, holding engorged flesh between his fingers, 'this this soon quietened 'er, took to it like a babby teks to a stick o' barley sugar, and you'll tek to it the same way.'

'More games, Zadok!' A crack of the whip flicked Zadok's bare bottom, causing him to roar as he rolled from its reach.

One hand pushing down her skirts the other drawing the torn blouse across her breasts, Saran felt the blood of shame flood her face.

'Come to me, my love, it's over, Zadok Minch won't ever touch you again.'

Relief adding to the trembling of every limb, Saran reached for the outstretched hand of Jairus Ensell.

# 28

'She went where!'

It was not a question, it was an explosion and the whole force of Gideon Newell was behind it.

'Brummajum,' Edward Elwell answered, confused by the other man's anger. 'The lad were tellin' how it were he got away from the man who had 'im, said a woman...'

'A woman!' Gideon's nerves jarred.

'Ar,' Edward nodded, 'said the woman were good to 'im, seen to it 'e were fed...'

'The name ... did the boy say the woman's name?'

'Not so my Livvy remembers.'

No name! Gideon struck restlessly at the doorpost of Edward Elwell's house. So why had she gone careering off like a demon was at her back? Without a name there could be no telling who the woman was, though he knew who it was Saran Chandler wanted it to be. But what were the chances that woman would be her mother?

She would be in Birmingham by this time. Gideon looked at the sky, the moon hidden by racing clouds. The night was bringing a storm and no coach ran at night; would she find lodging or would she walk home?

He had come to the Elwells in answer to the message brought earlier that day by Saran and had found a still tearful Livvy, and Edward seething yet with an anger that had burned the entire afternoon.

'Why did you let her go?'

'Weren't my choosin', lad,' the older man answered the question he knew was an accusation. 'I wanted to go find that swine, to rip 'is filthy heart out ... all I could think was to kill 'im for what he'd done to my boy; but Saran, her were all calm, said that I 'ad no proof, that to injure that scum of a man without evidence would put me on the gallows, and where would my loved ones be then? Her said to wait a while 'til I was calmer.'

Where would Edward Elwell's loved ones be without him!

Gideon almost groaned at the hopelessness encasing his heart. Where was Gideon Newell without his love ... where would he be when Saran became the wife of Jairus Ensell?

Had she gone to him, had Ensell escorted her to Birmingham? A thread of hope piercing the worry of what might be, he looked again at the man beside him. Edward Elwell was no coward, he would not have stayed behind willingly.

'I told 'er,' Edward booted the door frame venting a little of the frustration which, during Saran's absence, had turned to guilt. 'I told 'er it should be me go to Brummajum but 'er wouldn't listen.'

He could well believe that; Saran Chandler could be anything but biddable when she set her stubborn mind to a thing. Gideon touched the other man's shoulder. 'Don't blame yourself, Edward, I fear the Lord and His entire heavenly host couldn't have stopped her once she heard of that woman.'

'What'll we do ... it be gettin' late for the wench to be on the road; Livvy already be beside 'erself worryin' what could come of it.'

'I'll go look for her.'

'I'll come with you, lad, and don't say no for I won't be put off a second time.'

He would rather be alone, Gideon thought as Edward called to tell his wife of his decision. But he could hardly order the other man to stay behind. Keeping silence until they reached the market square, he then said, 'Perhaps Saran went to ask the help of Jairus Ensell, maybe she is at his house now.'

'Seems like summat a wench engaged to a man would do.' Edward nodded agreement. 'P'raps Ensell went along of 'er to see Minch.'

'It would be the sensible thing to find out. If you would go enquire I will take the Birmingham Road. The quicker we find Saran the easier we will both be.' Leaving the other man, Gideon ran in the direction of the Turk's Head inn. If there were a horse, Ben Mason would see he had the use of it.

She had clung to Jairus. Safe now in his carriage, Saran used the darkness like a cloak to hide the shame of what had happened, but the need now driving like wild horses deep within her she would never hide, she would let it blaze, let it burn on until revenge was hers.

She had taken Jairus's hand, had hidden her fear on his shoulder, wanting only to be out of that house, but as Zadok had laughed, as he had spoken her mother's name, she had turned to look at him.

Standing upright, making no effort to conceal his bare flesh, he had laughed but deep in those fat-shrouded eyes had gleamed the fires of hell and his words had spat like molten lava from between clenched teeth.

*'You asked did I whip your mother half to death same as I whipped the boy?'* he gloated. *'The answer be no, it wasn't* half *done, I finished that job ... down there in the kitchen I made the whip sing, I finished the worn-out bitch and her young 'un along of her!'*

She had stared at the heavy face, the world withdrawing then sweeping back, all she could think of was where ... where are they buried?

*'Buried?'* He had laughed at the question she had not realised she asked. *'I neither knows nor cares, a sovereign took care o' that, same as it sees to all the shit needs collecting from my house.'*

Jairus had raised the whip then but, suddenly calm, strangely in complete control and all fear of the nail master gone, she had laid a restraining hand on his arm.

*'No,'* she had heard herself say in an even voice. *'Not that way.'* Then freeing herself of Jairus's hold, she had taken one step forward. *'I have hated the thought of you ever since the night you bought my mother and my sister, purchasing them as you might a dog; hated you though I did not know you; now I do and that hatred has become loathing, a detestation. You are an abomination, one which I swear before God I will remove. I will destroy your life as you destroyed those of my mother and sister. From*

*this day I make this my solemn oath: I will tear down your life, piece by piece. I will not stop until I see you grovel as you made my family grovel. The whip I use will not be of plaited leather and its slash will leave no weal, but its bite will be every bit as deep, every bit as painful. The strokes I make will not cut into your flesh as yours cut into that of my mother and sister, but each will take a little of your life, it will slice away your arrogance and pride until nothing is left. This is my promise to you, though it should take my own life I will see you ruined!'*

Words! They had been her only ammunition. But they would not become an empty threat. Somehow she would find a way to give them meaning, one day she would see them fulfilled.

Curled in upon herself in the dimness of Jairus's carriage Saran did not notice the dark outline of a horseman rein in to watch the vehicle go sweeping past, nor did she hear the softly spoken words which said, 'Thank God, she's safe.'

'The candle lamps bobbin' in the distance said as it were a carriage and we guessed it would be Ensell. We thought he were coming to call on Saran but her were in that carriage along of him.'

Sat on a pile of iron tubes Gideon listened to Luke's explanation as they ate their midday meal.

'Don't ask how he knowed Saran were at Minch's house, but I thanks God he went there.'

How had he known? Gideon chewed on bread and cheese. Was the girl the real reason of Ensell's visit to the nail master or was his finding her there a surprise? Whichever way it didn't much matter so long as Saran had been escorted safely back to Brook Cottage.

'Saran wouldn't say what had gone on atwixt her and Minch, said only as her family weren't at that house.' Luke bit into his own sandwich, juggling the food in his mouth in his eagerness to talk. 'But Mrs Elwell could see her were upset and went to take her on up to her room. It were when Ensell were 'anded back the coat he had wrapped around Saran that it were seen...'

Seen! Gideon's breath held in his throat. What was it had been seen ... an injury ... had Saran been harmed in some way?

'Mrs Elwell, her screamed so I nearly jumped into termorrer!' Luke continued. 'At first I thought something must be wrong with Saran but then I seen for meself, it weren't no such...'

Relief almost painful, Gideon released his pent up breath. Had she come to harm he would have killed Minch with his own hands.

'Livvy ... Mrs Elwell,' Luke corrected himself, 'her caught sight of what Saran were holdin', it were a bit scruffy and screwed up but you could tell it were a doll. Her kept saying it were her Martha's doll, that her had stitched it from a wornout frock and sewed eyes and mouth with bits of wool on a piece of cloth to make the face; kept cryin' that her babby, her little wench had took the doll with her to the workhouse.'

'She said it was the same doll she had made for her daughter?'

'Ar.' Luke bit again into his sandwich as he nodded. 'Said her would know it anywheres, said it had a rip along of its back and the rip were pulled together with stitches big enough to anchor a warship, that were due to Martha sewin' it up herself, and sure enough there it was, 'zactly as her said.'

So how did Saran come by it? She couldn't have had it before leaving for Birmingham or Livvy would have known of it.

Almost as if the thought had been spoken aloud, Luke answered it. 'Saran were flummoxed, we could tell the way her looked at the thing that her hadn't the knowing of how her 'ad come to be holdin' it.'

She hadn't known of it. Gideon took a swallow from the jug of cider the errand runner had brought in from the inn across from the Bullen. The only other explanation was Ensell!

'Saran couldn't say how her had come by that doll but Ensell was quick enough to answer.' Luke took the jug and quenched his thirst. 'He apologised for having forgotten about the doll, said all thought of it went right out of his mind when he heard Saran had took the coach for Birmingham.'

'But how come he had it in the first place?'

The steam whistle announcing the ending of their meal break, Luke shook the crumbs from the cloth which had held his sandwich, folding it so it fitted into his pocket. 'Said as a collier had found it out on the heath near to Ryders coal pit but seeing as his family were all lads he had no use for a wench's toy. Ensell heard the others playin' the fool, pulling the pitman's leg sayin' he should keep the doll against his missis havin' the next babby, and him shakin' his head and sayin' there wouldn't be no more now he'd found out what caused 'em; seems at that he throwed the thing back over his head and it landed in Ensell's carriage. He had been about to reach it out when a business colleague had called to him and after that had forgotten all about it.'

The toy had been found over against Ryders colliery! Following into the heat and noise of the tube works Gideon frowned. That whole area of Wednesbury was riddled with abandoned gin pits, their open shafts deep enough to swallow a man without trace; those spending all of their lives as miners treated that part of the heath with caution, but a child...? It would have no chance!

Manoeuvring short iron tubes heated to the point of fusion on the draw bench, Gideon hammered the two pieces, butt-welding the iron into one longer tube before signalling for it to be removed. Supposing Livvy's daughter had somehow come to be on the heath, how had she got there? Busy as his hands, his mind formed question after question. Somebody had to have taken her there ... somebody perhaps wanting rid of her!

With his hammer ringing on iron, he let his mind run free. The governor of the workhouse had said the child had been taken by a gentleman... Jairus Ensell was naught but a fogger, a middleman who got his living by taking every farthing he could slice from a nailer's earnings, but those slices added up to a nice fat whole; but was it that whole or was it his grandmother's money paid for clothes and carriage which marked him as a gentleman?

Pausing to wipe perspiration from his brow Gideon caught Luke's smile across the body of the factory. Luke had no love for Jairus Ensell, seeing the man as no partner for Saran. Returning to the iron tubes glowing on the draw bench Gideon owned to the reason of his wild thoughts. They were the product of bitterness, of jealousy. Jairus Ensell had taken the girl he loved, leaving him prey to every kind of feeling. But much as he cared for Saran he should not give way to thoughts such as the ones edging into his mind, making him ready to suspect Ensell of...

'Hey up there, Gideon, be you butt-weldin' them toobs or be you hammerin' 'em flat!'

Recalled to the task in hand Gideon smiled, but somehow the smile was empty.

'Be you calling on the Elwells later?' Having said goodnight to the watchman at the works' gate, Luke turned to Gideon.

'Not tonight, Livvy needs rest and Edward will do best to stay with her. The work on the warehouse will take no harm from being put back for a while, but you might tell them I was asking after them.'

'I'll do that, and should I tell Saran the same?'

For a moment it seemed Gideon would not answer, then already turning away he said quietly, 'Please give Miss Chandler my regards.'

*'give Miss Chandler my regards'*

Irritatingly the words played in Luke's brain. Regards ... tcha! What was the matter with Gideon, why the hell not even try for Saran, why give Ensell a clear field! Leave it much longer and it would be too late, she would have married the man, would be the wife of Jairus Ensell... Christ, the thought alone gave him the creeps! Lord, if only he were older he would try for Saran himself... What would it take to make her see, make her realise that one was not a man for her? They hadn't exactly known him for years but one thing Luke Hipton were sure of, the centre of Jairus Ensell's world were Jairus Ensell, he...

A slight movement, a rippling of the shadows to his left had the thoughts slip from his brain like water from a jug. The heath was empty, devoid of movement, yet it was a movement had him suddenly still. From the distance the clang of nailers' hammers echoed faint in the darkness, their beat challenged by the thump of Luke's chest. It was not wages day, he had no tin, surely any thief would know that. His breathing slow and shallow he listened to the song of the night. Rustlings in the coarse grass, the whisper of leaves tossed by a light breeze, the hoot of a barn owl. But it was none of these had lifted the hackles on his neck.

Above his head clouds, dense and thick, cleared momentarily, flooding the heath with silver light, yet it showed Luke's swift gaze nothing but the ribbon of road leading to the villages of Ocker Hill and Gospel Oak, and the track he was standing on. But he was not alone, his every fibre told him something watched, waiting its chance. Was he to suffer the same fate as little Martha Elwell ... would he find a hard bed at the bottom of some pit shaft? But his death would not be as that of Edward's child, his would be no accident as a result of wandering across that mine-pocked heath; whatever it was waiting beyond the edge of sight would find Luke Hipton no easy prey!

Thought was simple, but persuading himself to move on that was something else. Pulling in a breath he forced his legs to move. Why was it waiting ... but then why call what watched from beneath the cover of darkness a thing? There were no wild animals roamed the heath apart from foxes and rabbits and they were hardly likely to stalk a human.

Behind or beside! His nerves stretched taut, veins throbbing from the pain of blood suddenly turned solid, he strove to define where the sound had come from. It had not been his own breathing yet it *was* breathing; short, rapid, nervous as himself, something breathed close by. Hands doubling into fists, teeth clenched, Luke began a slow turn, his gaze scything the shadows. Nothing! Brook Cottage was within shouting distance, he glanced at the oblong of light that was a window. But what stalked his steps would strike at the first call, better to go on, get as close to the house as he could.

His senses strained to the limit he moved, then froze as a hand gripped hard to his shoulder.

Livvy had been a woman demented. Having stayed with Ezekiel only long enough to agree to his proposal to fill several more casks with wheat wine, Saran had finished her bread deliveries with the same speed then hurried home to throw herself into the making of the next day's supplies. She had not truly realised what a help Livvy was with the baking. She lifted a flour-covered hand to her hot cheek, pausing long enough to draw a tired breath. But Livvy would be in no state to work for days to come.

She had snatched the little rag doll, holding it to her face, crying her daughter's name over and over. Setting dough to rise in the corner of the hearth Saran relived the heartbreak.

*'My babby be dead, my little wench be dead.'*

The repeated words had drifted behind as Edward had half carried the distraught Livvy to their home.

They had got her at last to bed and she had stayed in the room with Edward until sleep claimed Livvy, then she had returned to Brook Cottage. Jairus had gone. Saran straightened from the hearth, only now remembering he had offered no help to Edward, given no assistance in getting Livvy to her own house. But that was understandable, Jairus would feel responsible ... feel he was to blame by having left the toy in his carriage; feel he had, although unwittingly, brought more grief to the Elwells.

But what Livvy felt was more than grief, more than sorrow. The woman knew, as she herself knew, the misery of heartbreak. Her little girl was lost to her for ever, as Miriam and their mother were lost. The child was dead as surely as they were dead and, like Livvy, she would never know the lonely grave that held her dear ones.

A tap at the door claiming her attention Saran turned to see Edward, cap in hand, standing just inside the scullery. He looked so desperately tired. She felt her heart go out in sympathy. He could not have slept at all yet had insisted on carrying on with the day's work.

'I brought the tallies for the day.' He held out a fistful of paper slips.

He would not agree to let things lie over until tomorrow. Saran thought quickly, searching for a way which would do no injury to the man's quiet pride.

'Edward,' she glanced meaningfully at the evidence of her own exhausting efforts, 'would you mind if we did not fill in the accounts tonight? I ... I'm so tired I really need to rest. Perhaps we can do them tomorrow.'

'You does too much, me and my Livvy 'ave said it afore now.' He laid the slips on a board set close to the scullery sink. 'That don't be all we've said and now I be saying the same to you; God bless you, Saran Chandler, God bless you for your kindness to me and mine.'

It had been several hours since Edward had called. Glancing at the tin clock set on the mantelshelf Saran felt a tingle of alarm. Luke was never long in coming after Edward brought the day's tally. His own day's work finished he would sit with her and she would teach him accounting as her father had taught her. But tonight Luke had not come home.

Trying to take her mind from worry she moved about the kitchen moving things, tidying what had been tidied a dozen times before. Where was Luke? He had never been as late as this!

Too restless to sit she wandered to the window, staring out into the blackness. The heath was dangerous even in daytime, open shafts overgrown by heather and ling dotted every part of it, waiting for the unwary. Could Luke have strayed from the track, had the tragedy of Livvy's daughter happened all over again? No... She rejected the thought. Luke was too wise for that, he knew the hazard of the heath at night. Yet where was he? Turning, she glanced again at the clock. Perhaps the owner of the tube works had asked him to stay on, to help complete some urgent order. And if he had not? Catching up her shawl Saran wrapped it over her head.

There was a way in which to find out!

# 29

Zadok's visitor stretched long legs, crossing one leatherbooted foot over the other.

'I don't want it!' Zadok kicked at the brass fender set around an ornate fireplace.

The nail master's temper had not been improved by the attack made upon him. A knife the woman had used... Zadok had not seen that coming. An amused smile stayed behind the visitor's closed lips. The great Zadok Minch attacked by a woman! And one no doubt already half dead from neglect; anyone need only look at the man's wife to see how servants were treated in this house.

'You can tek it back where you got it from for I wants no truck wi' it!'

His long fingers tapping against a well-formed mouth Zadok's visitor remained silent. Let the nail master rant on, let him get some of his anger out then it could well be business as usual.

'A knife blade in the arm,' Zadok fumed, ''ad I not been so quick it could 'ave been in the heart ... in the bloody heart, I tells you! But her paid. Oh, her paid all right, that seen her off!' Eyes hot with unspent fury glanced at the long-handled whip stood beside the fireplace. 'Knife be no match for a whip ... seen her off, it did.'

'The woman ran away?' It was asked merely as a vent to syphon more of the wrath. The sooner the steam had gone out of Zadok the sooner he would settle to business, and business was all he himself was here for.

'Ran away!' Zadok laughed harshly. 'Her couldn't stand let alone run, not after I were finished with her! Her were bloody well dead and serve her right ... nobody raises a knife to Zadok Minch and walks away; and that one paid the penalty. Like I told that Chandler wench when her called here, nobody raises a hand to Zadok Minch.'

Seeing his visitor's eyebrows raise Zadok growled. 'Ar, and afore you gets any bright ideas, her weren't invited. Come off her own bat, but I sent her away with a flea in her ear!'

'And that was all she was given, a flea in her ear ... nothing between her legs? Not becoming choosy, are we Zadok?'

'You knows me...' the heavy jowls moved as the rumble of a laugh threatened the older man's still uncertain temper, 'swings and roundabouts, I likes both.'

Watching the older man, Zadok's visitor gauged the situation. Flatter the man's sexual ego and the deal was as good as done. 'And ride both equally well, I've no doubt,' he smiled.

'I gets my entertainment...' This time the laugh rolled free of the heavy chest. 'I sees to that.'

'So why not the Chandler girl?'

'I likes to choose who I teks my pleasure with and that one I had no liking for ... too skinny by 'alf; a man gets no enjoyment from lying on a hard bed, and tumbling a bony woman be the same ... no pleasure in it!'

A little longer, lead the nail master just a little further before returning to business. He must get the man to buy the goods, money was in short supply and any chance could not be allowed to slip from the fingers. Keeping his face blank Zadok's visitor rearranged long legs before asking, 'So why, if you had given no invitation, why did the Chandler girl come here to your home?'

As he touched a hand to his wounded arm, Zadok's face darkened. 'Bloody cheek!' he spat. 'And that one downstairs bringin' 'er up to the sitting room! That were summat *her* paid for an' all. My word be law in this house and everybody best see they sticks to it!'

'That is only as it should be.' The dark head nodded in sympathy.

'I allows nobody to question me, nobody meks accusations! I be master ... the wench found that out when the whip caressed her shoulders. I could 'ave finished her then, dealt with her as I dealt with the one give me this...' Zadok rested his free hand gently on the arm caught up in a silken sling. 'I could have seen her off for good 'cept I wanted to see her face, see the look on it when I told her the mother and sister her asked about were dead, courtesy of that whip.'

There had been enough questions concerning the Chandler girl, any more and the nail master's vitriolic temper would flare again, and spending half an evening soothing this man was not the object of the exercise. Drawing in his long legs, Zadok's visitor leaned forward in the deep leather armchair, his dark eyes approving.

'I've no doubt you had worthy cause to do as you did, your judgement has always proved sound, as it will again if you accept this latest consignment.'

'The world be full of bloody fools!' Zadok's raucous laugh echoed from the walls of the tasteful room. 'I thought her downstairs were daft but you be more so if you thinks I be going to buy what you brought tonight. I told you, I don't want it; now you tek your nails and the rest of the rubbish you brought with you and sell 'em to whoever be willing, but that man ain't Zadok Minch!'

'Estate!' Charity Newell looked up from her mending. 'Whatever give you that idea?'

'One or two things Luke has said.'

'Then Luke has got it wrong, the lad be mixed up in his thinking.'

It would be unlike Luke to get his facts wrong. Gideon rested his head on the back of the chair which had been his father's. The boy was sharp in his thinking, he carried a wise head on young shoulders.

'I don't think so.' Gideon put thought into words. 'Luke has mentioned it more than once in conversations, the estate belonging to Jairus Ensell's grandmother.'

The mending resting in her lap Charity looked at her son. 'Mebbe it don't be as wide known as it were, not now so many of the old folk 'ave gone to their rest but there still be one or two in Wednesbury can tell you the same as I tells you. The only estate Jessie Tandy ever knowed was that belongin' to Silas Thursfield, the owner of several collieries. Flighty piece, were Jessie, flaunting what her had wherever her thought it would do her a bit o' good. Well, her flaunted her charms one time too many and tumbled to Thursfield. The fact her were pregnant cut no ice with that man's wife, Amelia Thursfield sent her packing ... only her give her naught to pack. Seen her off without the shillings Jessie had worked for, said her had the pay her deserved. So what does Jessie do then but play her game with Thomas Ensell. That man had no more than a tiny cottage and half an acre of land out along Moxley way, but he could give name to the child he knew nothing about, so Jessie dupes him into marrying her and that half acre were the only estate Jairus Ensell's grandmother ever had, and, so far as be known to me, her lives there still. So whoever be filling young Luke's head with a different tale be–'

A knock at the door breaking off her account Charity set aside her mending, going to open it.

'I beg pardon for disturbing you...'

Gideon's heart stopped, then began a race which churned the blood in his veins. Saran! It was Saran had knocked at the door.

'It is a liberty coming to your home but, please, I had to ask... Is Luke here, is he with Gid– Mr Newell?'

'Luke? No, wench, the lad don't be here, but come you in.'

'No, no I must not impose.'

The trembling voice answering his mother's firm one brought Gideon to his feet.

'There is no imposition in your calling here, Miss Chandler,' he said, 'but please accept my mother's invitation to step inside.'

'It's Luke.' Hazel eyes wide with worry looked first at Charity then at the man beside her. 'He has not come home ... I thought perhaps he might be with you.'

Frowning, Gideon shook his head. 'He left the works with me, we walked across the Bullen together, same as always, the watchman will tell you the same.'

'I called at the tube works, the watchman said Luke and you left together that is why I thought–'

'The lad ain't been to this house,' Charity answered. 'I bet he be dawdlin' in the town somewheres, lads of that age find mischief in the most unlikely places.'

'Luke would not loiter in the town.' Saran pulled her shawl closer. 'Forgive my intrusion, Mrs Newell...'

'Wait up, wench!' Charity said quickly. 'You can't go searchin' on your own and as for crossing the heath and nobody with you...'

'My mother is right.' Blood still pumping like a steam engine Gideon reached for his jacket. 'It isn't safe for you to return to Brook Cottage alone and certainly not to enquire in some of the taverns. I will take you home and if Luke is still not returned then I'll look for him.'

There had been no 'will you allow me'. Charity Newell closed her door, her mind thoughtful. Gideon had not asked would the wench allow him to see her home, and his eyes as he'd looked at her... Oh, it had been Mr Newell and Miss Chandler between them, but Gideon's eyes...

Returning to her chair she picked up her mending but her fingers remained still, her glance lost in the heart of the fire.

Gideon had appeared cool, his words calm, but his eyes they had told a different story.

He had looked in every place he had thought Luke likely to be and in several he had hoped the lad never to be. Where in the name of heaven could he have got to ... where else was there left to look?

From the hill overlooking the town the parish church of St Bartholomew chimed eleven. It had been several hours since his leaving Saran at Brook Cottage. He had suggested she stay with the Elwells 'til his return with Luke but she had refused, saying they had troubles enough without sharing hers.

Her face had been so pale, her hazel eyes glistening with tears she was fighting so hard to hold back, and himself? Gideon's mouth tightened. He had fought hard to prevent himself taking her in his arms, to tell her of the feelings that made his nights unbearable, to tell her of the love that burned so deep his heart was afire. But he had not, he had simply promised he would find Luke.

That was proving a promise he could not keep. Had he searched as thoroughly as he might or had he been somehow sidetracked? Or was it an accident, had Luke daydreamed as he crossed the heath, had the mouth of some gorse-covered shaft opened beneath his feet? Gideon rejected the thought. Think, he told himself, think logically. But hadn't he done that already and got nowhere! So do it again. Trying to remember every word of the day's conversation with Luke, Gideon analysed them carefully, trying to discover in them some clue which he had missed, something which might tell where it was the lad had gone.

A burst of laughter from across the way breaking his concentration he glanced towards where a black-lacquered carriage was drawn up at the entrance of the elegant George Hotel. Elegant the building was, Gideon thought acidly, but many of its patrons left a great deal to be desired.

The laugh pealing again he looked more attentively at the well-dressed figure highlighted in the doorway, a silk-gowned woman to each side of him.

Jairus Ensell! Luke had talked of the man and of his grandmother's so-called estate, but Luke had not gone there. Watching the man, one woman clinging close on his arm, Gideon felt a rush of distaste; this was the man who was to marry Saran but that fact obviously did not preclude his sporting with other women.

Grabbing the second woman giggling at his shoulder, Jairus bent to kiss her and as he raised his head his eyes closed with Gideon's.

'Well, well!' He laughed again. 'We have an audience, my dears. Good evening, Mr Newell, you find our entertainment to your liking?'

'Will you not introduce us, Jairus?' The woman he had kissed giggled again.

'To a workman! I hardly think so. Come, we

must not embarrass the poor man, once is enough for any evening.'

The several lanterns illuminating the façade of the gracious George Hotel caught Ensell's eyes as he looked directly across the narrow space and Gideon saw they were laughing.

Just as he had laughed earlier! That was the once Ensell had spoken of as being enough. The bitterness of distaste was gall in Gideon's throat as he watched the carriage and its occupants drive away. Walking slowly into Union Street and on into Dudley Street Gideon followed the road towards the heath which bordered the town. Luke had talked of the man's grandmother so that had seemed a likely place for the lad to have gone, but the cottage had been locked and barred, the woman likely in her bed. So he had made his way to Ensell's house.

*'Luke has not honoured me with a visit, but then what would a foundry rat have with me?'*

Gideon remembered the smirk with which it had been said, and the almost uncontrollable urge to punch away the supercilious smile; but he had made do with words, words that for an instant had brought fear to that arrogant face.

*'Maybe he doesn't believe in fairy stories, the kind that tells of an old rag doll being found near the coal shafts then being tossed into your carriage, maybe the lad thinks as I do, thinks you too know fairy tales aren't true!'*

*'Doll?'* Jairus Ensell's finely marked brows had drawn together. *'Oh, but of course, the toy Saran tells me belonged to the Elwell child; but that was no fairy tale.'*

It had been said carelessly but, sensing the fear behind the smile, Gideon had left nothing to be guessed from his answer.

*'The doll, no, but how it came to be with you ... that* is *a fairy tale. I think you are lying, Ensell, I think you know a damn sight more than you've said, and should that prove no fairy tale I will break every bone in your body before throwing* you *down a mine shaft!'*

*'How very distasteful.'* Ensell's arrogance had returned. *'It strikes me you think I have something to do with the child's disappearance even though the workhouse could give no name to her benefactor... Perhaps you think her here in this house, in which case I insist you look in every room.'*

Ensell had not expected the invitation to be taken up. Gideon recalled the surprise on the handsome face as he had pushed past into the house. But the child had not been there ... and neither had Luke.

Nobody knew what he was doing or where he was. Luke gently lifted the window he had prised open, holding his breath against a possible sound. Saran would wonder at his not being home at the usual time but he would make some excuse of throwing dice with some of the men he worked with and forgetting the time. The window wide enough to afford entry he slipped easily inside the house, his breath returning as it lowered again without noise. Standing in the silent darkness he listened. Had he been seen ... heard? With his heart beating rapidly he waited, flinching nervously, as the sounds of old timbers creaked and groaned from the roof. Would he find anything of value here, enough to make the risk worth while?

What would Saran think if she knew what he was doing ... what would Gideon Newell think of him? For a moment Luke felt a twinge of guilt then quickly pushed it away. It didn't matter what they thought, they or anyone else; he had lived long enough under the eye of people who had him do as they thought he should, but now he was free of the workhouse and its warders, this was his life and he would live it as he wanted!

Around him the darkness began to take on darker shapes, silhouettes of chairs, cupboard and a deeper central pool of blackness which had to be a table. Accustomed now to the change from clouded moonlight to the gloom of the unlit room he moved cautiously to a door, listening intently as he eased it open. To be caught would not mean the workhouse, it would mean years of hard labour or even the gallows; the law did not look kindly on people breaking into the homes of others.

Taking one slow step at a time, listening at intervals, he moved along a short corridor coming to what the dull glow of a low fire showed to be the kitchen. Fire! Luke's nerves twitched. There must be someone in the house!

In the room he had just left a clock chimed, but soft as the notes were they sent the blood racing along his veins. Every sense telling him he should leave, go now before he was discovered, Luke gritted his teeth. He wouldn't go with nothing!

Resolution firm in his mind he moved cat-like in the darkness, touching lightly against furniture, intuition warning him when to stop. Forcing himself to concentrate, to ignore the settling of embers in the grate, which jangled his already taut nerves, the continuing crack of age-old timbers, he sought in his mind the location of the stairs. In this type of house they always led off the kitchen. His feet making no sound on the stone-flagged floor he edged carefully between the clutter of furniture. Knock anything over and it would ring through the house like church bells!

There had to be a door! Taking a deep breath Luke let his brain take over. Acting like a blind man he listened to his innermost sense. The wall opposite the fireplace, that was the most likely place for a door giving on to stairs.

It had been a fruitful guess. Testing each bare wooden step with a light press of his foot it seemed to Luke's pressured nerves that years passed before he reached the top. On the small square of a landing he paused. That fire in the kitchen grate said the house was occupied ... whoever lived here would be in a bedroom, but which bedroom ... and were they asleep or awake and listening? Waiting for him!

The thought adding to the tumult in his veins Luke pondered again the results of being caught. Twenty years ... thirty ... death? It was a mindless risk to take, a crazy stupid risk! In the darkness of the landing Luke smiled grimly to himself. Luke Hipton had so often been called stupid by those warders ... why deny it now!

Heart rapping in his chest he moved towards one of two closed doors. Stupidity was about to be tested.

The room had proved empty of people. In the half light provided by a low window he had probed every corner, satisfied with what he found ... but there was still the second room.

Downstairs the clock chimed the quarter hour, the sound echoing through the silent house while Luke's stretched nerves played the same tune. He really should go while the going was good! Back on the landing he looked at the second door. He had come this far, he wouldn't go before seeing whether that last room held anything of interest.

The doorknob felt solid in his hand and he breathed long and slow. If those inside had heard him, were waiting for him to step inside that room...! But nobody would have remained silent for so long, the alarm would surely be on by now. Painfully slowly he turned the handle, his teeth clenched so tightly they hurt in his jaw. This was mad! Sheer lunacy! Every fibre of his body tingling, Luke closed his mind to the warning and gently pushed back the door.

Becoming accustomed to the deep gloom his eyes picked out vague shapes, a chair, a bed, but the room was tiny, no more than a cupboard. Keeping his hands stretched out in front he felt his way, moving carefully until the sound of horses' hooves halted him.

'Damn,' he swore under his breath, moving more quickly to the window whose light was almost obscured by the overhang of a thatched roof. It was tucked beneath the eaves and with any luck he would not be noticed. Pressed close against the wall he peered into the yard below.

'What the devil...!'

Startled words floated on the night silence.

'Not the devil,' a rougher voice answered the first, 'but somebody who'll give you a worse time than him should I not get what I be here for.'

'And what might that be?'

'You knows well what that be...'

Making another of its coquettish appearances the moon spread the scene with silver and Luke strained to see who it was outside the house.

'I wants what be owing, the money for doing your dirty work.'

'I told you.' Irate, the answer came quickly. 'You will get your money when the goods be sold.'

'I be fed up with waiting, I've done my part and now I want the pay for it, or else I might be obliged to–'

'You'll do nothing!'

The cold snarl had Luke pressing closer to the window. Through the silvered pane he saw one figure grab another, shoving it savagely against a small pony cart.

'You say one word – you hear, one word – and you won't live to see the next day!'

'I just wanted my money.'

The strangled words floated up to where Luke stood listening.

'You said I would 'ave it tonight.'

Overlooked by Luke one figure released the other.

'I thought I would but the deal did not go through, seems what we have is no longer of interest, I will have to find another buyer.'

'And if you can't?'

For a moment there was silence then a harsh

laugh followed the grated reply: 'In that case you will have one more job to do.'

'I ain't–'

'You will do exactly as I say!'

The taller of the two shot out a fist, knocking the other figure to the ground before taking the horse's bridle. As he turned to lead the animal into a stable a shaft of moonlight illuminated his face, and in that darkened room Luke caught his breath. This must be the owner of the house ... and he was here to stay!

# 30

'I am sure you have done your best, Mr Newell.'

Her lips trembling with worry and disappointment, Saran tried hard to hold emotion in check as she thanked the tall man stood in the kitchen of Brook Cottage.

'There was no other place I could think of but if you know of somewhere he could be, I will go...'

'No.' Saran shook her head. 'Thank you, but you have done enough, besides which I would not have your mother fret on my account.'

Watching her struggle to keep her lips from quivering, to stay the tears glistening in her lovely eyes, the longing to take her in his arms, to whisper his love against soft shining hair, was almost unbearable.

'My mother realises the child is grown, she no longer has a boy for a son but a man grown,' he answered sharply.

She had annoyed him, and after he had been so kind.

'Mr Newell,' she said as he turned from her, 'I did not mean... It is just that I know how worrying it can be when someone you love dearly is from home so late; please forgive...'

'There is nothing to forgive.' The gruffness of emotion in his voice, Gideon did not turn; he knew that to face her now, to look into those tear-filled eyes, would have the barriers of his reserve crumble, that he would not have the strength of will to prevent himself reaching for her, babbling his love like a moon-struck fool.

'I ... I was about to make some tea, would you care for a cup ... or maybe a bowl of soup? I have kept some hot against Luke returning.'

The last word came on a sob, whirling Gideon around. In the second it took he saw the helpless drop of her arms, the fall of her head, and his heart pivoted. Forgetting they were alone in the house, forgetting she was promised to another man, forgetting everything but that he loved her, he drew her to him, wanting his arms only to shield her from hurt, his love to guard her from sorrow.

His lips touching her hair, her face pressed to his shoulder, her warm body trembling against his own, Gideon drank the moment deep into his soul. This was the only time he would know this joy, the one time he would hold his love in his arms ... it must last him for a lifetime.

'No tears.' They were not the words he longed to whisper, the words crying in his heart, but even as hunger for her racked him Gideon knew those were words he must never say. 'No tears,' he murmured again lifting a hand to stroke the gold-tinted softness of her hair. 'I will find Luke, I promise.'

Held against him, Saran lifted her head and for a moment her lips called to him and his senses leapt. He could so easily take that soft mouth, crush his own to it...

'You should not stay here alone.' The effort of denying himself that which every atom of his body craved, of releasing her from his hold had Gideon striving to keep his tone even. 'I will take you to the Elwells before I go look again for Luke.'

She was gone from him! His need raw and painful, he watched the slender figure move to stand staring into the red heart of the fire.

'Livvy must not be disturbed,' she said, brushing a finger over tears which had spilled, 'and I will not leave this house. I understand your care for my welfare, Mr Newell, but I assure you I am quite accustomed to being alone here.'

There was a determination in that quiet voice he knew would not be broken and though his very being cried out against it Gideon nodded.

Stood at the door Saran watched the light of the lantern she had handed him bob like a yellow star amid the blackness of night and suddenly the fear and emptiness inside her – a feeling which until now she had thought solely due to Luke's absence – became stronger, cutting with breath-snatching severity until it was no longer simply an emptiness ... it was a desolation.

The figure sprawled on the ground got to its feet. As the head tilted, Luke shrank back, wary of being seen at the moonlit window. Waiting several seconds before edging nearer he saw the figure turn away, becoming lost among the shadows. One gone. He loosed the breath held in his throat; but the other, the man gone into the stable ... he would not take the horse in there had he intended to leave again; no, that one was home to stay.

Could he get from this room, down the stairs

and out of the front entrance before the man came in? Perspiration damp on his palms Luke calculated his chances of escaping without detection. If that door were locked and then bolted ... no, he could not risk it, old locks could be the devil to release; the window, then, perhaps he could climb out of the window and jump to the ground – it wasn't so much of a drop! Grasping the sash he tried to lift it but the window refused to budge. Luke swore again, the sash probably hadn't been lifted in years!

So what now? He couldn't just stand here waiting to be discovered, and though the first bedroom had been empty that carried no guarantee it was the room the man slept in, it could quite as easily be this one.

The banging of a door resounded through the still house. Luke's tight nerves vibrated. Whatever he decided to do it had to be done quickly. Almost with the thought the sound of a footstep came loud on the stairs. Quickly wasn't enough ... it had to be *now*. The moon, obscured by cloud, withdrew its light and plunged the tiny room into pitch darkness, leaving him with only a vague picture of where the shape seeming like a narrow bed had been.

Had it indeed been a bed ... was it where he thought it was? The steps ominously near to the door, Luke knew he had no time to wonder. Taking one deep breath he launched himself into the blackness.

His heart had to be heard! Luke pressed close to the floor, hearing the brush of the door as it opened. If he heard that whisper of sound then whoever had opened the door must hear the drum beat thumping in his chest; breath he could hold, but how did he stop what seemed a cannon roar in his ears?

This must be the man's bedroom, why else would he have come in? Tension increasing, adding to the tautness of his nerves, Luke prayed the man would light no lamp, for if he did then all chance of remaining unseen could be kissed goodbye.

Why the hell had he come into this box of a room? Holding his breath in his throat, Luke cursed himself. Why couldn't he have been satisfied with what he had ... left the house while he had still had the opportunity?

From the shadows a murmur touched the riot in his brain. What was the man doing? Undressing ... reaching for a lamp? Fingers curled into fists as Luke assessed his situation. He knew the other man was here while his own presence was unknown, surprise was on his side and it was an element could prove as valuable as any weapon. A few minutes, allow the man to become totally relaxed and he would strike then run for that open window... Pray! he told himself. Pray the window hasn't been closed!

And if it had? The question formed as the swish of sound repeated itself and a quiet click of the door closing was followed by the sound of a key turning in the lock. Silently releasing pent-up breath, his body suddenly feeling ten times heavier than normal, Luke remained face down in the darkness. He was locked in! He had let himself get locked in this house!

With the coming of morning he would almost certainly be discovered, the man need only walk into the room! The window ... this time it had to open, but not yet, the fellow was probably not asleep yet.

Waiting what to him was the whole of eternity Luke stood. Moving cat-like to the window he looked out. The rim of the horizon was not yet edged with that faint band of grey which heralded dawn. Tentatively he tested the window, feeling it move slightly beneath his fingers. Sighing with relief he relaxed, two minutes and he would be away...

It was then the voice spoke!

He had come this way earlier. Gideon glanced along the faintly gleaming ribbon of grey that was the Bilston Road. Retracing it would prove a useless exercise but he had promised Saran he would search again and he had also promised himself, when Luke Hipton was found, to give him a sound remembrance of this night. All right, so the lad hadn't thought ... but next time he would, and hard!

Across the heath a dog fox barked, answered by the mournful howl of a vixen. Despite himself Gideon smiled. If Luke had heard that then hopefully it had him as scared as his going off had scared Saran.

Saran! The smile vanished. He had held her in his arms, felt the soft yield of her body against his own, and for a moment he had imagined she was there from love of him. And that was all it had been, imagination ... a pretence; but it was one he would treasure, conjure again and again through the long years without her. If he had taken John Adams's offer of post as overseer, if his mother had agreed to leave the cottage...? But moving place of work, moving home would not have wiped Saran Chandler from his mind, she would be with him always, a part of him, a part of his heart.

Was what he felt visible? His eyes scanning the rough ground to either side Gideon felt the warm blood surge in his face. Did his mother suspect ... had she guessed? He had called in at his own home after leaving Brook Cottage, told his mother of his intention to go look again for Luke, that she should go to bed and not worry. His mother had nodded when he'd said it was the least he could do for the lad but her eyes ... her eyes said she understood a different reason.

As a shift in the clouds allowed a brief illumination to push aside the barriers of darkness, Gideon halted. There! He had not been mistaken, there ahead ... something was moving ... it was moving towards him!

Straining to see into the regrouping shadows, to discern which moved and which did not, Gideon waited. The something was coming on but its speed was restricted, encumbered by something it carried.

'God Almighty, Luke! Where have you been?'

'Give ... give me a minute!' Panting with the effort of running Luke lowered his burden to the ground, slumping beside it.

'You bloody little fool!' Gideon hid his relief

behind anger. 'Do you know the trouble you've caused, the worry to Saran by running off without a word! I ought to take the skin off your backside! What the hell did you think you were doing ... and what's that you have? Luke...' Gideon paused, staring keenly at the boy he would have trusted with his own life. 'Why, why steal, why have you become a thief?'

His breath laboured and gasping Luke took a minute before replying.

'See ... see for yourself.' Throwing a blanket from the bundle beside him he stared up at Gideon. 'That be why.'

'You're going to show me!' Gideon straightened from looking at Luke's trophy. 'You are going to show me where you got what I'm looking at, and you are going back.'

Luke's explosion rang on the night, sending tiny unseen creatures scuffling among gorse and heather. 'Tek back! I'll be buggered if I does!'

'You'll be walloped if you don't.' Grabbing him by the collar Gideon hauled Luke to his feet then took up the bundle. As he gave Luke a shove in the direction he had come only minutes before, Gideon's voice was harsh. 'Lead on ... and no tricks!'

'Here?' Gideon frowned when a short while later Luke halted before a low-eaved cottage standing alone on the heath. 'But I came here earlier and you were not here.'

'Mebbe not when you come,' Luke's grin showed white in the moonlight, 'but this be where I've been and if you still intends to return what you be holdin' then this be the house.'

The lad knew what to expect if he was lying. Handing the blanket-wrapped bundle to Luke he banged a fist hard on the door. Barely had it opened when Gideon asked quietly, 'Light the lamp, please ... I have something here to show you.'

Waiting until the request had grumblingly been fulfilled he pulled the blanket aside.

Even in the sparse light shed by the lamp Gideon saw the face pale as it stared at him.

'What is this ... why come to my house at this time of night?'

'I'm sure you can see what it is and that must tell you why we are here.'

'If this is some kind of game, then I'm not amused.' In the anaemic glow dark eyes narrowed. 'But then perhaps it is not a game but rather something your devious mind has dreamed up in order to place me in a bad light.'

'No, it is not a game, and you don't need my help to place you in bad light. Just tell me how...'

His composure restored, the other man glared. 'I have only one thing to say to you and to the brat with you, leave my house or you will answer to the magistrate!'

'Tomorrer will see you answer to the magistrate!' Luke flared. 'He'll know what it were I found in your house.'

'Now that will be interesting!' The sneer was obvious. 'And how will you prove what you say is true?'

'It be the truth, I was upstairs watching when you come home, when you knocked a man sprawling cos he asked for money owed by you; I was in that bedroom when you come in, the one you locked after leavin'.'

'And that is the proof you intend to offer the magistrate?' A short laugh echoed in the gloom. 'You will own to the fact you broke into a man's house then, because you were disturbed by him before you could steal anything, you came back with a cock-and-bull story–'

'It be no story!' Luke's anger boiled. 'It be the truth, I found–'

'You found nothing!' The curt answer split the silence. 'Go to the magistrate, tell him what it is you accuse me of, but who do you think he will believe, a jumped-up upstart with the workhouse as his background – or will he believe the word of a gentleman?'

'What he says will carry weight with the law,' Gideon intervened. 'We have no real evidence, it will be your word against his.'

'Then he be going to get away with it?' Luke spat, disgusted. 'So why, if you knowed that, did you drag me all the way back here? Why not just forget everythin'!'

'I have my reasons.'

Standing an arm's length from them the man's sneering laugh broke once more. 'Oh, and what might they be?'

'This!' A fist shooting out caught the jeering figure, flinging it half across the dimly lit room. 'And this!' Following with a second stinging blow, he hauled the half unconscious man to his feet, holding him with one hand. 'You may have evaded the law,' he growled, his free hand doubling, 'but you haven't evaded me!'

That sixth sense, which had warned Luke of unseen eyes watching from somewhere beyond the fringe of sight, of that same something which had followed close on his footsteps on his way to Brook Cottage, had warned again of the closeness of danger and as the touch had brushed his shoulder instinct born of years spent in that workhouse, years where every moment must be one of self-protection, had come automatically to his aid. Walking beside Gideon he smiled at the memory of what had happened next. He had lifted a hand to his shoulder, grabbing what touched him, holding on as he had allowed his legs to fold and his body to roll, pitching a weight over his head.

Walking beside Gideon it seemed he heard again the thud as that weight had hit the ground. He had not given the initial surprise of being discovered the chance to wear off, instead he had flung himself on his stalker, fists flying. Several blows had found their mark before the resulting cries had penetrated the anger clouding his brain and he had let Joseph up.

The lad had mumbled an apology for creeping up on him, stumbling over the words, and it had taken a while before Luke had fully grasped the reason for the boy's lying in wait for him.

'So why did he wait for you?' Having heard part of the story Gideon was interested to hear the rest.

'Said he couldn't tell nobody else,' Luke replied, 'said he couldn't tell his mother on account of her not bein' able to stand the pain of it and he didn't want to worry his father more than he was already, then said he couldn't say nothin' to Saran but ... well, he said he had to tell somebody.'

Matching his steps to Gideon's he saw the scene again in his mind's eye. They had stood together, himself a head taller than the boy, and while a quixotic moon had darted in and out of heavy cloud he had listened to his garbled explanation, then, when it was done, had ordered him home. That part had not been so easy. Joseph Elwell had pluck, he had argued his rights until Luke's fist had waved beneath his nose and his tone had become threatening.

'And he thought the best somebody to tell would be you? So what exactly did he tell you, and whatever it was why do anything on your own?'

Glancing at Gideon, at the bundle in his arms, Luke could not determine if the tightly spoken words were a criticism.

'Joseph wanted to come but I told him I wouldn't have his mother worry over his not being home.'

It hadn't been quite like that, in fact it had been nothing like that. Luke hid the grin rising to his mouth. He had growled at the lad to *'go afore I lowks your ears'*, then when Joseph had argued he had grabbed his collar, his fist brushing the end of his nose while he repeated the threat to box his ears. Joseph had stepped quickly out of reach as his collar was released, then, when Luke had called a warning that no word be spoken to Saran – or else! – he had answered, *'I knows, I hold me tongue or you'll lowk me ears!'*

'Joseph told me he'd seen the man who took him to Minch's place.'

Gideon's glance shot to the boy at his side. 'The one who took him from the workhouse?'

'He wasn't sure of that but said definite it was the man took him to Minch, said he caught a glimpse of the face afore the fellow slipped a hood over his head and bundled him into a carriage or some such; said it were only a glimpse but the man he saw today were the same one.'

'Where did Joseph see this man?' Gideon hitched the bundle in his arms to a more comfortable position.

'Top end of Meeting Street.'

The street of the workhouse! Blood chilled in Gideon's veins. Had another child been taken?

'I would 'ave come for you but I thought there might not be time,' Luke went on hastily, 'so I described him at the kitchen of the Turk's Head and was told of the place I went tonight.'

Seemed the man was known for more than a thief! Gideon's mouth tightened.

'I got in through a window at the back and though I weren't sure of what it was I were looking to get I went into every room. It were after I seen him go into the stable I knew I had to get out but the window were stuck and ... well I had to dive under the bed. I don't know how long I waited afore crawlin' out but I went straight to the window, that were when I heard the voice. I swears there were nobody in that bed when I went into the room, it were gloomy but I would 'ave seen; he must have carried it upstairs and put it there when he come in. I tells you, Gideon, when I heard it I nearly done it in me trousers.'

'Serves you right,' Gideon smiled, 'p'raps that's the kind of lesson you need.'

'I wondered whether to run downstairs or dive right through the window,' Luke grinned, 'but then I heard this voice ask were I lost an' all? And when I turned to look there was this figure sittin' up in the bed, its face all white and scared. I were feared the man might hear and come bustin' in so I whispered there was no need to be frightened for I was leaving. I had the window up when I felt this tug on my jacket and heard the voice saying, "Please, do you know where my mammy be ... will you tell her to come get me ... I be frightened." It were then I looked closer ... I were looking at Martha. It were all a bit of a scramble after that. I couldn't tek time to look for clothes to cover her nightgown so I snatched a blanket from the bed and chucked it to the ground before climbing over the windowsill. Telling Martha to climb on me back, I let meself down the ivy and ... well, you knows the rest.'

Yes, he knew the rest. Gideon stared ahead to where a pinpoint of light beckoned. But the Elwells and Saran? They would know only that the child had been found by a workman crossing the heath on his way back from work.

# 31

The returning of Livvy's daughter to her had been heartbreaking to watch but beneath the tears had shone the parents' joy. Saran rested the long-handled pen, staring at a picture her mind showed so often. Livvy had screamed, staring as though at a ghost, but as Gideon had placed the child in her arms she had cried as if her heart would break and all the time had held the child as if against the world.

It had been a miracle her being found wandering the heath, she might so easily have fallen into some old mine shaft. God had been good returning both children to their home, but her family would never return, they lay dead with not even a marker to say their names.

*'a sovereign … it sees to all the shit needs collecting from my house.'*

The words rang in her brain. Zadok Minch had paid to have her mother and sister taken away like so much rubbish, their bodies probably thrown into a midden. But she had not forgotten her vow of revenge.

Returning her attention to the accounts book she so meticulously kept she felt a wave of satisfaction. In the months since Martha's return Livvy had thrown herself into the bread-making business with a will, and together they had increased the output tenfold and could increase it yet again except they were worked to the limit. It meant she would have to refuse William Salisbury's request that she make bread for the party he was throwing for his workers to celebrate the queen's coronation. It was something she hated having to do; after all, had it not been for the Salisburys there would be no Brook Cottage and no business.

'Don't the numbers add up as they should?'

Glancing up, Saran smiled. 'My mind keeps straying.'

'And where does it stray to?'

When had Luke suddenly grown so tall? Saran watched him cross the room, lithe and easy as a cat.

'To the night you and Gideon brought Martha home. Luke, was it truly the way Gideon told it, was the child found on the heath?'

He had not wanted the truth to be hidden, it should be told. But, as Gideon explained, they could prove nothing. To involve the Justice would only bring fresh grief to the Elwells and no benefit of seeing the man answer for taking their children. So why had he taken them? It had been several moments before Gideon had answered, telling him some men preferred children in their bed. That was when Luke had agreed never to let the full story pass his lips and had later made Joseph swear the same; what mother could live with the fear of what might have been? But the man ... somehow, someday he would get what was due him.

'Why would he lie? What good would it do him?'

Blue eyes vivid in the light of the lamp smiled at Saran but behind the smile was a flicker of unease. This was how it had been whenever she asked about that night, as if Luke knew more than he would say ... but why hide anything? Was it for the good it would do others rather than Gideon himself?

'None,' she shook her head, 'I'm just being silly.'

It would serve no purpose to pursue the happenings of that night. She had spoken of it several times to Gideon Newell as well as to Luke, but neither varied from the one fact that a child had been found by a workman who had taken her to his wife to care for. Luke had heard it being talked of as he crossed the market square and raced off to Bilston to find if it was Martha and that is where Gideon had caught up with him.

'And them figures...' Luke sat at the table, 'they bein' silly too?'

'My father wouldn't say so.' Leaning back in her chair Saran closed tired eyes. 'He would say it was not the book but the book-keeper; if figures did not add up then it was his work should be looked to.'

'Let me look at them.' Expert now as Saran herself he ran a finger down each column.

He would be a handsome man. She watched the concentration trace tiny lines between his brows. Handsome as Gideon? Quickly she pushed the thought away, conscious it played in her mind too often. She was to marry Jairus; he had been patient, understanding when she said that before she wed she had a promise to keep, a promise made to herself; and she was already keeping it. Edward reported that almost every nailer in the town now brought their product to Brook Cottage.

'I see nothing wrong with the figures, they looks well.' Luke looked up from the ledger. 'But I don't say the same of you, you be tired, Saran, you needs to let up.'

'I will, once the festivities for the coronation–'

'No!' Luke's answer was sharp with concern he had been feeling for some time. 'You need to let up now or else tek on some extra help.'

'It would take some of the strain off Livvy, but the amounts Edward records against the nailers' names shows the women have no time to spare, they work as many hours as their men.'

'I wasn't thinkin' of the nailers' wives.' Luke hitched his chair closer to hers. 'I were thinkin' of the women shut away in the bowels of hell, tek one or two from the workhouse and they'll be so grateful they won't never let you down. And the same goes for your wheat wine. Ezekiel be gettin' on in years, he won't be up to the work for many more years so tek a lad or a man from the same place and let him be trained to the job. I thinks you'll not regret it.'

The man in Luke had once more shown the way. Tomorrow she would take his advice.

'Jairus ... what are you doing here?' Saran looked at the tall figure leaving the workhouse, seeing the momentary confusion cross the handsome face as he saw who it was spoke to him.

'My dear.' He caught her hand, holding it protectively between both of his, using the moment to banish surprise. 'It is myself should ask you that.'

Glancing about them as he kissed her hand, Saran pulled shyly away. 'I am thinking of taking on a woman to help with the baking, it ... it was Luke's suggestion.'

Hipton, that young toad. He really must do something to rid the world of that particular vermin! Jairus's smile hid the poison of his thoughts as he answered.

'It is a very good suggestion, my love, one I wholly applaud. These poor people need all the help we can give, which is why I come once a month to make a donation which will buy them a little extra comfort. But maybe it would be well for me to go in with you.'

Suddenly feeling this was something she should do alone, Saran shook her head. 'No, Jairus, thank you, but really there is no need, I can manage perfectly well, besides which you must have other things to attend to.'

'There is business needing my attention,' he smiled apologetically, 'so if you are sure?'

She had been. Saran followed the grey-gowned wardress along dim corridors which so often haunted her nightmares. She had not wanted Jairus to see her face the man who had tried to abuse her.

'Chandler ... Chandler?' The governor looked at the wardress as she announced his visitor. 'Tell her to come back tomorrow.'

'I have business tomorrow.' Amazed at her own

courage Saran stepped into the room, dreams of which still disturbed her sleep.

'Then say what it is you have to say and go ... and *don't* come back tomorrow or any other day!'

He remembered their last meeting ... and it smarted! Saran kept her glance firmly on the heavy face.

'I have come–'

'Wait!' He waved the wardress out of the room and for a moment Saran felt a wave of the same fear she had felt on that other visit, but the hard ways of the world had added a new facet to Saran Chandler. Let this man touch her again and that same world would know of it, regardless of how it labelled her.

'Well, well!' Close-set eyes ran deliberately over the plain brown skirt topped by a cream cotton blouse, over which the threadbare shawl was drawn tight. 'You've found no man who can afford to dress you decent, I see! You shouldn't have been so quick to refuse what I offered.'

'Don't let appearances fool!' Saran returned acidly. 'Fine feathers do not always make fine birds, as you yourself show very clearly.'

From behind his desk the small eyes gleamed murderously. 'Get out,' he snarled, 'get out afore–'

'Afore what! Afore you try rape, before you abuse me as you did before?' Calmer than she thought she could ever be, Saran stared coldly at the face contorting with rage. 'I advise you think twice before you do.'

There was something different about her. His hands tightening on the desk, the governor strove to contain the urge to strike the young woman watching him with open defiance. The clothes were not so patched but neither were they quality, they had not cost a deal of money ... so what was it made her different, gave her such an air of assurance?

'I told you, say what you have to and go!'

He had not offered her a chair, but then he had not made to leave his own to come towards her as on that other occasion. Saran breathed quiet relief. Her tone calm and matter of fact, even though her pulse pounded, she said, 'Circumstances dictate I take on more labour. I believe the workhouse can provide that labour.'

'Circumstances! You need tek on labour...' a loud laugh filled the room, '*you* tek on labour ... and pay with what, chickenshit?'

Waiting for the laugh to subside, Saran stared steadily at the mocking face.

'A little more than chickenshit. I believe the rate for the release of an adult is five pounds, I shall be needing two people, one man, one woman.' Reaching into the pocket of her skirt she placed several gold coins on the desk.

Ten sovereigns! One finger spreading the coins the governor of the workhouse stared at the shining array. Where the hell had the wench got this! Whoring? Not many men he knew would pay more than sixpence for a woman like her ... yet she had got it somewhere. Ten sovereigns ... he felt his mouth salivate, he could buy many sixpenny women with those. As his fingers played over the coins a picture formed in his mind, the picture of this same woman snatching back his head ... sending him sprawling across this very room, and he shoved the coins savagely across the desk. A smile touching flabby lips, he looked at Saran.

'I remember on your last visit you offered money. I told you then to keep your sovereigns and I tell you the same again. Keep your money and I will keep the inmates ... *all* of the inmates!'

'The same way you kept the Elwell children?'

There was no mistaking the look that flashed across those fat-encroached eyes. He had heard, the whole town had buzzed with the news for weeks after their return; yes, he had heard ... and for some reason he was afraid.

'Well, no matter.' Saran drew the coins towards her. 'I will just have to make application to the Board of Trustees, no doubt they will be interested to hear why you refuse to release people offered work, people whose release would lighten the burden on the parish... Oh–' clear in the message they held, her eyes fastened on those of the governor '–and of course, whoever it was you released the Elwell children to... I hope you recorded the amount received for them.'

'You 'ave the bloody cheek to show your face here!' Zadok roared at the visitor his wife had shown into the room. 'You come here bold as brass after what 'appened! Well, you get your arse outta my house quick afore I kicks it out!'

'You can hardly blame me for–'

'Hardly blame you!' Zadok's face was purple with rage. 'Then who be it you suggests I blame? You be the fogger, you be the one creamed a profit off every pound o' nails sold to you; not satisfied with what I paid to you ... no, you had to tek more, and what did that cause? I'll bloody well tell you what it caused, it sent every nailer in Wednesbury scurryin' to another nail master, leaving my tekins down, and what do you do? You whine that it hardly be your fault.'

'They'll come back.'

'Come back!' Zadok almost choked. 'Would you come back when doing that meant a cut in wages? But I don't want 'em back, Zadok Minch be droppin' the nailin' business altogether.'

'Dropping the nailing?' Brows creasing, dark eyes looked concernedly at Zadok.

The nail master's mouth curved in a spite-filled smile. 'You heard me, I be finished with nailin'.'

Standing opposite the shorter, more heavily framed man, Zadok's visitor looked taller than ever. Dark eyes gleaming, he breathed deeply. 'And me ... what about me?'

'What about you?' Zadok laughed. 'You do what the hell suits you but don't come callin' for employment at the Coronet Tube Works.'

'The Coronet–'

'Ar, that's right,' Zadok interrupted. 'John Adams has sold out and I be the one has bought, and I tells you again I 'ave no further use for you!'

For a moment, silence, broken only by the tick of a clock, wrapped the elegantly furnished sitting room, then Zadok's visitor spoke.

'No further use?' He smiled. 'Does that include my acquiring of the special goods, the ones you enjoy so much?'

Leaning heavily in his winged chair Zadok eyed his visitor. That part of their business association had gone well, the goods he supplied had proved satisfactory and when no longer required had sold on at a decent profit, but then, like foggers, sellers of more special goods were not difficult to come by.

'What were got from you can be got elsewhere,' he said, touching a bell cord which would summon his wife. 'Now you tek your hook, and mind ... if you was thinking of opening your mouth, Ensell, then don't. Not lessen you wants it closed for good!'

'I see no reason to wait, my love, we can marry now. I want to be with you, take care of you.'

Held in his arms Saran tried to find the reason those words brought a kind of panic to her heart. Jairus loved her, hadn't he proved as much when searching for her family ... for Livvy's children? Yet still the thought of marriage disturbed her.

'Please, a little longer.' She drew away. 'I ... I have not yet kept my promise to avenge the killing of my mother and sister.'

Jairus's insides raged. Marriage to her was not his heart's desire but it was one way of keeping his head above water. Minch had been adamant, there would be no more money from him, so this was his only recourse, she *had* to be made to agree to an immediate marriage.

Drawing her back against him, his dark eyes darkened still more, his mind already playing on another vengeance. He, too, would see Zadok Minch destroyed.

'Then let me help you,' he murmured. 'Marry me and, as your husband, I will have the right to see that monster put where he belongs, where he can never harm another woman.'

'But there is the bread and ... and the nail-makers, so many people depend on the business ... on me.' It was her last excuse, she could not extend her prevarication much further.

'I will take all that pressure from you, my darling, you need have no worry. The business will go on as you wish. Marry me and together we will see your promise to your loved ones fulfilled.'

Lips pressed against her hair hid the smile as she nodded. Jairus Ensell would keep his word ... the word made to himself.

'I begs your pardon, I d'ain't know you had a visitor. Livvy, her said...' The woman she had taken from the workhouse bobbed an awkward curtsy as Saran wheeled free. 'I begs pardon ... you too, sir, I–' Her eyes wide, she stared at the man smiling across at her, then, still mumbling her apology, she ran from the house.

'We will marry very soon.' Jairus had no intention of letting the interruption spoil his advantage. 'Next week, my darling, no ... no, I will have no argument,' he touched her lips gently with one finger, 'next week you will become Mrs Jairus Ensell.'

Following behind as he walked to his carriage, Saran felt dazed. Mrs Jairus Ensell! It should be the epitome of everything she wanted, everything she could ever hope for ... so why did she not want it at all?

'Jairus, I–'

'No more words,' taking her into his arms he smiled, 'except the ones I shall say to you every day of your life... I love you, I love–'

'You bastard, Ensell, you took my lad and my little wench and I'm going to cut your slimy heart out!'

Pushing herself free of Jairus, Saran gasped at the sight which met her eyes. Holding an axe above his head Edward Elwell was running towards them.

'I knows it were you,' Edward screamed his anger, 'I've been given proof and now you be goin' to die. You took my lad, took him to be buggered, and my little wench ... was it to be the same for 'er?'

'Edward, stop!' Hardly aware of her action Saran ran to meet the furious man, hurling herself at him, holding on with all her strength. 'Edward, you don't know what you're saying, there must be some mistake.'

The strength of madness in his arm, the glint of it in his eyes, Edward Elwell pushed her aside. 'There be a mistake all right,' he breathed, 'and he made it by comin' 'ere, but it'll be the last he ever meks.'

'Please, Edward, stop ... think what you are doing!'

'No, Miss Saran...' Edward Elwell walked slowly towards the man stood beside the carriage, 'I *knows* what I be doing, that which I vowed I'd do should I find the one stole my young 'uns. That man be Ensell and I be going to cut his evil heart from his body!'

'Don't be stupid, man.' Jairus Ensell, his face pale, placed a hand on the carriage. 'What gives you grounds to accuse me?'

'You've been marked!' Edward raised the axe higher. 'You've been recognised. It were *you* took my Joseph, *you* went back for my Martha; two children, one of 'em no more'n a babby, but that made no difference, did it, Ensell; you could get money for 'em no matter the age, and that were your only concern. 'Ow much did Zadok Minch pay you for Joseph ... 'ow much was you to get for Martha?' Near enough to see the fear in the other man's eyes, Edward halted. 'Tell the truth, Ensell, clear your conscience and mebbe the Lord will forgive what I never will.'

Zadok Minch! Edward had spoken of Zadok Minch! Saran's mind reeled. Jairus and Zadok Minch!

Seeing the horror in the eyes that lifted to his, Jairus knew his last chance had failed. Even could he prove the man wrong, Saran Chandler would never marry him now! Swinging up into the carriage he grasped the reins in one hand, the other fastening on a short-handled whip.

'Your children!' he snarled. 'What better purpose can scum like that serve than to bring one man money and another gratification! They are worth no more to the world!' Flicking the whip so it caught the handle of the axe he snatched it from Edward's hand, then flicked it again, slashing the snake-like leather across the man's face and, even as Saran screamed, slashing again. 'Keep your brats,' he snarled again, the whip whistling through the air, 'you will never have Jairus Ensell!'

Bringing the whip across the flank of the horse he sent the carriage hurtling forward on the track leading towards Wednesbury, his laugh floating to where Saran knelt beside the bleeding Edward.

# 32

'He did what!'

Gideon Newell's grey eyes darkened, anger making them glisten like black diamonds.

Her nerves still jangling from the experience of the afternoon, Saran repeated, 'Jairus ... he slashed Edward with a whip.'

'Why?' The question was Luke's.

'He said ... he said... Oh God, I can't believe it...' The trauma of it all suddenly coming home to her Saran couldn't hold the tears any longer. 'I almost ... I almost...'

Scraping back his chair Luke rose but before he had taken a step Gideon was across the kitchen, the weeping Saran in his arms.

'Did he hurt you?' Gideon's normally strong voice cracked. 'Did ... did Ensell touch you at all?'

'No, no, he ... we...'

We! Gideon's world rocked about him. We – Saran and Ensell! What did that word mean, why had the man been here? But he had every right to come to Brook Cottage, he was engaged to Saran.

'Jairus was insistent...'

Gideon's brain suffered a minor explosion. He wouldn't knock hell out of the man, not this time; this time he really would kill him!

'He said there was no need to wait any longer, he ... he said we should marry next week. I ... I agreed and he left.'

The trembling explanation a hymn in his brain, Gideon's arms tightened. Ensell had not forced himself on her, she had not been harmed; but next week...

Seeing the look that crossed his friend's face Luke smiled to himself. That was where Saran should be, in Gideon Newell's arms, not those of that snake Ensell. Mouthing that he was going to see the Elwells he slipped from the kitchen. Left alone Gideon allowed himself to feel the joy of holding close the girl he loved, the girl he would give his life for, but who in a few days would be lost to him for ever.

'I didn't know, believe me, I didn't know Jairus was...'

She had lifted her head, those quivering lips were just beneath his... Gideon's mouth tightened against the rush of fire surging through his whole body. To hold her another minute would be too long, he would not have the strength to deny himself that which he longed for, to feel that soft mouth beneath his own. Releasing her gently he helped her to a chair.

'The woman I took on to help with the bread, she came into the kitchen while Jairus was ... was still here.' Saran continued as if in a dream. 'She apologised for intruding and went out again. I saw Jairus to the door, that was when Edward came with an axe in his hand screaming that his children had–'

Whatever Edward had screamed was obviously painful but to bottle it up inside herself would see it grow more so, it had to be spoken of. Quietly

Gideon asked, 'What did Edward say?'

The question acted like an open door releasing all the horror pent up inside her, words tumbling over words until the whole story was told.

'The woman you took on, there was no mistake?'

Still flooded with tears Saran's eyes glistened as she answered, 'She was certain. She said she felt happy for Joseph the day she saw Jairus leave with him. Thinking it must be the lad's father come to take him out, she thanked God for His mercy. But then later, when she saw him again – this time with a little girl – she wondered why he had not claimed both children at the same time.'

'But was she sure the girl was Martha?'

'She did not say the name.' Saran sniffed back threatening tears. 'She said the child was small and thin, "too thin for to 'ave had a easy life" were her actual words but then said that was not what she noticed most, for that was normal in this town where bread was snatched from the mouths of babes by the greed of foggers and nail masters. What most had caught her attention was the doll a wardress handed back to her, a rag doll with a face stitched from wool.'

'But surely rag dolls are not so uncommon, many mothers in Wednesbury must make them for their daughters.' Gideon pressed the point gently, he had to be sure.

Twisting a handkerchief between her fingers Saran nodded. 'I thought the same thing and when I asked I was told yes, they did, but how many of those dolls had a line of stitches big enough to anchor a dray cart along its back?'

The same doll Saran had unknowingly taken from Jairus Ensell's carriage! Gideon breathed deeply, swallowing the disgust rising from his stomach. Saran was upset enough, his anger would only add to that.

'Where did Jairus go?' It was a lame question but he had to say something.

'I don't know, he whipped the horse along the track but he must have heard Edward shout that every man in Wednesbury would hunt him down.'

'And that includes me!' Luke entered the kitchen. 'We should have killed that swine the night I found Martha in his house...' The rest tailed off as he caught Gideon's warning look.

'You found Martha in Jairus's house?' Blank disbelief chasing the residue of tears from her eyes, Saran looked from one to the other. 'You knew all along yet you said nothing to me? Why, Luke ... why?'

'It wasn't Luke's idea to keep it from you,' Gideon answered before Luke could. 'I thought you would not believe, that it would seem something concocted in order to–'

'Gideon thought you'd see it as jealousy,' Luke broke in, 'you knows well enough neither of us saw him as the man for you.'

'But you would have let me marry him, you knew what he had done ... what he was ... yet still you would have stood by and let me become the man's wife!'

Her disbelief turning to anger she rounded on Gideon. 'And Joseph – was he fed the same story, was that why he too said nothing, was he supposed to see it as jealousy?'

'Saran...'

'No, Luke.' Gideon kept his eyes on Saran, his look candid and open. 'Joseph is young but he has a shrewd mind. We told him the truth but he chose to keep silent, wanting to protect his mother from a grief which could easily have proved too much. Time will heal and when it had the whole truth would have been told, at least that was what Luke and I planned; unfortunately fate had its own plan.'

'And by that time I would have become Mrs Jairus Ensell. Did you not once think what that would have done to me? Finding I was the wife of a ... a child stealer!'

Could he have allowed that to happen? Would his stupid pride have got in the way of truth, would he have ruined her life as well as his own? Beneath Saran's scathing look a medley of thoughts cascaded through Gideon's mind.

'That wouldn't 'ave happened!' Luke's glare was mutinous. 'He might not 'ave told you cos of ... well, he knows why he mightn't, but I would.'

Because of what ... why might Gideon Newell not have told her? The question in her eyes she looked at him, but as quickly he turned away, leaving without another word.

So Jairus Ensell was dead, his carriage found half buried in a collapsed mine shaft. Well, that was no great loss to the world and none at all to him. Pleased with the way events had turned, Zadok Minch stood in the yard of his newly acquired tube works. True, the man had kept him supplied with the playthings he liked but they were always to be got elsewhere, all it took was a sovereign or two and he would make those in plenty with the tubes. That had been another stroke of good fortune for him, p'raps if the nailing had gone on he would never have thought of buying this place, but here was where he would make a real fortune ... tubes were the future and it would all belong to Zadok Minch!

Holding a short length of iron in his hand he surveyed the wide heaps of finished tubing. All his, it was money in the bank. Slowly, a satisfied smile spreading over his jowled face, he turned half circle then halted, his eyes narrowing viciously as he caught sight of a slight figure standing at the gate.

Brown skirts, cheap cotton blouse, a shawl he wouldn't give a dog to lie on ... all the same, they were all the same! But it was the hair, that he could not be mistaken about: fair with streaks like beaten gold... No, he could not be mistaken about that.

The bar gripped between fingers tight as iron bands, he stepped forward several paces before yelling, 'What is that bloody woman doing at my gate?'

Surprised by the shout the gatekeeper turned, two wrapped sandwiches almost falling from his grasp. 'This 'ere be Saran, Miss Chandler, her always calls at this time.'

'Not any more, her don't!' Zadok's little eyes glinted his pleasure.

'But Mr Minch, sir, her brings mine and Luke's dinner, her brings it every day.'

'Not to my works, her don't, and if you don't like what I says then you can bugger off along with her. In fact, it don't matter whether you likes my sayin' or you don't, you can get your tin, you be finished 'ere!'

'There is no call to let our differences spill on to others.' Saran stared at the face flushed now with the colour of advancing anger. 'You have no call to sack–'

'No call, no call!' The interruption echoed over the yard. 'I needs no bloody call, I be master 'ere, do you hear that, you smart-mouthed bitch, *I* be master and if I says a man be sacked he be sacked, and when I tell a scruffy-arsed woman to leave my gate then by God her had better leave quick or this iron will knock in what words don't.'

'Don't, sir, the wench didn't mean…' Seeing the iron bar raised the gatekeeper hobbled towards Zadok but one vicious swipe of it sent the old man tumbling to the ground.

'How very applaudable!' Saran's searing glance strafed the flushed face. 'You are as skilful at hitting crippled old men with a bar of iron as you are at beating helpless women to death with a whip. Tell me, do you take lessons in brutality or does it come naturally to you?'

For a few seconds words seemed to clog Zadok's throat then he raised the piece of iron while his fat-encased eyes spat pure venom. 'It comes natural!' It was hissed like a snake poised to strike. 'And I gets much pleasure from it, same as I be going to get when I bends this iron over your head!'

‘Try bending it over mine first!’ Gideon snatched the bar away, at the same time spinning the heavy frame of Zadok Minch around to face him. ‘There you are...’ he handed back the weapon, smiling as the other man’s hand closed over it, ‘try bending it over my head, but I warn you I am no helpless woman nor am I a crippled old man ... but don’t let that stop you.’

It seemed the rage in Zadok would carry him beyond common sense, that he would in blind fury strike at the man now facing him, but then his fingers parted and the iron bar clattered on the hard ground; yet there was no defeat in the stare that rested on Gideon.

‘You can get your bloody tin an’ all!’ he growled. ‘You be finished, same as the cripple, but afore you goes I ’ave a warnin’ for you. Zadok Minch don’t tek to threats and he always finds a way of repaying ’em, and once be all it teks!’

Glancing first to where Saran stood with her bread cart, ensuring the set-to had caused her no hurt, Gideon helped the crippled gatekeeper to his feet before going back into the works.

‘Gideon!’ A puzzled Luke watched the jacket being shrugged on broad shoulders. ‘Be you going somewhere?’

‘I’ll talk to you tonight when your shift ends.’ Gideon picked up the hammer belonging to him.

The move was not missed, Luke touched a hand to the older man’s sleeve. ‘You never teks that hammer home nights, not once since I’ve knowed you, so there ’as to be summat up... What is it? I wants to know now not tonight.’

‘I told you, same as I told the wench at the gate,

bugger off ... or do I get half a dozen of this lot to throw you off the premises!'

The roar had Luke twisting to face the works' new owner. Wench at the gate? The only wench ever to come to the Coronet Works was...

'Saran!' His own shout ringing above the sound of hammer on iron he launched himself at the heavy figure. 'If you be talkin' of Saran ... if you've hurt her...!'

'Luke.' Gideon's curt voice mingled with one cracking with anger. 'Luke, she is all right... Luke!'

So this was Luke, Luke Hipton. Zadok's brain cleared, leaving an unhindered path to memory. This was the lad Ensell had told him of, the one who had probably had a hand in the returning of that brooch to Salisbury. Oh yes, Ensell had told him all about that! A fortune ... the brooch must have been worth thousands and it could have been his had it not been for this brat and a slut of a wench ... a wench who had dared tell him she would destroy his life. He had waited his chance to take recompense for the losing of that brooch and right now he could begin with Hipton ... and the girl? He could deal with her anytime, swat her as he would a fly.

It was her fault. Gideon and Luke both sacked and it was her fault; if only she hadn't gone to the works! Spirits which had drooped since it had happened drooped lower. Luke had tried to cheer her, vowing he was thinking of leaving the tube works, Minch had merely pushed him along a little. But that was all his words could have been, an attempt to restore her spirits, they could not possibly be the truth.

Truth. She stared at her reflection in the mirror Luke had hung in her bedroom on one of those first few days they had come to live at Brook Cottage. Who was she to speak of truth when...

Picking up her hairbrush she touched it to hair already brushed and plaited, then, impatient with herself, she replaced it.

She had accused Luke of being untruthful, accused Gideon Newell of deceit! Luke had gone to the house he thought was that of Jairus Ensell's grandmother but there had been no woman there, young or old ... so Jairus, too, had lied.

Crossing to the bed, she knelt, forcing her mind to concentrate on the prayers she never forgot to say, prayers asking eternal peace and rest for the souls of her mother and sister; but the moment that was done the thoughts she had banished came crowding in on her brain.

Jairus had lied when saying he was searching for the Elwell children, had he lied also when saying he had searched for her own loved ones? And that day she had met him leaving the workhouse and he had said he was there to make a monthly donation, was that also lies? Had he in fact been there with the loathsome intention of taking young children to sell to the likes of Zadok Minch?

Lying in the semi-darkness of her room she winced at the horror of it all. Now Jairus was dead and, dreadful as it seemed, she could feel no sorrow at all. The man she had been ready to marry, to give her life to ... and she could not mourn for him.

*'that wouldn't 'ave happened'*

The words leapt at her. Luke's words, not Gideon's. Luke might have intervened before the final moment, might have told the truth about Jairus and thus have prevented her marrying him, but not so Gideon.

It was a pain so strong it was almost physical. Closing her eyes she tried to shut out all memory of the rest but like river water they kept on flowing. The boy's stare had been more angry than she had ever known, their reproach brilliant. It seemed on reflection that he was censuring her, blaming her for something he felt she should have known; but what, what was the something she should know?

*'he might not 'ave told you cos of–'*

Luke's words battered her mind, demanding they be let in, that they be understood.

*'he knows why he mightn't'*

Wouldn't they ever go away, the thoughts that had tormented every long hour of her day! What did it matter the reason he would not speak to her of Jairus Ensell's activities? The fact was she was of so little importance to Gideon Newell he had been prepared to stand by and watch her throw her life away.

She was of no importance to him! The breath which followed was short, almost a gasp which caught and held in her throat. He had no feeling for her at all except perhaps that of cold dislike.

But it had not seemed like that when he had held her. His touch had been gentle yet strong;

held against him she had felt safe, protected. It had been simply an act of kindness on his part, though, a comfort he would have extended to any woman in those circumstances. But with Jairus she had never felt as she had in those few brief moments. His touch had not aroused that deep disturbing tumult in her stomach.

Truth! Her eyes opening slowly she stared into the moonlit shadows of her room but inner eyes watched different shadows. Slowly, like drifts of mist on a summer morning, they floated across her mind, thinning into long hazy fingers reluctant to part and when finally they melted her breath caught again in her throat. She had accused Gideon of deceit but was her own any less? It had been deception when she had told herself she loved Jairus Ensell, lies when saying to herself she was content to marry him. There had been no wild frenzy deep inside her whenever he smiled, whenever he took her in his arms.

Who was she to speak of truth when – the thought came again and this time it spoke on – when truth said it was not Jairus Ensell's arms she wanted to be in but those of Gideon Newell!

# 33

Lack of sleep had kept her listless all day. Her head aching, Saran closed the accounts ledger pushing it away from her across the kitchen table. So weary her legs screamed, she rose when sounds from the scullery told her Luke was home.

He had said he had been thinking of leaving the tube works and she had not believed him, yet there had been none of the despondency she had witnessed in other people when losing their livelihood; in fact, it was the opposite, Luke was nothing if not cheerful. And what of Gideon Newell, was he so full of spirits? That was a question she could not answer for she had not seen him since that day he had stood against Zadok Minch, nor could she bring herself to enquire of him from Luke.

'That be it, signed and sealed ... the whole thing be done.' Luke bounced into the kitchen, flinging his arms about her, swirling her around the table in a wild dance.

'What is signed and sealed? Luke, put me down!'

'The deal with John Adams.' Planting a kiss on her cheek he set her on a chair, his hands on her arms, his eyes dancing with excitement.

A deal ... with John Adams, something else she had known nothing about! Saran's head throbbed. Why the secrecy, did Luke no longer trust her as he once had, was he growing away from her? Of course it must happen ... but so soon?

'You sit there while I make us a cup of tea to celebrate.'

His grin wide as the canal which ran past the cottage given over to the Elwells, he danced to the fireplace swinging the teapot about his head, but Saran felt none of his elation.

'Luke,' she asked quietly, 'what is it we are to celebrate, and why could I not be told?'

The flatness of her tone reaching through to him Luke set the teapot down. 'It were me this time.' He sat opposite, her hand in his. 'It were not Gideon, he were against it but I told him it were my business.'

'Gideon ... does he have something to do with this?'

Hair which fingers must have driven through several times during the day flopped over his forehead as Luke nodded.

'He be three-quarters of Newell and Hipton.'

Pride shone on the young face but a sudden snatch at her nerves kept Saran silent. What had Luke done ... and what part had Gideon Newell played in it?

'That be why I wouldn't tell you, I knowed it would worry you.' Luke had read the expression on her face. 'But it were my money to chance, my life to live, and going into partnership with Gideon is the future I want.'

He was defending himself, explaining himself to her. But why should he when what he said was right? Luke Hipton's life belonged to none other than Luke Hipton.

She looked at the hand holding hers, a hold that was so surely being broken and her heart twisted. Luke had never been a child and now the man she had many times seen just beneath the surface was finally breaking through. 'Luke,' she swallowed, the words an obstacle in her throat, 'Luke, you do not need to explain, you are not tied to this house nor to me, if you have decided to leave–'

'But I ain't!' Luke's retort was swift. 'It ain't that at all, I don't never want to part from you and even when I be of an age when it be indecent for me to live in this house I'll find a place close by. It ... it were the money. I thought that by not tellin' you what I planned you wouldn't have any worries if I lost it, though I've set some by against my keep.'

'I don't care about the money.' Saran smiled. 'It was yours to do with as you wish.'

'And that *were* my wish.' The returning excitement added fresh lustre to vivid eyes. 'To have a place if not all my own, at least to own a part of it. Gideon gave me that when he agreed to me becoming his partner in the property he purchased from John Adams.'

'But John Adams sold his property to Zadok Minch.'

'Not all of it.' Eyes like blue stars glittered their enthusiasm. 'He didn't sell that he built on Monway Field to Zadok Minch, he sold that to Gideon ... and to me. The money I had saved together with that given by William Salisbury bought only a small share, but it's a start, Saran, it's a start and I mean to make it grow.'

'That's all very well, but what is it you intend to make grow, have you and Mr Newell decided to go into farming?'

Catching the twinkle behind the tiredness Luke laughed then dropped a kiss on the hand he still held. 'Smart, Miss Chandler, but wrong. Newell and Hipton are going to grow iron!'

Luke was part-owner of an iron foundry. The ledger put away she set the table for supper, Luke's whistle floating in from the scullery where he was washing his hands and face. And Gideon Newell was his partner. He had worked at the Coronet from being a boy, Luke had confided, and had saved every last penny he could so one day he could buy his dream, and that day had come when John Adams had agreed on a down payment to be followed by annual instalments until the whole were paid. What it amounted to was that Luke was in debt ... and when the flush of excitement finally died away would he regret it?

The queen had been crowned and thanks given to God, the country had rejoiced and sang but then it was over and once more the realities of life had fallen into place. It had left her exhausted, the extra bread-making for the workers of William Salisbury. She had been obliged to take on three more women in order to fulfil that request, finding each of them a place to stay with widows who had no other source of income. Then the coronation was over. But how could she send those women back to the hell she had taken them from, return the men taken on to give Ezekiel extra help with the brewing, or the young boy whose task was scrubbing the bread cart every evening? He had the cart almost as white as the linen cloth which covered the loaves. Remembering it now Saran saw the grin which greeted her each time the task was finished, the pride with which he took the pay she knew would go to help feed brothers and sisters. How could she take that away from him?

*'The way be not easy.'*

Harriet Dowen's words, spoken so long ago, had crept into her mind as they often did. Over the many months since being forced from her home, seeing her mother and sister led away, bought like chattels in a market place, her own humiliation on that auction table, Enoch Jacobs offering her like so much meat, those words had proved ever more true.

*'the path which fate unrolls before you be pitted with grief and anguish, pocked with bitterness and misery'*

Those, too, had not been empty words. Had Harriet Dowen's special sight shown that which she had not been told? Had that kind-hearted woman thought the horror of hearing her family were doomed to die beneath the lash of a sadistic whip too much for a young girl to bear? But she had borne the misery, and would to her life's end. And the bitterness? Would that, too, live with her for ever?

In the coach taking her to Birmingham, Saran now remembered the events of a year ago.

*'There you be, wench.'* Sat on a stone enjoying the June heat Ezekiel had smiled, one tooth sitting in lone splendour in his gums. *'That there*

*bread carries the scent of 'eaven.'*

Handing him his usual loaf she had rested on the stone beside him, her brown skirts spread about her feet.

*'Be you feelin' poorly, wench?'* The old man had looked piercingly at her tired face.

*'I'm well enough, thank you, Ezekiel ... just tired.'*

*'No.'* He had shaken his grey head. *'It be more'n just tired ... you be fretted over summat. Tellin' what it be might see the easing of it.'*

It was the tap which had released the spring of her emotions. Sat beside the man who had become a support as well as a friend, she had let it all pour out.

*'It be a great responsibility for one so young,'* Ezekiel had said when the flow slowed to a drip. *'Bein' nail master to every nailer in the town, tekin' on folk to work at the brewin' and the bread; but the Lord don't place burdens He thinks be too 'eavy for the shoulders given the carrying of 'em.'*

It had been meant as comfort and she had smiled her gratitude, but words did not diminish the worries of paying those extra wages.

*'Wench,'* Ezekiel's hand had touched her arm, staying her as she made to stand. *'I be an old man and not spritely as I once were but I sees things mebbe the young be too rushed to see. I've been on this earth many years and been witness to many changes yet I knows there be more still to come and that be good, for change be the fresh water which keeps the channels of life clear, without it the world sleeps and man stagnates. Try not to be afeared of life, wench, nor of the changes it brings. This Black Country of ours be small but it will grow, grow so all the world knows it.*

*It will rise to stand tall; held on stanchions of iron, the arteries of its industries will reach beyond boundaries not yet dreamed of.'* He had looked at her then, and in those rheumy old eyes had gleamed a confidence which even now, more than a year later, she remembered with vivid clarity. He had patted her hand, the gnarled touch seeming to transfer a strength she had almost felt flow into her own body, and with it he had nodded. *'Accept the challenge,'* he had said, *'face the future, child, and rise you up with it.'*

As the coach drew to a halt a man sat opposite raised his tall hat, wishing her a polite good morning. So very different from that other ride to Birmingham!

The brief stop over, the coach resumed its journey and Saran's mind, lulled by the steady rhythm of horses' hooves, continued her own journey along the road of memory.

She had forgotten her tiredness, the old man's enthusiasm had been invigorating. He had gone on to talk of the success the wheat wine had been with people celebrating the queen's coronation and of the daily requests of hotel managers and tavern-keepers for more of the same.

*'You be lettin' opportunity slip away.'* Ezekiel's words were loud in her reverie. *'That there wine could bring a fortune were it to reach further across the land.'*

*'But I don't want a fortune, I just want enough to pay my workers.'*

Staring out of the window Saran's gaze saw nothing of the fields, their crops dotted with the brilliance of wild flowers, seeing instead the old man's look as he shook his head slowly.

*'Think you only of a few when there be so many needs the lift of yer hand?'*

It had sounded almost like a reproach and she remembered the surprise and stab of hurt it had brought.

*'The nailing will be teken from folk, done by machines I already hears talk of; when that day comes they be going to need new work and you can give it to them.'*

He had hushed the protest on her lips, talking softly of the ideas in his mind. They had been shrewd. No more selling of the 'uisge' by the barrel. He had used the term by which his forebears had known the strong drink brewed from wheat. *'Put it in bottles of clear glass so the beauty of its colour shines through, place upon each a label elegant and distinctive, give the brew a name the little queen herself might have chosen so the high ones of the land, as well as those building their money from industry, will be proud to serve it in their homes.'*

She could smile now that time was proving the old man right, but that same evening it had taken Luke's support for Ezekiel's proposals to reinvigorate her own. Luke … as always he had been so wonderful. They had sat for hours dreaming up fancy names, him laughing at some she suggested, flatly denying it be labelled just plain whisky. Ezekiel was right, he had declared, when she had tried to argue in favour of plainness. Fine feathers made birds which caught the eye, it must be the same with her whisky. It was then Gideon had come for the discussion he had arranged with Luke to talk of their own business.

Her heart had quickened as it quickened now remembering the tall straightness of him, the ghost of a smile that had touched his strong mouth as he greeted her, but most of all she remembered his eyes. Guarded, cautious, yet with a wistfulness sheathed in a second, those grey eyes had held hers then looked away.

*'If, as Ezekiel says, the whisky will sell to gentlemen of wealth then they should be made to feel it is something is reserved solely for them. Why not label it so?'* He had returned his glance then, looking her straight in the eyes, saying quietly, *'Even though hope can never be realised, men still hope the best is held in reserve, that it is for them alone.'*

*'So what would you call it?'*

Luke had not seen that look in Gideon's eyes, felt the lurch his quiet words had jolted in her stomach, but his question had been enough to break the moment.

*'What else?'* Gideon had smiled but it was not for her. *'What else but Gentleman's Reserve?'*

And so it had become. Bronzed gilt paper finely edged with a band of gold enclosed the elegantly scripted name:

*Gentleman's Reserve ... the spirit of character for gentlemen of character*

It had proved an astounding success, so much so that Ezekiel had allowed his property to be extended ... property his death showed had been willed to her. And she had used it to fulfil that old man's vision of the future. 'Gentleman's Reserve' had been quickly followed by:

*Lady's Cordial*

a softer, gentler fruit drink, then by:

*Renaissance ... a restorative wine aiding recovery of energy after illness*

Each label had been carefully designed to be tasteful rather than glaring, as had their containers. The glass bottle works at Greets Green had been happy to oblige her request for the varied shapes, valuing the extra work her custom provided.

Her success had been rapid. She had kept her workers and employed more, taking her bread business a stage further to produce pies and savouries, releasing many from the hopelessness of the workhouse, the drudgery of a life in servitude to hell. She had brought happiness where the very meaning of the word had been forgotten, but where was her own happiness ... the happiness of vengeance?

She had sworn to destroy the life of Zadok Minch piece by piece, but as each piece was cut away she felt none of the pleasure she thought would come of revenge. Beyond the window, fields and cottages passed swiftly by but Saran saw only the pictures in her mind. First it had been the nailing, slowly at first then in ever growing numbers until every nail-maker in the town came to her. She had saved every farthing she could, seeing them grow into pennies and pennies into the sovereigns which would fulfil her vow, and as they had become a large enough sum she had purchased the Tommy Shops, those shops Zadok Minch had owned, where his nailers had been forced to buy their provisions with the tokens he paid in lieu of wages.

Then the columns in her accounts ledger had shown she was capable of buying the coach axle works Zadok Minch had put up for sale. Luke and she had discussed the buying of it, Luke telling her to offer a lower price, the grapevine had it Minch was in poor straits. The offer had been accepted. Another piece of the man's life had been sliced away. But he had bought the Coronet Works ... had the grapevine been wrong?

Time had answered her. More of its workers had been given their tins, men and boys coming to Brook Cottage asking for employment. Somehow she had always managed to help, the relief on their faces speaking their gratitude. She had given them happiness. But for herself there was none. The dream she had lived with, the dream of being reunited with her family, had shattered in Zadok Minch's house, had died beneath his cruel laughter as her loved ones had died beneath the vicious lash of his whip. And that other dream, the one so secret she let it creep into her heart only in the silence of the night? Saran felt the familiar twist of pain in her chest. Being loved by Gideon Newell ... that was all it could ever be: a dream.

'Brummajum, miss ... it *were* Brummajum you were wantin'?'

The strings of the present jerking her like a puppet Saran hesitated, then smiled her thanks to the coachman waiting to help her down.

'You won't go forgettin' the time of the last coach back, now will you, miss?' He touched a hand to his forehead as she reached into her bag for a coin. 'There'll be none runs after eight o'clock tonight.'

Summoning a hansom cab she relaxed, allowing thoughts to rush in like a tide yet keeping back the one which held her dream. It would never be realised ... contrary to Ezekiel's belief, not all dreams could be lived.

What was happening to his bloody world! Zadok Minch slammed shut the ledger on his desk. First the nail-makers, they had shifted to Elwell, and his profits had taken a downward turn one after another, all of his holdings had taken the same! Now the tube works had followed suit and he faced bankruptcy!

Adams had said nothing of the smaller place he had built on Monway Field. Was that because he'd somehow found out that he, Minch, hadn't the money to pay for it, or had there been some other motive? Hadn't the fellow heard of mortgages ... bank loans, any one of which would have bought the property. Instead it had gone to Newell and the brat he called a partner. A bloody partner. Christ, it was laughable! The kid could be no more than fifteen years old, sixteen at the outside. But the profits they had turned in less than two years weren't laughable! Zadok stabbed the pen savagely into the polished surface of the desk. Iron foundry were what it had started out as and smelting iron should have been what it kept to; but not them, they had incorporated the mekin' of tubes into their little business, mekin' 'em to a new process invented by the smart-arsed Mr Newell ... and one he had the foresight to protect by Letters Patent. This new process of tube-making worked by means of heating iron in a blast furnace rather than a forge and immediately on withdrawing the plate iron passing it through swages, an instrument he had designed to bend the metal up on both sides until the edges almost met, giving the form of a long cylindrical tube. That was then returned to the new-fangled blast furnace until the iron was almost to the point of fusion. When that point was reached it was removed by means of chain attached to a draw bench and passed through a pair of dies by which means the edges of the iron were pressed together and thus the joint was firmly welded in a smooth seam, creating a tube much preferred by the manufacturers of steam engines for making steam cylinders, water boilers and pistons.

That was the brainchild which was grinding his business into the dust. Butt-welding iron strip into tubes meant joining together lengths not much more than four feet, hammering the red-hot iron end to end, and the more joints it took the more the labour ... labour he must pay for. Oh, he'd found out about this process of Newell's but the copying of it he could not do.

'God damn!' Zadok swore loudly. He would be out of business altogether by the time that patent expired!

'What the hell do *you* want?' His anger added

to by the interruption, he rounded on the mousy woman stood hesitantly at the door.

'You were asked to be told when your visitor arrived.'

Zadok glanced at the mantelpiece. Ten o'clock. Punctual, he liked that, liked it as much as the pleasure this visit would give him.

'Out o' the way!' Pushing his wife aside he strode to the stairs, the remainder of his growl trailing their long flight.

'And keep you outta the way, the less my eyes sees of you the better I be pleased!'

Watching the heavy figure pass along the landing and into the bedroom he referred to as his games parlour, guilt marked a deep shadow on the woman's lined face.

# 34

'So you comes again to Zadok Minch, an' what favour does it be you expects to get?'

'No favour.' Saran ignored the hand waving her to a chair. 'I have come with a business proposition.'

'Business ... the only business you 'ave to offer be one I can get anywhere in the town for sixpence.'

The same words! Saran swallowed hard, the same words Gideon Newell had said to her a lifetime ago. But they were as wrong then as they were now. Keeping her voice even she looked at the man she detested as much as ever.

'Not quite,' she answered coldly. 'My proposition is worth several thousands of sixpences.'

Heavy jowls wobbling he laughed. 'Thousands... I wouldn't pay that kind o' money to tumble the queen herself, virgin though her undoubtedly be; but if you be sellin'...' He glanced towards the large bed set to one side of the room.

Time had not changed this man except to make him more odious. Saran watched him pour himself a drink, noting with satisfaction the label announcing it as Gentleman's Reserve. Zadok Minch would choke on it were he to know who it was made his whisky. But, like the rest of her acquisitions, it was registered to S.C. Enterprises.

'I am not here to sell, I am here to buy.'

The drink tipped off in one gulp, Zadok stared at the young woman eyeing him icily. The patched skirts and moth-eaten shawl were gone, replaced with velvet and a feathered bonnet. Her'd found herself a lover, one with money to throw away on scum! Well, money was money no matter where it came from and he needed it. Swallowing back the contempt coating his tongue he refilled his glass.

'To buy!' He raised the glass, watching light dance in its amber contents. 'And what is it you wish to purchase ... a painting, a Dresden figure–'

'No.' Saran cut the dialogue short. 'We both know the valuable contents of this house were sold long ago. I am here to buy something of a different nature.'

How the hell could her know what he'd sold? Anger flicked the edge of contempt. He would find the one who had been talking, and when he did the bastard would talk no more, he'd have the tongue cut from his head.

'I asked to see you for two reasons.' Saran spoke again. 'The first being to offer you four thousand sixpences in exchange for being told where the bodies of my mother and sister were taken.'

One hundred pounds! Christ, he could do with a sum like that; he could tell her anything, take the money and...

Spreading twenty five-pound notes like a fan Saran watched greed narrow the small eyes, intent spread the essence of a smile over flabby lips, and she tapped the notes against gloved fingers. 'This,' she said, 'will be paid once the remains of my family are found.'

The bitch was smart! Already whip-like inside him, his anger flicked harder. Her thought to 'ave got one over on Zadok Minch but her could keep her hundred pounds, use it for arse paper!

'That be the proposition you spoke of?' Anger hid behind a laugh. 'It be as well for women they don't engage in business for they don't 'ave the brains of a fly ... if they had to live by their wits they'd die of starvation. I told you the answer to what you ask some years gone, told it for free. Them folk o' your'n was took wi' the rest of the shit and I don't ask where shit be dumped. However...' a smirk spread further over thick jowls as lecherous eyes followed the length of her, '...Zadok Minch be a generous man, so pay what I asks, though it don't be money, pay what I asked afore, lay that body o' your'n under mine, pleasure Zadok as you be pleasurin' some other man, and I'll find out where your folk were thrown.'

Bitterness and acid burning her throat, Saran fought the wave of nausea threatening to engulf her. Slowly, using the moments to regain enough composure to answer, she replaced the banknotes in her bag, and when she looked again at that mocking face her own showed every atom of her loathing.

'Perhaps, as you said, it is as well women do not engage in business, but it is not all women who do not have the brains of a fly. This woman comes to tell you to vacate this house by the end of the month.'

His glass lowering with a jerk, Zadok loosed a roar of laughter. 'That be a bloody good joke, do you 'ave any more like that?'

'A few.' Saran's tone was cold and even as sheet ice. 'But they are not jokes. You mortgaged this house in order to raise the money which bought the Coronet Works. In its turn that also was mortgaged to meet other debts, the loans being made by Morton's Bank who, because of repeated failure on your part to comply with the agreement regarding repayment, foreclosed on that property at noon yesterday. The mortgages were redeemed and you are to leave by the end of the month.'

Narrow eyes narrowed further, Zadok's fury spitting from slits between folds of flesh. 'Do you think I be bloody stupid ... do I look daft enough to tek a tale like that?'

Withdrawing a folded paper from her bag Saran held it out. 'How you look revolts me, but I am certain the look you will have once you have read this document will prove very pleasant to me.'

'You know what you can do wi' that!'

'Then we will leave it for a solicitor to deliver.'

Solicitor! Zadok's smirk vanished. This bitch had already showed her was smart ... smart enough to somehow 'ave got wind of his finances? Was some man whispering more than sweet nothings in her ear? Snatching the paper with his free hand he shook it open, running a glance swiftly over the neatly written words, then, looking back at her, he flung the empty glass against the wall.

'Has the fool who be buyin' you fancy clothes, the one you be sleepin' with, let you bring this 'ere?' he shouted. 'Then tell 'im I'll see him gaoled for lettin' a bloody woman know my business.'

'I came to this house for two reasons; one you have already rejected, the second you cannot reject. I came to say what I told *you* some years ago, told it for free: you would be destroyed piece by piece. And that promise has been kept. The nailing was taken first, then the strip-iron works which fed that trade, that was followed by the Forge Pool coal mine, the last one you owned. It took time but finally they were all gone and you were left only with one thing to raise money on, this house. Now that, too, is no longer yours.'

'So the one bedding you be the one cutting the ground from under me! Well, I tells you this – and this be for free an' all – you won't get nothing from my going under, the one you be pleasuring will tek that pleasure and when he be tired will 'ave you thrown out along o' the shit, same as I 'ad that scum of a family o' your'n throwed out; you'll get nothin'... you hear me? ... nothing!'

'I hear you.' Quiet as a mill pond Saran's answer followed the bellow. 'And you are correct. The one I sleep with is the same one cutting the ground from under you.'

'And that don't be you,' Zadok yelled again. 'It don't be no bloody woman!'

'Can you be certain of that? I did tell you it is not all women do not have the brain of a fly. The bills of sale transferring the properties–'

'Were signed S.C. Enterprises, a firm backed by

money not by some cheap little whore auctioned to the highest bidder by Enoch Jacobs!' Zadok beamed triumphantly seeing the words strike like a blow. 'See how soon your bedfellow rids himself of you once Zadok Minch tells him what you really be, tells him how many men rode you in the fields along your way, how many times Enoch Jacobs sampled the goods he offered for sale.'

Closing the bag held open all this time Saran looked straight into the mocking narrow eyes. 'You can tell the one I sleep with nothing which is not already known. You see, the fool who buys my fancy clothes, the one cutting the ground from under you, the S.C. Enterprises who now own everything you once had is me. Saran Chandler Enterprises. The same person once offered for sale by Enoch Jacobs.'

Beyond the door a mousy drab woman smiled as she hurried down the stairs.

'I'm sorry, but your coming might be a waste of time.' Zadok's wife smiled apologetically at the attractive figure stood in the hall. 'When I was sent to invite you I was unaware Zadok had also invited a young man.'

'A young man?' A painted mouth tightened.

'More a boy really, someone from the works no doubt. He has left now but I fear my husband was tired by the visit, business often leaves him exhausted. Maybe I should see if he is awake.'

'Please don't bother. If he is sleeping I will just slip away.'

Watching the exquisitely dressed figure walk up the stairs, Zadok's wife smiled to herself.

'Your wife said you were tired.' Red lips smiled as Zadok's naked figure half lifted from the bed. 'Does that mean I should go home?'

He hadn't expected this, but then he wasn't going to turn it away either. His flesh already stirring, he lay back. 'It means you should get them clothes off, I be a hungry man.'

'I don't know whether I should play with you...' the full lips pouted, 'your wife tells me you have had a visitor already today.'

His wife wouldn't be able to open her mouth for a week after he'd dealt with her! Hiding the thought behind a toss of the head, Zadok answered, 'A solicitor. Called with some figures I'd asked him to collect. But who wants to talk legal business when there be more pleasant business to hand?' He stretched out his hand in invitation.

Lie number one! While the podgy outstretched hand was ignored, the violet eyes hid irritation. How many more would he tell?

The throb in his loins demanding attention, afraid his attractive visitor might leave, Zadok thought quickly. It was a case of say something or waste what could be a most amusing evening.

'It be the Coronet Works.' He slid a gaze over the elegant figure. 'I be thinking to sell it and this house along wi' it.'

Finely arched brows drawing together, Zadok's visitor expressed surprise. 'Sell this house ... but why ... where would you live?'

Impatient with the questions and with being kept waiting for the satisfaction his body shouted for, Zadok's reply was snapped. 'The why should be obvious, I be fed up with tube-mekin' and with this house, as for where I'll live ... the house you be in belongs to me, I shall live there.'

'Your wife, too?'

'Who said anything about her living there? I 'ave ways of gettin' rid of shit!' Spread-eagled naked on the bed he smiled to himself. He had gotten rid of that bitch Chandler's mother and sister, and today he had taken steps to get rid of her. Tomorrow would show just whose life it was were destroyed!

In the next room, with an ear pressed to the wall, Bridget Minch drew a long breath then, moving quietly, returned to her kitchen.

Livvy was happier than she had ever seen her. Holding her skirts free of evening dew Saran made her way across the rough open ground towards Brook Cottage. Her family safe around her, training others to the making of bread and savouries, the woman had blossomed in health and in confidence until now she could run the large specially built kitchen like a trained chef; and Edward he also was happy, keeping a sharp eye on the quality of the nails brought to him, buying in only the best iron for their making. Ezekiel too would have been content at the success of the brewing. They were all happy, including Luke. At the thought of him she smiled. He had grown so tall, almost as tall as Gideon ... Gideon! Her smile faded. He rarely came to Brook Cottage any more, business meetings between himself and Luke taking place at the works they ran together. He was polite on the odd occasion their paths crossed but it held no warmth. The grey eyes were always guarded and the mouth tense. She had lost the friendship of Gideon Newell long ago and he made it clear in his every look and movement that he wanted no renewal of it.

This evening had been no different. He had come not to Brook Cottage but to the home of the Elwells, bringing a birthday gift for Martha; but all during that time he had spoken only briefly to herself, wishing her good evening. It had become more than she could bear – the nearness of him yet the distance – and so she had begged the excuse of doing her accounts.

Entering the house by the scullery door she paused, a quick shiver tracing her spine; had something moved in the shadows? Holding her breath for a moment she strained to hear the shuffle again but all was silent. Releasing the pent-up breath she reached for matches and candle kept just inside the door. It was only her imagination, the tension of the past hour. Lighting the candle, turning to set it on a shelf, she gasped as the silver blade of a knife flashed in its yellow glow.

'I don't want to do this.'

A low voice spoke against her cheek as she was pressed face down on the stone-flagged floor.

'You ain't never done nothin' to me and I be sorry for what it is I 'ave to do to you ... but I've no more choice.'

Pressure in the middle of her back squeezed the air from her lungs, pounding blood crashed in her ears as Saran tried to twist her head.

'Stay still!' Fingers closed in her hair, holding her head down hard against the stone.

Was it rape? Was that blade against her neck to hold her, a threat of what would happen if she tried to resist?

Fear, wild and uncontrollable, sweeping a whirlwind through her mind Saran screamed, the sound choking away as the hand twisted into her hair slammed downward.

'Don't scream.' The voice was hushed, urgent against her face, breath jagged and snatched. 'It won't mek no difference ... I can't let it mek no difference ... I 'ave to do it ... this be the only way.'

'Please,' squeezing the cry from crushed lips, Saran tried to turn, 'there is money–'

'Don't look at me ... please!' Trembling almost as much as her own the voice interrupted quickly. 'This be hard enough to do ... if you looks at me–'

'But I'm looking at you, you bastard ... and I'm going to kill you!'

The weight on her back was gone, the knife touching her neck was gone but, caught in the grip of terror, Saran could not move.

'I don't be going to do what you meant to do, rape ain't to my taste, but I be going to take that knife and carve you like a bloody Christmas chicken!'

That voice throbbing with anger was Luke's but the one murmuring was not. Lifted from the ground, arms close about her, she felt safe, closed in a world of love, the same feeling she had had once before when– 'Gideon!' The name broke on a sob, her whole body shaking with the after-effect of terror ... and of something else.

'It's all right ... you're safe, my love... Oh God! If anything had happened to you!'

The words had only been whispered but her heart had caught them. He had said the words she had once ascribed to imagination, he had called her 'my love'.

As she twisted to look up at him the hold broke immediately and he stepped away, the light of the candle reflecting on features drawn tight.

'Luke has the culprit,' he said tersely, 'you are quite safe now but perhaps you would like me to ask Livvy to...'

Disappointment stealing her voice Saran shook her head. They had been simply words after all, she was a fool to have dreamed otherwise.

'Then we had better see who it is lay in wait for you before Luke kills him.'

Sat in the kitchen, hands clutched in her lap to still their trembling, she watched the man Luke had thrust on to a chair, but every fibre of her was aware of that other figure, of the anger brooding in grey eyes. She must not read that false, he was reacting in the way any man would on finding a woman being attacked in her own home, she meant nothing else to him; but the words *my love?* They were a common enough term, words she had often heard spoken to children hurt in a fall. Was that how Gideon Newell thought of her, as a child?

'What the hell is this all about?' Stood over the spare-framed man Luke doubled his hand to a fist.

Dropped over the chest a tow-haired head

swung slowly. ‘I ... I told him... I said as I didn’t want–’

Patience, never much of a virtue with Luke, slipped from him altogether. Grabbing the tow hair he jerked the head so he could see the face. ‘Told who? Out with it afore I beat your brains out!’

‘You best call the Watch...’

‘You ain’t never going to see the Watch, you–’

‘Luke, wait!’ Gideon was beside them, easing Luke’s grip. ‘It makes no sense to beat this man before he tells us why he tried to harm Miss Chandler.’

‘I didn’t want to, miss,’ the man threw a distressed glance to where she sat, ‘and he didn’t say why it was he wanted you done away with...’

‘Who?’ Luke demanded again. ‘Who didn’t say?’

The man’s head swung again but more violently this time and words that had come slowly and reluctantly tumbled quickly over each other. ‘I don’t care about meself, don’t matter what ’appens to me, but my wife ... my babbies ... he’ll kill ’em ... said he would kill ’em if I breathed a word.’ He looked up then, eyes dilated with fear. ‘And he’ll do it, mister ... he’ll do it, he’ll kill my family.’

Responding to the emotion racking the thin body, recognising fear she too had felt, Saran rose to her feet, shakily going through the ritual of making tea. It was an absurd thing in the face of what had happened but it gave her mind and fingers something to do.

Seeing Luke almost bursting with anger,

Gideon gave a brief shake of the head in the direction of Saran, her back turned to them. Reading its instruction Luke stepped away.

'Miss...' a trembling hand fastened on Saran's wrist as she set a cup of tea before her attacker, 'I didn't want to harm you ... as God be my witness I didn't want ... forgive me, miss ... I only agreed so I could feed my little 'uns, now they'll starve sure as anythin'.'

Gideon's hand releasing her wrist Saran's senses lurched, sending a tremor along her arm, and at once his fingers broke their touch. His face hard as the tubes he forged, he spoke briefly to Luke who eased her back into her chair, standing protectively beside her.

'This person who threatens your family.' Gideon had already turned his attention to the seated man. 'If you give us his name I guarantee your family will not be harmed.'

Hands shaking the man replaced the cup, shedding tiny droplets of liquid into the saucer. 'Won't do no good mekin' agreements with that one ... he don't keep his word.'

'But I keep mine,' Gideon answered quietly, 'and you have it. Tell us who put you up to this and I promise your family will not suffer in any way.'

'You ... you means that?' At Gideon's nod some of the fear left the man's eyes. 'That be more'n I deserves, mister, God bless you forrit; and God damn Zadok Minch for what it were I almost done.'

# 35

He had lied about his visitor and lied about the reasons for selling both the Coronet Tube Works and this house in saying he was tired of them. Zadok's visitor smiled at the man lying wide-legged on the bed. Zadok Minch never tired of anything which made him money or gave him physical pleasure, that meant only one thing ... the man was no longer making money, and a man without money was a man without attraction.

'So what will you do without the tube works to occupy your time?'

'Spend it on more satisfying pastimes.' Zadok reached again for the figure smiling down at him.

But just who was it he would be satisfying? Violet eyes showed no indication of the thought. He had said he would have no other lover, no trivial affair, yet only hours earlier he had entertained a man, a solicitor. But he would not be lying naked had that business been simply one of delivering information.

'We'll live in that house together, there'll be no more coming and going.'

'But your wife, will that not be awkward, three of us living in the same house?'

Shifting a little on the bed Zadok studied his attractive visitor; mahogany-brown hair dressed high on the head, the shapely body enhanced by the elegant cut of velvet, the face of a goddess and eyes ... eyes which smouldered like the devil's own. The comparison between lover and wife was wide as an ocean and he knew which shore he meant to stay on.

'There won't be three.' He smiled satisfaction. 'That one downstairs be going to a sanatorium, I be going to 'ave her put away. So you see, my pretty love, there'll be just you and me. Now, show me the games we'll play.'

*'just you and me'*

Fingers eased free a line of tiny buttons allowing the mulberry velvet jacket to slide from smooth shoulders barely masked by palest pink chiffon. How many times had those words been said, and how many more times had evidence of the lie been found in that dressing room? Zadok was a generous lover ... but he liked too many! How soon would it be before boys were brought to the house as they had been brought here, how long before the house he planned to live in no longer had room for this lover?

'I think you have had your games already, maybe I should go.'

Soft and seductive as silk the words creamed out, fingers halting teasingly on pink chiffon.

'If you do then you'll never know what it is be in that drawer.' Zadok's glance swept to a tall chest of drawers stood beside the door leading to his dressing room, then back to the figure stood a little away from the bed. 'You can look at it now if you be interested.'

A sultry smile curving the full red lips, smoky eyes stroking with a slowness that had Zadok moan with desire, the answer was low and musical. 'I'm not. How could I be interested in anything other than what I see now?'

With no more haste than moments previously, the velvet skirt was loosed, sighing to the ground in a whisper of promise fulfilled by falling lace.

Every line of the naked body highlighted by lamplight, Zadok's hard flesh jerked against his stomach. He took his pleasure with boys but they were always afraid, too scared for a man to truly enjoy; but here was sophistication, a true skill which brought satisfaction in all senses of the word. Watching slender arms lift, long fingers free hair to tumble about the shoulders, his breath was quick and uneven. The one he had sent to murder the Chandler wench, the one whose life he had threatened, he could never have roused the feelings which racked now.

'I think you have been a naughty boy.' The violet eyes smiled as Zadok's hand closed over a shapely thigh. 'And we all know naughty boys must be punished.'

His eyes glittering with anticipation Zadok pretended fear as his companion came from the dressing room, a small whip in one hand, a bundle of coloured satin ribbons in the other. Christ, he couldn't hold it long enough for them to be tied!

'Now you must behave...' red lips touched the throbbing head, 'disappoint me and you will get no sweeties tonight.'

Gritting his teeth, fighting the craving that burned like fire along his nerves with every move of that sensuous body, every touch of titillating fingers, Zadok spread his legs wider, smiling at thoughts of what was to follow, his ankles being securely fastened to the bedposts.

There was soft laughter as a delicate hand pushed away podgy fingers brushing the glistening mahogany mound at the top of long legs, then fastened the wrist to the bedhead with yellow satin.

'Now!' Zadok moaned as the other wrist was secured. 'Do it now.'

Brilliant as gemstones the violet eyes echoed the sultry laugh. 'Soon, my love, but first we have to confess our sins.'

Veins pulsating, flesh jolting between his legs, Zadok shook his head. 'No more teasing... I want it now!'

The plait of the whip trailing up along his legs touched the hard mounds jutting beneath the jerking column and for a moment the lovely eyes lost their smile.

'Naughty boys don't get what they want until they admit to what they have done ... and you have done wrong, haven't you?' The whip moved, drawing a finger of leather over the throbbing flesh. 'Tell what it is and you can have all of this.' Bent over the moaning Zadok, a wet tongue slid over his chest and along the line of his navel until lips touched once more against a rigid penis.

'Yes, yes, I've done wrong.' Zadok gasped at the spasms pulling at his body.

'That is not enough.' The whip slid silently over throbbing flesh. 'We have to say what we have done, we must be honest if we are to be forgiven ... and you do want to be forgiven, don't you?'

Christ how he wanted to be forgiven! Desire

thickening his throat Zadok nodded. 'A lad ... before you come ... a lad, but it were nothing more than petting.'

A lad! The whip twitched. So much for promises! Chagrin was veiled by a smile as Zadok's partner in pleasure laid the whip aside and reached for the cravat Zadok had carelessly left lying on the floor, stuffing it into his open mouth and wrapping it securely around with a scarf snatched from a drawer.

'You said there would be no one but me.' The violet eyes smouldered, the voice had lost none of its silk. 'You said I was your only lover, that I would share with no one else. But you lied, my love, you broke that promise and now you must face the consequences.'

Held fast to the bed Zadok watched the quick agile movements between bed and dressing room, his mind still playing on pleasures he had so often enjoyed before.

'You thought to share my house, no doubt to bring your little playthings there. But that house was promised to me, for my use alone, as was this.' A soft laugh trembled on the stillness while tapering fingers tied a white satin ribbon around agitated flesh. 'You should know, Zadok...' eyes of violet ice smiled, 'you should know I share with no one.'

This was a new facet to an old game but every little twist added savour. Relishing the thought Zadok watched the supple figure half turn, then the expectation dancing on every nerve died and narrow eyes dilated with fear as the figure turned to him and he saw what was held above his head.

Slow, sibilant as a slithering snake, the figure moved several inches towards the foot of the bed. 'You will never take my house, and as for this...' tender fingers lifted the organ suddenly robbed of its potency, 'you will never share this with anyone again.'

Craning his neck Zadok saw the painted mouth smile, caught the flash of lamplight gleam silver on the open razor, but his scream remained locked behind a silk cravat.

'Tut, tut ... white was a mistake, I should have chosen black to match your lying tongue. But let us not be bitter, kiss your love goodbye.'

Still smiling the figure leaned agilely across the bed, touching the gagged mouth with his own erect penis.

Fury sitting like a stone inside him Gideon urged the horse along, oblivious to the dangers of potholes hidden in the darkness. Zadok Minch had sent that man to lie in wait for Saran, Zadok Minch had been behind that attack.

He had listened to the fellow's story, the fear in his voice when he spoke of the threat to his family attesting to the truth. He had told it all, how the owner of the Coronet Works had given him and a dozen others their tins, how he – the only one of them all – had been ordered to come to the house in Birmingham. It had been there, sprawled stark naked on his bed, the industrialist had tried to induce him into acting the part of a woman, and when he had refused had said he would swear he, Minch himself, had been attacked and abused by an ex-employee out for revenge; that, he had said, would attract the death penalty in any court of law, the man would go to the gallows and his family put on to the streets to starve unless... That was when the proposition had been put: kill Saran Chandler and he would be paid well, refuse and his wife and children would die!

It had taken a while to calm Luke, to have the lad agree to wait until morning before taking any action, impressing upon him that Saran must not be left alone. But Gideon Newell would not wait. Zadok Minch would answer before morning, he would answer to him.

'He will answer to no one.'

Her eyes fever bright, the wife of Zadok Minch answered the demand of the man who had hammered on her door.

'He will answer to no one.' She glanced towards the stairs and as Gideon sprinted up them she followed slowly.

'God Almighty!'

Soft as Gideon's exclamation was, the drab little woman heard and laughed, a bitter wild laugh that died to a sob in her throat.

'Yes, God Almighty. It is His vengeance for what was done to that woman and her daughter, for another I found whipped almost to death in my own sitting room, for all the young boys made to play his filthy games... It is the Lord's vengeance upon me for being too weak to oppose him, for the law will say I did this. But I will not care nor fear the scaffold, only bless the name of the one who had the courage I lacked, the courage to kill Zadok Minch.'

Stood in the lamplit bedroom Gideon looked at the scene before him. Bound and gagged, his lower body sprayed with blood, Zadok stared with sightless eyes at the ceiling, his severed penis, like a small ribbon-bound final parting gift, laid reverently on his chest.

'It is no more than he deserved ... and no more than I deserve.'

No, that was wrong. Gideon's mind refuted the admission. The man lying on the bed had been the one had taken the Elwell child, tried to force him to do God knows what, he had whipped Saran's mother and sister until they had died of it and only hours ago had ordered a man to kill Saran herself... That was Zadok Minch, he and he alone was responsible, he and he alone should pay.

'I wanted to stop it.' The quiet voice trembled on. 'I thought once that I had found the courage to do so but Zadok ... the whip, it hurt so much ... and my cowardice meant pain and harm to others, that is the cross I bore so long; but now I can lay that burden down, the Lord in His mercy grant me a quick death.'

There would be no more death. Gideon breathed deeply, the resolve firm in his mind. Why should a woman Minch had terrified for half of her life hang for a man who was no better than a devil from hell? Given what he knew, he believed Zadok Minch had deserved to die a long time ago ... and the one who had caused his death? Whoever that was had removed a scab from the earth. Lord, he would give the culprit a medal!

Stepping to the bedside he looked once more at the blood-soaked body. Yes, it was no more than he deserved. 'Get water and a cloth then bring clothes he wore for business,' he said. Then, as the lined face frowned, he snapped, 'Do it ... now!'

The barked order more to her understanding than softer sympathetic words the woman scurried like a dark shadow to do as she was told.

Waiting until she was out of the room Gideon took the blood-soaked ribbon between finger and thumb. Minch did not deserve burial as a full man. Disgust thick in his mouth he flung the organ into the fire.

Why had he not come to Brook Cottage? Her heart heavy inside her, Saran pushed the ledger to one side. Luke had told her how Gideon had ridden to the house of Zadok Minch only to find him dead of an affliction of the heart and his wife distraught. He had been so kind easing the shock of Zadok's wife who had thought her husband sleeping following a fraught day at his business. It was Gideon who arranged for the death certificate, he who organised the funeral, even going with the woman to the interment. But then that was Gideon, ever ready to help, to offer assistance where he realised the need, as he had once tried to offer assistance to her.

But she had thrown it in his face, accused him of thinking her a common prostitute. A sixpenny girl! Drawing the ledger to her again she opened it, her glance following neat columns of figures. She was worth a great deal more than sixpence now.

*'as you walks you casts a great shadow, a shadow*

*that covers many'*

Out of the past the words returned. Her shadow did indeed cover many, earning their living at the jobs she had provided. But the prophecy muttered so long ago had spoken of things other than shadow, it had told of grief and anguish, of bitterness and misery; and just as one part had proved true so had the others. Grief had come of being unable to find her family, and anguish at learning of their terrible death, anguish that remained with her still, that came again and again out of the loneliness of the night; and bitterness? That had been born of her accusing Gideon Newell of something she had learned over the years he would never think. And the misery? That came from a love she held yet could never share. She loved Gideon Newell but it was a love too late. Luke in his awkward way had tried to show her she was wrong to trust herself to Jairus Ensell, Luke had always championed and admired the man who was now his partner in business, but she had been stubborn, stubborn and blind. Luke – she smiled – forthright dependable Luke who had stayed with her through the hard times, who was with her yet.

*'there be one walks beside you'*

Luke had walked beside her, but one day Luke would marry, one day his life would be locked with another.

Her thoughts interrupted by a knock, Saran felt the colour rise in her cheeks as she opened the door to Gideon Newell.

'Luke ... Luke is not here,' she stammered, 'he is with the Elwells.'

‘It is not Luke I came to see ... it was you.’

Quickly turning back into the lamplit kitchen she crossed to the fireplace, hiding her blush beneath its crimson glow.

‘Would you care for some tea?’ The question asked to cover the sudden emotion whirling inside her Saran kept her back to her visitor.

His refusal abrupt, Gideon looked at the slender figure. He had argued with himself over the stupidity of coming here, of having to look at the woman his heart cried out for but whom he must never touch, of having to talk with her when all he wanted was to hold her, to whisper he loved her. Why could he not have asked Luke to deliver the message, why cause himself so much pain?

‘Then what can I do for you, Mr Newell?’

She had turned to face him. Light from lamp and fire combined to sprinkle red-gold glints among pale hair caught from a face whose lovely eyes gleamed like dew on grass. Breath caught in his chest, Gideon could not answer for a moment and when he did it was with a sharpness directed against himself.

‘I suppose I should have given Luke a message but...’ he hesitated, ‘this is a matter I prefer to put to you myself. Bridget Minch–’

‘Luke has told me of the death of Zadok Minch, of his wife finding him in his room. An attack of the heart; it must have been very frightening for her. It is kind of you to have helped as you did.’

Luke could not have told the whole story for he himself had not been given it. Seeing compassion darken those hazel-gold eyes Gideon knew it was right to have kept the details secret. Like the man's wife, Saran Chandler had suffered enough from Zadok Minch, it was useless to add the burden of pity.

'I have not called to discuss my actions, suffice to say the business is all but over.'

He was finding his visit far from his taste. Saran felt the brusqueness of his answer sting inside. She must make it brief for him.

'Then say what it is you *have* called for, Mr Newell, as you no doubt noticed I am very busy.'

The mouth had tightened at her reply and the eyes had hardened. 'Miss Chandler, I am not here for myself.'

*'not here for myself'*

The words had rocked her world. Gideon Newell had not called with a wish to see her but on behalf of someone else.

Sat once more at the table, the ledger opened in front of her, Saran's mind played over the events which had followed.

He had come on behalf of the wife of Zadok Minch, come to ask Saran to agree to meet with her. How could he ask that, ask her to visit the house of the man who had killed her mother and sister, who had offered to tell where their bodies lay only if she would lie with him, a man who had sent another to kill her?

But he had asked. The pen falling from her fingers she stared into the past, stared at a heavily jowled face, narrow ferret eyes gliding slowly over her while thick lips shone wet with the lust of imagination.

*'None of that was his wife's doing,'* Gideon had

remonstrated at her refusal to meet with the woman. *'She was as badly dealt with as you, maybe more so for she was married to the swine; she felt his cruelty every day, for her there was no escape.'*

*'There was no escape for my mother and Miriam! Have you forgotten that?'* But even as the words had been flung from her she had known he had not. Once again she had accused him. The look of hurt in those grey-blue eyes swam now before her own, clearing her vision of Zadok Minch, of the heavily jowled face mocking from the shadows of her mind.

Gideon had stepped to the door and when he turned to look at her again the hurt was gone, but her own hurt would never go, that deeper hurt which came from not being able to speak her love for him.

*'I thought you to be of finer stuff than to refuse a woman who has done you no harm.'* It had been cold, cutting deep as a blade, the sting of it bringing sharp breath from her throat as if he had stuck her. She must have cried out for he was suddenly so close she felt the warm breath of him. But he had not touched her. Instead he had spoken gently, as to a child, and for the first time he had said her name and not retracted it.

*'Saran,'* he had murmured, *'for your own sake if not for that of Bridget Minch, I ask you ... meet with the woman. Trust me, just this once.'*

That had been all, no goodnight, no word for Luke, and none of any regard for her. Gideon Newell had simply turned on his heel and walked out of her house ... walking once more out of her life.

# 36

Dressed head to toe in black, Bridget Minch looked at the young woman sat facing her. She was beautiful, her face almost a replica of the child that had once been in this house, a child whose mother had died trying to protect her.

'It makes what you have suffered no easier, but before the Lord I swear to you I had no part in my husband's doings.'

She had no need to apologise, the deep-grooved lines on that tired face stood witness to the fact she had been no more than a tool in that man's hands. Saran had sat in silence listening to the woman's sobbed account of her husband's sordid life. How had she borne such treatment ... but then had her own mother not borne much the same at the hands of Enoch Jacobs?

'Joseph Elwell told us of how you tried to be kind to him, that you did not try to prevent it when the other woman's attack on your husband gave him the chance to get away. You must not blame yourself for lack of courage, that is a thing we all experience, especially in the face of such cruelty.'

'That, child, is the one thing I will never forgive myself for.' The grey head swung slowly. 'But I did not ask you here to talk of my failings, I wish to–'

'Mrs Minch,' Saran interrupted quickly. 'Luke

and I, we want to return this to you, please ... don't refuse.'

Opening the parchment given her the woman's hands trembled, her faded eyes sparkling with tears as she finished reading. 'This house,' she murmured, 'you return this house to me, after all–'

'No more talk of that, it is over and done.'

Laying the paper aside the older woman smiled. 'No, child, not quite over. I have not yet asked what Gideon Newell said I should ask for myself. He said I should ask you come with me to the cemetery.'

Gideon had said she should ask that ... he could be so heartless as to suggest this woman ask her to visit the grave of a man who had murdered her mother and sister! Aghast, Saran stared at the face watching the nuances of emotion play over her own.

'Please, child, it would mean so much to me.'

*'I thought you to be of finer stuff than to refuse'*

It sang in her brain. He had known what it was this woman wanted and yet he had spoken those words!

'I see you cannot, but then I should not have asked.'

It wasn't this woman should not have asked but Gideon Newell. He would have known the feelings such a request would arouse yet still he had suggested it. But in respect of Bridget Minch he had been right, she could not be held to account for the evil done, and refusing her one request would undo none of it.

Rising to her feet at the same time as her

hostess Saran swallowed the bitterness of what she saw as betrayal, saying she would accompany the woman.

The hansom ride was short but to Saran, struggling with her emotions, it seemed like half a lifetime.

'Your usual day, mum.' Her bonnet wide as her smile, a flower-seller seated at the tall iron gates facing the cemetery exchanged a posy of violets for the coin Bridget Minch handed her.

'It's this way.'

Boots crunching on dry stony ground the woman walked quickly, leading the way past ornate tombs, their stone figures bent on prayer, past headstones carved from white marble or black granite, their floral tributes stood in tiny vases beneath lavish phrases. Which would mark the resting place of Zadok Minch, what words would speak to the world? None which would speak the evil which their stone covered.

'It's here.'

The black-robed figure had stopped and now stood looking at a small stone half covered by a great yew draping its branches protectively over it. Surprised at the unexpected simplicity Saran waited while the older woman laid the tiny offering against the stone, whispering words she could not discern. Only as Bridget Minch rose did she see the carved inscription.

*Sacred to the memory*

The letters danced before her eyes, twisting wildly together as she read again.

*Sacred to the memory of Rebecca Chandler*

Her mother! It was not the grave of Zadok she

had been brought to visit but that of her mother! The carved letters drowning in the ocean of her tears Saran flung herself across the grass-covered mound.

'Mother,' she sobbed, touching a hand to the name cut deep into the headstone. 'I looked for you... I tried so hard to find you... Jacobs, he ... he said who bought you and Miriam. Oh, Mother! I tried so hard...'

'The stone is so very small, but I did not have a deal of money and I dared not ask Zadok.' Sat once more in the hansom Zadok's wife spoke quietly.

Eyes brilliant with tears resting at their brim, Saran's answer throbbed with emotion. 'He said they had been taken with ... with...'

Behind her black veil Bridget Minch's mouth portrayed her feelings. Zadok had bought people like others bought household utensils, using them, selling them on when he had no further need for them, even destroying them if they failed to please him. This girl's family had been no different in his eyes: they were simply part of the 'goods' he brought to the house. 'I can guess what he said,' she answered, 'but like always when temper got the upper hand I was left to clear away the results. Zadok never asked of your mother and I never told him she had been laid to rest in holy ground. Oh my dear, believe me. I asked Gideon Newell what he knew of you, other than Zadok's attempt to have you killed. He would not speak at first, but when I told him of that grave and who lay in it he, too, thought the woman had to be your mother.'

Gideon... Gideon had known, that was why he had urged she meet with this woman.

'The words on the stone,' Zadok's widow went on quietly, 'it was virtually all I knew of her, she never said the name of her husband.'

Her mother had not spoken of Enoch Jacobs, had not once mentioned the man who had bartered her for beer money; had not owned to his name while in that house! She would not be made to own to it in her grave.

'What you did for my mother I will never be able to repay. I have lost her but now my mind can rest, knowing she received a church burial. I will always be grateful.'

The hansom rocked on its springs, the driver calling the horse to a standstill. Glancing from the window Saran's brow creased. They were driving to the coach departure point but the large house set behind tall ornamental gates was no coaching inn.

Alighting, Bridget Minch glanced back to Saran. 'Forgive my not asking if you would mind my calling here before taking you to catch the coach but this house it ... it makes me so nervous ... please, Miss Chandler, would you come inside with me?'

Missing the coach would mean a wait of hours until the next one, but what was that against this woman's kindness.

At the door the older woman hesitated, and behind the fine gauze of her veil her faded eyes held a new light. 'Miss Chandler,' she whispered, 'what I say while in this house ... support me, please.'

It had been too late to ask why. Sat in a leather-upholstered chair in a book-lined, tall-windowed room, Saran remembered the agitated shake of the older woman's hand on her arm as the door had opened immediately on her words. Something here frightened Bridget Minch.

'I received the letter from your solicitor, Mrs Minch. Allow me to express my condolence, your husband was a fine, well-respected man.'

'Thank you.' Bridget's handkerchief lifted to her mouth.

'So what is it I can do for you?' His hands folded on the large leather-topped desk, a well-dressed man watched Bridget with shrewd eyes.

'The truth, as my niece here will adduce to and my solicitor will no doubt corroborate, is that my husband died virtually penniless. The businesses he had, even the house we lived in, are gone...' the handkerchief rose again, 'so I am afraid there can no longer be payment made to this establishment.'

As if by some unseen hand the suave smile was wiped from the man's face. Glancing at Saran, who felt herself nod agreement, he cleared his throat noisily.

'I see.' The hands moved out of sight. 'That creates something of a predicament. This sanatorium is not a charity, we cannot house and feed without the necessary fee. You must understand, Mrs Minch, much as I would like–'

Behind the handkerchief Bridget sobbed. 'I do understand, Doctor Spence, that is why I have called today. My niece,' she reached a black-gloved hand to Saran, 'has offered me a place with her but she ... she finds herself unable to continue paying the cost of keeping my daughter here.'

Her daughter! Saran's nerves jolted. Zadok Minch had a child, a daughter of his own, yet he could do what he did to children! But why put that daughter here in an institution? Was she disabled in some way ... did she suffer from a feeble mind ... or was there some more sinister explanation?

'It is regrettable, Doctor,' Bridget sobbed again, 'but I must take my daughter away.'

White hands reappeared, splaying dramatically above the desk. 'My dear Mrs Minch, as our annual report to your late husband disclosed, your daughter, though well in health, has made no recovery. She still does not speak, extreme care is needed if she is not to relapse into the same severe state of shock she was in when she was brought here to this sanatorium. I must advise your niece that proper medical supervision...'

The gloved fingers pressed slightly, the woman was asking for support. Looking directly at the doctor, Saran nodded. 'I agree, medical supervision is best for my cousin but sadly my finances do not run to providing your fee. However...' she stood up, helping Bridget also to stand, 'if you can arrange for her to remain here without that fee then both my aunt and myself–'

'I explained, we are not a charity!' The doctor interrupted, bringing both palms flat on the desk.

An arm about the older woman's shoulders, Saran felt the quiver run through the thin body. Was it simply tension or was it fear ... fear that somehow her daughter could be kept from her, locked away for ever behind these high walls?

Voice and eyes a match in coldness though her nerves burned, Saran looked directly at the man who had not risen from his desk.

'Precisely so, Doctor,' she said icily, 'neither am I, and as I have no intention of wasting time repeating that, either you release my cousin to her mother's keeping or we bid you good day!'

He had taken no further persuading. Bridget's hand clutched to hers Saran waited as the uniformed nurse he had rung for stalked away on her errand.

How long had it been since this woman had seen her child? What had caused the severe state of shock the doctor had spoken of, and what was hindering recovery? Thoughts tumbling through her mind Saran watched the pen whisk busily over the paper which she guessed was to be signed by Bridget to say she had withdrawn her daughter from this man's care. As her glance returned to the trembling woman she saw the lips form a silent warning: Remember you are her cousin!

'Sign here!'

The paper shoved ungraciously across the desk Saran released the other woman's hand and as Bridget bent to sign turned towards the nurse re-entering the room.

It had felt like being caught in a dream. Sat at the bedside of the sleeping girl, Saran watched the face which had held such a hopeless lost look, the dark-circled hazel-green eyes empty of all save deep unhappiness when she was brought to that doctor's office. Remembering now, Saran felt again the pain-filled surge that had rushed through her, snatching at her breath, tipping her heart sideways. The child had stood silent beside the white-aproned nurse, her small hands twitching nervously, her whole thin frame jerking visibly when the doctor told her sharply to hold her head up.

The child had obeyed like some wound-up toy then those vacant eyes had filled with tears and the thin arms had reached out, one word whispering across the room.

Her own breath quivering as it had then, Saran's veins quickened with the same overwhelming rush, but now pity was mixed with happiness.

Bridget Minch had given one sideways glance to Saran's own face then had taken the trembling child into her arms, hurrying her out to the waiting hansom, and only when the sanatorium was out of sight did she release her. Then, the veil still lowered over her face, she had smiled, her voice low as she said, *'Take her, Miss Chandler, take your sister.'*

'I don't understand.' Livvy Elwell spoke quietly, breaking the reverie. 'I mean, why say she was her daughter?'

'I asked the same.' Saran touched gentle fingers to the fair hair so like her own. 'The woman was forbidden ever to see or communicate with Miriam, she had to take the chance Zadok had given no name to the institution, and that they therefore would list her under his name.'

'But at least Zadok paid her keep.'

Saran shook her head, the pain of the full story still raw in her mind. 'No, not Zadok. That was done by Bridget. She knew he had wiped his hands of the child, put her away for life knowing, when the promised fee did not arrive, that she would be turned out on the streets. Bridget could not bear that. Out of all the children her husband had used and then sold on, this girl was the only one she might have the chance to help, so though the thought of being found out terrified her she sold anything it was hoped he would not miss, putting as much of the housekeeping to the proceeds as she dared, and that way found enough for Miriam to be kept at that place. But even so she was put as a maid in the scullery.'

'But why not just turn her out, why did Zadok Minch put himself to so much trouble?'

Meeting Livvy's eyes across the bed, Saran's face showed the strength of her feelings. 'He could not take the risk of her telling anyone of his vileness, of what he was trying to do with her, how she had been stripped, how his filthy hands were stroking her when my mother burst into that bedroom, how he whipped her to death before Miriam's eyes then did almost the same to her when she screamed, whipping her until she went into so deep a shock she could not speak; but there was always the danger she would recover her voice, therefore it was the institution for her. No doubt she was handed over with a host of lies about delusions and self-torture.'

'The scars on her back ... that was how he explained them! May the man rot in hell.'

'She never did tell anyone.' Saran's eyes sparkled

with silver tears. 'She never spoke a single word from that day, not even her name.'

Sighing heavily, Livvy rose. 'Thank God Bridget Minch remembered it, and thank God Gideon Newell told her of you. We all have a lot to thank that man for.'

Kissing the brow of the sister she was almost afraid to lose from her sight, Saran followed the other woman downstairs. Alone in the bright kitchen the echo of Livvy's words played in her mind. They did all have much to thank Gideon Newell for, but when she had tried to express hers he had simply nodded then turned and walked away.

Luke had brought the answer. Gideon Newell would come to Brook Cottage.

Nerves throbbing more than they had in that sanatorium Saran smoothed her green skirts for the tenth time. This was ridiculous, she told herself sharply. Gideon Newell was not some monster from a childhood fairy tale, he was a perfectly ordinary man, so why did her hands shake and her heart beat like a drum? Because Gideon Newell was no ordinary man, not to her: he was the man she loved.

Luke had refused to stay with her. 'This be your business, Saran,' he had declared emphatically. 'I'll have naught to do with it one way or the other.'

He had never refused her anything before but in the question of the Coronet Tube Works he had proved adamant. The tube works was hers, she must do with it as she saw fit; all he would say was she should ask the advice of Gideon Newell.

Would he tell her what Luke had already told her, that she must run her own business her own way? Should she even ask his advice? He and Luke had enough to think about with their own works.

The knock at the door ended the thought abruptly. Saran's hands brushed her skirts again, then fell to her sides as she admonished herself for being a fool. She would say exactly the words rehearsed so many times in her mind ... no more and no less.

'Luke said you wanted to speak with me.'

Yes, I want to speak with you, I want to tell you I love you. Blushing at the words springing silently to her mind, Saran led the way towards the parlour she had furnished with pretty chintzes and deep comfortable chairs, the gleam of amber-shaded lamps casting a glow whose gentle light usually served to calm but tonight seemed to add to the turmoil inside her.

Why did he not sit! Twisting her fingers together, conscious of the even stare of those blue-grey eyes, she sought for a way to begin.

'Has...' she swallowed but the tightness in her throat refused to release its grip, 'has Luke intimated what it is I wish to speak with you about?'

Why was he making this so difficult? Saran watched the curt nod. Had he already decided, like Luke, that she should be responsible for herself, make her own decisions? Well, if that was so she should begin right now. Drawing a deep breath she looked at the man who smiled at her only in dreams.

'Mr Newell,' she said, praying her voice would not tremble, 'the iron works you and Luke have on Monway Field I believe does not have the capacity to produce enough metal to meet with the orders placed your way, this results in a loss of business. The Coronet Works, too, has that problem, therefore I suggested Luke discuss a merger, one works producing only iron, the other concentrating on tubes; a joining between us–'

'No!' The vehemence of the word seemed to vibrate from every part of the tiny parlour, bouncing from glass vases set above the fireplace, ringing from crystal pendants hanging from the pretty amber lampshades. 'No!' He said it again. 'There can be no merger between us!'

Taken aback by the veracity of the reply, Saran took a moment before asking, 'Why? Why will you not join with me – is it because I am a woman?'

The question hanging between them it seemed he would turn and leave without answer, but of a sudden his hands clenched and his brows drew together, words grinding like pebbles between his teeth. 'Yes, yes, it is because you are a woman! But you are not any woman, you are the one woman in the world I could not stand to speak with every day, to look at and be with...'

The almost savage virulence, the cold anger drawing the handsome face into peaked lines, the eyes which seemed to burn with fury were too much to bear and Saran turned away, a soft cry trapped in her throat. He must hate her so much.

'I'm sorry,' she said quietly, 'I should not have

asked you to come to this house. I ... I did not realise you felt so strongly ... please forget the joining of...'

'I can forget that easily enough, for that is not the joining I want.'

The anger had gone as swiftly as it had flared, the words spoken so quietly he could have meant only himself to hear. But it was not what he said had the heart turn in her body, it was the way he had said it, with a tenderness, a softness which was almost a yearning. Turning quickly she saw, for one unguarded moment, the echo of that tenderness reflected in the look he played on her, but on the instant it was masked.

But her own emotions were not so easily hidden, and when she turned to face him her eyes sparkled with the sheen of tears.

'Saran! Saran, for God's sake!'

It was the cry of a man at the end of his tether but as he swept her into his arms Saran felt no pity, only a wonderful heady joy, an exquisite rush along every tingling nerve.

'Saran!'

The whisper became a kiss as she lifted her face to his, a kiss whose demand rocked the world.

'Now you see!' He released her abruptly. 'Now you see why I could not stand to be with you every day, it's because I love you. Perhaps, now it has been said, I can forget it.'

He loved her. He did not hate her, he loved her! The room about her was filled with a golden haze of happiness and she smiled. 'Gideon, I don't want you to forget, I don't want you ever to forget, because I love you, I think I always have.'

For one eternal moment Gideon did not move, then, with a catch of breath that might have been a sob, he snatched her to him, his mouth crushing hers, his arms locked about her as if he would never release her again.

'Oh, my love,' he whispered when his lips left hers, 'my one love, I've wanted you so long.'

Held against his strong body Saran felt her whole world settle into place.

*'But there be one walks beside you, his future locked with yours. Give him your trust, for through him you find what it is you seek.'*

A whisper in her mind, the words of Harriet Dowen returned. It had been Gideon had persuaded her to meet with Zadok's widow, through him she had found her family.

*'through him you find what it is you seek'*

The words persisted, and now she understood. Her family had not been all she had longed for – she had longed for love, the love of the man who held her now.

*'give him your trust'*

Lifting her lips, her eyes closed beneath his kiss. For the rest of her life he would have that trust.

'The Coronet Works?' It was a lifetime later she asked the question. 'Will you agree to their being joined?'

'The only joining I want is ours ... in marriage,' Gideon smiled, 'but if merging the businesses is what you want then, if Luke agrees, so will I.'

'And Luke, he will be a full partner?'

His eyes filled with love he caught her again in his arms, his words a gentle song against her hair. 'Not in everything,' he murmured. 'Luke will be

a full partner but only in the business. You, my dearest, are mine alone, I will never share you with anyone ... my darling little sixpenny girl.'

The publishers hope that this book has given you enjoyable reading. Large Print Books are especially designed to be as easy to see and hold as possible. If you wish a complete list of our books please ask at your local library or write directly to:

**Magna Large Print Books**
Magna House, Long Preston,
Skipton, North Yorkshire.
BD23 4ND